Family Reunion

**Center Point
Large Print**

**This Large Print Book carries the
Seal of Approval of N.A.V.H.**

ॐ श्री गणेशाय नमः

Family Reunion

Carol Smith

Center Point Publishing
Thorndike, Maine

This Center Point Large Print edition
is published in the year 2001 by arrangement with
Warner Books, Inc.

The text of this Large Print edition is unabridged.
In other aspects, this book may vary from the original
edition. Printed in Thailand. Set in 16-point Plantin type by
Bill Coskrey.

ISBN 1-58547-076-7

Library of Congress Cataloging-in-Publication Data

Smith, Carol, 1938-
    Family Reunion / Carol Smith.
        p. cm.
    ISBN 1-58547-076-7 (lib. bdg. : alk. paper)
    1. Family reunions--Fiction. 2 Large type books. I. Title.

PR6069.M4215 F36 2001
823'.914--dc21

                                                        00-065678

*For all the many descendants
of William Henry Smith (1867-1941)
and Gwenllian Edith Thomas*

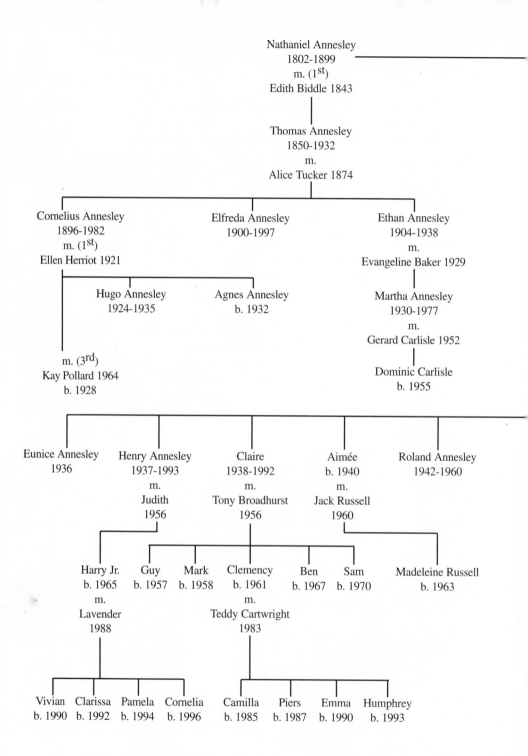

Nathaniel Annesley
1802-1899
m. (1st)
Edith Biddle 1843

Thomas Annesley
1850-1932
m.
Alice Tucker 1874

Cornelius Annesley
1896-1982
m. (1st)
Ellen Herriot 1921

Elfreda Annesley
1900-1997

Ethan Annesley
1904-1938
m.
Evangeline Baker 1929

Hugo Annesley
1924-1935

Agnes Annesley
b. 1932

Martha Annesley
1930-1977
m.
Gerard Carlisle 1952

m. (3rd)
Kay Pollard 1964
b. 1928

Dominic Carlisle
b. 1955

Eunice Annesley
1936

Henry Annesley
1937-1993
m.
Judith
1956

Claire
1938-1992
m.
Tony Broadhurst
1956

Aimée
b. 1940
m.
Jack Russell
1960

Roland Annesley
1942-1960

Harry Jr.
b. 1965
m.
Lavender
1988

Guy
b. 1957

Mark
b. 1958

Clemency
b. 1961
m.
Teddy Cartwright
1983

Ben
b. 1967

Sam
b. 1970

Madeleine Russell
b. 1963

Vivian
b. 1990

Clarissa
b. 1992

Pamela
b. 1994

Cornelia
b. 1996

Camilla
b. 1985

Piers
b. 1987

Emma
b. 1990

Humphrey
b. 1993

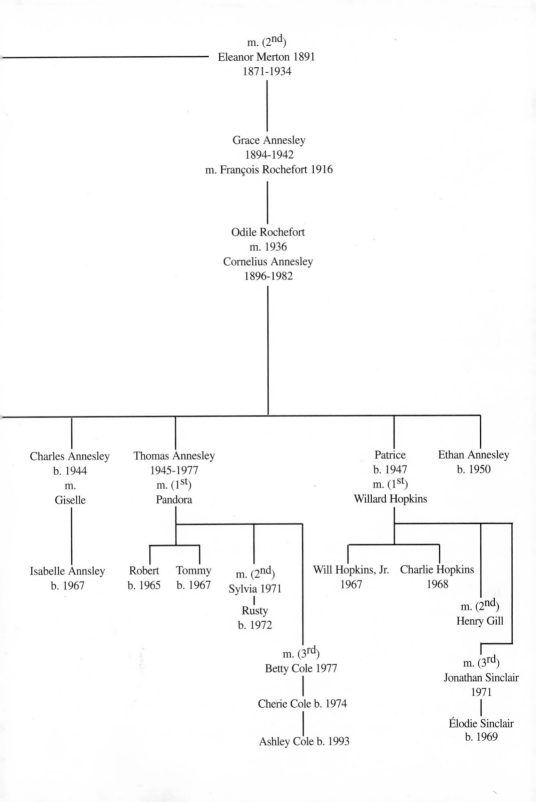

m. (2nd)
Eleanor Merton 1891
1871-1934

Grace Annesley
1894-1942
m. François Rochefort 1916

Odile Rochefort
m. 1936
Cornelius Annesley
1896-1982

Charles Annesley
b. 1944
m.
Giselle

Thomas Annesley
1945-1977
m. (1st)
Pandora

Patrice
b. 1947
m. (1st)
Willard Hopkins

Ethan Annesley
b. 1950

Isabelle Annsley
b. 1967

Robert
b. 1965

Tommy
b. 1967

m. (2nd)
Sylvia 1971

Rusty
b. 1972

Will Hopkins, Jr.
1967

Charlie Hopkins
1968

m. (2nd)
Henry Gill

m. (3rd)
Betty Cole 1977

Cherie Cole b. 1974

m. (3rd)
Jonathan Sinclair
1971

Ashley Cole b. 1993

Élodie Sinclair
b. 1969

Acknowledgments

Again, thanks to my agent, Sarah Molloy, and my editor, Caryn Karmatz Rudy, at Warner Books. Thank you, too, to Sir David Smith, F.R.S., of Wolfson College, Oxford, who let me pick his brains for some of the science.

Prologue

The girl in the silver sequined boob-tube was without doubt giving him the eye, up there on the bar again, precariously balanced, leather skirt barely clearing her crotch as her feet, divested of their trendy platform wedges, moved faster than a hummingbird's wings. Through the fug of too many cigarettes, he watched with slanted eyes as he strummed, no longer infected by her near hysterical excitement, impervious to the lascivious glances she threw him each time she swung her enticing little bot his way.

"Lucky or what?" Greg had muttered, eyeing the long legs, the sinuous thighs, as he humped his bass up on to the improvised stage, but this particular circus has run its course. He was jaded by the unending testosterone challenge; weary of too much willing flesh. Time to move on.

Outside, even in the small hours, Hong Kong maintained its frenetic pace, a city that never sleeps. He jostled his way through unyielding, pleasure-seeking crowds and up the stairs of a narrow, jolting tram, inhaling the mix of garlic, sweat, and something intangibly Eastern that gave the place its exotic flavour. Two more weeks and the gig would be over, though it went unspoken that they could renew any time they liked. This traditional Irish music, with its jaunty rhythm and catchy beat, went down surprisingly well with the newly liberated island's cosmopolitan mix. Bankers, brokers, market traders, airline personnel; an exciting hodgepodge of creeds and colors, all races and ages but predominantly young. Anything was available if you knew where to look for it in this pulse-spot of the immediate; no law was inflexible, if it existed at all.

But there comes a time when the juices flow more slowly and even the hardiest hedonist feels the need to come up for air. This is what he was feeling now. He'd been on the road for far too long and the time-scarred face he regularly eyed in the shaving-mirror belied the fact that he was actually still in his prime. It was time for a change of pace and some sober reappraisal. To quit running and turn and face up to things, things that had haunted him since early childhood. Memories that must inevitably be confronted before he could even think about a normal life. Time, in fact, to go home.

After he'd sorted out a few loose ends.

1

*M*artha took the scenic way home as she often did, across the wide sweep of sand at St. Brelade's Bay and up the path next to the Fisherman's Chapel, which led around the point to the house she shared with Auntie. They'd kept her talking longer than she'd intended, those two old queens in the Portuguese café who amused her by being straight out of an E. F. Benson novel.

"How's your auntie?" they'd asked as she sipped her sherry, and she'd told them as well as could be expected, considering her age. Ninety-seven come February and still keeping active, though the eyesight was no longer as good as it might be and she suffered quite dreadfully from arthritis, poor love. But, all in all, Martha couldn't really complain. They'd rubbed along nicely, the two of them, these twenty-two years, since the tragedy of Gerard and all the anguish that had entailed. And you needed someone to keep you company, particularly in the twilight of your life. A dog wasn't enough.

She paused to gain breath at the top of the steep climb and gazed back over the flat steel-grey water of the Channel. Odd the way things happened, that here she was, a resident of Jersey, where Gerard had been born but never returned to since he left it in his impatient teens. It was a good place to grow old and Auntie liked it too, the friendliness, the healthy living, the mellow climate and lack of traffic or fuss. No crime either, which was a boon to two old ladies, rattling around together in more rooms than they could use, yet able to leave the door unlocked both day and night. Where else in this tough old world could you find that sort of safety? Certainly not in America, where both of them had been raised; not any longer.

Martha never tired of this breathtaking view, though she knew it now as well as her own face. It gave her a reassuring sense of peace and stability, missing through all those hectic years as the wife of a man continuously on the move, with all the to-ings and fro-ings and ups and downs such an existence demanded. Not that she'd begrudged him a single second. When Gerard died, so horribly prematurely, she'd thought her own life had come to an end. She glanced back towards the hillside cemetery where her darling now rested in peace. Where she could tend his grave at her leisure and really keep her eye on him at last, bless his heart.

The front door of the ochre-tinted house was slightly ajar, which was not a good thing. Martha frowned as she pushed open the gate. Lately Auntie had been growing careless. Lack of fear was one thing, but allowing easy access to any passing goat or cat or chicken quite another. She tutted as she walked up the path between the geraniums and sea pinks and meticulously scraped the sand from her sensible brogues. She and Auntie needed to have a word. Else she wouldn't feel easy at leaving her alone next time.

"I'm back!" she called as she slipped out of her light-weight mac in the shady hall, but the air was as still and undisturbed as when she had left, and the door to the sitting room, which they still called the front parlour, wide open and welcoming and clearly hiding no secrets. It was ten past four. The walk to the village had taken longer than she'd intended, but these days what was there to hurry back for? Except Auntie, who shortly would be wanting her tea.

Martha headed towards the kitchen to put on the kettle but paused at the foot of the staircase.

Damp footprints, just discernible on the pale beige of the serviceable carpet, led upwards in a single row, drawing her eye. Footprints from heavy rubber boots, it would appear; a man's boots.

"Hello there!" she called, more jauntily than she felt, venturing up a couple of steps and peering through the banister rails towards the landing, but there was no response. Only the heavy ticking in the hall of Thomas Annesley's clock and the distant skirling of the inevitable seabirds. Apprehension clutched at her throat; all of a sudden the house seemed unnaturally still.

"Auntie!" she called, with a confidence she didn't feel, tripping lightly up the staircase and around to the master bedroom, where the door, unusually, was flung wide open. One glance confirmed her worst fears, though nothing appeared to have been disturbed apart from the awfulness on the bed. Across the crocheted bedspread, like a broken doll, Auntie lay draped with her hair shaken loose from its combs, head down dangling towards the floor, eyes popping out in terror, clearly dead. The dressing-gown cord that had been used as a ligature was still twisted tightly around her throat and mindlessly Martha moved to touch it, then froze as she sensed the slight stirring behind her.

She turned. And gaped incredulously, clutching her throat. After all these years, this couldn't be happening. It took her a moment to come to her senses. Too long.

"You!" she breathed, dumbfounded. There was so much she suddenly needed to ask, but time had already run out for her. The automatic was raised to the center of her forehead and she was dispatched, cleanly and effectively, with a single shot.

"Too terrible," said Douglas in the bar. "We were only talking to her yesterday lunchtime, weren't we, Lionel?" The older man nodded. Tall and stoop-shouldered and defeated by life, he had seen it all in his time and then some. But cold-blooded murder in a place like St. Brelade's was worse than anything he could recall. Especially of such a refined old lady. There was something, they'd always said, well . . . classy about her. As if she had secrets she wasn't betraying, though she lived quite quietly up there on the cliffs, with only her ancient aunt for company. Bette Davis, they'd called her privately, because of her elegance, that self-contained hauteur that belied what was actually a far gentler nature.

"They say she was once married to a very distinguished man," said the barman, polishing glasses. "A composer, or something, who came from these parts. But that was all a long time ago."

"American, I'd guess from her accent." Douglas prided himself on his powers of observation. "And a right beauty she must have been too, in her time. Pity, really, we never got to know her. I'll bet she had a tale or two to tell."

"What have the police to say about it?" Lionel, a former navy man, cared about these details, liked to see things ship-shape and in their place.

"Not a lot," said the barman, scrutinizing a glass. "A competent job, neat and efficient. Nothing stolen, nothing displaced. Almost like an ordered execution."

"Goodness me!" Now Douglas was seriously shocked, his

13

reaction tinted by a tiny chill of pure terror. Thrilling, really, in a forgotten backwater like this. Whatever next!

"You'd better watch it, son," said the barman mock seriously, choosing his words with care to titillate and entertain. The old codger was well into his seventies but still enjoyed being teased. The eyes behind their bottle lenses fairly gleamed with excitement. Worth making that steep climb for; better than *The Archers.*

"Come along, Lionel," he said, draining his glass. "Time for beddy-byes. Doesn't do to stay out late these days."

"Watch out for the Big Bad Wolf," called the barman.

"Behave!" said Douglas with a saucy wave of the hand.

Alone in her farmhouse kitchen, Odile Rochefort Annesley stood motionless, gazing across the silent vineyards as a sepia sun sank in a leaden sky. At this time of year there was nearly always a storm brewing and soon she would check the shutters before she set about preparing a meal. It was midafternoon but almost dark; the daylight hours were short. There was no electric light in this stern old house, but that's how she preferred it, *au naturel,* the way it had been since her parents' day.

What was exercising her mind right now was something she had just read in the newspaper. *France-Soir* lay spread across the old oak table, her neat gold pince-nez resting upon it where she'd flung them down in anguish. Was this endless nightmare never to go away? Had she to go on fighting even after all these years? She twisted stray ends of her thick grey hair, which she still wore up in the style of her girlhood, and pushed them severely back into the knot on top of her head. With her slight figure and erect carriage, from behind Odile still resembled the lissome seventeen-year-old who had first caught the eye of Cornelius Annesley so fatefully and so long ago. But closer to, in the dull, dying rays of the almost extinguished sun, the fine parchment skin revealed the fact that she was now an old woman.

Something must be done and without further delay. With the gritty determination for which she was noted, Odile swept out of the kitchen and into the dim front room, where she lit the gas brackets, opened her writing desk and settled down to compose a letter. It was time she told someone, and told them fast; this latest occurrence was her responsibility and might not have happened had she been a little less stubborn. A flash of Cornelius's beloved face came and went swiftly at the back of her mind, but she pushed it away. She sighed. It had been a long, hard struggle, these past forty years, and not for the first time she questioned her decision. No time, however, for futile self-recrimination. Unless she acted swiftly, it might be altogether too late.

2

*D*id you get Mémé's Christmas card?" called Clemency from the kitchen. The children were sitting in a row on the settle in the hall, removing their Wellingtons while Clemency had hurried on ahead to put on the kettle. Two fair heads; two dark sleek ones, clones of their father. Clemency had done well for herself. Not for the first time, Isabelle found herself envying her.

"Containing her letter to us all?" Clemency appeared in the doorway, brown and sleekly plumaged as one of the well-fed hen pheasants they had seen on their walk.

"No, of course you didn't," she answered her own question. "Your mail will still be going to Canada, won't it?"

Isabelle followed her on stocking feet into the drawing room, where a huge fire blazed. Dogs and children came pushing past her and someone turned on the television with a blast of unwelcome sound in the still Sunday afternoon.

"Switch that thing off," came Clemency's voice authoritatively. "Now is not the time, darling, not when we have a visitor."

"If you still haven't worked off your lunch, young man," said Teddy mildly, pulling the heavy curtains, "I'll take you on at Ping-Pong. The four of you, if you like."

Isabelle watched, impressed, as he winked at her and ushered out the children. He was a big man, running to heaviness, with florid good looks and a shock of greying hair, and she was rapidly growing fond of Clemency's indulgent husband.

"He is a poppet, isn't he?" said Clemency, reading her thoughts. "Now, where did I put it? Let me read it to you." She fumbled among cushions, discarded Sunday papers and some put-aside knitting, a sweater for one of the boys. Complacent as a mother hen, Clemency dominated this house. Her touch was on everything, her signature unmistakable. Again Isabelle envied her; next to her she shrank to being invisible. But that was nothing new to the shy Canadian, a person accustomed to not being seen.

"She addresses it to all of us. Or so she says in her letter." Clemency found the stiff, cream envelope with its foreign stamp and familiar spidery writing, located her reading glasses and began to read.

Her grandmother had written in French, finding, as her age

increased, a more natural facility with her native tongue and knowing that, as they had all been raised bilingual, her grandchildren would have no trouble in deciphering it. Clemency, from the habit of a lifetime, automatically translated into English as she read, ignoring the fact that her houseguest, who hailed from Quebec, was probably actually more at ease with the original than the translation. But that was Clemency all over.

She began by wishing them all *une bonne année,* then progressed abruptly to the main message. Mémé rarely wrote these days; when she did, as they'd all learned over the years, it was worth sitting up and taking notice.

"How old would she be now?" asked Isabelle, unable to calculate.

"Shush, she's coming to that. Wait a bit."

Addressing collectively her fifteen grandchildren, Odile wanted to let them know that she thought of them often even though present circumstances prevented her from seeing them these days.

Clemency paused. "That's rich," she snorted. Mémé had deserted them all abruptly, for reasons of her own, when most of them weren't even born. Leaving their grandfather heartbroken with a house full of kids, to follow a selfish whim to strike out on her own and try to make it as a painter. At a time too when such radical feminism was not yet fashionable. Clemency had often longed to talk to her about it but never, so far, had the chance. She had dim recollections of the house among the vineyards where she'd sometimes visited as a doted-upon grandchild, but those visits had come to an end, she didn't know why, years ago when she was still very young.

But now, Mémé told them, she was growing a little frail and this coming September would mark her eightieth birthday. Grandfather Cornelius had been dead these past seventeen years (though she didn't mention that) and she thought the time had come for her to make peace with her family and let them know the terms of the will she was drawing up. Clemency riffled through the pages and glanced up to make sure she had her companion's full attention. Isabelle, spellbound, was gazing into the heart of the fire, dark head bowed, intent on the glowing embers. Her feet, in their thick woolen socks, were baking slowly in the heat. There was something soporific and wonderful about these weekends in the country with the Cartwrights. Home away from home, if only it had ever been like that, back there in Quebec with a mother who drank and a father who hardly ever communicated in any fashion at all.

"Does she live there all alone, or don't you know that?"

"We know very little." Clemency shrugged. "I seem to remember there was one old retainer, but it's years since I've been there. Since I've been invited, in fact." There was no electricity, that's what stuck in her memory most. Those frightening summer evenings when it was just growing dark at bedtime and she was forced to go upstairs alone with only a flickering candle for company. And a dormouse nesting in a corner of the eaves that made gnawing noises at night while she was trying to sleep. A less sensible child might have been permanently damaged, but Clemency, from a houseload of boisterous brothers, had survived unscathed. Though she was extra careful with her own cherished four, mindful of those infant panics and the way, unless carefully watched, simple anxieties were apt to grow out of all proportion.

To her ten grandsons, Mémé now announced, she was leaving her money, to be evenly divided. She didn't say how much it was, but she'd always been thrifty, and what could there be, in the heart of the French countryside, on which she was likely to spend it?

"Do we know if she manages to sell her paintings?" inquired Isabelle, but Clemency shook her head. Her grandmother's life was a mystery to her, to all of them, even her reasons for having deserted them so abruptly, leaving so many young children to fend for themselves.

Everything else, her furniture and possessions, was to go to the five granddaughters, to be sensibly shared as they thought fit. To Clemency, the eldest, the one she knew best, she also left as a special bequest her gold and pearl crucifix, a gift from her own parents on the occasion of her first communion. Clemency was pleased.

"I remember that cross," she said, "even after all these years. She always wore it around her throat on a black velvet ribbon. Look," she said, waving her hand in the direction of the piano. "It's there in her wedding pictures and all the others."

"Is she dying, do you suppose?" asked Isabelle thoughtfully. "And putting her affairs in order before she goes?" Or was this just the contrition of a selfish old woman who had abandoned her family quite dreadfully on a whim and now was hoping to make the best of the situation? So it was with many of these zealous Catholics. Putting their so-called faith before the ordinary needs of those who cared for and relied upon them. Or so she had always found. If his mother had not walked out when her own father, Charlie, was only sixteen, who knew how his life might have turned out for the better? With a proper mother to watch over him, the way Clemency watched over her children, he might never have been allowed to drift off to Canada and end up washed up in a dead-end job with a slut of a wife whom he didn't even love.

"What do you think?" asked Clemency, breaking into her thoughts. "Shall we go down there in September and surprise her? Just the five of us, maybe, the granddaughters, as a demonstration of support. It might be a bit of a lark, don't you think?"

Teddy surprised them by flicking on the light. In the glow of the firelight, with their matching pink cheeks and dark curls, they looked, he thought, like sisters or even twins. Closer by far than the cousins they actually were. An odd thing, heredity, a fact fully demonstrated by his own raucous brood.

"Mum," said Camilla, bursting in behind him, blond, bossy and self-important from being the eldest. "Have you shown Cousin Isabelle Harry's Christmas letter?" The whole family hooted with laughter.

Harry Annesley, famous architect, lived in fashionable Barnes, West London, with his saintly wife, Lavender, and four perfect children. For some odd reason, perhaps because he traveled so often to the States, he had evolved the habit over recent years of sending his relatives and friends a Christmas round robin crammed with details of his burgeoning riches and the dazzling achievements of his unparalleled family.

"Pompous prat!" muttered Teddy, as they read it triumphantly aloud for the umpteenth time, putting special emphasis on the doings of those tedious gifted children. He never had had much time for his wife's cousin; considered him a prig and a hypocrite as well as an insufferable bore. Luckily they didn't see too much of him these days. Teddy suspected it had something to do with their own comfortable lifestyle, which somehow seemed to stick in the architect's craw. Though for no apparent reason, since all he could ever talk about was money and material advancement. The Cartwrights's gorgeous home was right up his alley. It was strange, in fact, that he didn't visit them more.

Isabelle hadn't met him yet, not since she was a child; was, in any case, finding this huge and complex family hard to cope with.

"Can we go through it again?" she pleaded. "And sort out who is descended from whom?" Her own father, Charlie, the sixth of the Annesley children, had wandered off abroad while still in his teens and never really been reconciled with them since. Apart from a fleeting visit as a schoolgirl, this was Isabelle's first time in England. She had a lot of catching up to do.

"It's quite straightforward, really," said Clemency. "There were nine children, of which five are still living, and all had issue except three." Put that way, it did sound simple, but Isabelle knew it was not.

"Plus Grandpa's other children," piped up Humprey, the pedant.

"Hugo, who died as a child," explained his mother. "And Agnes, who is a nun."

"And what about Thomas and Patrice, the serial marriers?" said Teddy. "Don't forget them. They really snarl things up."

"And Eunice and Ethan, the oldest and youngest, neither of whom ever married at all, let alone begot children."

"Stop!" said Isabelle, in mock despair. "You're going to have to draw me a family tree. Else, goodness knows, I'll never get it straight."

"Mummy, I've counted and counted," said Emma, "but can only ever get it to eight."

"Eunice, Claire, Henry, Aimée," recited her sister.

"Charlie, Thomas, Patrice and Ethan," finished Emma. "Eight."

"You're forgetting Roland," said Clemency. "The one who died. I'm sure we've got it all written down somewhere. It's a pity family bibles went out of fashion."

"Why did our grandparents have so many children in the first place?" Piers had never really thought about it till now.

"Mémé is a Catholic."

"Though that's not really the reason. Grandpa wasn't. I think it was just because they loved each other so much."

"One of life's great love stories. Truly romantic."

"So what went wrong?" All eyes turned to Clemency.

"I don't really know"—she shrugged—"but something certainly did. Mémé just upped and offed in 1961, and that was that. The end of an idyll. It almost destroyed your grandfather."

"Though he married again."

"Eventually, yes, but his heart was never in it. Kay was just a substitute, and a pretty poor one at that, though I'm really not blaming her. She worked with him in the department and was conveniently there to cook and clean and mop up after him, particularly as he got older. Like wives the

22

world over, if we're honest about it."

Clemency beamed. She wasn't like that and the world didn't need telling. She presided over this cozy family of hers with an astounding capability, while also sitting on the parish council and effortlessly juggling other part-time causes. In the short time she'd been over, Isabelle had grown to respect her; love her too. A family to warm your hands by, that's what the Cartwrights were. An only child herself, she was grateful for their generosity, for including her when they still hardly knew her at all.

"A paragon, that's my wife," said Teddy fondly, dropping a light kiss on Clemency's abundant hair. "Goodness knows where we'd all be if it weren't for her."

"Which is how it must have been in the Annesley household when Mémé took it into her head to jump ship."

"What did happen to Roland?" asked Isabelle as they cleared away the tea things. His photograph, identical to the one in the hall, also hung in her own parents' apartment, though she'd never really thought about it till now. Just another faded picture of another unknown relative. There were so many she'd never met, they all merged into one. Until now, since she'd been here, and the family was at last beginning to untangle and take shape.

"He drowned when he was just a boy," said Clemency, stacking the dishwasher. "Diving off rocks at Christmas Cove in Maine. It was a frightful tragedy at the time."

Isabelle wandered back into the hall for a closer look at this long-dead uncle. It was a formal portrait, typical of the period. He had short, dark hair and a serious expression but a quite discernible twinkle in his eye.

"He was certainly good-looking." A bit like her own father but better, though probably the pressure of years had taken their toll of Charlie. Clemency came up behind her.

"From all accounts, a bit of a daredevil too. My mother always said he missed his true calling by being too young for the war. He was fighter pilot material, fit and fearless, destined to die young. And when he did, it broke his mother's heart."

"Is that what happened to the marriage, do you suppose?"

"It's never been stated, but I've always thought as much. Losing a child at any age must be devastating. And Roland indisputably was her darling." Clemency shuddered. It was bad luck even thinking about it, though she tried not to be overprotective. Accidents did happen and among all those children it probably fitted the statistics. All the same. She ushered her visitor back into the warmth.

An academic herself, Isabelle was impressed by Clemency's knowledge.

"You've certainly got it down pat," she said admiringly. There seemed no end to her cousin's accomplishments. "You ought to be a biographer. If not a novelist."

Clemency laughed. "I've always been fascinated by the Annesley clan," she said. "They're living history in the making, part of my own children's heritage. You can learn an awful lot, you know, just from looking at your own immediate past."

"Now, what exactly was the story about Aunt Effie?" asked Isabelle later after they'd eaten, the children safely out of the way, packed off to bed. It had happened only a few months earlier, but she'd missed the details, as she was then in transit and taken up with her move to Oxford. Her father, never much of a communicator, had mentioned it only in passing.

"We never did find out," said Teddy, relaxing comfortably in his favorite armchair with a glass of the claret he'd brought from the supper table. Clemency was knitting, frowning slightly as she pored over the complicated cable pattern. They made a handsome couple and, again, Isabelle felt the smallest prick of envy. So far this sort of happiness had eluded her, though she knew she could never even hope to catch up with the blessed Clemency, on whom the sun seemed ever to shine.

"They think it was an intruder," said Clemency, relaxing her concentration and leaning back to ease her neck. "Someone walked into the house in Jersey and killed both her and Aunt Martha too. Just like that, without apparent motive. Nothing was taken, there was no sign of a struggle. And none of the locals saw anything out of the ordinary: no stranger, no unfamiliar car, not a thing."

"Why would anyone want to do that?"

"You tell me." Clemency shrugged. "They were just two inoffensive old ladies living in quiet retirement. Had been there years, knew everyone in the village."

"The only clue," said Teddy, searching for cigarettes, "was a row of footprints from a man's seaboots. Or so the Jersey police decided."

"So the intruder came in by boat?"

"Looks that way. Though what he was after, Lord knows. They weren't rich, not as far as we know, and had never done anyone the slightest harm."

Isabelle pondered. "Were there any children? Any direct

relatives, I mean."

"Effie never married, kept house for her widowed father and her brothers. And Martha had been widowed for years."

"But she had a son."

"Our second cousin. Can't for the life of me remember his name right now. Dropped out of university in his second year and went off abroad, never to be heard of since."

Clemency shook her head as she stitched. Her own childhood had been close-knit and very happy; she was doing her best to reconstruct that security among her own four children in this beautiful house.

"We don't even know if he knows about the murders. No one's heard a word from him in years."

3

Élodie Sinclair stood at the window and watched the morning traffic stream towards the Champs-Élysées. It was already six-thirty and time she was at work, but she lingered over her latté, warming her hands around the comforting ceramic mug. Behind her, on the bed, last night's conquest still snored it off, tanned torso sprawled across the sheets, those strange, far-seeing slate-grey eyes veiled in sleep by lashes as thick and luxuriant as a girl's. She turned to look at him. It was chilly up here in her fifth-floor attic studio, and the thin satin slip she wore did little to warm her. But last night had been worth it; she didn't regret a moment of it. A small smile curved the corners of her mouth. It had been a long time since she'd enjoyed sex that good.

She'd spotted him quite by accident, at the pulsating nightclub two streets away that she occasionally visited for a late-night booster on her way home from the fashion house. At this time of year, with the spring shows imminent, Élodie worked around the clock, and last night's madness was the kind of delicious R and R she felt she richly deserved yet rarely found. Certainly not of that caliber. She'd been sitting with her cognac in the corner of the bar, catching up on the day's news, when the live music trio had emerged for their session and she'd found herself drawn both to the music—the sort of melodic jig with a kick that she found more emotive than the usual tuneless racket—and to the mesmerizing looks of the lead singer. His voice was raw and husky, with a primeval sexiness that instantly aroused her, and his entire persona fascinated her so much that she ordered another cognac, something she rarely did, and settled back to give him her full attention.

He was certainly worth it. Beneath the pounding rhythm and through the massed dancers on the pocket-handkerchief floor, she watched him as he sang and found she could not look away. He was of fairly average build, just under six feet she'd guess, with thick, dark hair and those startlingly pale, almost luminous eyes. The eyes of a wolf, she now observed, or some jungle predator. He was dressed conventionally in jeans and black T-shirt and the fit of his worn Levi's left little to the imagination. Élodie's hormones began to zing and she knew she had to have him, and have him soon. The leaden weariness brought on by too many nights of too little sleep lifted magically; almost before she'd realized what she was doing, she was out there, moving unpartnered to the music while fixing his eyes with her own. And he, receiving her message loud and clear, grinned broadly back at her as he played and sang, and she knew she'd snared him, at least for that night. So much for the chic Parisian teenyboppers in their ultra-cool outfits that barely skimmed their cute little bums. Élodie, dressed down in stark leather drainpipes and a skimpy chiffon T-shirt of her own design, wiped the floor with the lot of them, though she probably had a good ten years on most of them. Which didn't say a lot for the much-trumpeted French mystique. It took a streetwise New Yorker to score with style, once she'd reactivated her flagging energy and thrown herself into the beat.

By three in the morning the dancers were dropping off and the boys of the band stubbed out their cigarettes and began to dismantle their equipment. This was Élodie's cue to depart. She left a loose pile of francs on top of the bill, rose languorously and slowly stretched, letting him see everything she had to offer, then swung her Chanel purse over one shoulder and sauntered out of the bar without a backwards glance. It was two blocks to her apartment building; she walked quite quickly and held her breath that he would follow, knowing with fatal certainty that he would.

As he did. He caught up with her just as she was reaching for her keys, took them wordlessly from her fingers and ushered her through the massive main door, letting it glide silently shut behind them. There, on the unlit staircase, he took her in the way she'd always dreamed of being taken, ripping up the thin, expensive chiffon to uncover her boyish breasts, yanking down her leather pants while he fumbled with his own belt buckle. It was thrilling beyond belief and Élodie found herself in a spasm of electrifying shock. *Do it, do it, do it,* hammered her brain and he was in there in a trice, hard and urgent as a steam hammer, splitting her up the middle and opening the way to ecstasy. He covered her mouth with his own and his saliva tasted of brandy and stale tobacco while the smell of his sweat mingled with hers and added to the force of their coupling. *Unreal.*

They had staggered up the darkened staircase, half clothed and gasping, grabbing at each other on every landing for another grapple. The building appeared to be asleep; not a sound emitted from any apartment as they silently wrestled and tugged at each other's clothes. Then he'd remembered his guitar, abandoned at the foot of the stairs, and went down after it, leaving her laughing weakly outside her own door. Once he'd safely reclaimed it and lugged it up all those stairs, the whole performance had started over again. She didn't know where they found the energy, but they were at it all night, until dawn rose over the Paris rooftops and the sounds of early traffic began to infiltrate her battered consciousness.

So here they were now, in the aftermath of passion, and she realized she knew nothing of him, least of all his name. She couldn't even recollect the name of the group, though it had been emblazoned across their purple drum kit. Well, that was how it went these days, the way she infinitely preferred it. She'd tried Grand Passion, and look where that had landed her—pushing thirty, alone in a foreign city, reassembling her shattered life and trying hard to reinvent herself. She wasn't even sure what nationality he was. Irish, possibly, from his slightly unraveled look and the beat of the music he played. If they'd spoken at all, it had only been in grunts. For all she knew, that was the best he could manage.

The thought amused her and rather turned her on. Well, so

much the better. Words got you nowhere; she was sick of high-living smart-asses. A bit of the rough was every woman's fantasy, and certainly tonight she'd lucked out and found it in spades. She turned for another peek and was startled to find him awake, those disconcerting eyes studying her with the same frank appraisal she'd already given him.

"You're awake."

"So it seems."

"You're American."

"Smart girl."

"Passing through?"

He laughed. "Something like that."

He sat up bare-chested and scratched himself under one arm. Charming. His beard stubble was heavy, but she still found him irresistible. Sharp desire tugged at some molten spot deep within her so that, drawn irresistibly, she found herself back on the bed, fighting him and struggling as he swiftly overpowered her. He was strong and muscular and carried no superfluous flesh, a man who lived an active life or perhaps fanatically worked out.

"You're certainly a goer," he admitted with an element of grudging admiration, as he collapsed, replete, on the tangled sheets and Élodie, slick with sweat and finally sated, lay there, eyes closed, wishing she need never move again.

Eventually she stirred and glanced at the clock, then shot upwards like a jack-in-the-box and stumbled from the bed. *Merde,* where had the time gone? She had a catwalk rehearsal and five sulky supermodels waiting for her at the studio. And she wasn't even dressed yet.

"If you need coffee, it's on the stove," she directed from the shower. Then: "Guess you'd better get a move on. I need to be out of here like now."

When she reemerged minutes later, toweling her short, dark curls, he had roused himself and was zipping up his jeans, a cigarette already in place on his lower lip, guitar case by the door. He stood for a moment appraising her with those disconcerting, vulpine eyes, then opened the door without a word and began to descend the stairs.

"See you 'round," was all he said, and all of a sudden Élodie felt like a tart. Could he really be leaving her just like that, without so much as a second glance, outsmarting her at her own sophisticated game? She knew nothing of him except that she still fancied him and would kill to do it all again right now. She couldn't allow him to walk away, out of her life, just like that.

"Wait!" she called, hating herself, as he reached the main hallway. "What's your name?"

He paused a second, thoughtfully glancing up. Then wagged his fingers and let himself out into the street.

He was still very much on her mind that night when she got home, wearier than ever and with a throbbing hangover to boot. She really shouldn't abuse her body this way. She was almost thirty and, by rights, should be slowing down. All her life she'd had the energy of a whippet, which was how she stayed as thin and supple as the models she so much despised. And still there was scarcely a line on her olive-skinned face. But enough was enough. She continued to be in a towering rage when she thought of how he'd abandoned her. Like a piece of trash, trodden under the heel of his boot as he walked away. Nobody treated Élodie Sinclair that way; it was as well for him that he *wasn't* on the doorstep

31

when she finally made it home after ten.

Once inside the flat, however, her anger began to abate and she even considered freshening up and popping back to the bar down the road in case he was playing again tonight. But pride prevented her, just. She'd never in her life had to chase a man; she wasn't about to start now. If he didn't appreciate quality when he found it, well, that was his own damn bad luck. And if he was, as he'd said, just passing through, it was as well not to get too fixated on him. She'd been that route before and knew how self-destructive it could become. From this moment on, Élodie was determined to travel alone and travel light. She'd carefully shed all her surplus baggage and was not in a hurry to gather any more. Though it was a tragic waste of a brilliant fuck.

She flicked through her mail, which the concierge had left on the mat. Bills and more bills, plus a few late Christmas cards. And a hand-addressed letter in an expensive cream envelope in her grandmother's spiky writing. So what was the old trout after now? It had been years since Élodie had heard from Odile, despite the fact that they lived in the same country. She had little feeling for this woman she'd never known, just a faint, apathetic curiosity. Odile had fled the nest when Élodie's own mother, Patrice, was thirteen, deserting her at the crucial age when a girl most needs her mother. Patrice had never really recovered from it, had spent the main part of her adult life searching for a love she could trust. Élodie opened the envelope, nevertheless, and smiled a thin smile when she read its contents. So now the old bat was beginning to sense her own mortality and looking to her descendants to bail her out. Well, count me out, thought Élodie, angered anew. No way was she even going to respond.

Cousin Harry's Christmas letter was another matter entirely and served considerably to brighten Élodie's spirits. What a jackass he was, what a total jerk. She whistled cheerfully as she chopped fresh herbs and flipped herself an omelette. It had been years since they'd actually spent any time together, but he went on writing regardless, usually postcards from exotic, faraway places, more to impress than to maintain any real connection with a cousin he'd never taken the time to get to know. She'd forward it to her mother in Connecticut for a laugh, though in all probability Patrice would have had one, too, if he wasn't too cheap to pay the excess postage. Harry Annesley had some mistaken feeling of family and rank and seemed to consider himself leader of the pack, at least of his own generation.

"A busy year for the Annesleys," ran this year's letter, tastefully printed on holly-garlanded paper with a color photo of the six of them superimposed at the top. Harry, with those strange, pale eyes and perfect features that echoed his grandfather's distinction, was standing beside a stiffly smiling Lavender with his arms around two of the daughters. They were a bunch of creeps as far as Élodie was concerned, but she couldn't resist rereading the smirking self-assurance of this letter couched in the inimitable jargon that was recognizably Harry's own. *"My new development on the smarter side of the river grows apace and rumour hath it that we may receive a special Aims for Industry Award for technical innovation and design. Gratifying to be filling a national need while doing the thing one loves best. Lavender is keeping busy with her charity work. Her October ball for the Asthma Foundation chalked up a*

record £150,000. *And, it can be safely reported, a cracking good time was had by all."*

Élodie chuckled. Harry really was a jackass. She dimly remembered Lavender from the wedding, a slim, neat creature with a glacial smile, but hadn't seen much of her since. Not exactly overflowing with the milk of human kindness; that, at least, had been Élodie's impression. Harry was the one who seemed to have some sort of family feeling. Whatever his faults, she had to give him marks for that. Or was he merely posing and bragging?

"Vivian has reached Grade Eight on the violin, the youngest boy in the school to scale those heights, while dancing continues to be very important to Clarissa and a week's summer school with the Rambert Dance Company has fueled her enthusiasm. Next year she will have to choose between her dual images of danseuse extraordinaire *and brain-on-legs . . ."* What prissy names they all had, to be sure. The choice, no doubt, of the upwardly mobile Lavender, the bank manager's daughter from Brighton, with an elevated perception of her own social importance. *". . . while Pamela and Cornelia excel on the recorder and hope soon to form a family quintet."*

There was more in the same vein, but Élodie couldn't be bothered to reread it. She changed her mind about her mother, screwed it up, and tossed it contemptuously into the bin.

"Jackass!" she hissed again, but at least he'd made her smile. And banished momentarily from her mind all thoughts of the elusive stranger.

4

O dile's New Year letter had had a far more electrifying effect on her oldest grandchild, Harry Annesley. It lay now on his office desk where he'd brought it after breakfast and he leaned back in his leather swivel chair, fingers looped above his head, gazing out at the famous Barnes duck pond and pondering its precise significance. A small cute daughter wandered in, recorder in one hand, but he ordered her abruptly out of the room, commanding her snappishly to close the door behind her. Bloody kids. Working from home had at first seemed a brilliant idea; lately he was not so sure.

Lavender stuck her head around the door, making him wince once more.

"Why's Cornelia out here crying?" she asked disapprovingly. Then, without bothering to wait for an explanation: "I'm off into town to look for a hat."

"Then take her with you." Why wouldn't they understand, the lot of them, that working from home did not automatically mean he had nothing better to do? True, the original plan had been, supposedly, to spend more time with the family—that's how he'd got his wife to agree to letting him intrude his business affairs into the tranquillity of the house she so much loved. But also to save money and be closer to the site. Or The Site, as he was apt to think of it now, his ambitious Thames-side development, just a half mile down the road, which was taking up more and more of his waking time and starting even to intrude into his dreams.

He wandered through to the room overlooking the garden, which Lavender had dubbed his "trophy room," and stood looking out at the river beyond. Rows of squash cups and cricket photographs lined the paneled walls, with crossed sculls over the doorway and his Bisley shooting certificates framed on a shelf. The rest of the family entered here at their peril. Selfish it might be, but Harry never saw it that way. He'd renovated and paid for the ruddy house; it wasn't a lot to ask for a bit of territory all his own.

The truth was that, despite his confident bragging to anyone who cared to listen and a widening list of recipients of the annual newsletter, all was not as rosy in Harry's life as he would have the world believe. Certainly not on the business side, not right now. To begin with, the property market had not boomed at quite the expected rate and the crippling funding he had had to raise in order to develop his riverside scheme still occasionally made him feel giddy. Especially when he woke in the early hours, anxious and sweating, and found himself wondering if he'd bitten off more than he could chew.

Even apart from the finance, he'd encountered unbelievable calamities. The emergence of an underground spring, not marked on the out-of-date maps he had used, had led to soil subsidence and, in its turn, inevitable trouble with some well-heeled Barnes residents who'd objected to the noise and intrusion of his bulldozers with the resulting mud and brick dust. They had petitioned the council, who had, in their turn, ordered all work to cease until the finer legal points had been ironed out, a matter which had spread into months. Which meant he was now running more than a year behind schedule and the markup on the flats he was building was not keeping abreast of inflation. His financiers were starting to make ominous noises and a lot of his time these days was spent dodging their calls.

The brutal truth was simply that what Harry needed now, and fast, was an infusion of hard cash to see him through this unfortunately sticky patch. Which was why, at first, Mémé's letter had seemed such a godsend, until he got to thinking about its fuller implications and the fact he was expected to share with so many others what he considered to be his lawful inheritance. Harry was the oldest grandchild, born ahead of even Clemency's brothers, and he saw no reason at all why he shouldn't scoop the lot. The custom of primogeniture being such, in his mind there was no question at all that his grandmother should even think of dividing her estate. Not, of course, that he wished her any harm, but she'd had a good innings, and eighty was quite old enough for a woman who'd served all apparent useful purpose.

He glanced again at the letter. Cash to the boys, to be divided ten ways, and the rest to go to the girls. There was no telling how much she was likely to leave, but it stuck in his craw that it should be diluted this way when he almost certainly needed it most and would undoubtedly put it to better use. The girls were to get her "personal effects," but there was no mention, not here, of the house and its land. And that was what Harry really coveted. Had done since his early manhood.

He had tried telephoning the old-fashioned firm of Toulouse lawyers who had traditionally handled the affairs of the Rochefort family, only to find himself rebuffed in stiff though courteous French. Madame Annesley, he had been informed, was these days in touch with them solely by letter. They had no instruction to deal with anyone else and were therefore regretfully unable to answer his queries.

When Odile Annesley fled in 1961, taking with her only the bare necessities, to seek refuge alone in her old family *mas* among the vineyards of provincial France, all further mention of her had been forbidden in the home she had lately abandoned. No one spoke her name anymore, at least not in Grandpa's presence, and if the children ever whispered it to each other, it was only privately, behind closed doors. Harry was scarcely born at that time so had no real memory of her at all, nor had he ever experienced firsthand those Camelot years, part of family lore, when the Annesley clan was a tight-knit unit and Cornelius and Odile were still so much in love.

Which doubtless helped to add to the impact when, as a student backpacking across Europe, he'd eventually seen for himself Mas des Vignes and had fallen so desperately in love with it. An old stone farmhouse dating back to the beginning of time, improved and added to over the centuries, it stood alone in the midst of acres of wine-growing land and, with its closed courtyard and heavy wooden gates, was as private and impregnable as a fortress. Any budding architect's instant dream; a heritage to be coveted and to brag about.

Along with Ben, a pal from Oxford, Harry had rented a Fiat and driven the five kilometers or so from Uzès, the nearest market town. They hadn't warned Mémé they might show up; in retrospect, perhaps they had been wrong. It had simply not occurred to the youthful Harry that he might not be welcome whenever he chose to call. He might not actually have seen her since childhood, but this was, damn it all, his own father's mother and he took it for granted she'd be thrilled to see him. All his life till then he had lived a charmed existence, confident and exceptional at all he did. He'd inherited some of his grandfather's stern handsomeness and also his intolerance of anyone he deemed a fool. He had also, in a lesser degree, a modicum of Odile's artistic talent, which had helped him in his rapid ascent of the foothills of fashionable architecture. The golden boy, in short, returned in triumph to lay claim to the fatted calf. Which is why the reality had come as such a shock.

They'd arrived in late afternoon, which seemed a perfectly reasonable hour—time enough for an early supper yet not so late as to inconvenience her. Harry was full of excitement, not least when he saw Ben gawking at the handsome old farmhouse with its fortified entrance. And all the land.

"Is that hers too?"

"Absolutely."

Though raised comfortably in a middle-class suburb, Harry liked to cultivate an upper-crust veneer and claimed finer breeding than he actually possessed, a fatal flaw that had led him to Lavender, whose high-boned haughtiness implied bluer blood than she actually had. Two frauds together, inevitably fated. But that had been all still in the future, a different story.

The huge wooden gates were tightly shut and secured with a padlock which, from the look of it, was rarely undone. The boys wandered around the perimeter wall and found a side door with an old-fashioned bellpull. Harry jerked at it. Nothing happened.

"Hello there!"

They circled again, peering through barred windows, but

could see no light, no movement, nor so much as a flicker of a sign of life within. Which was bloody inconvenient after the distance they'd just traveled, on the road since the early hours. They were desperate for a pee and something to eat and drink, and it was spoiling Ben's first impression of Harry's ancestral home.

"Was she expecting you?"

"Well, no, not exactly. But where else could she possibly be in this out-of-the-way hole—an old girl like her, living on her own?"

To Harry, around whom the universe revolved, there was little consideration of the requirements or convenience of others. It was jolly thoughtless of her not to be there after all the effort he'd put in. They considered telephoning, but it was the days before cellular phones and the farmhouse stood alone amid acres of vineyards. Anyway, as sharp-eyed Ben had pointed out, there weren't any visible wires. True isolation, this; she had gone to ground in the heart of the countryside without a connection to the outside world. What a way to live.

They ended up having to relieve themselves in the bushes, then circuited a final time while Harry rang the bell again and rattled the door. Where could she be? Having a nap in the garden, perhaps. Eventually they heard distant noises from inside the house and the welcome sound of bolts being drawn. Slowly the door was opened a crack and a dark, faintly menacing face peered out.

"*Oui?*"

"Madame Annesley?" asked Harry brightly, flashing the orthodontic excellence his parents had paid so much for.

"*Qu'est-que vous cherchez?*"

"*Madame Annesley. Ma grand-mère.*"

The man, what they could see of him, was tall and power-fully built, with heavily weathered skin. He was roughly shaven and dressed like a peasant in a dark blue work shirt and shapeless dungarees. His eyes bored into them. His boots were ancient and cracked and heavily laden with mud. He made no attempt to widen the gap; merely stood there in the doorway, glaring out.

"*Et l'autre?*" He indicated Ben.

"*Mon ami. Nous*—what the hell's the word for travel together?"

"*Voyagons,*" supplied Ben helpfully.

"*Votre nom?*" His attention returned to Harry, who was by now back in the car, scrabbling in his backpack for his passport.

"Harry Annesley," he called. "*Je-suis-le-grandfils-de-Madame.*" His accent might have lacked finesse, but he spoke slowly and distinctly in condescending Brit manner, with carefully raised voice, while waving his passport in the man's face. Surely even this French clod could understand him; it wasn't that difficult.

But the man remained immovable and showed no sign of comprehension. Harry, with difficulty, held on to his temper. Whoever this fellow might be, his attitude was insufferable. Wait till he did get through to Mémé; heads were going to roll in a major way. The man continued to block their entrance, scrutinizing them both with glittering eyes that gave nothing away. When Harry made a move as if to force his way inside, the door swung sharply inwards.

"Now, look here, my man," said Harry at his most author-itative, abandoning all attempts to deal with the damned

41

lingo. "I insist on seeing my grandmother, *tout de suite*. I've come all this way from England. It's my right." Suddenly inspired, he dug deep into his pocket and brandished a five-hundred-franc note in the man's face.

This, to his surprise, simply made the Frenchman grin, with the flash of a gold tooth through his heavy stubble. What exactly was so amusing was not at all obvious. The brute still blocked the entrance and showed no interest at all in being bribed.

"Mémé!" screamed Harry eventually, losing it and trying to push past the brute. The man's face darkened instantly, all humour fled. "*Non*," he said menacingly. "*Pas ici.*"

And closed the door firmly in Harry's face.

Later, once he'd calmed down and they were comfortably settled in a nearby hostelry, Harry tried his charm again on the friendly innkeeper who luckily spoke passable English. Yes indeed, he told them, Madame Annesley was well known in the village, though he'd seen her around less frequently in recent years. A veritable beauty in her day, the man kissed his fingertips expressively, as well as a talented painter. Such a waste to hide herself away like that, alone apart from some domestic help.

"And the man?" asked Harry, curious. The thug who had refused them access.

"Oh, he is, how you call it—her odd-job man. Her help."

"Does he live there?"

"*Oui*, in the barn, so I'm told."

"He's certainly hostile."

The man laughed. "Just an honest French citizen, protecting his property."

And that, so it appeared, would have to be the end of it. They did, however, make a brief detour next day on their way through to Avignon, to check out the house one final time and see if anything had changed. Although it was a fine, bright morning, they still could see no sign of life. Not a window open, not a shutter unbarred, the gates still heavily padlocked. This time he didn't even bother getting out of the car, though he did take a few quick snaps, which he still had tucked away somewhere. Evidence of a dream that, over the years, had refused to go away, something that now might soon be within his grasp. If he played his cards right. What was it that was struggling to come to the surface of his consciousness? A distant whisper from his early youth of some family scandal that had been hushed up. Mad Aunt Effie, was it, who had let it slip? Or garrulous Pandora, Tom's first wife, with a mouth that was always on the gab? He strained his memory and almost got it; something to do with one of the girls, a baby born on the wrong side of the blanket. Well, that was what he needed now, proof that would get at least one of them excluded. Every little should help.

But time was growing short and he needed professional assistance. Harry switched on the computer and flicked to his personal organizer. Somewhere he knew he had the address of a family ally he reckoned he could trust, with just the right credentials for the job and similar motivation. Before he was through, he meant to get possession of it all. Especially Mas des Vignes, which had dwelt so long in his dreams, the ideal bolt-hole in which to plan the start of a whole new life.

5

*M*adeleine Russell stood in the early morning sunlight in her beautiful state-of-the-art kitchen, sipping herbal tea as she watched *Breakfast News*. She had to be in Baker Street by nine, but that still gave her tons of time. She was fresh from the shower but already immaculate, with her flawless skin and pale gold, drip-dry hair which fell automatically into a heavy, silken bob. Thank God for London and the magic scissors of Nicky Clarke. Her fingernails were perfect too and she studied them now as she listened to the weather forecast. Cold but dry; that suited her just fine. She was taking a client to view a building development that wasn't yet finished. A little rain and it would be filthy underfoot. First impressions were always the most important, as Madeleine knew from experience.

She chose a Joseph sweater in heavy cream and teamed it with a matching skirt that barely skimmed her knees. High-heeled boots in caramel suede completed the ensemble, which would look stunning beneath her cashmere coat. Provided the rain did hold off. She shook her head until her hair fell perfectly, then lacquered it lightly to preserve the casual look. A touch of pale blusher on her arctic skin and Madeleine was ready to confront the day. Huge dark glasses, for effect rather than protection, a whisper of lip gloss, and she was set to go. She picked up her car keys and suede driving gloves from the glass-topped table in the hall. Figaro sat forlornly beside them, tail wrapped tidily around his paws, striking an upright, noncaring pose like an ancient Egyptian cat on a tomb. But there wasn't time for any of that right now.

" 'Bye now, lambkin," she said as she left, kissing his sleek head. Today was the day her cleaner came in; he'd have plenty to occupy him until she got home, chasing dusters and stalking the hoover.

The Porsche was a luxury she couldn't really afford, but it was worth any number of skimped meals and missed holidays just for the lift it gave her in the mornings. That envious stare from strangers, usually men, as she shot past them in the rush hour and wove her way expertly into the fast lane. Today the traffic on the Bayswater Road was unusually light, so she made it in record time. Enough to fit in a few vital calls before the client arrived. She closed her door to indicate she was not to be disturbed and settled down for a fast half hour of power bargaining. Selling property was not what she'd set out to do in life, but she seemed to have a natural flair, so it was okay for now. Until something more inspiring came along.

Sometimes she fantasized that that something more inspiring would turn out to be a man, to whom she could devote her life. People who barely knew her, which was most, would have been surprised to learn that such sentiment could exist beneath the ice maiden's super-cool exterior. To the world at large she appeared to have it made, to be working up her career curve ruthlessly and methodically, totally in control. They were wrong. Inside her head, Madeleine was a mess, a tangle of mixed emotions and childish terrors, amazed at the end of each day that she'd managed to get there at all. She was thirty-five and beginning to lose hope. No matter how many dates she might

45

have—and her answering machine worked overtime—usually she came home with a hollow feeling that all this socializing was a futile waste of time, such shallow encounters meaningless and demeaning. For that special someone continued to elude her no matter how hard she searched. Back in the States, when she occasionally visited her mother, she found all her former classmates busily engaged in blind dates, very much *de rigeur,* it seemed, among singles of all ages. Older people, in retirement homes and the like, she could just understand; after a lifetime devoted to that one special person, making do the second time around was perhaps acceptable. But she hadn't yet met that one and her skin crawled at the idea of advertising her need. How totally humiliating; she'd prefer to remain a spinster.

It did seem at times an impossible quest. Looking at things logically, any man designed to turn her on would need to be at least her financial equal, and these days she was earning considerably more than most. No matter what they said about equality, she knew she could never find sexy anyone younger or less high-powered than herself. There could be no shopping down for her; she knew she wouldn't respect any bloke whose ambitions and achievements did not match her own. It might seem hardheaded, but that was how it was; at least she was honest about herself.

"Lighten up," her best friend, Julie, told her. "Fucking is fun provided you don't take it seriously."

Julie was a journalist on a glossy magazine whose main pursuits, outside work, were shopping and screwing around. She was bright and feisty with bold black eyes and an unabashed come-hither look that nearly always brought results. Madeleine admired her for her fearlessness and spirit but knew that, in a million years, she could never possibly act like that herself. Not, indeed, that she'd want to. Her mother, Aimée, had brought her up carefully to behave like a lady and not let the family down.

"They won't respect you," she had always warned, and even though that attitude was way out of date, Madeleine stuck to it as far as she could. Her sexual life had started relatively late and even these days, in the emancipated late nineties, there were few men she'd allow into her confidence, let alone her bed. Not that it damaged her social rating; quite the reverse. Madeleine was becoming something of a legend in Notting Hill; men fought for the privilege of being rebuffed by one of those glacial stares.

The client today, a stockbroker in his fifties, showed signs of wanting the meeting to continue through lunch. He'd liked the new flats, was a possible buyer, but thought he'd prolong the pleasure of looking around, provided this delectable salesperson would continue to be his guide. Madeleine made a swift decision. She hated having to chat to them after hours but could sense a possible sale a mile away. And this man was a sucker just asking to be led over the edge.

"Just a quick one, then," she told him as he directed the cab to his St. James's club. They always did that, as if it would impress her, when really boys' food did nothing to turn her on. If they only knew it, they were far more likely to score in an atmospheric trattoria or sushi bar. But since she had no intention of ever seeing this man again, not once he'd signed on the dotted line and she knew the sale was safely in the bag, she was quite content to play along with his vanity and suffer another uninspired offering of potted shrimps and an unpalatable steak.

She asked politely about his wife, which usually brought them to heel, and watched with satisfaction as he squirmed and shifted his gaze. She was "in the country," which was what they always said. Madeleine suppressed a grin as she watched him wriggle and try to bring the conversation back to a satisfying level of flirtation. Any minute now and he'd be telling her the poor woman didn't understand him. She glanced swiftly at her discreet gold watch. Ten past two, must go. Every second spent in this stuffy men's club was time away from the telephone and the market. She extracted a promise that within the week he'd bring his wife to view the property, then streaked back to the office, leaving him to deal with the bill. If she ever did find her prince, the man of her dreams, she'd certainly not risk leaving him, alone and dissatisfied, to philander away his days and evenings like this.

After a grueling day spent viewing other people's homes, many of them seedy, some even verging on the horrendous, it was always a pleasure to return to Chepstow Villas and let herself into her own cool and spacious flat. Madeleine had struck lucky with this particular purchase and bought at a time when the area was just on the turn. Speed was essential, as she knew from her job, and she'd put in her offer on the spot, without waiting for a survey or even trying to bring down the price. The vendor, a first-time owner starting to work up the property chain, had been so startled by her positive attitude, he'd been instantly on his guard.

"Well," he said thoughtfully, stroking his chin. "I *have* had a couple of offers already. . . ."

Madeleine recognized an opportunist when she saw one;

she was one herself. "The offer's on the table but only for three days," she snapped, feigning a sudden loss of interest as she pulled on her driving gloves and picked up her keys. Beneath the elegant cashmere, her heart was beating wildly, but a glance at her untroubled beauty gave nothing away to the casual observer. Porcelain looks occasionally had their upside, though Madeleine often cursed them and wished she could look sexier and more of this world. But this time the advantage was all hers. Seeing the doubt flicker across his face, she pulled out her checkbook and swiftly uncapped her pen.

"I'll give you a deposit right now," she said smoothly, praying the bank manager would play ball and not let her down. "Does that clinch it?" She hadn't been long in the business at that time, wasn't seasoned enough to be certain of her ground, but it was clear that the vendor was also at sea, so she pressed her advantage.

"I'm offering you the asking price," she said reasonably. "Why bother messing around?"

She had a point and he knew it; shopping offers was illegal. In only seconds, he'd conceded her victory and pulled the cork of a bottle of passable wine in order to toast the deal. Madeleine left with a smile on her face and joy in her heart that knew no bounds. Even the disbelief on the face of her lawyer—"You gave him money? You don't even know that he owns it!"—or her accountant's anguished cry—"For such a short lease! What a terrible invest-ment!"—had failed to get her down. Madeleine lived for the moment, and that was now. The home of her dreams in an area she loved; security over gilt-edged investment every time. Surf-riding, that was her forte, and she rarely lived to regret it. Luckily there was no one she needed to clear it with; any mistake she made was entirely her own.

But it had worked. Always spontaneous, except when it came to love, Madeleine acted on impulse and usually proved herself right. The cashmere coat that had cost her an arm and a leg; the string of real pearls bought on auction at Bonhams, even the Porsche. Extravagance on the surface, enough to keep her awake at nights sweating, but in the end pure value, justifiable even to the bank. Go for quality, her mother always told her, shop at the top of the market, and that was what Madeleine did. Chepstow Villas was an up-and-coming area and quick-witted Madeleine slipped in there just ahead of the trendies. Four years before the common-hold law became valid.

The cleaner had been and the place smelled wonderfully of beeswax, with everything in order and fresh flowers in the hall. Figaro lay sinuously sprawled in the center of the impressive Chinese rug, welcoming her home with splayed legs and his head turned coquettishly to one side.

"Sausage!" She dropped her bag and keys and swept him up, rubbing her cheek appreciatively against his thrumming, dark brown velvet body. On a good day, this was all the company she needed, the constant adoring presence of her beautiful Burmese cat, another impetuous purchase made at a cat show when she could barely afford it.

She tossed her coat onto her immaculate white bed, then went on into the kitchen to give him his supper before he began asking for it. It was dark already, but the myriad tiny daylight bulbs that lit her kitchen ceiling bounced off her stainless steel fittings and the dazzling white-on-white effect

50

she had laboured so long to achieve. White with a touch of lemon. Minimalist and perfect, like Madeleine herself, and every bit as unsullied. She winced. It was an easy joke, one which her friends liked to make, but deep inside she'd begun to resent it. On an impulse she exchanged the blond wool for jeans and a suede jacket. The ice-maiden image was beginning to pall; it was not her fault that her father had Norwegian blood. She was tired and depleted and in need of a meal and a rest, but every now and then it seemed life was threatening to pass her by. Madeleine dropped her car keys and walked around the corner to the pub.

At first she couldn't see if he was there, but then, as the crowd shifted, she spotted him in his usual place, settled in the corner with the *Independent* and a pint, deep in his reading, close to the blazing fire. Something knotted inside her began to relax, a sense of well-being that came from within. She loved her local and there he was, lately the one consistent in a callous world. She edged her way closer to the bar and ordered a gin and tonic. Double.

"Hi there, Madeleine. What gives?"

A nice man she'd encountered at Clifton Nurseries hailed her and made room beside him at the bar. It was a good crowd, this. Local and familiar and easy to relax with. Made her feel ordinary and at home. She glanced towards the inglenook and was relieved to see the man still there, engrossed in his newspaper, quietly sipping his beer. Dark and slightly disheveled, in jeans and a leather jacket, with eyes that she knew when he raised them to hers would be bright and perceptive and welcoming, with that slightly droll smile that made her go gooey inside.

She didn't know his name or even what he did; nothing

about him at all, in fact. Just that he'd been coming here regularly these past few weeks and that even though they'd never even spoken, he was as aware of her as she was of him. It had something to do with the way he shifted his gaze whenever she happened to glance his way; his habit of lingering while she was there, then immediately folding his newspaper and collecting his change when she started making obvious moves to leave. So far he had not attempted to speak to her or even accost her in the street. She wasn't quite sure what she'd do if he tried. Just that she ached to get to know him, that just his presence in the room made her senses hum.

Jack, she'd decided his name was, and, judging from his appearance and sloppy way of dressing, probably a newspaperman. One who worked long hours for far too little money, always putting his beliefs way ahead of his earnings. A foreign correspondent, maybe, or a campaigning journalist. She knew she was only fantasizing, but that's the way she was. Beneath the outer cool lurked a true romantic. A writer would do, or possibly even an actor, though she wasn't sure she'd be able to cope with that amount of ego. Anyway, Jack was too scruffy to be that aware of his looks, always a giveaway with performers, she'd found. Julie, who hadn't seen him, said he was probably a teacher— *boring*— but something about his alertness, the way he seemed aware of his surroundings even when his attention was glued to his reading, made Madeleine certain there was more to him than might appear. Much more.

He was looking at her now with that frank, appraising gaze, speculative and knowing, as though he could read her thoughts. His eyes were somehow penetrating and his thick, dark brows expressive. Madeleine found herself reddening and fumbled in her bag in confusion. It was after ten, high time she was heading home. No, she wouldn't have another, she told the nice man from the nurseries, then buttoned her suede jacket and headed off into the night. Jack would keep, at least for a while, until she had summoned the courage to work out exactly what she really wanted and possibly take the next step. Time now for bed—Figaro would be waiting—with another hectic, work-filled day lined up for tomorrow. And the next day, and the next.

The light on her answering machine was blinking and she hesitated before picking it up. There were several people, bores and discarded admirers, she was on the alert to avoid. But this late it could be urgent, so curiosity prevailed.

"Hi!" said a warm and breezy voice, surprising her because it was so long since she'd heard it. "It's your cousin Clemency calling from the country. Ring me back, will you, when you've got a minute?"

In spite of herself, Madeleine smiled. That was Clemency all over. Ever the organizer, the leader of the pack. Never too shy to come forward and speak her mind. But it warmed her heart, it really did, just to hear again that confident school-prefect voice. Families did have their place, provided they kept to it. She'd call her first thing when she wasn't quite so tired.

6

*G*et a move on, you little bleeder! We're late enough as it is." Cherie Cole stood stamping her feet with fury while her hyperactive child ran riot through the house, adding to the chaos while he sorted out things for school. "And leave those bloody kittens alone!" she shrieked with sudden cold foreboding as he raced upstairs and out of her sight. She need not have worried. When, seconds later, she followed him into the bedroom, she saw the mother cat had herded her new litter back into their box at the bottom of the wardrobe and was there in alert attendance, eyes slanted, ears flattened warningly, warding him off.

"Come along, Ashley, stop messing about." Cherie's temper was already almost at the breaking point. If he didn't stop acting up, he'd get a good belt around the ear, the least he deserved after all he'd put her through lately. She grabbed him by the arm and dragged him reluctantly back down the stairs and into the chill, dank morning outside. It was frigging miserable and she shivered in her thin jacket, but all her spare cash had gone on things for the boy. Cherie lit a Silk Cut, then clumped off down the cul-de-sac, Ashley dragging along behind her. She wore skintight jeans from the boys' department of C & A, a shiny Lurex anorak and ludicrously high wedge-heeled shoes that accentuated the frailty of her spindly legs. Her face was painted deadpan white, with ghoul-like black shadows around her eyes and glossy purple lips, though all that would have to come off once she got to work. The job at Tesco was like going to prison. All they ever thought of there were rules and regulations. Even smoking was forbidden, and that was just cruel.

The bus came late, and then it was crammed. Cherie, squashed between two beefy factory workers, felt her nose beginning to dribble but couldn't get her hand into her pocket for a tissue. She hated this life, which was worse than the salt mines. Living purgatory, with nothing to look forward to but debt. The school was several stops away and then they both had to get off so that she could drag him to the gates. No use trusting him to cover the last few yards alone. Last time she'd tried that, he'd disappeared for the day and she'd had the school inspector banging on her door.

"Got your sandwich box?" She smoothed his tousled hair. "Give Mummy a kiss, then, lovie." He wasn't really a bad kid, not deep down. It was just all this damned superfluous energy that kept him going like a wild thing day and night. He wriggled out of her grasp and ran towards the gates. Already, at five, he hated to show affection. Cherie lit another smoke and stood and watched him go. What she'd done to deserve this burden, God only knew, and He wasn't telling.

She was late again, by twelve and a half minutes, but still took the time, once she'd washed off her makeup and changed into the insipid pink overall she was obliged to wear, to snatch another illicit smoke on the fire escape outside the ladies' lav. Once she got in there, it would be solid grind for three hours before she was relieved and allowed to go for her dinner break. Talk about prison conditions. Those desk workers inside didn't know how fortunate they were not to have to battle against the real world.

Life had not been easy on Cherie Cole. Raised by a barmaid mother whose drinking had led to her early death, she'd been placed in foster homes since early childhood until she ran away at fifteen to look for a life of her own. She'd hung around the sordid streets of Solihull, finding work where she could, and lived on her wits quite effectively until, at nineteen, fate had intervened again and she'd found herself up the spout with a baby of her own. That had been the final straw and Cherie's fierce determination crumbled. Hating herself for her weakness, she'd given in and written to the one person in the world to whom she knew she had a genuine blood tie. Her absentee father's own mother in France, Odile Annesley.

Cherie had never really met Thomas Annesley, who'd died in a car crash along with the drunken barmaid, leaving her an orphan at the age of three. She knew very little of him except that he'd been a silver-spoon-in-mouth type who preyed on women as feckless as her mother and had littered the world with his children. So they said. There'd been two legal wives already, Pandora and Sylvia, by whom he had had three sons before he'd hit an all-time low and taken up with her mother, Betty Cole. He must have been aware of her, however, because his mother had written at the time of the crash and threatened to come and get her and take her back to France. But Betty Cole's half sisters, Rita and Irene, had had other ideas. To hell with the father, these two staunch Midlands housewives had decided; blood was blood and they'd see that the bairn was cared for, though neither was willing or able to give her a home. They'd arranged for her fostering in nearby Dudley and only lost their grasp on her when she'd run away and left no trace.

Odile's letter had been part of Cherie's inheritance, along with the god-awful French name her father had saddled her with. The Annesley family, who'd always ignored her, had a lot to answer for, she felt. So she swallowed what little pride she had left and wrote to this foreign woman who claimed to be her grandmother, but all she'd ever got for her trouble was a condescending visit from Harry Annesley, who'd turned up unannounced one day on her doorstep, declaring himself to be her cousin. The memory still made

Cherie grin, though why, she didn't quite know. What an utter prat he had turned out to be, with his posh BMW and swanky manners and a la-di-da accent you could cut with a knife. He'd taken one look at Cherie's swollen belly, glanced around the hellhole she had then known as home and written her a check for five hundred pounds to give the baby, he said, "a proper start in life."

Some laugh! She'd spent the money on food, cigarettes and baby things, then managed to get rehoused by the council. What they had now wasn't Buckingham Palace exactly, but she was proud of her small concrete house on a run-down estate and the fact that they hadn't removed Ashley from her custody. So take that, Cousin Harry, and ram it up your bum! A fat lot of good those posh connections had proved to Cherie Cole when she needed them.

Harry, however, had not seen it that way and obviously viewed himself as some kind of benevolent philanthropist. For the past five Christmases, since Ashley's birth, Cherie had been the privileged recipient of a Harrods hamper containing all kinds of ridiculous things she'd never heard of and didn't like. Gentleman's relish, indeed! Along, of course, with Harry's annual message, which did make her laugh, if only for its absurdity.

So you could have knocked her down with a feather this year when the Christmas post had brought, along with Harry's latest piece of pretentious showing-off, a letter from her grandmother in France, written in a language she didn't understand. Which was typical of the family thoughtlessness. Curiosity had conquered, however, so that she'd bitten back her resentment and taken the letter around the corner to an old lady she chatted to occasionally in the supermarket, who used to teach French. And that was when she'd discovered—with a jolt—that she was a potential heiress and that there might be something in these supposed family connections after all.

The kitten idea came from a glossy magazine she'd read at the clinic, in an article listing "Ten Ways to Earn Extra Pocket Money" or some ridiculous rubbish like that. Not that it was pocket money Cherie was after; clearing some of those threatening bills was more what she had in mind. She hit lucky with the first cat who turned up, pregnant, at the local branch of Animal Rescue and somehow got into Cherie's hands without them realizing or, at least, caring about her worth. She carried the nervous beast home carefully, made her a bed in an old cardboard box at the bottom of the wardrobe, then found herself forced to spend money she could ill afford on food, litter and vitamin pills to boost her health and keep her coat glossy. Breeders, she found out later, recommended a daily dose of egg yolks beaten up in Carnation milk, but Cherie thought to hell with that. Enough was enough, and she wasn't planning to show her.

Not then. Although not a touchy-feely sort of person herself, she was surprised how quickly she warmed towards this small, graceful creature whose pale tabby fur was as soft as cotton-wool and had a distinguishing silver undercoat, implying a breeding unheard of on this downtrodden estate. Mimosa, she called her, because she was exotic, and when the four kittens arrived, she sold them locally for a satisfactory profit. And that was how it got started.

To make real money out of this cat-breeding lark, Cherie discovered she needed formal proof of their pedigrees. So she'd joined the local Cat Fanciers' Association and boned up on the tips and pitfalls of becoming an authorized breeder. An unexpected windfall, in the shape of another check from patronizing Harry, had enabled her to invest in a pair of Burmilla kittens, a new breed evolved from a cross between a Burmese and a Chinchilla, and Cherie found herself in business. She now had three adult queens and this latest litter of five, and although it was hardly riches, it did help cover the more essential outgoings and the cats were company for her and Ashley. Though she hated to let them go, when the time came, and Ashley was a bit of a liability when it came to having these tiny, helpless creatures swarming all over the bed.

She stood by the school gates at three-thirty on the dot and silently observed her hyped-up child intent on some private game of his own which involved two sticks and an inordinate amount of humming. What went on in that small, tortured head no one could really account for. She dragged him to see doctors who had given him all kinds of tests, but so far none of them had come up with any answers and she hadn't the time to keep on with it. It wasn't that he was insensitive or rough; there were times, when he wasn't racing around like a headless chicken, that his lightness of touch quite startled her and she saw flashes of a talent she couldn't account for. Finger painting, for instance, was something that came to him naturally, from the moment he could first grab up handfuls of mud. Down at the community center they'd been impressed and asked if there was any artistic talent in the family. The well-meaning social worker wanted to know about his dad, but there Cherie couldn't oblige her. Which of those layabout lads it had been, she wasn't able to say. As far as she was concerned, each was as useless as the rest. The main thing was, none had stuck around.

Grandma Annesley, however, whom Harry rather pretentiously called "Mémé" was a painter of some repute in France and she was Cherie's granny too. It wasn't impossible, Harry said, that she'd passed on more of her genes than just the stubbornness and some of that talent might have filtered through to Ashley. Cherie knew nothing of these things, but Harry was strangely family-minded. Sometime, if she ever came to visit, he told her, shuddering inwardly at the very idea, they'd go through the family photo albums together and she could look for clues. Ashley certainly had the familiar slate-grey eyes. No one could deny that.

She grabbed his hand and broke into his reverie, but he kept up the high-pitched humming as he shuffled along beside her, still playing with the sticks. She asked him routine questions about his day but found he wasn't listening so let it drop. He wasn't really a bad kid, when all was said and done. She just wished sometimes she had someone to confide in, someone altruistic who'd help take off the pressure.

There was another letter waiting among the bills, addressed on expensive stationery in a bold, firm hand. This was obviously Cherie's week. She squinted at it as she closed the front door, but it wasn't writing she had ever seen before. She soon found out. A breezy note from another cousin, Clemency Cartwright, inviting her and Ashley for the weekend. All expenses paid.

7

*S*pain had exactly the ideal climate for golf, thought Pandora, as she stepped smartly out of the hotel entrance and shaded her eyes against the afternoon glare. Here, on the coast just south of Barcelona, it was clear and sunny, though not yet too hot. Not for bashing a little white ball along the fairways, even with a skin as delicate as hers. Muriel was waiting in the golf cart and they trundled off happily and on to the first tee, as bright and perky as two divorcées of a certain age can be. Well, if the truth be told, more than middle-aged, but Pandora rather hoped it didn't show.

She had always been pretty, and age had added an element of elegance that sat well upon her as she stood, feet apart, and gripped her number four iron. She had kept her figure and neatly turned ankles and the checked divided skirt she wore looked good with the pink La Coste shirt. That and the St. Andrews sunshield gave her a professional air that pleased her. She had worked hard on her game since her marriage broke up and was proud of the fact that she was now down to a nifty twenty-six handicap.

"Good shot!" yelled Muriel as she raised her iron and the ball flew high and clear. They made a good team and were comfortable traveling companions. Pandora had discovered, after all that upset, that there *was* life after marriage, after all, with far more warmth and camaraderie in it than during those turbulent years. Tom had dumped her when the boys were still small and she never had managed to find a permanent substitute, not that she cared that much anymore. She was still bright and chattery, for all the knocks she had taken, with a shallow gaiety that attracted a certain type. A good-time girl, was Pandora Annesley; always had been, always would be.

Life right now, all things considered, was treating her rather well. Her mother had died, after a lingering illness, leaving her a small bequest that provided a few modest luxuries. Living in Tunbridge Wells since the divorce was pleasant enough but low-key. This timely windfall had brought her the extras, a regular facial, a smart new car and a few trips abroad on an annual basis. Once they'd finished here, she'd decided with relish, they'd take a small detour up into France and pay a surprise call on her onetime mother-in-law. It had been years since she'd last seen Odile, probably only on a couple of occasions since Roland's funeral. Odile was already out of it by the time Pandora had caught and married Tom, the only reason she had managed to get away with it.

Pandora Clay had grown up with the Annesleys, practically part of the family, sharing their summers in idyllic Christmas Cove while her less fortunate parents remained out of sight in Portland. Though originally Aimée's friend from school, she had attached herself to the family as a whole and dated three of the brothers in turn. Roland first, her real true love, then—after his premature death—both Charlie and Tom in succession. She was older than Tom by a good five years but had married him defiantly when Charlie went abroad and Odile was no longer there to get in the way. Sharp-tongued Odile, who had never quite got over Roland, was inclined to be possessive of all her sons and had once observed sourly that Pandora's failing was that what she was in love with was the *idea* of the family and almost any one of them would do.

As it turned out, Odile need not have bothered worrying. Tom had never given up his philandering and their brief marriage had proved as rocky as a roller coaster. They'd been on borrowed time right from day one so that when Pandora finally caught him red-handed, it had come almost as a relief. Robert and Tommy were aged five and seven then, old enough to help her cope but not too advanced to miss their dad.

She missed his family, however, and often thought of those distant golden summers. Which is why, when Robert was born, she'd used it as an excuse to reestablish contact with Odile in France and still kept in touch by way of the occasional chatty note, even though they usually went unanswered. So she'd been thrilled and delighted this Christmas to receive an unexpected letter in Odile's austere hand, mentioning her forthcoming birthday and setting out her plans for her grandchildren's inheritance. Both boys were included in the financial share-out; although she had no idea how much they were likely to get, it would pay to stay in with her ma-in-law for her last remaining years. You never knew, this could be Pandora's lucky year. Everything comes, they say, to she who waits.

"And that part of France is supposedly delightful," she told Muriel as they pored over road maps as they planned their golfing holiday. "Close to both Avignon and Arles and only a stone's throw from the Pyrenees." And if they were lucky, she'd even invite them to stay. Pandora had long been curious about Odile's new life and would welcome the opportunity to linger and snoop. She had, after all, very little to return to and Muriel seemed game. So she'd dropped

Odile a card, announcing her impending visit, and packed her Michelin to be on the safe side.

The course was deserted as the sun rose higher, and Pandora was beginning to feel the heat. Once this game was over, they'd retire to the pool and waste away another few hours just lounging and gossiping and knocking back a few martinis. Good old Mummy, providing her with this cushion; at this time of life, a girl needed all the perks she could get. And last night in the bar Pandora had spotted a distinct possibility; slightly on the red-faced side, perhaps, and pompously English but fit and definitely in the right age bracket.

"You and your eternal romanticizing," said Muriel with a twinkle, but she had no objections. She was easily led.

At the thirteenth hole they ran into difficulties, but what could you expect, said Muriel, the superstitious. Pandora took a herculean swing and landed her ball into scratchy desert scrub.

"Jolly bad luck!" called Muriel cheerfully from the cart. "I'll head on over and meet you on the green."

She might have stayed to help, thought Pandora grimly, but suspected her friend was feeling the heat too. And in this sparse scrubland it couldn't be too hard to spot a ball; she'd be on it in a jiffy and then she'd show Muriel who was the better player.

She was wrong, though, and had been at it at least twenty minutes when she finally heard a rustling in the bushes and knew triumphantly that her friend had come up trumps. About time too, she muttered through gritted teeth, and waved her club without bothering to turn around.

"Over here!" she shouted, still kicking her way through

sandy soil. "I can't imagine where the damn thing's disappeared to. Ought to be obvious, I would have thought, amongst all this dratted dead grass."

Muriel didn't answer and Pandora went on looking until soft footfalls just behind her announced her presence.

"Shall I cheat?" asked Pandora, without looking around. "Drop another ball on the edge of the scrub and pretend you didn't see?"

Muriel stayed mute, which was not like her at all. Maybe she thought Pandora was serious and disapproved. That was the trouble with the Brits, no humour about the game. Muriel was ladies' captain at the club back home and took it all so seriously, even on holiday when she ought to be relaxing. Pandora straightened and turned to her with a smile, but the quip on her lips was wiped clean away when she saw who was standing there, silently watching.

"Lord!" she breathed, "wherever did *you* spring from?"

They were the last words she ever spoke.

Muriel found her when she eventually got around to looking, then screamed her lungs out and set off in the cart to get help. She'd only been dead a few minutes, was the steward's expert opinion. Face down in the sand with her skull caved in like an eggshell from that terrible blow from the sand wedge.

"Someone must have taken it from her bag," said Muriel dully, practically mute with shock. "She had lost her ball in the scrub and was looking for it."

"So it was probably just a random killing?" said the Spanish policeman thoughtfully. Maybe some local maniac with a special aversion to lady golfers. Perfectly possible, especially in this sun. He found women like this fairly irritating himself, though he doubted if he'd go quite so far, even if provoked, to suppress them. He took down some details, then snapped his notebook shut. Siesta time had come and gone; he had pressing business at a bar in Sitges. If they couldn't look after themselves, they really oughtn't to travel.

"*Adiós, señora,*" he said gravely as he replaced his cap and climbed back on his bike.

8

*W*e decided not to bother with Harry and the rest this time," said Clemency with a twinkle as she carried in the roast. Teddy was busy sharpening and she placed it before him with traditional reverence. "We thought we'd keep it to just immediate family and you girls. A chance to get to know each other better."

She had included her brother, Guy, however, a typical army officer, suntanned and fit, doing the honours with the rather good wine he'd brought.

"It's rather a case of coals to Newcastle here, I'm afraid," he said, grinning at Teddy. "But what the hell? It certainly beats chocolates."

They were twelve in all, including Ashley, at a table that could well have taken thirty, in the long, low-beamed room off the kitchen that led through French windows into the flower-filled garden. A house like this, four artisan's cottages skillfully knocked into one, was worth a cool half million in the current market, estimated Madeleine, possibly more. Fifteen minutes from Marlborough in a picture-postcard village. The Cartwrights had bought shrewdly when they'd first set up home together.

She caught Élodie reading her thoughts and grinned. This cousin from Paris whom she rarely saw was chic and funky in her own original way, skinny as a model in a tight boat-necked sweater with a multicoloured skirt she had apparently made herself. Élodie wore her dark curls cropped short, with huge silver earrings that swung as she gestured. She saw Madeleine watching and grinned right back. Of them all, that was the one she warmed to most, her sort of woman: modern, sophisticated and slightly detached.

Isabelle, the Canadian, looked nervous; and Cherie, the unknown quantity, sulky and a little scared. What an interesting bunch they were, all here together, five quite different women who shared the same blood. Ashley, for once, was behaving himself—sort of—banished to the far end of the table among a bubbling mass of Cartwright children.

Teddy carved and Clemency ladled out vegetables. They worked so well together as a team, Madeleine thought as she watched them. She got on well with Clemency, even though she found her inclined to boss, and had always been fond of Teddy, who was a love. By no means her sort of man, but that was okay. Madeleine was so fussy and her tastes so rarefied, she could never ever settle for this kind of low-key domestic coziness. Though it did have its attractions, she could absolutely see that, particularly on occasions like this. Again, she caught Élodie watching and was pretty sure she agreed. She didn't know much about her cousin's life in Paris except that she'd been there two years and seemed to love it. She had subtly altered since her New York days and now looked entirely French. It was funny how different aspects of your heritage could emerge at various times. Mémé's foreignness was clearly stamped on this grand-daughter, thin and high-charged with frenetic, expressive hands.

Cherie was feeling miserably out of her depth and trying hard not to hate them all. At least they weren't patronizing like Cousin Harry, well, Clemency was a bit but didn't mean to be. She had welcomed the Coles with warm hugs and an open heart and was doing her absolute best to make them feel at home. Even Ashley seemed to be subtly changing; his boisterous second cousins had got him surrounded and so far there'd been no embarrassing explosions of temper. Cherie glanced nervously along the table, not certain which knife and fork to use, and caught the eye of Guy, who winked. Nice man, less aware of his own importance than Harry, but with the same plummy voice that made her want to puke.

Teddy finished his carving and raised his glass in a toast.

"To the Annesley clan, God bless 'em. And all who sail with them!"

He looked around the table at the five different women and could already see strong resemblances there. Clemency and Isabelle were both chunky and dark-haired with wide, pale eyes and the same lustrous skin. Cherie and Élodie shared similar birdlike looks, thinner and nervy with natural curls. While Madeleine, the superior blonde, made a striking contrast with her silvery Nordic beauty. Yet they all had one thing in common, and that was truly amazing. They had identical noses, thin and straight and slightly too long, an echo of generations of bourgeois French farmers, evidenced by old photographs and family portraits. Most interesting.

"Come on, eat up. There's plenty more." Clemency passed the gravy boat and they all tucked in.

"Dreadful news about poor Pandora," said Clemency, once they were settled. "Beaten to death on a golf course with her own club."

"Felled by a sand wedge, how utterly poetic. Couldn't have happened to a more deserving woman."

"Bet she was winning," said Guy with a chuckle. "These golfing ladies are formidable when it comes to stealing a few strokes."

"Which one was Pandora?" Isabelle, bewildered, was at it again.

"Tom's first wife," said Clemency, glancing at Cherie. Did she know her true heritage and was it possible she'd care? Born out of wedlock and abandoned as a baby; surely she couldn't view her father with anything other than disgust.

"Tell us more about yourself," urged Clemency, to cover the awkwardness. The youngest of the cousins so far had scarcely contributed a word. Cherie, embarrassed to be the center of attention, shrugged. What was there to say? She was wearing her purple satin bomber jacket with jeans and her cumbersome footwear and sat hunched between Teddy and Isabelle, dying for a smoke and wishing she hadn't come.

"Where exactly is it you live?" Clemency was quite unstoppable. Somewhere in the Midlands, she knew from the strong accent, but couldn't now pinpoint precisely where.

Solihull sounded truly weedy when compared with London, Paris and Quebec, but it wasn't her fault that she'd been born a bastard, and she wasn't about to be made fun of now. Cherie scowled and pushed aside her plate.

"We live in a council house on a terrible estate," she said flatly. "Just the two of us with a load of cats."

"Cats?"

"Cats." There was a pregnant pause while everyone waited, so Cherie, reluctantly, was forced to expand. She explained about the kittens and how the hobby was beginning to work out. Clemency cooed and said, "How lovely," and even the children began to take notice.

"Darlings, once we've finished our meal," said Clemency brightly, "take Ashley down to the barn to see what we've got there." She smiled at the silent five-year-old, but he didn't respond. Just sat there stolidly staring at his plate, making that unnerving high-pitched humming sound as if he were run by machinery.

"I've got a Burmese," contributed Madeleine, and Cherie looked at her in sudden gratitude. She hadn't taken to this cousin at all, thought she looked superior and condescending. But when she spoke, she turned out to be perfectly human and the smile she gave Cherie was kind and perceptive. Poor little thing, she was silently thinking. There, but for the grace of God . . . Well, maybe.

After lunch they all repaired to the drawing room and Clemency produced the promised photo albums. The children trooped off to the barn to see the chickens and the pig, while Guy and Teddy slipped away to the study to watch the match.

"Gather 'round, girls," ordered Clemency, and spread the musty-smelling, leather-bound albums on the carpet where they could all get to look at them at leisure. And a lot of them there were.

"My mum was the second oldest girl and inherited them from Grandpa when he died," she explained. "Eunice didn't seem interested and Mum had a special involvement, I suppose, since she had more kids of her own than anyone else." It was a much-acclaimed fact that Clemency was the indulged middle child of five, the only girl among four adoring brothers. Here again, Isabelle envied her. What a wonderful childhood Clemency must have had, all that love and security, which she was now handing on to her own four children. A great start in life. She remembered Clemency's mother, her aunt Claire, who had died a few years back from wrongly diagnosed breast cancer. She'd been a brisk, jolly woman with the most wonderful smile, as capable and giving as her daughter. No wonder life had turned out so well for Clemency, with that gilded childhood behind her.

"I guess I was just lucky with my genes," beamed Clemency, spreading recent family groups on the floor. "And the boys, bless 'em, always took such care of me. Escorted me to parties, fought off schoolyard bullies, helped me with my homework. Even dated my friends." She laughed. Guy and Mark and Ben and Sam Broadhurst were bywords for perfection, with wives that got on and children who played together and even liked each other.

"Next time," promised Clemency, "I'll invite the lot of them too. Only they do take up so much room and I thought you might find it confusing."

Isabelle had been confused from the start, still was. Her own pallid childhood had been very humdrum, living in cramped, rented accommodations with parents who scarcely spoke. Just the list of names and the sight of all those smiling faces, staring up at her from the carpet, filled her with awe and a weary suspicion that she'd never truly get the hang of it, nor be able to remember who was who in this vast, colorful clan of which she was part. Still, it must be loads worse for Cherie, the real outsider.

She looked across at the younger girl, scrunched in a corner of the massive sofa, a glass of wine in one hand, a cigarette in the other, looking bored and miserable and slightly cross. Well, she might make a bit of an effort.

"Have you met many of the family?" she asked brightly, and Cherie turned on her a baleful stare.

"No," she said abruptly, as if she were indifferent to the whole tedious subject. "Just Harry." The saint. And her benefactor, though she didn't add that. Cherie was not herself charitable by nature; her complicated childhood had seen to that. And now she was resenting these intimidating cousins, all so confident and carefree and well set up in life. Try bringing up a child like Ashley alone, she thought savagely, and then see how pretty and well-dressed *you* can afford to be.

The mention of Harry brought forth the usual laughs. All of them shared the same opinion, it seemed, that he was comic and pompous and overly pleased with himself. Pretentious, in a word.

"Have you met Lavender?" asked Élodie with a grin. She recalled the time they'd visited her in Paris and she'd ended up spending nearly a month's salary giving them dinner, because they'd made it clear they had certain expectations.

"At that time I was pretty hard up, doing sketches for St. Laurent. Yes, there's money in designing but only eventually, once you've made it."

"And you hadn't then?" Clemency eyed her with warmth.

"Haven't now. I'm still learning." Yet the chic, understated clothes she was wearing certainly came from no High Street chain store. And this for just a weekend in the country.

"And what about those dreadful kids?" Madeleine was warming to the subject. Although she lived the nearest to Harry, she avoided him like the plague when she could. She found his wife chilly and his children too much, with their musical instruments and private tuition and the monotonous regularity that they all came out top. Vivian was the worst, a right little know-all. Still only seven yet a musical genius who also had a precocious talent for soccer.

"Do you get the Christmas newsletter?"

"I do indeed." And then they all cracked up laughing, Cherie included.

All in all, it was a success, reckoned Clemency. The more they laughed, the more they relaxed, so that soon even Cherie had forgotten to scowl and her small face softened into a natural prettiness that had been hard to detect beneath all that makeup. What a shame. Clemency longed to scrub her and turn her into a real person, a twenty-something with bright, merry eyes and her grandmother's nose into which she'd stuck a diamond. And a silver ring, for defiance. What on earth had Uncle Tommy been up to, when he'd conceived this sad little misfit out of wedlock and then, apparently, abandoned her? She found the appropriate album and shoved it across the rug to Cherie, pointing out her grandparents in the heyday of their first love.

"There they are, Odile and Cornelius. Don't they make a handsome pair?"

Cherie peered. Odile was slight and upright with a tiny waist and piled-up hair, looking more Edwardian than the thirties flapper she must have been when she met her husband. Cornelius towered above her, tall and imposing and a little like Harry, with beetling black brows over disconcertingly pale eyes, and a shock of dark hair that was just turning grey. An intimidating figure, one she was glad she'd never met.

"He was older than her?"

"Much. More than twenty years."

"And already married," piped up Madeleine, "with a wife and two children in Maine."

"One child," corrected Clemency, who always knew best. "Hugo was dead by then."

There was Hugo in an older photograph, a pale, pinched child, a little like Ashley, leaning against his younger, bolder-looking sister.

"Agnes." Clemency answered the unspoken question. "Who is now, would you believe it, a nun? In a closed order."

"What happened?" Isabelle's curiosity was piqued and even Cherie was beginning to show interest.

"It's a long story," said Clemency comfortably, never happier than when she was holding the floor. "I'll tell you later. They were actually first cousins who fell in love. But first let's discuss this trip. Who's in favour of motoring down to Uzès in September? To give her a surprise birthday party, catch her unawares?"

"What, all of us?"

"Why not? It should be a bit of a lark. We've never had a proper family reunion, and what better occasion than

74

Mémé's eightieth birthday? And that part of France is simply beautiful. It'll knock her out, bound to, particularly after all these years."

"Where will we all stay?" asked Isabelle, aware of her limited finances.

"The house is vast, with a barn alongside. The children can bring sleeping bags and, if necessary, camp out."

"Or we could all stay in Uzès," added Madeleine, who liked her creature comforts.

"No need, I promise you. There's loads of room." Too much, if anything; Clemency had never forgotten those long, dark corridors and a row of rooms that ran into each other. Perfect for Sardines or Hide-and-Seek. Even Murder in the Dark, if that wasn't too scary.

"Should we invite Harry and company?" asked Élodie, hoping not.

"Oh yes, let's make it a proper reunion," said Clemency. "Not just Harry but all the rest too, kids and all. There are bound to be a few who can't come, like Aunt Eunice, but at least I feel she should be included."

They groaned. Eunice Annesley, the eldest of the uncles and aunts, was a formidable spinster, now living back in New York. Most of them gathered in this room had stories to tell about her, not all of them pleasant.

"She used to give us face flannels and soap for Christmas," Clemency said with a chuckle. "And once, when she asked Sam when she should visit us again, he said: 'Come back when we've forgotten how nasty you are.' "

"And when she stayed with Harry she kept upsetting the kids by switching off the telly in the middle of *Blue Peter*."

But Clemency stuck to her guns. "Nevertheless, she has to

75

be included. Ethan too. All the direct descendants with their children and other halves. It's history in the making and we might not get the chance again."

9

*T*he Annesley tribal history, as explained by Clemency that Sunday afternoon, was neither as complex as Isabelle had feared, nor as dull as Cherie had expected. Backed up by albumsful of faded photographs, she sat in the center of the rug and held forth, pushing the albums to her attentive listeners whenever she felt the need to illustrate a point. It all began with Nathaniel Annesley, or at least as far as photographic evidence went, a printer from Devon who took his chances in the New World and married Edith Biddle from Philadelphia in 1843. Then, after she'd given birth to Thomas, their own great-grandfather, and presumably died of fatigue or simply run her natural course, as women of that era were prone to do, he married again in his seventies, one Eleanor Merton, whose forebears were not recorded, and produced a sister for Thomas, Grace, a whole forty-four years later.

"Dirty old devil!" exclaimed Cherie spontaneously, making them all laugh. Shades of her own father, she was thinking, and she guessed her cousins were thinking it too.

"Probably there were loads of dead ones in between," explained Isabelle. "Women in those days didn't have an easy time."

As if she did or ever had. But Cherie remained silent. Against her will, she was beginning to get fascinated, dragged into all this family stuff by her far more knowledgeable cousins.

Thomas married Alice Tucker in 1874 and from that match came their own grandfather, Cornelius, his sister Elfreda and brother Ethan. Grace, the daughter from the second marriage, who was only two years younger than her nephew, Cornelius, ended up marrying a Frenchman, François Rochefort, and had lived in Europe ever since. Until her death in 1942, during the war.

"Are you keeping up?" whispered Madeleine, aware of the rapt expression on Cherie's face. All this was entirely new to her and pretty indigestible.

"Sort of," muttered Cherie, fascinated in spite of herself.

Cornelius himself was born in Maine in 1896. Since his father was a scholar of some distinction, it seemed perfectly natural for his elder son to follow him into an academic career, which he did *cum laude,* graduating from Bowdoin College with an armful of distinctions and moving south to take up tenure at Harvard with a full professorship by the age of twenty-nine. By then he had also married the blue-blooded Ellen Herriot, a true New England prize, and they had an infant son, Hugo, on whom, she doted. Cornelius, however, even as early as that, had reservations about the child which he tried to keep to himself.

Cornelius was a tall, imposing man, athletic and out-standing at all sports (though not, as it turned out, in the league of his younger brother), with a glacial stare and withering tongue that terrified and intrigued students and fellow academics alike. He possessed an apparently unconscious feeling for style, favouring sightly foppish cravats and corduroy jackets, and had the eloquence and showmanship of the flamboyant matinee idol he so much resembled. Women especially idolized him; dazzling good looks were offset by those startling slate-grey eyes that gave him the dangerous air of a jungle predator and drove them quite crazy with frenzy and desire. Wherever he went, they threw themselves in his path, only to be rebuffed by a biting sarcasm which served to intensify their yearning. Yet Cornelius, for all these many temptations, remained faithful, more or less, to the coolly detached Ellen, whose breeding prevented her from showing much in the way of passion, other than for her ailing son, who was always a bit of a lost cause.

"How do you know all this?" asked Élodie, frowning.

"The aunts," said Clemency gaily, warming to her subject. Eunice, Aimée, Patrice and her own mother, Claire; put them together and they were as vocal as a skyful of starlings. As the oldest of the girl grandchildren, fourth in all after her two older brothers and Harry, she'd been privy to conversations the others hadn't, was the only one of the lot of them to be privileged as a child to visit their grandmother's hideout in France. Just by hanging around and keeping quiet, she had garnered a whole lot of family lore and scandal she was now prepared to share with her cousins.

Hugo was delicate and disappointingly slow to develop, but his father endeavoured to mask his frustration by showering him with some of the love he found it harder to give to this wife. The boy was fair, with transparent skin and virtually colorless hair, and the fine, long fingers that were the heritage of his mother's family. On Ellen they looked artistic and refined, seen to best advantage when arranging flowers or coaxing a complex Scarlatti sonata from the ivory keys of her genuine eighteenth-century spinet. But for Hugo, his father thought privately, they were altogether too effete and unmasculine, the waxy appendages of a decadent or, worse still, some kind of artisan or permanent dropout. Cornelius had the highest respect for the intellect but was inclined to be dismissive of things not directly cerebral. He planned for his heir a distinguished career, as a thinker rather than any sort of doer. Hugo's eyes, however, were pure Annesley and this his father found reassuring. Pale and direct and surprisingly alert, though he had a habit of skewing them sideways if anyone returned his gaze too long, while a strange, muted mewling emitted from his throat as if from an animal at bay. After years of trying in vain to find some sort of expert on this unnamed condition, Cornelius put it firmly to the back of his mind and tried not to worry.

They spent their semesters in Boston, in a tall, elegant house on Beacon Hill, but moved back up to Maine for the long vacation, to the steel-blue-with-white-trim clapboard summer home in Christmas Cove that had belonged to the Annesley clan for generations. There they would be joined by friends and other family members; Cornelius's sister, Elfreda, who had not yet managed to hook herself a husband; and his younger brother, Ethan, a bit of a wild man with his dashing good looks and amazing prowess both on track and field. All in all, they were an impressive bunch, the Annesleys, and had many hangers-on, who lasted no longer than they were tolerated.

"Like the Kennedys."

"I suppose. But our lot were slightly more moral."

"You think? Wait and let the story unfold."

Those were happy times, those early prewar summers, seemingly interchangeable from the sepia snaps that covered the pages of the photograph albums, with white-clad figures playing tennis and croquet on the lawn, while discreet servants flitted in and out like ghosts, with trays of tea and jugs of lemonade. Cornelius had his books and boats and Ethan his interchangeable women, while poor, silly Effie would sit and just gab on, crooning over baby Hugo in his bassinet, all the while fluttering her eyelashes at any of the young men who would look at her.

Ellen would sit sightly apart, in a basket chair under the trees, quietly reading or sewing while keeping a vigilant eye on the child and the sister-in-law she didn't entirely trust as the men prepared to go out in the sailboat, to battle with the crashing waves beyond the cove. Later, as the sun began to falter, she would hand little Hugo back to his nursemaid and, skirt tucked up, wade bare-legged around the rock pools, scooping live clams from the pulsating sand to simmer in wine and garlic on an open fire on the rocks while Cornelius mixed them all sundowners on the terrace.

Isabelle sighed involuntarily and they all looked up at her, startled, then laughed.

"Those certainly were the days," said Madeleine.

"Decadent and extravagant," added Élodie disapprovingly, grabbing for her lighter as she reached for another cigarette. She pushed the packet across the carpet to Cherie, who accepted one gratefully. This was beginning to be great stuff. Living history, as Clemency had put it.

Ethan Annesley, though less academically brilliant than his brother, excelled at sport of all kinds and was chosen to represent his country for the long jump in Amsterdam at the 1928 Olympic Games. There he was in action in one of the faded snaps, a lithe, shock-haired figure in white, hurtling through the air as if on wires. His parents rather hoped he would become a lawyer, but by the time of the Olympics, when he was already twenty-four, he still showed little sign of taking life seriously or settling down. He sped around the quiet Maine lanes in his dashing racing Chevrolet, fluttering the hearts of the local girls and terrifying his mother nightly when he failed to return by midnight. His father urged on him caution and suggested he think about getting himself a job, but he startled them all unexpectedly when he met a shy, pretty teacher at a local dance and fell head-over-heels in love.

Evangeline Baker was around his age, with soft reddish hair and an appealing smile, and before the Annesleys had even got used to the idea, Ethan was married and had found himself a job, as a high school teacher in Ellsworth, Maine. Where he taught geography, coached the local athletes, and satisfied his yearnings for greatness by playing semiprofessional basketball. So that was that, relief all around; madcap Ethan off the streets and grounded. With a pretty shingled house, with its own back yard, and a baby already on the way.

"Well," said Clemency, stretching. "Who's for tea?"

"Where does Agnes fit in?" asked Isabelle.

"We're coming to her, be patient."

The match was over and the men had rejoined them, and Teddy was sifting through photographs and passing them over to Guy.

"Good God, was that Effie as a girl? She was quite a beauty." They all looked. Effie wore a pale summer dress, midcalf, with glossy black Mary Janes and the sweetest smile on her sunflower face as she glanced up shyly at a tall man in tennis whites.

"Why is she wearing white socks at her age? She must have been well into her thirties by then."

Teddy shook his head. "I really don't know. She was always a bit dotty, or so they say. Though I only knew her as a very old lady."

"Who died just recently, slaughtered in cold blood. Along with Aunt Martha."

"Poor soul. She can't have deserved that. What a truly terrible way to go."

"And after living so long too. Almost a century."

"Well, whoever did it must have had a reason."

"Which it looks as if we'll never know."

Agnes Alice Annesley was born in the summer of 1932, two years after her cousin Martha, Ethan's daughter, when Hugo was almost eight. Her parents had deliberately held off having another baby until they could discover what was wrong with him, but now he had moved into permanent care, in a discreet institution that could provide the necessary nursing. Ellen was initially heartbroken when they took him away, but she was strong and sensible and knew it was for the best. She could visit him regularly and take him out for drives. And buy him cream teas and generally spoil him, knowing she wouldn't have to deal with the aftermath when he was back in the institution and reaction set in. And even though it hurt her, she knew he didn't care, that he was content to be with the nurses he didn't know and didn't appear to miss his home or his mother at all. They never did discover the cause of his illness, the shifting gaze and inability to talk. He appeared quite normal, did well in his aptitude tests, could dress himself and take care of his natural functions. But he either couldn't or wouldn't learn to talk and he ran around in circles like a thing demented whenever anything upset him. Luckily or not, depending how you looked at it, he died of a fever in 1935.

Agnes, however, was different entirely, a lusty, dark-haired beauty with none of her brother's delicacy but her father's heavy brows and disconcerting stare. And, as they were quickly to discover, his intellect too. Cornelius took one look at her and found himself falling in love. This was his true child, rare and perfect, there was no mistaking it this time. They bonded the instant he first took her in his arms and he knew an emotion he had not experienced before.

In 1936, Ethan was sent to Germany as a stringer for the Ellsworth American, to cover the Olympic Games in Munich. As a former Olympic athlete himself, he was often called upon for similar services and rather enjoyed the extra glamour it gave him. This time, however, he came back shaken to the core. Changes had occurred in Germany that were not yet apparent to the United States; the Munich stadium was festooned with enormous Nazi banners, and Wagnerian overtures blared out between events. Something terrible was taking possession of Europe; the dark hand of evil just beginning to show its strength.

"For the first time ever, I felt like a foreigner," he said, and hugged his daughter, Martha, extra hard, relieved to be back in the land of the free.

"Hitler!" hissed Élodie, seeing the puzzlement on Cherie's face. Where on earth had the child been dragged up? Did she know nothing at all?

So it really came as no surprise to Cornelius when, later that summer, as they lounged around in Christmas Cove enjoying their sybaritic pleasures, a letter arrived from Grace Rochefort, his father's half sister, whom none of them had seen since her marriage. They had decided, she wrote, as American as ever, that in view of the current political climate in France, their daughter, Odile, should continue her studies back home and had accordingly enrolled her at the School of Fine Arts at New York University.

"She's a talented painter," wrote Grace, *"and I'd like her to see a little of her homeland. And perhaps get to know her relatives."* She was not quite eighteen, a child.

"That's nice, darling," said Ellen brightly over breakfast. Agnes, as always, was seated on her father's knee and Ellen didn't really approve of such laxity. A semester away from Cornelius would do the child no end of good, so his forthcoming sabbatical was more than a mixed blessing. Do them all good, in fact, to have a bit of a break. The marriage, though still civil, had lost a lot of its guts since Hugo's death. They needed a breath of fresh air to blow away some of the cobwebs.

"You can keep an eye on her while you're lecturing at Columbia. Show her New York." That should put a dampener on his libido. Chaperoning can work two ways.

How could she possibly have known, Ellen Herriot Annesley, the pragmatist, that that innocent suggestion was to herald the end of her marriage?

10

*T*he marriage of first cousins had long been a point of contention, mused Isabelle, pedaling cautiously through heavy Oxford traffic, right back to biblical times. Mendel and Lévi-Strauss had both had a fair bit to say about it. Except, of course, in the case of royalty or where there was money or land to be protected. Which wasn't so with her own grandparents, though this was the first she'd heard of the closeness of their blood. That's what came from having a taciturn father and a mother who simply wasn't interested. Who lived on the other side of the world and didn't maintain close ties with the family. The weekend with Clemency had certainly been an eye-opener; Isabelle was still considering its implications.

She'd enjoyed meeting the cousins, had warmed to Élodie, been a little scared of Madeleine, was sorry for Cherie with that hyperactive child to raise alone. Remembering Ashley reminded her of Hugo; could there, she wondered, be any genetic connection there? Or weren't these things hereditary—she'd have to check it out. Though from what Clemency had said and the faded old photographs, Hugo looked to have been more of a Herriot than an Annesley. Sadly, only Agnes remained from that branch of the family and she had, by her own choice, for years been incommunicado, incarcerated behind thick walls in a closed order of nuns in Normandy. Which seemed an extraordinary path for such a free spirit to have chosen, throwing in her lot with the Poor Clares just a year before Mémé's own defection. There was clearly a lot more family history to be explored. Her appetite well and truly whetted, Isabelle could hardly wait to talk to Clemency again and dig a little deeper.

She reached the cloistered entrance to Magdalen and dismounted. It was wonderful how times had changed in recent years so that she could now be part of the same distinguished college as her grandfather before her. His name was still commemorated here, so that people were inclined to know who she was. The Annesley Fellowship was one of the best endowed in Oxford; she felt intimidated and was determined to do her utmost to live up to him. She padlocked the bike and lugged her heavy briefcase up the narrow staircase to her own suite of rooms on the second floor, from where she had a splendid view of the quad and the college grounds. Oxford turned out to be as magical as she'd imagined; she tossed her gown over her shoulder and fumbled for her keys.

Footsteps were descending from the floor above and a pair of suede brogues, followed by jeans and a leather jacket, came into view. Dr. Carlisle, her mysterious upstairs neighbour who seemed to come and go with no apparent pattern.

"Hi!" he said, smiling, as she moved to allow him past. But he stopped for a chat, clearly in no hurry.

"How's it going?" he asked her kindly. They had met only fleetingly and exchanged the time of day in the three weeks since Isabelle had arrived. Once he'd dropped in a note, inviting her up for sherry in his rooms, but she'd had a tutorial that night and hadn't been able to make it. She hadn't actually seen him since. She was sorry about that; she liked the way he looked. And his accent was reassuringly North American too, which meant he might turn out to be a natural ally.

"Okay," she said, finally locating the key. "It's all a bit confusing at first, but I guess I'm slowly getting the hang of it."

He laughed. "They're a quaint bunch, the Brits, aren't they, but good-hearted under it all. I've only been here a couple of months myself, but already they acknowledge me in the local. Even allow me to pay for my round."

He had thick, dark hair, faintly grizzled with grey, and eyes that were disconcertingly pale as well as oddly familiar. She realized she knew nothing about him except his name. Oxford was comfortingly casual. She guessed him to be a few years older than herself, late thirties perhaps or even a little more. A visiting professor? Or a research graduate? She was too shy and awkward to ask. She felt foolishly inept as she waited for him to leave, but he showed signs of lingering so she invited him in instead. He picked up her briefcase and followed her with unfeigned curiosity, crossing immediately to the casement window which she always threw wide open whenever she entered these musty rooms.

"Nice view. I've got the identical one above, only your windows are less obscured by ivy." He peered out. A bunch of undergraduates in gowns were strolling across the sunlit grass while tourists took pictures. Oxford on a Saturday afternoon, city of dreaming spires and mellow fruitfulness and all that. While she made tea he had a good snoop around, unembarrassed by his own obvious nosiness. She liked the way he fitted right in, the easy intimacy as if they'd known each other for years.

"You're a scientist?" He was looking at her books.

"Genetics."

"Me too. Behavioural sciences."

She paused and raised an eyebrow in inquiry as she poured.

"Princeton," he said. "Among other places." And there the conversation pretty much petered out.

"Carlisle?" said Clemency, sounding startled when she told her. "Don't laugh, but he could turn out to be a cousin of sorts."

"You're kidding!"

"No. Martha Annesley, Ethan's daughter, married a Jersey composer called Gerard Carlisle. They had one son, Dominic. About my age and American."

"That fits."

"Well, it's a huge coincidence but certainly worth a check. Dominic's definitely rather dishy and could easily fit your Dr. Carlisle. Though I'd no idea he was in Oxford."

"You've met him?"

"Briefly." Clemency, for once, was unusually unforthcoming and offered no further information, not like her at all.

"So what's he doing here, at Magdalen?"

"I really wouldn't know, I'm afraid. Try asking him."

Isabelle conjured up the attractive, humourous face with those strange, slate-grey eyes that seemed to bore right into you. Grandpa's eyes, now she came to think of it, or was she being overly fanciful? And did she really want this charming stranger as a blood relative, just when she'd discovered him in the wasteland of her life? She knew what Mendel would have to say on the subject, then dismissed the speculation as foolish and immature. But she'd ask this Dr. Carlisle, she would most certainly, the next time she got the chance.

. . .

"Cornelius Annesley was my grandfather."

"I know." He looked up from the book he was reading and returned her gaze impassively. Isabelle shuffled her feet uncomfortably. His calm stare made her feel foolish; she wished now she'd left him alone.

"Mine was his younger brother, Ethan," he said more gently. "Pleased to meet you, coz." He held out his hand in a slightly mocking gesture. Isabelle reddened.

"So why did you say nothing?" she asked, perplexed, settling down beside him on the grass.

He shrugged. "Didn't see the point. Wanted to get to know you first. Something like that. Does it make a difference?" Not really, she thought, put that way, but still. She felt faintly offended, as if she didn't matter, and realized how much she had wanted to impress him. He grinned, friendly creases warming his face.

"I'm a behaviourist by training and I guess old habits die hard. There's something sneaky in my makeup that compels me to want to spy."

She laughed. He really was awfully nice, and now, like it or not, she felt he was a bit of an ally. "So where exactly do you fit in? To the family, I mean."

"My grandfather settled in Maine," he said, "and married a local teacher. Had one child, Martha, who married my dad and spent the rest of her life traveling the world. That's how I grew up something of a mongrel. Rootless all my life, a bit of a rolling stone."

"Which makes you . . . ?" She couldn't quite work it out.

"Your second cousin."

"Or is it first cousin once removed?" A scientist herself, she ought to do better than this. But, for some reason, he made her feel oddly nervous.

"Something like that. Not too close for comfort." To demonstrate his point, he leaned forward and kissed her lightly on the cheek. Isabelle flushed scarlet. Physical contact always scared her hugely, perhaps because of the way she had been raised, and he was far too attractive for his own good. She recoiled slightly and, aware of it, he laughed.

"Don't worry," he said easily. "I promise not to pounce. Not without prior warning."

She looked at her watch in confusion, then scrambled back to her feet. Her heart was pumping hard and her palms were damp; cool it, she tried to tell herself, but found she couldn't comply.

"You've already met Clemency," she burbled defiantly, with a note of something sharp that was almost jealous.

"I have indeed. Our cousin." His eyes continued to hold hers steadily, calm and searching and quietly amused. He must think her an awful ass, she thought as she stumbled away. Crass and awkward, a real backwoods girl. While he was obviously so easy in his own skin, so relaxed. A seasoned world traveler who had probably seen it all. And then she remembered that his mother had recently been murdered and felt a shocking pang of remorse. She ought to have mentioned it, should have let on she knew. If only she weren't so clumsy with men, particularly attractive ones who fluttered her pulses. She reported back to Clemency, who sounded exasperated and oddly on the defensive.

"Oh really, Isabelle." Couldn't she get anything right? For one reportedly so brilliant academically, the Canadian could be such a clodhopping dolt. "We'll just have to arrange another cousins' get-together, in Oxford this time so that we

90

can count him in. Corner him and find out when he's likely to be free and I'll give the others a bell. A Saturday would probably be best."

Despite her love of fixing things, for once Clemency was curiously reluctant to share this new cousin. But if Isabelle had already met him, there wasn't a lot she could do now. Might as well include the others too, perhaps not Cherie but certainly Madeleine. Élodie was back in Paris and would doubtless consider it too far to travel.

But when Isabelle finally summoned the courage to leave him a note, the porter told her frostily that he had closed up his rooms and left.

"Don't know when he's coming back," he said. "Or even if he is. Dr. Carlisle is a force unto himself. Makes his own arrangements and never thinks to share them with the likes of me." He gave her a wintry smile. He had been in this post almost forty years and what he didn't know about the Magdalen inmates could be graven on a grain of rice. Other than Dr. Carlisle, that was; that one was definitely a cat who walked by himself. And this silly woman, judging by the idiot flush on her cheeks, was finding him irresistible along with all the rest. That's what came of letting them into men's colleges. He'd always known no good could ever come of it. Pursing his lips in disapproval, he returned to his scrutiny of the racing news.

Clemency came, regardless, but on a Thursday and without the others. Teddy was staying over in London, where he kept a convenient *pied-à-terre*. Over lunch by the river she cross-examined Isabelle; she wanted every tiny detail about Dominic.

"It's odd he didn't identify himself," she said. "Since the

91

Annesley name is comparatively rare and Grandpa was such a big shot at Magdalen. You'd think he'd be keen to flaunt the connection, particularly to a known relative."

Isabelle agreed. Most odd; almost as if he had some devious purpose, had somehow crept up on her without wanting to be noticed. Odder still that he'd departed without a word, but then, he probably hadn't given her a second thought. Isabelle was well used to being ignored. She looked at Clemency, so serene in her gorgeous splendour, over-weight yet flaunting it, with a beautiful caramel knitted linen smock and amber beads to die for. In actual fact, they were of similar build, heavy with lustrous hair and glowing skin. But that was where the resemblance ended, other than the nose. Clemency swept along, like a ship in full sail, while Isabelle crept like an apologetic mouse. Again she found herself envying this cousin with her devoted husband, four bright kids and that beautiful, sprawling house. It all had to do with the way you'd been raised and Clemency, daughter of Claire, the second oldest, had certainly come up trumps. Plus she'd grown up in the middle of those four protective brothers. With that sort of kick start in life, how could she possibly have failed?

Isabelle, an only child, always found male company rather daunting. Her father had remained detached and, without any brothers of her own, she'd found it hard to mix. And her mother had insisted on a convent education, which had only made matters worse. Being brainy didn't exactly help either and only added to her isolation, so that the move to Oxford in her early thirties had come as something of a relief. A new start with a new decade; a chance to reinvent herself. Though sitting here beside her glamourous cousin served only to make her feel even dowdier than ever.

Clemency, chattering and watching the river glide by, was privately thinking along similar lines. Isabelle needed taking out of herself; the raw material was there and she was, after all, an Annesley. With a better haircut and some stylish clothes, who knew what might be achieved? There was nothing Clemency liked better than fixing things, and the moment this lunch was over, she knew exactly what to do.

"Come along," she said, calling for the bill. "I think we could use a little retail therapy before I return to the wilds."

11

*T*he truth was Clemency had a secret of her own which was making her feel quite skittish, a state that didn't come naturally to one as steady and commonsensical as she had always been. Several weeks earlier, while loitering in the village after an afternoon meeting of the parish council, a silver Mercedes had drawn up alongside her and a stranger in dark glasses inquired the way to Tall Trees Lane.

"*He's* pretty tasty," remarked Tessa, the vicar's wife, approvingly after they had set him on his way. "I wonder what he wants."

"Now, now."

There wasn't much up there apart from grand houses, the most impressive of which was Clemency's own, where Teddy also based the headquarters of his wine business. But Teddy, just now, was away. The *pied-à-terre* in Covent Garden had proved a blessed convenience at times like this, when trade was booming and meetings thick on the ground.

And it meant he didn't have to drive home to Wiltshire after being at tastings all day.

"We could always follow him and see," suggested Myrtle, a divorcée, but Tessa had her children's tea to get and, besides, that was hardly fit behaviour for the wife of a man of the cloth. Not that she wouldn't if she could think of an acceptable excuse. Things around here could be very tame at times.

"Must be getting back," said Clemency, though actually her own children were all taken care of and for once the big house would be gloriously empty and peaceful. She was consumed with curiosity. In a village like this one, more manicured than serviceable, there was far too little novelty to exercise the mind and, truth to tell, she'd been more than a little beguiled by the stranger's friendly manner and heart-stopping smile. American, she would place him, from the little she'd heard him say. Not that she was susceptible, not even remotely. She had loved Teddy Cartwright from the age of nineteen, when her brother Guy had first brought him home, and married him with all the trimmings once he'd finished at Oxford and settled into gainful employment.

Health, happiness, domestic bliss; Clemency Cartwright had it all and bounded through life with a confident smile and a heart overflowing with good intentions. She was, in her mother's tradition, a contented woman with a husband she adored, and little time for moaning minnies or the feminist angst she read about in the papers. Flirtation and adultery had no place in her life; nevertheless, she was intrigued. Even more so when she turned into her lane and saw the silver Mercedes parked silently under the trees.

"Hello, again!" she called, winding down her window as

she pulled up beside him on the corner of her own drive. The Willows was looking especially beautiful today, slumbering in late sunshine with newly clipped hedges and an uncluttered lawn. He seemed faintly startled, then leaned across to roll down his passenger window.

"I think I'm probably a little lost," he admitted. "I was looking for a wine importer's, but this all seems to be residential."

Clemency beamed. "It's Teddy Cartwright you want," she said. "And I'm his wife. He's not here, I'm afraid, not for a couple of days, but do come into the house and make yourself comfortable." Always hospitable, that was Clemency, as if life were one vast cocktail party and she its hostess.

She drove up into her circular drive and parked by the triple garage. The Mercedes followed slowly and the driver got out and offered her his hand.

"Sorry to intrude like this," he said, removing the dark glasses. "I know I probably should have phoned first, but I didn't have a number and this trip is a tad haphazard since I'm trying to cram so much in." His accent was, indeed, American—soft and well modulated, almost certainly East Coast.

"No problem at all," said Clemency easily as she led him into the shade of the porch. "I'm only sorry it's been a wasted journey, unless there's anything I can do for you instead?"

She was glad now she'd taken the trouble to dress up; she carried clothes well but looked bulgy in jeans. Feminine suited her best and this simple lilac smock lit up her wonderful complexion while also concealing her worst excesses. And it stopped just short of the knee to display her impressive legs. She looked good and knew it, knew also that he saw it too.

"Come on in and make yourself at home," she said, throwing caution to the winds. Anyone who was an associate of Teddy's must be all right and nothing bad ever happened in this respectable neck of the woods. Also she found she was reluctant to allow him to leave. Not just yet, till she'd got to know more about him.

"What a beautiful house," said the stranger, following her inside, stopping admiringly in the wide bright hall with its low oak beams and handsome antique furniture.

"Tea?" asked Clemency, heading towards the kitchen. "Or, since it's already gone five, perhaps you'd prefer a gin?"

She returned with a tray to find him still rooted in the hall, staring at the photo of long-dead Roland.

"My uncle," she said, preceding him into the living room. "Drowned in a tragic accident while not much more than a boy."

She opened the French windows to allow the air to circulate and the heavy scents of the garden filled the room. This was the best time to show off the house, when the shadows on the grass were lengthening and the birds beginning to cluster. Now he was over by the piano, looking at the rest of her pictures, and she started to feel uncomfortable, as his curiosity seemed unnaturally intense.

Who are you? she wanted to ask. *And what exactly is your business?* But she feared sounding inhospitable, so held her tongue. Instead she perched on the arm of an easy chair and allowed her visitor to examine her room at his leisure. He was around six feet tall and athletically built, with thick, dark hair, just touched with grey. Her own sort of age, late thirties, she would guess, in a well-cut suit that he wore with ease. When he turned to smile at her, she was startled by his eyes; a keen slate-grey with an almost luminous quality.

"Family?" he inquired, indicating the framed photographs, and she nodded and went to stand beside him.

"My grandparents had nine children," she explained. "And all of them survived and most of them married." There was one group shot of the lot of them together, taken informally on the lawn at Christmas Cove. Late fifties, she would guess from the way that they were dressed, when Roland was still alive and she not yet born. He traced his fingers lightly over the glass as he studied them intensely. For a stranger his interest seemed eerily obsessive; a chill took hold of Clemency and she moved abruptly away.

He glanced at her. "I'm sorry," he said, gently replacing the group. "I can't resist snooping into other people's lives. It's a nasty character flaw, I know. Please forgive me."

She relaxed. This was not the smile of a loony, just a pleasant, straightforward American with a healthy interest in the world around him. Nice; unusual too, especially in a man. They settled with their glasses to look out at the garden, and she told him a bit more about the Annesley clan. It was funny how lately the family kept cropping up. First Isabelle's arrival, then the cousins' lunch, now this.

"So you're American too," he said, surprised, focusing now upon her. Her accent was pure Cheltenham cut glass; he never would have guessed.

"Half," said Clemency. "My father was a Brit. Actually, only a quarter, since my grandmother is French."

The light was beginning to go, so she switched on a couple

of lamps and glanced at his glass to see if it needed a top-up. He still hadn't mentioned his business but seemed entirely absorbed in her reminiscences. Catching her glance, he looked at his watch and made polite noises about keeping her so long.

"I'm sorry to have missed your husband," he said, rising. "Perhaps I'll catch him next time I come this way." He pulled out his wallet and selected a card, which he placed on the piano alongside the framed photos. Rising also to show him out, Clemency picked it up and glanced at it idly out of curiosity. *"Dominic Carlisle,"* it said, *"Wine Importer."* And that was when she knew right away he was not at all what he seemed.

Imposter was too strong a word, but she used it, nonetheless, because she was angry.

"How dare you come in here," she said, "pretending to be a friend of my husband, preying upon my good nature." She stood tall and imperious and would have quailed most men, but he gently drew her to him and kissed her softly on the mouth.

"I'm sorry," he said. "I simply couldn't resist it. It's a terrible habit I've had since childhood and, besides, I find you utterly adorable." He laughed.

She backed away, one hand to her mouth in protest. "You know you shouldn't have done that," she said. Her dignity was wounded, but she found his eyes compelled her and a forbidden thrill shot through her as she knew she wanted more. She also knew that he saw that too and suddenly she was afraid. Her safe little world was shifting on its axis; supposing Teddy were to come home now and catch them.

"Come here, coz," he said gently, reaching for her again. He kissed her a second time, lingeringly and with expertise, and this time, against her best intentions, she let him.

Clemency's childhood, for as far back as she could remember, had been a storybook one of warmth, security and endless treats, blazing log fires and idyllic summer picnics on the banks of the Cherwell, where her mother had continued to live long after her parents had gone their separate ways and her father returned to the States. Claire, the second daughter, had married early a dependable solicitor with firmly planted feet and started her family right away. Two boys within a couple of years, then a three-year gap followed by Clemency, Ben and Sam. Nicely tucked in as the middle child among four brothers, Clemency had grown up cherished and fearless, her father's little sunshine, her mother's longed-for daughter, as well as a loved and cared-for sister to the boys. Which is why, she always said in later years, she got on so well with men. All men regardless, whatever their age or status, plumbers and deliverymen as well as her husband's peers. A tomboy who grew up to be startlingly pretty, she learned to ride and climb and fight, to throw a cricket ball and tickle a trout. And then, in her teens when she'd shed her puppy fat, to snare the friends the boys brought home, culminating in Teddy, whom she married.

This, to Clemency, was the ideal way to raise children, and she was trying to emulate her mother's pattern with her own brood. Two girls and then two boys, again in rapid succession; she loved them and ministered to them without cramping and allowed them space in which to grow and develop. Teddy was both temperate and sound, as solidly dependable in his own way as her father. In Clemency's book, unlike her more caustic contemporaries, men were people you could look up to and trust. None of this aggravated nonsense for her about equal opportunities and sexual parity. He was the provider, she the nurturing mother. Like swans who mate for life, the Cartwrights performed brilliantly as a team and the four sturdy children they were raising as such individuals were a credit to this unity.

She'd had her setbacks, of course, who hadn't, but they had been nothing more than glancing blips in the general contentment of her life. After Emma's birth and then, again, Humphrey's, she had shocked herself by giving way to depression, but after a course of Valium and some stirring advice from the health visitor, she'd managed to pull herself together and return to her habitual serenity. Both times. She often wondered about her mother's pregnancies and if this erratic hormonal state could possibly be inherited, but Claire had been strangely reluctant to discuss it and always changed the subject. Women of her generation were far less forthcoming about these matters, even to their daughters.

One thing her aunts made no bones about, however, was the euphoria Claire had felt at Clemency's birth. After textbook pregnancies and the easy delivery of the first two boys, her heart had been broken by the birth of a stillborn girl, apparently perfect in every way but with the umbilical cord wound tightly around her neck. Claire had given way to an almost suicidal depression, which had lifted, magically, three years later with the timely advent of another girl.

"You never saw anything like it," recalled Aimée. "She was a totally changed person and snapped back to normality in a trice."

"You were always a very special little girl," explained Patrice. "Smothered with love, right from the start, the apple of everyone's eye." Particularly her own mother's, she thought but didn't say. Odile had always preferred boys to girls; of Clemency she had made a rare exception.

"It's a wonder you didn't turn out a brat. But even the boys were thrilled with you."

"Nurturing, not nature," Clemency explained. "You get what you deserve, depending how you train 'em."

"Like husbands," said Patrice, already on her third.

"I was thinking more of labradors," said Clemency with a grin.

If anything was lacking in this life of total contentment, it might be, dare she admit it, a certain absence of spice. Eighteen years of marital commitment during which, she knew without having to think, she had not so much as glanced at another man. Her friends had their peccadilloes and she wasn't so preachy as to condemn them, but truthfully, as she tried to convince them, she'd already got all she wanted. Good, solid Teddy with his warmth and laughter and cheerful bonhomie; how well she'd chosen and what a brick he'd always been. Alone among her friends, she was almost maddeningly complacent. They laughed at her, the ladies of the village, but always with an element of respect.

Now, all of a sudden, here she was, faced with a dazzling stranger, and all she was aware of were his eyes, his lips and her own rapidly beating heart. His kiss was soft and persuasive and the arms around her unyielding; she liked the way he tasted and the smell of expensive cologne.

"Nice," he muttered, echoing her thoughts, moving his lips to her hair, and she felt herself drawn more tightly against his body as a frightening vulnerability opened up within her.

She was saved, quite literally, by the bell, a cheerful, apologetic neighbour ferrying home the children from the gymkhana, tired, muddy and babbling with excitement.

"Mum, I won a rosette!" said one.

"Mum, we stopped for McDonald's on the way home."

"Sorry about that," said the neighbour apologetically, but Clemency ruffled their heads and simply laughed.

"Don't give it a second thought," she said. "Saves me having to cook."

Her hair was ruffled, her eyes unnaturally bright. A damned fine-looking woman, thought Fiona's father, not for the first time, and in any other circumstances . . . well. But everyone knew she was hopefully besotted by Teddy, more's the pity.

"Come along, kids," said Clemency, waving him off. "Wipe your feet, then into the living room to meet another relative."

"I'll be off, then," said Dominic after he'd been introduced. "And I'll call again, if I may, one of these days. I rather think we have unfinished business." And he laughed with enjoyment as he watched her confusion. Definitely ripe for the picking, she was, and he had never been one to pass up an opportunity.

12

*H*arry was high on scaffolding, wearing his hard hat and arguing with the foreman, when the crash came. At first he thought it was distant thunder, rolling across the river from an ominous sky, but then he heard urgent shouting and running feet and, looking down from his precarious perch, saw workmen excitedly converging on one spot. Something had happened.

"Shit, what now?"

Both men looked at each other, for one split second alarmed into complicitous silence, then, with a single accord, began to edge back along the planking to where a makeshift ladder descended to the ground.

"It's Darren, guv. He's only gone and fallen off the top." Taking a chunk of the building with him, it appeared.

"Stay here. Don't move him. Call an ambulance." Harry was already fumbling for his mobile phone as he barked out orders, too stunned by this latest piece of misfortune to think it through. The fit young workman lay unnaturally still in a position that looked chillingly unlikely. The men stood around him, hard hats in hand, mopping their brows and muttering among themselves. Then Lenny, the foreman, shouted in sudden horror:

"Hats on, lads, and back away. Quickly, now. The whole bloody lot is coming down!" Whereupon, with another threatening rumble, a corner of the building began to cave in as if in slow motion, entirely obscuring the injured workman beneath a pile of broken concrete.

"Bloody hell!" Through a thick cloud of stone dust Harry bolted forward, unmindful for one moment of his own personal safety, anxious only to see the extent of the damage.

"Back off, guv'nor. It just ain't safe." Lenny had him by the sleeve and dragged him forcibly out of the range of falling masonry.

"But what about the lad?"

"Ain't nothing we can do. Not until the services get here; till the slippage stops."

Harry slapped his forehead in consternation and walked away. On cue, hard rain began to fall, icy and unrelenting, punishing him for his carelessness. In minutes the site had become a chalky swamp, with the men standing around unheeding in the downpour, worrying about their workmate, who was now entirely obscured. This was all he needed, an accident on site, when they were already running so far behind schedule and the bank was growing antsy about its investment.

A couple of fire engines arrived, followed by a police car and an ambulance. Amid the torrent, the firemen began to dig, though when Harry stepped forward to offer his help, he was brusquely waved away.

"Let them do it, they're the experts." Lenny's firm hand on his arm was eloquent in its sympathy. "Also they've got the equipment."

They all stood around and watched for what seemed like hours as the crane driver edged his huge contraption back onto the site and the firemen directed him to move the heavy broken slabs. Eventually the victim was uncovered, which was when the paramedics came into their own. They lifted the damaged body gingerly onto a stretcher and carried him carefully into the waiting ambulance.

"Alive, apparently; well, that's good news," said Lenny. But Harry was thinking differently, thoughts he dared not utter. Dead was one thing, one single contrite settlement, but alive and crippled could prove to be far worse. A vision flashed past him of years of endless payments stretching ahead, with a wife, perhaps children to support. A court inquiry with the resulting bad publicity; his whole career could well be on the line. This he most certainly didn't deserve.

"You'll come to the hospital?" asked Lenny anxiously, having ascertained where they were taking him.

"I suppose so." Hard hat rammed down on his head and his heart in his boots, Harry led the way through the sludge to his opulent car.

It was worse even than he'd thought. No wife nor kids, as it turned out; just a widowed mother with arthritis and a Down's syndrome sister to support. But that wasn't nearly the half of it. Would that it had been.

"We've been looking into the cause of the slippage," said the surveyor, unrolling plans on the table. "And it would appear there was something faulty with the mortar."

"What?"

"The mortar. The mix was obviously wrong, the proportion of water to sand. Nothing in the foundations gives cause to believe that the building is not properly underpinned. The ground is firm, the underground spring diverted. Look, here's a copy of my original survey, and all the points we raised back then have been sorted."

He shoved papers across the table to Harry, but Harry was preoccupied.

"No, it's clear from what happened and the way the whole structure subsided that the fault lies in one basic factor, the mix of the mortar, which, as you well know, is crucial."

"Jesus!" If that was so, the whole building would be unsafe and would need to be shored up or even demolished.

"Indeed." The surveyor's eyes were flinty; this was

serious stuff. "Only a madman could have let that happen. Whoever was responsible is in major trouble. A multimillion-pound court case, at the very least, not to mention full liability for that poor young man's injuries. I only hope you're sufficiently insured."

Suddenly dizzy, Harry closed his eyes. This went beyond his wildest nightmares; he couldn't believe it was happening to him.

"There's bound to be a witch-hunt once the press get wind of it. If I were you, I'd get in there first, seek out the culprit and make a public sacrifice of him. It's the only way. Otherwise you're facing certain ruin and I wouldn't like to be in your shoes."

The man leaned over and pulled back his plans, rolling them efficiently and sliding them into a tube. His eyes, when they met Harry's again, were suddenly sympathetic. For all his bluster and braggartism, Annesley wasn't an entirely bad chap. Full of himself, yes, but not without some cause. His skills as an architect were demonstrably formidable; he'd won a lot of awards in his time. The man had always respected his utter professionalism; now his heart went out to him. He headed towards the door.

"Let me know what happens," he said. "Hope you identify the blighter."

Blindly, Harry nodded. Somewhere in his records, neatly filed, would be the document giving instructions for the mixing of the cement and authorizing building work to commence. He didn't need to search for it; he knew without a shadow of doubt. The signature on the offending order was his own. It was only a matter of time before the world knew too.

Lavender was peeved by the time Harry eventually reached home. She was banging about in the kitchen, making heavy weather with her color-coordinated cast-iron pans, and gave a great sigh of resignation when he finally walked through the door.

"At last. I'd given up on you."

"Don't start." He crossed to the freezer and pulled out an ice tray. What he needed, above all things, was a good, strong drink, though his slightly slurred speech was a dead giveaway that he'd started already on the short journey home.

"Now what? I thought we were going to see that flick."

"Not tonight. I have things to attend to."

She sighed theatrically and pulled a casserole from the oven. The children were fed and out of the way. One plus point about Lavender, she was certainly efficient. Efficient and unsmiling like a put-upon P.A.

"When don't you?" she said, banging dishes onto the table. She was heartily sick of Harry and his histrionics. With the money he earned, he should be taking things far easier. What was the point of all the hassle if you couldn't, when it came to it, relax occasionally and enjoy it? She wanted to talk to him about the Hurlingham Ball, but one glance at his doom-filled face told her this wasn't the time. Instead she settled down like a martyr to pick at her food and have a thoroughly miserable time.

It was around the time the bank was giving him the most grief and his mind had been full of their obstacles and demands. He ought to have allowed the development his full attention, of course he should, but he was the boss and a man can only be stretched so many ways. In addition to which, Vivian had been sent home from school for stealing and Lavender was blaming it all on Harry, who never had time for his children. Also Cornelia had begun to wet her bed.

"We never do anything as a family anymore," whined Lavender. "No wonder they are growing up so badly." If she'd only sort her own life out and spend less time at the hairdresser's; but he was tired of these marital conflicts. He had enough friction as it was, on the site. Let her get on with it and drag them up as she liked. It was woman's work, being a mother. He'd never really wanted them in the first place.

Harry paced his trophy room, whiskey in hand, and watched the rain destroy the elaborate garden. He groaned as he thought of the probable repercussions bouncing and reverberating from that single moment of carelessness. Not only a man's livelihood but almost certain financial ruin, with a permanent slur on his professional reputation that would be there for life. Lavender might be complaining now; it was nothing to how she would react when she learned the truth. He crossed to his desk and opened one of the drawers. There, at the back, were the snaps he'd once taken of Mémé's house, grey and dignified, rather like the woman herself, nestling among the vines. What a haven of peace it looked to him now, with its fortified courtyard and solid stone walls. All of a sudden Harry longed to be up and out of here, to walk away from his troubles and responsibilities, just as his grandmother had done almost forty years before.

He remembered something Clemency had said about organizing a reunion to tie in with the old girl's birthday. Originally she had intended it to be just for the female cousins—sucking up to Mémé again in that particularly odious way she had—but had let something slip when she'd phoned to tell him about Pandora. And Harry had instantly locked on to the idea. If his cousins were going, he was definitely going too. He was, after all, nominal head of the family; as the oldest grandchild he certainly had that right and was damned if he'd ever allow Clemency to steal a march on him. September, she'd said, and he'd marked it in his diary. That gave him just six months to get things organized, which ought to be time enough, even by Annesley standards.

He wished it could be sooner; he might well be needing a bolt-hole. But at least it would give him the chance to have another look at the property and insinuate himself into his grandmother's affections. He thought about taking his children to enchant her. Few could resist Pam and Cornelia when they really turned it on. But that would be impracticable; he dismissed the thought. Taking the children would mean coming back and he suddenly knew for certainty he was nearing the time for flight. He thought of Pandora, dying like that on the golf course, and his gloom began to grow. She had always been an irritation, but this latest piece of timing beat it all. It was only a matter of days, he was sure, before the authorities moved in to question the family, and the last thing he needed, on top of everything else, was anyone poking around in his life. They were a large family and he had no obvious motivation, but he wasn't inclined to chance it now, not with those other deaths in Jersey so recently too. If someone was bumping off members of the clan, the police would quickly put two and two together. It was only sense.

Lavender would just have to take her chances, but she'd always been an opportunist and would survive. Harry paced the room again, then poured himself another large whiskey. Drastic action was called for now; he dared not put it off any longer. Somewhere at the back of his troubled brain a distant memory was beginning to stir. Of crazy Aunt Effie sitting blabbing on the lawn about some long-suppressed family scandal that had happened before he was born. If only he had listened properly, it might prove invaluable to him now. It was vital he got control of his grandmother's estate without having to share it with the others. Something to do with a baby.

He was standing on quicksand and couldn't afford to waste time. The cavalry was called for now, and fast. He made his decision and reached for the phone. It was chancy, maybe, but he really had no other choice.

13

*E*than Annesley poured coffee into two BBC mugs and carried them through to his cluttered front room, where the stranger was making himself at home. If there was one thing Ethan especially hated it was people poking around among his things, but he could hardly say so now, not after such a short acquaintance.

"Milk and sugar?" he asked awkwardly, slopping coffee all over the *Listener* as he clumsily tried to clear a space on his desk.

"As it comes," said Dominic smoothly, edging the letters he had just been reading back beneath the shelter of a covering file. The curtains were half closed even at almost noon and a bright shaft of sunlight pierced between them to spotlight the dust he had stirred up. This was, most definitely, a bachelor establishment that had probably never encountered the touch of duster or mop. Dominic swung his attention to this, the youngest of Cornelius's children, named in memory of his own long-dead grandfather. They were riveting, this brand of British single men, not to be found in any other race.

Of course Ethan worked in radio, he had institution stamped all over him. The balding head with its straggling hair, the flannel shirt and shapeless corduroys, even the dangling reading glasses, one arm stuck together with a paper clip. A cliché BBC producer without a trace of American in his speech, but then, Ethan had spent his entire life in England. Minor public school followed by a spell with the British Council; Dominic had done his homework well and was fully prepared for the interrogation. Provided he could get his prey to spill the beans. Ethan was fidgeting now, clearly wishing his visitor would state his business and leave, but Dominic was in no hurry and quite enjoyed the small anxiety he could see his presence here today was causing. He sank onto the lumpy sofa, coffee in hand, and continued to survey the untidy room with its plaster cornices and rather fine fireplace.

"Adam?" he inquired, genuinely interested. Ethan shook his head.

"Not in Kentish Town," he said. "A clever replica picked up in a junkyard. It's the right sort of period but certainly not the quality." He shrugged and grinned. As if he could afford the real McCoy on the salary Auntie paid him. This smooth American cousin with his black velvet jacket and cashmere polo shirt appeared to be having a whale of a time, silently mocking his threadbare relative. Well, that was all right with Ethan, provided he left soon. He had piles of work to get through before the evening's recording and had not expected this unannounced intrusion.

Just passing through, Dominic had said when he called. Would love to catch up, won't take a minute. But he'd been here already for a full fifteen and looked as if he was settling in to stay.

"I'm afraid I've not much here that would interest you," said Ethan apologetically. "No family records or photographs or anything." All that sort of thing had been corralled by his sisters long ago; besides, he had never really been very interested. Only eleven when his mother pushed off, he had been raised by his sister Eunice, with a very bad grace, until his father had let her off the hook by marrying again. Ethan was sick and tired of the Annesley family and tried to stay away from them as much as that was possible.

Since early adulthood he had struck out on his own and after his spell in the British Council had moved over to Broadcasting House with a relieved feeling of finally reaching home. Among the warren of corridors in the rambling thirties building, he had constructed a proper life for himself which absorbed almost all of his time, enabled him to keep his mind busy and effectively shut out the past.

Until today when this cousin had popped up out of the blue to beset him with questions and force him to face truths he thought he had managed to blot out. How old was

Dominic, nine or ten years his junior? He remembered him now as a smart, cocky child with a shock of dark hair and his bottom hanging out of his pants. What a world of difference thirty years or so could make. This one and Henry's boy had caused havoc when they got together and made his life a misery at a most impressionable age.

"How is Harry Junior?" asked Ethan awkwardly. "Do you ever get to see him these days?"

Dominic shook his head. "I've been traveling for the past eighteen years and only came home when my mum was killed."

Ethan was embarrassed. Ah yes, the murders, which had had their moment of tabloid notoriety. So detached was he these days from the Annesley clan he had almost overlooked the fact that his name was a dead giveaway.

"Relatives of yours?" his colleagues had clamoured, and when he had reluctantly nodded yes, distant ones, had plied him with the usual sort of questions that snoops and hacks reserved for matters of vulgar titillation. As if they could possibly care. Luckily, as is the way, some other sensation had quickly come along to distract their prurient curiosity and Ethan had found himself safe once more to slip back into his accustomed anonymity and finger his memories silently and selectively on his own.

Pandora's death had occurred while he was out of the country, on a cycling holiday in the Pyrenees, collecting and cataloguing rare species of butterfly. Her name, of course, had appeared in the local newspapers but had gone unnoticed by him because of the language difference, and by the time he had finally pedaled back to Portland Place, another family secret had been laid to rest and Ethan had not been faced with awkward explanations.

His sisters, all older, had long had the habit of trying to mother him and fussing over him from afar; one of the reasons he stayed firmly put in London with the width of the Atlantic Ocean to divide them.

"Does Ethan have a . . . friend?" was a regular question, when the sisters got together or the phone wires hummed. "He was always such a quiet little boy. It's hard to know what turns him on these days."

"If anything does," remarked Patrice, the nearest to him in age. She had reacted to her mother's defection by throwing herself early into matters of the heart and constantly seeking, for the rest of her life, that unconditional love to which she felt entitled. Not so Ethan. Barely eleven and always a secretive child, he had hugged his misery fiercely to himself and betrayed little sign of what he was actually feeling. Eunice had returned to chivy and scold him and take out on this hapless younger brother the anger and frustration she felt at the loss of her one chance of love. But Ethan remained apparently unscathed. Wildlife and plants became his absorbing interest and he was never happier than when wading in a pond or laboriously making intricate flower drawings, stamen by delicate stamen.

"I shouldn't remotely think so," was always the sisterly verdict on his sex life. Pale and underdeveloped, he had slipped through adolescence, and the middle-aged man now being grilled by Dominic was not a lot different from the schoolboy of thirty years back. Except that the hair had receded and the teeth, when he displayed them, were visibly decaying, proof that he took no interest in his physical health.

Poor sap, was Dominic's private opinion as he nursed his cooling coffee and attempted to bring him around to the point.

They were wrong, however, about Ethan's emotional state. He did have a love, one that was overpowering, which had occupied his thoughts for more than a decade. Emily Ransome was eight years his senior and he'd loved her from the minute he'd first glimpsed her striding by. Emily had a doctorate in archaeology and had joined the BBC as an arts producer. Ethan worshiped her but silently and, as the years went by, gradually insinuated himself into her circle until he was, by now, her closest friend. Occasionally, if he was honest, he saw flashes in her of the mother he had once adored, but he tried to keep such thoughts firmly at bay, though people did occasionally ask if they were brother and sister. The truth was, Emily was his goddess, plain and simple. That was all the insight anyone need have.

It was Emily who had helped widen his horizons, who led him across the world, stage by stage, visiting sites while he catalogued the flora and fauna. His lifelong hobby fitted in well with hers and they found each other's company absorbing. None of the family had ever been allowed to meet her, but Patrice had seen some snaps in which she featured and noted instantly the resemblance to Maman. Though she had never been able to winkle out what Emily's exact place was in her repressed brother's life.

"I think they're just companions," she reported to Aimée. "Colleagues with similar tastes who work well together. I can't imagine Ethan actually doing it, can you?" Then giggled smuttily and moved the conversation on to Eunice. The sisters talked, on average, at least once a week. Though not particularly alike in temperament or tastes, they shared an abiding fascination with gossip and found the family an endless source of small salacious titbits that could be wondered over at length without much harm.

It was Emily who'd been with him, cycling in the Pyrenees, when Pandora had come to her sticky end.

"Tell me about your childhood," urged Dominic. "Those glorious summers we used to have in Maine."

Ethan visibly stiffened. He wanted to tell this impudent puppy to buzz off, to stop sticking his nose in where it wasn't wanted. What business was it of this second cousin to pry into family things that had long ago scarred over? All that was way in the past with the door firmly closed. But this mild-mannered man was unaccustomed to being aggressive. He fumbled with a pile of colored paper clips then looked his cousin in the eye and smiled an ingenuous smile.

"Oh, there's nothing really to tell you," he said. "There were lots of us kids, enough to get lost among the crowd. We were warm and well fed and the summers were long and hot." Especially the one he tried so hard not to think of, the year of the tragedy, which resulted in Roland's death.

It was frightening in the woods, cold and frightening, but the others wouldn't listen to him and would only call him a baby if he cried. They had managed to slip away after early supper and headed for the trees that surrounded the Annesley territory.

"Where are we going?" hissed Charlie as they ducked under branches and slithered through fallen leaves.

"To the village," said Roland, swinging agilely over a stream. "Straight down the hill, then over the bridge."

Ethan was afraid and wanted to turn back. It was miles his brother was talking about and he wasn't sure he could make it. Besides, his bedtime was earlier than theirs. If Maman should notice his absence, there'd be trouble. But Tom, five years older, had urged him on.

"Don't be a spoilsport, scaredy-cat," he'd whispered, and, more frightened even of his brothers than his mother, Ethan had kept quiet. On and on they'd scrambled, unable to see in the impenetrable darkness, stumbling and falling and scratching their knees. Fleet-footed Roland had barely looked around.

"We must be there by nine," he said but beyond that wouldn't explain.

When they finally reached their destination, it was a quiet country lane with a farmhouse at the end. Ethan was disappointed; all that tribulation for this? Roland moved forward Indian fashion, stooping to avoid being spotted from the house. The porch door stood open and there was light from the family kitchen. Someone was playing a tinny radio, something loud and jazzy from the current Top Ten.

Then they spotted her, standing at a window, in a room lit dimly by lamplight; pale-skinned and luscious, naked to the waist. She just stood looking out at the empty night with a secretive smile on her lips as she languorously brushed her hair. Tom gave a catcall which Roland instantly suppressed, while Charlie stood there looking, his tongue practically hanging out. It was Ethan, however, who nearly gave them away. Eyes popping, practically strangling with distress, he gasped and almost shouted, "It's Gladys. Gladys Stott." One of their housemaids from Christmas Cove whom he'd known almost all of his life.

"Shut up, fool!" hissed Roland, practically striking him in his fury. "Babies shouldn't be in on this if they don't know how to behave."

It was clear that Gladys had done this before, a nightly ritual in which Roland was somehow involved. They hid behind a clump of conifers, then he whispered that he was going in and left them alone. They watched him sprint across the patch of moonlit lawn, then round the corner, out of sight of the porch, leaving them standing there, uncertain what to do next.

"I want to go home," wailed Ethan. It was late, he was cold and the whole thing was turning ugly.

"Go on, then," said Tom viciously, "if you think you can find the way. But not a word to anyone, mind, or we'll know you squealed and will kick you in the head."

It was the bravest thing he'd ever had to do, finding his way back blindly through the woods, panting with terror and crying under his breath, hearing animals stalking him, certain he was about to be eaten alive. Eventually he spotted the lights from the house and pushed his way through the brush without caring about his clothes. All he wanted was home and the safety of his mother's arms to make it all better again. He got away with just a mild scolding when he told her how he'd got lost, and soon was deep in a comforting bath while she got out peroxide for his scratches.

"Poor baby," she crooned as she smoothed back his hair. And when she asked where the others had gone, he told her he didn't know.

Ethan was asleep when the boys returned that night and

remained undisturbed when the police arrived next morning. Too young to be involved, was the family consensus, so while Roland, Charlie and Tom faced the third degree, Ethan was confined to the nursery with the nephews. Things had eventually calmed down and Cornelius had lifted his ban. The whole sordid business had been hushed up and they'd heard, much later, that a man in the village had been arrested. But Ethan had had nagging doubts until this day which he certainly wasn't going to share with his pushy cousin. Who was fast outstaying his welcome.

"And that's it?" asked Dominic, clearly disappointed.
  "That's it," said Ethan firmly. "Now I really must get on."

14

*I*t was on Eurostar that Élodie saw him again. She was sitting alone in a single seat in first class, absorbed in an in-depth magazine article about a series of unsolved murders in France by a killer dubbed the "Provence Predator," when she happened to glance up as someone walked by—and it was him. Unmistakably. Even though this time he was quite conservatively dressed, in a blazer and white shirt and with a reasonable haircut. She jolted upright and gasped involuntarily, but he was already at the end of the carriage, heading apparently for the bar. Élodie's heart beat wildly; seeing him unexpectedly like this was a shock and she was surprised to discover quite how much it affected her. It had been three months easily since their original encounter, yet she'd been incapable of putting him out of her mind. Selfish, arrogant, self-serving bastard that he was, just the lingering memory of his hands upon her body made her shiver.

But what should she do now? To blatantly pursue him would be uncool in the extreme, yet she ran the risk of losing him again. The train was due to stop at Ashford shortly and who knew where he might alight. On an impulse, she checked her lipstick and ran deft fingers through her curls. The hell with it, she was a modern woman. She closed her magazine and stuck it into her bag, then rose to her feet and strode boldly after him. She was a free spirit and would do as she damned well liked.

But he wasn't there. The bar was virtually empty, so Élodie bought herself a small red wine and balanced on one of the stools to watch the countryside sweep by. Perhaps he'd gone to the loo and would be reappearing shortly. But she waited in vain. The train reached Ashford International and she watched the passengers file out; not a sign of him. Maybe he'd been just a figment after all. She'd certainly had him on her mind a lot since that first meeting.

It wasn't typical of Élodie's luck with men. Love them and leave them had long been her motto, but she didn't expect the reverse behaviour. More or less, all her adult life, she'd been able to pick and choose who she wanted, and that's exactly what she had done. Apart from the single aberration of the New York banker, her heart had rarely been involved, but her sex life had continued to be spirited and regular. Now all that appeared to have changed. The stranger from the Paris nightclub had jolted her ego in some fundamental way and she had a nasty suspicion that what she was feeling went a whole lot deeper than just pure lust.

She remembered his strange, pale eyes and mocking smile, the smell of his sweat as they lay tangled together and the sharp rasp of his stubble on her skin. An animal reaction, and a powerful one. What she couldn't forget, and it sickened her still, was that he used her and dumped her without a second glance. Élodie wasn't accustomed to that. They had unfinished business; she needed to get even.

At Waterloo she grabbed a cart and pushed her single bag briskly through the crowds, heading for the underground that would transport her across town to Paddington. The cousins were meeting in Oxford this weekend; it was Isabelle's turn to do the honours and, against her normal instincts, Élodie was rather looking forward to it. As a single child of a second marriage and living away from her homeland, she was used to going it alone. Will Junior and Charlie Hopkins, her half brothers, were amiable enough but had families of their own and, besides, these days she rarely saw them. Now she found she liked the novelty of suddenly belonging, of having blood relatives with whom she could interact.

Suddenly, on the escalator, she spotted him again, several people in front of her, with a battered leather briefcase in his hand but no guitar. For a second she felt like shouting to attract his attention, then pulled herself together and tried to calm down. She couldn't push through to him, it was far too crowded, but logically she'd catch him when she reached the platform, unless, of course, he was traveling on a different line. With her blood firmly up, her excitement grew and the spirit of the chase took hold.

"Got you, you bastard," she muttered under her breath, straining to check that he hadn't eluded her, that she stood the chance of finally facing him again.

She liked the look of the back of his head, the slight wave in the thick, dark hair, the flecks of grey that added distinction. He looked so unlike the roving musician that for a moment she wondered if she'd made a mistake, but when he turned slightly to study an advertisement she knew from the lurch in her stomach that it was definitely him. Here in London and headed—where? From the way he was dressed he could pass as a Brit, but she remembered the American accent and that he was not quite what he seemed. Bastard.

At the foot of the escalator the crowd swirled thickly and while she was reading the signs to the Bakerloo line, she lost him again. In a panic, she looked wildly around, but this time he'd gone without trace. Curses. Finally forced to give up—she had, after all, a train to catch—she resigned herself to a monochrome existence and dragged her bag grumpily off to the Oxford platform. Loser, she told herself glumly, though she knew in her heart that he was undoubtedly a bad lot, one it made sense to steer clear of.

Clemency surprised her by meeting her at the station with Madeleine in the car beside her.

"Hi!" she called with her brilliant smile. "Good journey?"

Still hopeful, Élodie was glancing around, hoping to spot her stranger in the forecourt. There were loads of people waiting and a steady flow of movement, but she looked in vain.

"Fine," she said firmly, kissing Clemency on both cheeks. "Swift and uneventful. Beats flying every time."

"I love that train," said Madeleine. "Paris in less than four hours."

"So next time you can host it," said Clemency gaily. "And we'll all take lunch off you."

Élodie sank into glum preoccupation as they headed towards Magdalen, until finally Clemency came boldly out with it and asked what on earth was bugging her. Élodie paused, then told them, well, why not? These were, after all, her closest kin now. Sharing was part of having a family and it helped to get it off her chest.

"He was drop-dead gorgeous," she admitted at last, careful not to go into too much intimate detail for fear of shocking them. "And it's ages since I saw a man I really fancied."

"Tell me about it," sighed Madeleine surprisingly. She was thinking of her mysterious Jack, omnipresent in his corner of the pub. Though they now exchanged nods, they still hadn't spoken, and she was going quietly crazy thinking of ways to chat him up. She was positive he was interested, he appeared always to have his eye on her, but she really had no idea at all how to start breaking the ice. Which was pretty pathetic, she had to admit. A younger woman would plunge right in and boldly introduce herself, but Madeleine Russell had been raised a traditionalist. Her mother, Aimée, had drummed it into her that a lady should never be too available.

"They won't respect you," she warned and, even these days, Madeleine suspected she was right. She found herself telling them a bit about Jack. It was not in her nature to reveal her innermost feelings, but she felt surprisingly at ease with these friendly cousins.

Élodie looked scornful as Madeleine described her dilemma. Life was too short for such niceties, she said. "You'll be old before you know it."

123

Élodie scrutinized her cousin's porcelain skin but failed to detect so much as a line. Yet Madeleine was a good six years older. It must be the Scandinavian blood, she thought cattily, which, of course, she didn't share. Clemency surprised them by siding with Élodie.

"If you think he's that great, grab him before someone else does. Truly wonderful men don't grow on trees." And, though they couldn't possibly know it, for once it wasn't Teddy she had in mind.

They drove along Oxford High Street in thoughtful silence till Élodie suddenly inquired, "No brat this time?"

"Cherie?" said Clemency. "No, we didn't invite her. Thought it was somehow . . . inappropriate. And where, anyhow, would she park the kid?"

Élodie laughed. Cousin Clemency certainly pulled no punches. She said what she felt with no messing. Élodie approved.

"Snob."

"No, really. She can't have much money, poor sweet, and would be way out of her depth in these surroundings."

"But you're still including her in the trip to France."

"Absolutely. It's only fair. Illegitimate or not, she *is* Mémé's grandchild, as entitled to be there as any of us."

"Plus the kid?"

"If needs must." The thought of traveling with that hyperactive weirdo was not attractive, but in for a penny and all that. And he did have a look of the Annesleys about him which was bound to interest his great-grandmother. They all scrambled out at Magdalen while Clemency looked for a parking space. She opened the car boot and pulled out a hamper.

"A small contribution," she explained with a smile. From what she'd seen of Isabelle, she doubted she'd know how to cope. "Grab those bottles, will you, someone? A gift from Teddy, who's sorry he couldn't come."

Lady Bountiful personified, Clemency led the way grandly past the porter's lodge and up the stone staircase he indicated. Isabelle had certainly landed on her feet. There was a wonderful atmosphere in this fine old building which must be inspiring if you were here to study.

Isabelle opened the door rather too quickly with a flush on her cheek and hair that could do with a comb. Also they noticed that she wasn't wearing shoes; perhaps they'd arrived too early and caught her on the hop.

"Come on in," she said, slightly flustered, kissing them all dutifully and ushering them into her main room. Which was where they saw that the party had already started, that they weren't the first to arrive. A man was standing by the open window, holding a glass and gazing out across the quadrangle. He turned as they entered and they all gave an involuntary gasp.

"Oh," said Isabelle awkwardly, "have you guys met already?"

"Welcome," said the tall, dark stranger comfortably, holding out his hand. "Dominic Carlisle, your second cousin."

They all reacted in different ways, and this time it was Élodie who was cross. Seething, in fact, though she tried hard not to show it. How dared he keep quiet when he must have known? It was far too extraordinary to be a coincidence.

"I saw you on Eurostar," she said coolly, pretending she didn't care. But the eyes were as keen and appraising as ever and her heart gave a lurch when he pecked her on the cheek. There was a glint of mischief as he looked her up and down, openly admiring her understated chic.

"You should have spoken," he said easily, displaying no remorse. "We could have traveled together." Yet somehow she knew he was not being straight with her; that he had, in fact, been aware of her presence but for reasons of his own gone out of his way to avoid her. She couldn't for the life of her imagine why.

Clemency was pinkish and unusually subdued as she bustled about, opening her hamper and setting out homemade pies and assorted salads. Whereas Madeleine was frankly floored. What! Her mysterious Jack here with them in Oxford, not a stranger at all but in fact her own flesh and blood. She was fairly reeling with shock, unable to get her mind around it. He laughed when he saw her confusion and kissed her too.

"Well, well, well," was all he said, but the words spoke volumes in a kind of secret language. The others didn't notice; they were far too busy clucking. Each one of them had something on her mind but didn't want to share it with the others.

Clemency was the first to pull herself together and she commanded them all to sit and help themselves. No point letting all this good food go to waste; they could ask their burning questions just as easily while they ate. Dominic sprang rapidly into butler mode and pulled the corks of several bottles to allow the fine wine to breathe. He appeared completely at ease with himself as well as entirely unfazed by this odd confrontation.

Trying hard to control her rising temper, Élodie attacked. "So you knew all along who I was, but didn't say."

He laughed. "Guilty as charged, I'm afraid."

"But why?" She could see the others were listening hard but was damned if she was going to let them know the sordid details. She hoped she could trust him to be a gentleman, but from his behaviour so far, feared she was merely spitting in the wind.

"I guess it amused me. I also knew we were bound to meet again."

Wild with humiliation, she flounced across the room and planted herself on the window seat with her back half turned to the room. For this she had traveled all the way from Paris; if it weren't so far, she'd be tempted to leave right now. Dominic followed her in one swift stride, squeezing her shoulder to make her turn to face him.

"It wasn't just that," he said in a gentler tone. "You caught me at a time when I wasn't sure what I wanted, when I'd just returned from traveling the world and was trying to sort out my head."

"Which you've now done, I suppose." She was still shaking with fury, but at least he appeared sincere. The others, cut off from what she was saying, were helping themselves to food and starting to talk among themselves. Isabelle fluttered helplessly, out of her depth. She wasn't used to entertaining company and was finding it all a bit much. Just before the others had arrived, he'd given her a cousinly squeeze, thus throwing her into a spin. She felt lumpish and stupid while also yearning for more. This was the brother she had always dreamed of having, though at the same time she couldn't ignore his sheer physical pull.

She was terrified they'd notice, that her agitation would betray her. But Clemency, as usual, had everything under control, though below the surface her heart too was in turmoil. She'd thought her dalliance with Dominic was private; a cherished secret never to be shared. Yet here he was, as bold as brass, and apparently known to all four of them already. What in the world could he be playing at? Why the secrecy, the game of cat and mouse? She would almost consider it sinister if he weren't so utterly charming, treating each one of them with a playful dashing insouciance. This was a man well accustomed to women, adept at getting his way.

Over lunch they tried to sort out a few things. Clemency was never one to let things lie, and neither were Élodie or Madeleine. Dominic Carlisle might well be their second cousin, but he certainly had a lot of explaining to do. But first things first; Clemency was punctilious about manners.

"I'm truly sorry," she said, leaning over to press his hand. "Last time we met, I completely forgot to mention your mother's terrible death." In truth, she'd been so dazed by the confrontation that everything but his physical presence had been driven right out of her head. Poor Aunt Martha. Poor Aunt Effie too.

He returned the pressure of her hand. "That's okay. It was frightful, wasn't it, but at least she didn't suffer."

"And did you get to see her before she died?" Four pairs of matching eyes accused him.

He shuffled slightly in his seat and shifted his gaze uncomfortably. "I was on my way."

He'd been traveling, he explained, for most of the past

eighteen years but had, at that moment, ironically, been returning to make his peace. He hadn't seen his mother in ages but knew she was happily settled with Aunt Effie. He felt the usual guilt, well of course he did, but a child can't live a parent's life and he'd always been something of a rolling stone. Élodie nodded; of all of them, she understood. She had quit the security of Connecticut the minute she'd passed her exams. She adored her mother and really got on well with her, but Patrice was heavily embroiled in her own hectic life and, in any case, had Dad and the boys to see her all right. Élodie needed to strike out and make a life of her own. Madeleine too. And as for Isabelle, well, here she was, all the way from Canada for new beginnings.

"We're an odd bunch," she said shyly, "and certainly far-flung. I wonder what it is about the Annesleys that made them travel so far afield."

"Simple," said Clemency. "It's a case of the big bang. Their mother deserted them at an impressionable age, so they all shot off in separate directions. It's a wonder so many of us are here together now, considering the damage Mémé could have wrought."

"Well, I, for one, am glad you are," said Dominic. He, alone among them, was not Odile's descendant. His own reason for being here they had yet to ascertain. Though he did, of course, have Annesley blood and this was an Annesley college.

"Why Oxford?" asked Madeleine. "And what exactly are you doing?"

"I guess I just felt that the time had come to settle down." He was almost forty and still unrooted. He had interrupted his studies several times and followed his heart to all sorts

129

of unlikely places. Australia, Manila, Hawaii, Hong Kong. His father, before him, had been a restless spirit, musically gifted, which meant he could go where he liked. He had left his home in Jersey as soon as he was old enough and now his only son was following in his shoes.

"My grandfather, Ethan Annesley, was a bit of a disappointment who turned into a proper stick-in-the-mud after all that early athletic promise. Never left Maine once he'd settled down. And died in his thirties in a ridiculous freak accident."

That was news to Isabelle, who was still lapping up family lore.

"He drowned in Maine one morning when the family was asleep. Swept away by the current. His body was never found."

"But—" Isabelle was startled, but Clemency knew what was coming.

"Like Roland twenty-two years later. Strange how history repeats itself," she said.

They ended up traveling back together on the coach to Notting Hill. Madeleine hadn't bothered to bring the car, since the coach, which dropped her almost on her doorstep, was so direct and also so cheap. And Dominic, who'd half planned to stay on in Oxford overnight, decided on sudden impulse to go with her, much to Élodie's continuing rage. It was an opportunity to get to know her better and he'd finished his business in France, at least for the time being. Of all the cousins, Madeleine was the one who most intrigued him, yet was also the hardest to fathom. He knew he had to come up fast with some sort of a plausible explanation: of how he came to frequent her local when he didn't, in fact, live anywhere near; of why he was so much drawn to her remote beauty, even though he'd known all along of their blood connection.

Madeleine too was playing it cool, which was her way. Stuck right next to him, in this crowded coach, arm touching arm as cozy as kittens, she found it hard to maintain her aloof pose but did her best. It would never do to betray to him the quickened beating of her heart or the flash of jealousy she had experienced when she'd found the others knew him and knew him well. She'd seen the flush on Isabelle's cheek and the burning loathing in Élodie's eyes. Watched too, with surprise, Clemency's strange loss of confidence and wondered what game he'd been playing with her. Cousin or not, there were things about Dominic that certainly needed exploring. Men that attractive were most often lethal; from what she'd seen of his performance today, she knew he was not all he was cracked up to be. Each time he turned to face her, she found her eyes drawn to his mobile lips; could not stop herself wondering what they would be like to kiss, how it would feel to be snuggled up safe in his arms. Then she mentally slapped herself for being absurd. This man was dangerous and best left alone.

Dominic, to his secret surprise, was also slightly thrown and filled the journey with trivial conversation, which was not at all like him, asking about her work and marveling politely that she'd managed to do so well so soon. Patronizing sod, was Madeleine's first reaction, though she softened immediately as he continued to ply her with questions. She liked his voice, his smile, his bushy eyebrows, liked everything about him, in fact, especially that soupçon of mystery. When she tried to retaliate and cross-examine him back, his eyes glazed slightly and he grew instantly evasive. He had a doctorate from Princeton, he told her vaguely, and was also a Visiting Fellow of Magdalen. Among other things.

But now they had reached Notting Hill; it was time to part. He was reluctant to leave her yet wary of getting too close. He had managed, so far, to avoid the heavier questions. The thing about a gaggle of such strong-minded women was their habit of talking across each other so that nobody's line of inquiry got very far. Which, in his case, suited his purposes well. There were many things in Dominic's life he'd rather they didn't know just yet. They hadn't, for instance, asked if he'd ever met Harry.

He suggested a quick drink at their shared local, but Madeleine, recalling Élodie's scorn, boldly offered him supper at her flat instead. Nothing special, she warned him, just pasta and salad. She felt bitterly rebuffed when he said he hadn't time.

15

*H*arry called Clemency. The summer was creeping along and he was growing more and more anxious about his situation. The sooner he got away, the better. The injured workman was lingering on, not deteriorating but showing little sign of recovery, and the rumblings of authority were there in the middle distance, shuffling papers, drawing ominously closer.

"So what about this jaunt to France, then?" He could always go off on his own, of course, but this time needed an alibi. The house in France beckoned as the ideal refuge, remote, quite strongly fortified; best of all, without a telephone. But he didn't want to face Mémé without support. The memory of last time was still raw.

Clemency's spirits plummeted at her cousin's authoritative tone. She liked most men, rejoiced in their company, but made an exception in the case of Cousin Harry. She wasn't sure why, but he'd grated on her since a kid. Something to do with his general manner, pushy, impatient, barely concealing his dislike. It was clear he had little time for women: witness the uptight prune-face he'd married.

"September, I said September," she said crossly. "Her birthday's on the ninth. We'll go then."

"Does she know we're coming?"

"No, of course not. It's meant to be a surprise, remember?" Dumbo.

Harry bit back his impatience. It was the end of June already and the soccer fans were returning. At least they wouldn't get caught up in all that. Fighting and drinking and rioting in the streets. He liked his beer with the best of them, but the recent happenings had been disgusting, laddish behaviour of the very worst kind. If he had his way, they'd be lined up against a wall and shot.

"Have you been in touch recently?"

"Not for a while." Why did he always think he knew better? She had responded to Mémé's Christmas letter when she'd hinted broadly that she hoped to be seeing her soon. It was only fair to give her a little warning, but Clemency was keen not to ruin the surprise. A full-scale family reunion should be an enormous to-do. She sincerely hoped that her grandmother, at eighty, would prove up to it, but it was a

133

chance she was determined to take. They would motor down there in convoy, breaking the journey at overnight stops. Take their time and see a few chateaux, make it a real holiday, one for the family albums. She wondered if Aunt Eunice, the eldest, would be persuaded to fly over from New York. She was already compiling lists and had verbal promises from a couple of them, including Élodie's half brother Will Hopkins, Jr., who hoped to be in London at that time on fleeting banking business from New York.

Harry snorted with impatience. He needed to get out of the country right now. He hadn't discussed the matter with Lavender, was hoping he could manage to sneak away without her. With so much on his mind just lately, they weren't exactly communicating well these days. Two months was a long time to wait; who knew what disasters might erupt before then?

"And we can't go any sooner?"

"I don't see why we should." That was what she'd never liked about him. Always awkward, forever demanding his own way. Typical of the kind of man he was, a petty tyrant in and out of the workplace. She bet he was hell at home.

"The roads will be packed in a couple of weeks, anyhow, with all those schoolchildren on the move. And August is an impossible month. The whole of France takes its *congé* then."

She fancied she heard him mutter "harrumph" or something remarkably like it, fatuous fool.

"So what's your problem?" Faced with her cousin, all sophistication fled and Clemency's natural belligerence surfaced. She figuratively tossed her pigtails as she stood her ground. She'd bested him more times than she could remember, was secretly beginning to enjoy it.

Harry remained silent. He certainly wasn't going to confide in her, bossy, ball-breaking cow that she was. He changed the subject with a bad grace. "So who else is coming?"

"Don't know yet. Anyone who cares to, provided they fit the bill. I'm sending the invitation to all of Grandpa and Mémé's living descendants. Along with partners and children, of course." And significant others, if she only dared ask.

"Including Cherie?"

"Absolutely Cherie. Ashley too, he's the first great-grandchild." That settled it. Even Clemency had had her doubts, but now she was sure. Grumpy bugger, if he thought he was so clever, let him try organizing it himself next time. Which reminded her; she ought to get on with the invitations. A party this size took a lot of organizing and she needed to know how many to expect. She softened slightly as she made her farewells and promised Harry she would be in touch soon. She would find some basic chore to keep him occupied and salve his *amour propre* in an appropriate way. Anything for a peaceful life. Thank heavens for the sainted Teddy.

She wandered out into the garden where Teddy was weeding and surprised him with a spontaneous hug.

"What's that for, old thing?" he asked, gently disentangling himself. His shirt was filthy and he smelled enticingly of sweat. He mopped his brow and pushed back his heavy, dank hair. The image of another—younger, fitter and a lot less weighty—flashed treacherously through Clemency's mind, but she sternly repelled it and kissed him on the cheek. Dear dependable Teddy, what a brick he'd always been. All these years they had been together with scarcely so much as a cross word.

"Just for being you," she said archly, and went in to telephone Madeleine.

Who was feeling depressed, though she didn't let on. Sundays, on the whole, she usually found pretty cheerless and a whole two weeks had passed without a word from Dominic. It was partly her own fault, she supposed, since she'd started avoiding the pub. Well, she didn't want to appear too eager, especially after his brush-off over supper. But she did feel hurt; he could easily have rung. Now that she knew that he knew who she was, she felt he really had no excuse. Though maybe their blood tie made everything different and he looked on her merely as a somewhat close relative.

Élodie would tell her to be more bold if, that was, Élodie were not so keen on him herself. Something had obviously happened there; there was no ignoring the repressed fireworks and flash of anger in her eye. He was a dark horse, Cousin Dominic, and no mistake. She looked wistfully at the telephone, then remembered she had no number for him. Somehow they'd managed to part without him telling her where he lived. And she was damned if she'd sink her pride and call a cousin.

On cue, the phone rang, but it was only Clemency. Sounding spirited and cheerful, overflowing with her usual bustling bonhomie.

"Hi, it's only me. I'm not disturbing you?"

"No." Madeleine tried to dispel the gloom from her voice and knocked back the remains of a glass of lukewarm wine she'd been lingering over as she read the Sunday papers.

Clemency told her about Harry's call and they both had a giggle at his expense. He seemed to have a similar effect on all his female cousins; more's the pity he'd had no sisters of his own to beat him into shape. She then went on to outline her travel plans. They could all drive down together and double up in cars.

"We'll take Cherie and the kid," said Clemency. "If Teddy drives the Range Rover, we can all squash in."

Madeleine had room for only one passenger. She already had a fantasy which she wasn't about to share. In any case, not being Odile's descendant, Dominic didn't strictly qualify and wouldn't be on the list.

"What about Élodie?" asked Madeleine, anticipating trouble.

"She'll be going direct by train. On the famous TGV, which makes Eurostar seem like a snail."

"And Isabelle?" Isabelle on a bicycle; old family joke.

"Either with us or with you. Whatever."

Trust Clemency to have it all so well sorted. There was nothing really to worry about except whether he'd be there too. Which she didn't dare ask, since she didn't really want to know. In a social landscape as bleak as hers, a girl needed something to hope for. Even a dodgy second cousin with all the appearance of being a bit of a dirty dog.

Clemency rang Élodie, who seemed to be out of sorts too. What was it with these female cousins? They had all been such wonderful company when they'd met. She was positively monosyllabic, especially when she heard what Clemency wanted, and said she'd come if she could get away, though not to count on it.

"Oh no!" Clemency was genuinely dismayed. The deal had always been that they'd all go together. Now her plans seemed to be falling apart and they still had two months to go.

Élodie, detecting the concern in her voice, relented slightly, pushing away her dark cloud. "I'll probably make it. Keep your cool."

She liked Clemency, she really did, just reacted slightly to her perpetual assertiveness. Talk about school prefects, wow. If that's what growing up with four brothers did for you, she was thankful she'd been raised an only child. Though, come to think of it, Clemency would have made an acceptable older sister. Madeleine too. In spite of feeling out of sorts, Élodie found herself relenting and offered to take her turn at entertaining them when the grand influx of Annesleys hit Paris.

"Now, don't be hasty," said Clemency with a chuckle. "You've no idea what you're letting yourself in for. And besides, we'll almost definitely be bypassing the cities."

They discussed travel details and the guest list, then swapped routes. Élodie, the French resident, should prove a godsend once they actually hit the road. Unless she stuck to her plan to take the train. But all that sort of thing could be fixed later. It was a relief to know there was so much solidarity. And Élodie was feeling more cheerful by the minute, though she was too proud to let Clemency know what was really bugging her. That rat. What it boiled down to was, they could count on each other. Kissing cousins and all that was meant by that term.

That all sorted, Clemency decided it was time for proper

action. No point in putting it off one moment longer. Harry was right, though she'd never admit it. Her grandmother deserved to know at least something of their plans, to be forewarned. She was almost eighty and had lived alone all these years. A sudden invasion of exuberant grandchildren might prove too much for her delicate sensibilities. She settled down at Teddy's desk to compose a letter that was not too explicit. Best, though, to give her some sort of warning, even if it meant diluting the surprise.

16

O dile Rochefort Annesley sat on the stone stoop outside her kitchen door and painfully unlaced her strong, serviceable boots. Trips to the market grew harder each week and if it weren't for her friendly neighbourhood farmer, who gave her lifts on the back of his hay wagon, she'd not be able to make the journey anymore. As it was, her fingers were now so crippled with arthritis she could hardly undo her laces. Eventually, though, her feet were free and she walked in her socks back into the shadowy room and across the flagged floor to the dim passage beyond. Even in July, the coolness of the aged stone kept out the worst of the summer heat and the vegetables she stacked in their wicker baskets would retain their freshness till she was ready to cook them.

She placed a battered tin *cafetière* on the stove and lit the gas with a taper. There were spiders lurking in the darker recesses of this room, but they didn't trouble Odile, whose fading eyesight no longer saw them. Nearly forty years she had inhabited this house, alone except for sporadic domestic help, and had grown as gnarled and wizened as the sturdy vines in the fields all around her.

The mailman had left her letters in the box and she slowly sorted them on the table as she waited for the coffee to brew. Her statement from the bank, a letter from her solicitor and another in a sprightly modern scrawl which she recognized as Clemency's. Dear girl. A slow smile softened the old lady's face as she sought with shaking knuckles to undo the envelope. What a joy that child had been in those early formative years before her presence here had become a liability and her grandmother had been obliged not to ask her again.

So her ruse had worked and they were planning a trip down here in the early autumn, just a few of her grandchildren apparently on an extravagant whim. Odile sipped her coffee and gazed out over the vineyards; she was well used to her solitude but occasionally still craved company. Even Pandora would have been welcome after a gap of so many years. The foolish woman had kept in touch sporadically via her chatty, news-filled notes and had written recently to warn Odile she was coming, then mysteriously not shown up. Odile had barely given it a second thought till she'd heard, weeks later, of Pandora's violent death. That had really startled her, though there was nothing, by that stage, she could possibly do. She had put it down to a ghastly freak of nature and tried to push it from her mind.

The children would be well grown by now, the lot of them, with lives of their own and individual personalities. How she longed to get to know them, most of them born since her own withdrawal from life. She looked back over the years to those sunny, carefree summers on the Maine coast, to the laughter and happiness before the darkness came.

She placed her cup and saucer in the sink for Dominique to deal with and moved into the vaulted hall. This fine old farmhouse had been sturdily built, to last through the centuries and withstand the harsh extremes of climate. Two wooden-railed staircases swept up, one on each side of the vast front door, which was rarely unlocked these days. Odile took the left-hand one and climbed painfully and slowly up to the room that had long been her studio. The shutters were closed fast and it took her some effort to shift the rusting bolts with hands that no longer retained their suppleness. Once done, she pushed wide the creaking wood to allow the midday sun to come pouring in with the healing scent of lemon verbena, clear and nostalgic. The room was large and lofty and tiled in the same cold stone as the rooms below. A second door opened on to the narrow balcony that ran the length of the house and she unlocked that too and went to stand outside, gazing across the acres of vineyards which stretched as far as she could see.

The sun had parched the earth and the green of the vines faded to a dull, leprous yellow. They'd be harvesting soon and then her peace would be broken by the incessant humming of tractors as they worked the regimented lines of bushes, stripping the grapes that supported this community. Odile found it restful and serene even when the workers were moving across the land. She had been raised in this district and the wine was in her blood. Her years in America and later, Oxford, had receded so far that she scarcely gave them thought. Only the impending visit of her grandchildren forced her back to reality for a while.

She turned back into the cluttered room, where stacks of canvases stood facing the whitewashed walls, and inhaled the familiar smells of paint and old turpentine, an aroma that always brought her satisfaction. Odile had worked throughout her life and these past forty years had not been idly spent. She had her art as witness to that effort; a few paintings had been sold to importunate buyers, but by far the bulk of her oeuvre remained here, part of her bequest to her unsuspecting heirs.

Her back was aching after riding on the wagon and she shuffled painfully forward to her easel, shrouded with a paint-daubed cloth to hide from prying eyes the painting she had left in progress. It had been months since she'd last been able to pick up her brushes and she hesitated now to look at what she had done. She feared that her talent might recede like the rest of her senses, would rather destroy than leave a less-than-perfect legacy. Slowly, with throbbing knuckles, she raised one hand and pulled from the canvas the concealing cloth.

Despite the broad expanse of evocative landscape that greeted her eyes daily in an ever-changing panoply of color, Odile depended for inspiration on her memory. There were few French scenes among the massed canvases; her subjects were portraits and occasional still lifes. This one she'd done from inner vision and love: the head and shoulders of a stern, handsome man in his prime, with thick black brows and silver eyes that penetrated the viewer from whichever point they looked at it. Cornelius Annesley, her passion and obsession, her husband for twenty-four years until she'd abruptly abandoned him.

Odile stood silently for several minutes, contemplating the past and the life she had left behind. She would never know for certain if she'd done the right thing, had reacted to an untenable situation with the only course of action she could think of at the time. Flight. Dear Cornelius. She caressed the thick paint lightly with her finger, then carefully replaced the cloth to eclipse him once more. Best not dwell too much on the past. She had done her solitary grieving in the long years she'd lived here in exile. Her drastic action had been for a purpose and could not now be altered. She had made her decision at the full height of her powers, a passionate, determined woman of forty-two, and had fled from beloved husband and needy children in order to appease a troubled conscience. Rightly or wrongly, only time would tell.

She left the windows open to air the room and shuffled down the back stairway to the kitchen, where the coffee was still brewing on the old iron stove. The mail lay scattered on the solid pine table and she swept the few letters into a pile and carried them through to her writing desk. She would write to Clemency later in the day. It was good of the child to care about her still and she was touched by the news of the impending visit. But when she discarded the envelopes, she looked in vain for the letter, which appeared to have gone.

She'd be losing her head next if she wasn't careful. After a slow and painful search of the shadowy kitchen, Odile finally gave up and left it for her domestic to find when she came later in the week to sweep up. And it didn't really matter. Clemency's address was safe in her locked writing desk and she could remember the gist of the brief, cheery message. September the ninth she said they'd be arriving. Odile smiled at her granddaughter's ingenuous belief that she was now too senile to realize the significance of that date. But bless her, nonetheless. She filled a pan with water and shoved it onto the stove. She'd bought fish heads in the market, which would boil up, with a handful of fresh herbs, to make a nourishing broth, all she really needed these days, along with some goat's cheese and the fresh local bread.

Odile Rochefort was not quite eighteen when she'd looked up from her figure drawing and seen for the first time her cousin Cornelius. He was forty and already married with a child, but that hadn't prevented the searing flame that arose in both of them the moment they locked eyes. Cornelius's memory of that life-altering moment had been a slim, ethereal child caught for eternity in a slanting ray of light that came through the skylight of the School of Fine Arts at New York University. It was 1936 and she'd just arrived from France.

It was all the fault of Ellen, his first wife. She had saddled him with this family responsibility when the letter came from his cousin Grace, and the child's arrival had coincided with his summer sabbatical at Columbia.

"Make sure she's all right," Ellen had said, always more family-minded than he was himself, so he had, with a bad grace, made the fatal call and grumpily collected her to take her to tea. Cornelius had always been a bit of a ladies' man, though he scorned their attention and treated them with contempt, but he was quite unprepared for the impact of this French girl, young and virtuous yet with a strange, deepseated maturity. Her English was passable, through having an American mother, and once she'd got over her initial shyness, she had chatted quite comfortably in the plushy Russian Tea Room and won his heart with her sparkling, straightforward *joie de vivre*. Not like the jaded flappers he was used to; her innocent effervescence made him feel young again. Quite simply, he reported, the child was a delight, though he didn't embellish his telephone call home and Ellen had no idea of what was actually happening that fateful summer that was to alter all their lives.

By the end of the semester, when he was due to return to Maine, his heart was irrevocably taken and he made excuses to linger on in Manhattan when he knew he was needed back home to comfort Ellen. Hugo was only recently dead and the infant Agnes taking up all her time. Though passion had faded entirely from the marriage, they were still good friends and a mutually supportive team. Ellen had suffered a lot in the past two years but continued to smile bravely and soldier on, cushioned as she was by the Herriot wealth and the peace and beauty of their lovely country home.

It was only when he heard that Agnes was pining for him that he was forced to make a choice between his two important loves. And the four-year-old, inevitably, won the contest hands down, at least for the few weeks till the bombshell of Odile's news. She hadn't intended to be a home-wrecker, had never met Ellen and preferred to keep it that way. But when she knew she was irreversibly pregnant, she had panicked slightly in this foreign country and run to her only support, the paternal cousin and father of her unplanned baby, with whom she was so passionately in love.

They had met, the two wives, for the first and only time, on the lawn at Christmas Cove when the sun was stretching long shadows across the grass. And Ellen had taken one swift, cool glance at her rival and seen immediately the way things were, even though Odile was still svelte and boyish, with a figure that had not much altered with the years.

There was not much choice then; the ending was inevitable. It was the 1930s and the Annesleys had a name to protect. Odile had been raised a strict Catholic and in prewar America abortion was out of the question. There'd been tears, of course, though not many, and from Odile surprisingly rather than Ellen. Cornelius had sealed his fate in a couple of frenzied weeks. Tearing himself from the daughter he adored, he took the hand of the trusting teenager and whisked her away to Oxford, England, where he'd fixed to take tenure at Magdalen College.

Eunice had been born in the early spring, before the divorce was actually finalized, but the change of location served to conceal the truth and the residents of Oxford accepted the new Mrs. Annesley with fitting respect. And that's where they'd lived and flourished all those years, on the banks of the Cherwell, where they'd loved and raised their family. Nine sturdy babies, each as beloved as the next, four girls and five boys, in a period of thirteen years. Though poor deserted Agnes managed to hold her own deep in the heart of the father who had wronged her.

Odile had seen to that and also managed to grow closer to her stepdaughter despite the unfortunate circumstances surrounding their relationship. For a while, of course, there had been a natural break in communication while Ellen came to terms with her quiet bitterness and the war in Europe forcibly kept them apart. But once it was safe to travel abroad again, Cornelius was determined to see more of his best-loved child, and the long-legged teenager, who looked so much like him, had started visiting Oxford and his growing second family. Five years older than Eunice, she had rapidly been assimilated and Odile had warmed to her energy and spirited beauty. It was odd, she thought now, pounding garlic for the *aioli,* that the flighty, headstrong American girl should also be spending her autumn years in France.

Not that they ever met these days, nor had any contact at all. Normandy was a long way off and Agnes never emerged. She was as dead to the rest of them as the dimly remembered Hugo, and Odile feared she had never made her peace with Cornelius before he died. She did, however, think of her often and the way both their lives had turned out. The irony was not lost on her, and she smiled as she thought of it now, that they might as well have shared their self-imposed exile and, like Martha Carlisle and poor Aunt Effie, spent the last barren years together instead of separately and alone.

But now Clemency had written and everything would change. This stern old house could do with an awakening. She would unbolt the doors, throw wide the heavy shutters and allow at last the health-giving sunshine to flood in. Let them see what they saw, her grandchildren, and come to their own conclusions. For forty grim years she had nurtured her secret. The time was long overdue that she pass the burden on.

Acting on an impulse, she also dropped a note to Agnes. She was, when all was said and done, as much an Annesley as the rest of them and had every right to come here too. She sat there quietly pondering in the silent heat of the afternoon, then, hearing a step on the staircase, locked both letters in her writing desk to post next time she managed to get into town.

17

*T*here was a man talking to Ashley outside the school gates when she got there cursing, late as usual and in a thoroughly foul mood. At first she thought he must be a teacher, he was so respectably dressed, but his manner was less officious and she hadn't seen him around before. Ashley was telling him about the kittens, lucid for once and with a strange animation which showed him off at his very best. Warmth swept through her as she reached his side and planted a proprietorial kiss on the top of his smooth, dark head. But Ashley shrugged it off and went on talking. The man flashed Cherie a collusive smile but allowed the child to continue. She liked that. He appeared enthralled.

"Four you say? And all different colors?"

The kitten ploy seemed to have worked triumphantly and Ashley, for once, was hooked. His habitual clumsiness had toned itself down whenever he tiptoed into the bedroom to watch them feed and squirm about. He was even permitted to touch them now, though only under strict supervision. Now he beamed up proudly at the stranger.

"One stripy, two blue and the other Mum calls cinnamon."

They were six weeks old, not yet ready to leave the mother but old enough for showing to prospective buyers. Was this what was holding the stranger's attention so raptly? Eventually he turned to her, flashing a smile that lit up his face and immediately allayed her ingrained suspicion.

"Great kid," he said, appearing really to mean it, and Cherie's bitter and unyielding heart unclenched itself one notch. She still didn't know what he was doing here, but he'd certainly found a champion in her son. The child stood looking up at him, eyes alight with fanatical pleasure, transfixed by something not immediately apparent to her. Perhaps he was a school inspector or someone from Social Services. She'd fallen into that trap before, knew they had sneaky ways of creeping up.

"Come and see them," begged Ashley, pulling at the man's hand and turning huge, imploring eyes on his mother. "Can he, Mum?"

"Why not?" Despite herself, Cherie laughed. All those drummed-in lectures about not talking to strangers; this child was impossible, yet she loved to see him communicate. The way he was now, it didn't show that there was anything wrong with him. She was grateful for that and inclined to indulge him, though she didn't know the stranger from Adam. For all she knew, he might be a murdering rapist. She raised one querying eyebrow at the man, who smiled, shrugged, then nodded. Taking Ashley's hand, he glanced at his watch and said he could spare a half hour or so. Provided it wasn't too far.

"Ten minutes on the bus," Cherie told him, but he was fishing in his pocket for his car keys. He was certainly easy company, as if he already knew her, and she liked his smile and the direct appraisal of his eyes. For the first time in ages, he made her feel sexy, but she trod on that thought and ground it fiercely out. No way. She was through with all that rubbish, the certain path to disaster. At only twenty-four, she had seen all she needed of life.

"You live here alone?" asked the stranger casually as they drew up outside the concrete box of which, till now, she had been so proud. Seeing it through his eyes, though, she found it filled her with a feeling of depressing inadequacy. The trash collectors were due and the cul-de-sac reeked of rubbish. She gazed despondently at the trodden-away grass as she stood on the curb and watched him lock the car. A group of neighbouring kids were playing in the road and they shouted to Ashley, who normally would have joined them. Not today, however. He clung to his stranger, feasting his eyes. Sad little mite that he was, he had never had a father figure; come to think of it, neither had she. Like a new revelation, Cherie suddenly saw how much these things mattered.

She led the way silently into the house, where the kittens were playing all over the stairs and the odour of cat hung heavily in the air. She went around opening windows, ashamed of the mess. Whatever must he think? The stranger scooped up a couple of the kittens and held them gently under his chin. Their tiny vibrating bodies snuggled up close to him and Cherie glanced with appreciation at his strong, capable hands. She had an unexpected urge to snuggle too. It had been too long.

"So what is it you do?" he asked, glancing around. "Surely more than just breed cats?"

She cleared a space for him to sit, then stood there hovering, uncertain what to do next. They were out of biscuits and the milk was off, so she couldn't even offer him a cup of tea. But the man appeared entirely at his ease. He placed both kittens gently back on the carpet and made room for her to perch beside him. So she told him about Tesco and how much she hated it and he listened intently as though he had all the time in the world. It had been ages since anyone had paid her so much attention. Though naturally taciturn, she suddenly found there were things she needed badly to get off her chest. And he really seemed interested. Crossed his ankles and leaned back comfortably, showing no signs of wanting to leave. Ashley bored easily, which was probably just as well. He wandered off upstairs to change into his play clothes.

"And this little chap?" asked the man when he eventually reappeared, clutching his skateboard and heading towards the street. What powers of concentration he had, had always been pretty limited; already the stranger's fascination had begun to wear thin. She told him a little about Ashley's beginnings, amazed at herself that she could be so frank. And when he questioned her about her own parents, she told him that too. Her mother's early death in a car crash, the father she'd never known.

"Any pictures?" he asked, but she shook her head. Nothing, since the day she had run away from the home, escaping from authority and the interfering aunts. She knew a little about Betty Cole, dimly remembered a big, florid blonde with a hearty laugh, who was forever cuddling her and always smelled of carnations. But her father, Tom Annesley, remained an enigma, though she was piecing together, bit by bit, a jagged portrait from things she learned from Clemency.

Which brought her to Clemency and the other cousins. Proudly Cherie told him of the recent family gatherings and the fact that she'd just been invited to join them on a jaunt to France.

"That sounds exciting," said the stranger alertly. "Have you ever been there before?"

Of course not. Who did he think she was? She'd not been anywhere, apart from to Clemency's, and was secretly dreading it, though she kept a brave face. Abroad was a concept she found frankly repellent; all that froggy food and a load of garlicky foreigners. And she didn't much like the thought of taking Ashley; who knew what germs he might pick up in France? But she'd borrowed an atlas from the local library and was gradually showing Ashley the route they said they'd take. The least she could do was try to knock some knowledge into him. She was secretly proud of what she was learning too.

"And your cousins are nice." It was a statement more than a question, but she launched into details, keen to show them off. Clemency she liked a lot, though was still a bit in awe of her. She admired the French one, Élodie, and was a little scared of Madeleine. Isabelle was nice to her too, though a bit too brainy for her taste. And as for Harry, well, you really had to laugh. She told him about the newsletter, found herself rocking with laughter, and was gratified to see he was laughing too. She could tell he liked her, was enjoying this cozy chat. The kittens toddled around them both and started to swarm over his knees, and he caressed their tiny heads with delicate fingers and rubbed their tight little tummies.

Eventually, though, he had to leave and glanced at his watch with regret. He was headed south, he said, and it was a long way from Solihull to London. He hadn't told her a thing about himself, but she didn't realize that until she had waved him off. She didn't even know his name. Ashley, still playing in the cul-de-sac with his pals, saw the car start up and let out an agonized roar.

"No!" he screamed as he flung himself after the car. But he was too late; their intriguing visitor was gone. Without so much as a backwards glance at the savagely weeping child

152

he was leaving behind.

After she'd done the dishes, dried Ashley's tears and finally got him to bed, Cherie sat down and laboriously wrote to Clemency, telling her that they would definitely come. However she felt about traveling so far, she was warming slowly to the concept of family and didn't want to miss out on this excursion which seemed to mean such a lot. Also, she was intrigued to meet Odile. From all she had heard, her French nan was something of a card and secretly it made her feel exotic to think they shared the same blood. Ashley too. Perhaps it was true and he really had inherited her talent. Cherie had never even thought about such things, but it did begin to make sense.

She had no money, but Clemency had offered to cover their costs. All they had to do was get on the coach to Wiltshire and the Cartwrights would take care of things from there. It was the start of the school term, but she was sure they wouldn't mind. It should be educational and Ashley was off so often, in any case, that it was doubtful they would even notice his absence. She started to worry about what she was going to wear, then shrugged it off and lit another cigarette. To hell with what they thought. She would go as she was, they could like it or lump it.

At ten o'clock exhaustion claimed her, so she stopped what she was doing and dragged herself up to bed. It was a lonely life, living here with just the kid, and although it meant a roof over their heads, there wasn't a lot else she could say for it. The walls were so thin, she could hear the neighbours scrapping and the sound of their television, tantalizingly just out of reach. Top of her shopping list was a telly of their own, but first she had to deal with the more crucial bills. She had earmarked some of the kitten money for a secondhand set and was looking forward to the time this lot would be ready to go. The way things were developing, they could turn into a nice little earner.

Ashley, for once, was quiet and his light already off. She poked her head around the door and could see him lying there, all scrunched up, looking as peaceful and perfect as a little angel. Bless his heart. All in all, he wasn't a totally bad kid, though the intrusion of the stranger had made her wish he had a dad. She didn't see what she could do about that; it was nowhere on her agenda. She loathed and despised the disgusting local louts and couldn't afford to go clubbing or even to the pub very often. Life, she was aware, was rapidly passing her by, but that seemed to be the lot of today's young single mum; do-gooders were forever ramming it down her throat.

She stepped softly into the room to tuck him in properly but stopped stock-still when her hand brushed cold fur in the dark. It had been years since he'd last had a cuddly toy; with a hand that suddenly shook, she reached for the light switch. Then screamed at what she saw, waking him abruptly.

"You little bleeder!" she yelled in horror. "Now what have you been and gone and done?"

But she saw already that she'd arrived too late. Four little limp bodies lay strewn about the bed, their tiny necks broken like discarded toys.

18

*M*adeleine was still a bit fed up but managed to get a grip on herself. The property market was rumoured to be about to peak; she was determined to get in as many big ones as she could before that happened. So what if some treacherous man had failed to phone her? It was something she was so used to by now, it didn't cost her much sleep, though she did still jump and look furtive when the phone did ring. She was fleetingly tempted to confide in Clemency, then brushed the thought aside. From the way she had behaved at the Oxford lunch, Madeleine had a shrewd suspicion that Clemency had been bitten too, though she'd always made such a thing of her blinkered devotion to that nice, safe (and—dare she think it?—dull) husband.

In any case, what could sharing it with Clemency achieve? Confirm that Cousin Dominic was a rat and leave it at that? Or that he was seeing Élodie (it certainly looked like it) and possibly Isabelle too? Best leave the whole murky matter alone and seek elsewhere for reliable love. Family members were a bad idea, anyhow. Inbreeding, genetic weakness and all that stuff; witness the descendants of Queen Victoria. But it hurt, nonetheless, when she let it.

Clemency sounded sprightly when she phoned her and confirmed the September trip to France was definitely on. Teddy would drive the Range Rover and there'd be room for Madeleine, if she cared to squash in, along with the family, Cherie and the kid. And possibly Isabelle too. She didn't yet know what the others were doing or even how many there were likely to be.

"Harry's in for a cert," she said gloomily. "But he would be, wouldn't he? Can't afford to risk letting us girls steal a march on him; we might persuade Mémé to alter her will. I just hope he'll leave the dreaded Lavender behind. I don't see her roughing it on the road."

Madeleine laughed. Clemency was a tonic.

"Or those butter-won't-melt children either." With their party frocks and musical instruments and that ghastly little boy who was forever showing off. But Clemency was more sanguine.

"Mémé's house has no electricity," she reminded Madeleine. "So no creature comforts, and you'd better believe it. I have slipped that thought into Harry's mind and let's hope he passes it on. With luck, if they do come, they'll prefer to stay in a hotel." Secretly Madeleine could quite see their point.

Teddy would detour through London, said Clemency, and pick up Madeleine so that at least they could drive in convoy. Teddy was a saint by anyone's standards and went along with all this family stuff with scarcely a moan. Not for the first time, Madeleine envied Clemency her marriage, since it seemed to make her so happy. But men like Teddy were thin on the ground and also, in truth, a shade too amenable for her taste. She liked a man to have a little more grit, to be less dependable and more quixotic. But that was something she was trying not to think about.

There was no need for Teddy to pick her up, she said. She preferred to drive herself in any case. But Clemency, always the organizer, was adamant. It would be no trouble at all for them to drop by Notting Hill. The journey was a trifle; Teddy did it all the time. Two hours, door to door, if he really put his mind to it, and they'd got the Covent Garden pad if they felt like stopping over. Not that there was much room there, but they'd manage to fit in somehow.

There was no point even trying to argue with Clemency, so Madeleine didn't bother. But she fancied bringing the Porsche. She liked her independence and looked forward to the thrill of letting rip her expensive toy on those fast French roads. She ended the call, then shot off into the center of town for lunch.

Clemency drifted out onto the terrace, where Teddy was valiantly trying to cope with paperwork with a labrador's adoring nose on his knee and a couple of children playing handball on the lawn.

"What would you like for lunch, darling?" she asked, absently deadheading hydrangeas. Teddy grunted but didn't look up. More and more these days he sought solace in his flat; there, at least, he could concentrate properly and also have some semblance of a life of his own. Here was entirely his wife's domain, manicured, luxurious but bearing little trace of him.

"Quiche?" she suggested. "With a nice fresh salad?" And then, when he didn't answer: "Or pasta, perhaps? Artichoke hearts and tomatoes, you always like that. And the boys will be starving after all this exercise."

"Anything," said Teddy, still without looking up.

"With a bottle of Sancerre. Would you choose one for us please, love?"

Teddy went on stoically shuffling papers.

"Soon, please, dearest. The lunch won't take long and we'll need it properly chilled."

He sighed and laid aside his pen. She was a marvelous manager, a veritable field marshal, but with her constantly hovering it was hard to get anything done. He rose and stretched, gently pushing aside the dog. For the first time in his life, he found himself almost siding with Harry. Who loved to boast about that house but stressed the no-go areas. One thing was starting to dawn on Teddy after sixteen blissful years, and that was that man was not by nature a pack animal. Notwithstanding his easygoing exterior, Teddy Cartwright needed occasionally to shake off family constraints and walk by himself.

So when Clemency suggested he trim the edges after lunch, he reminded her fairly brusquely that he had to get back to town.

"This afternoon?"

"Yes, I've a meeting at six."

"So late?" It was the first she'd heard of it.

"A vintner from Bordeaux, only here for a couple of days. Promised to meet and have a bite together. Thought I'd take him to Rules."

"Well, don't go eating anything you shouldn't. Remember your cholesterol and that paunch, my love." Teddy smiled easily and helped himself to salad. She was constantly on at him, like a nervous tic, so regularly these days that she no longer even noticed. But he did.

"And wear your light suit. It should be hot tomorrow." After a truly dismal summer, it was finally starting to perk up.

"Yes, dear," said Teddy absently, inwardly beginning to seethe. Why wouldn't she remember that he was a grown man, not a child? Always fussing around him, straightening his tie, polishing his shoes. Tucking a clean handkerchief into his pocket and reminding him to wear a hat and not sit too long in the sun. She was a dear but, well. Teddy badly needed a bit of fresh air, and the place to find it was certainly not here in the country.

"Drive carefully," she said as she waved him off. "And ring me the minute you get there, promise. Just to make sure."

Yes, yes. And swallow his indigestion pills and be sure to change his socks. It was like a catechism, he had it off so patly, but the moment he was away from her, his mind readjusted and he wiped it clear. He hit the road at a quarter to four and drove like a mad thing until he reached Marlborough. He'd invented the vintner, as he so often did these days, but his wife was so preoccupied it didn't occur to her to wonder. Well, what the heart didn't know was really not a problem. Teddy struck out cheerfully for the city and his real life.

Clemency couldn't really help her bossy, mothering ways. Having been showered with love throughout her infant life, it all came quite naturally to her. Her mother had idolized her and so too had her aunts and Mémé. The oldest of the granddaughters, she was the only one ever to be singled out to visit the house in the vineyards and those few, far-off French summers were still imprinted on her brain. It was odd, now she came to think of it, for an apparently caring mother to have abandoned quite so abruptly her own grieving child, to cope with two small boys and a brand-new baby, and just wander off on some selfish whim in search of a career of her own. Feminism was one thing, but Mémé had

had heavy responsibilities as well as a husband who utterly adored her and had abandoned one family and his native land in order to spend his remaining years with her.

Mémé was an enigma; her behaviour simply didn't add up. True, the beginning of the sixties was when women started doing their own thing, but Odile Rochefort, with her strict Catholic upbringing, was just not the type to have turned into quite such a rebel. From all accounts, she had idolized her husband and raised all those children serenely and with care. Clemency suddenly realized that she could hardly wait to see her grandmother again and perhaps discover the truth about what had actually happened. And why the invitations to stay had ceased so abruptly.

The house in the vineyards was guarded and grim and the absence of electricity terrifying to a child. To anyone of any age, in fact. She must be sure to pack candles and make everyone bring a flashlight. Her own well-balanced children would take it all in their stride. They adored outdoor camping, and generally roughing it, and all had sleeping bags of their own. But she couldn't answer for any of the others, especially Lavender and her precocious bunch. Clemency enjoyed the idea of Lavender slumming and was pretty certain there'd be tears before they were through. All part of the fun, of course; developing the pioneer spirit. The reunion was such a capital idea, she was sorry now she hadn't thought of it before. They must all make sure that they made it truly memorable and gave the old lady the birthday of a lifetime.

It was slightly odd she'd not yet answered Clemency's last letter, but Mémé had lived so long alone, she had doubtless forgotten the smaller niceties of life. Clemency brought in great swaths of blooms from the garden and spent a contented hour in the flower room, arranging them in vases and distributing them around the house. Teddy hadn't phoned yet, probably caught in traffic. She wasn't really a worrier, just kept automatic tabs on him, everything in its place. She would try to bring some color to her grandmother's life. She remembered the house as dark and forbidding, with staircases not to be lingered on, and a small, familiar frisson of terror crept deliciously up her spine. It would be interesting to see it all again, after so many years, and try perhaps to relive some of her childhood experiences.

He rang at last, just as Madeleine was preparing for bed. Her heart started pounding, but she managed to keep her cool and let him know curtly that now was not a good time. He was sorry he'd been so silent, he said, but had only just got back from a trip to France. Yeah, yeah. If that was intended to endear him to her, he couldn't be more mistaken.

How is Cousin Élodie? she nearly asked sarcastically, but bit her tongue just in time. Dignity at all costs was what her mother preached. Never let a man know the effect he was having; keep the emotional seesaw balanced and you were unlikely to go too far wrong. If in doubt, do nothing, was Madeleine's personal mantra. Despite the advice of bolder spirits like Julie, she preferred always to be the pursued. Probably why she was still single, in fact, but a relationship was only worth having when the passion was at full heat.

"We need to talk," said Dominic urgently, but Madeleine firmly rebuffed him. She was busy, she told him, with house deals and such. And her diary was crammed to overflowing.

"I'll call again, then," he said, sounding slightly less

161

confident.

"Whatever," snapped Madeleine as she slammed down the receiver.

19

*É*lodie was positively dancing with delight as she strode along the Rue du Faubourg-St.-Honoré on her way to the fashion house for a fitting. Last night had exceeded anything her fevered imagination could have dreamed up. She was reeling from it, giddy with hysteria, finally obliged to face the fact that she was well and truly hooked. Today's valued customer was a pampered Parisian shrew and they were unlikely to get through it without some form of histrionics. For once, however, she simply didn't care. She hummed a lively tune in rhythm with the clacking of her heels while her heart serenaded his name over and over again. *Dominic, Dominic.*

He had called out of the blue to invite her to dinner, explaining he was in Paris on a flying trip and had things he would quite like to discuss. Élodie had wavered, uncertain how encouraging it was cool to be, but the fact that the visit was so fleeting had tipped the balance in his favour and she'd graciously agreed to this last-minute date. Had rapidly cut short her pattern-cutting session, in fact, and flown home for a shower and total makeover, sorting through her closet like a thing demented in search of the one subtle outfit that might make him take her seriously. Or, at the very least, rekindle his original desire. Pathetic, sure, she hated herself but for once had no power over what she was about to do.

They met at a bar on the Boulevard St. Germain on a fine,

162

clear evening when the streets were abuzz with strollers, and the second she saw him, relaxing at an outside table with a glass of yellow Pernod and a copy of *Le Figaro*, her heart lurched wildly and she knew she was in trouble. Big trouble, because she wanted him so much. He looked clean and well groomed and was wearing a sober suit, light-years away from the animal who'd first attracted her, but when she stooped to kiss his cheek, the familiar musk sent a delicious thrill right through her. *Let's get out of here,* she wanted to shriek, *back to my pad to fuck the night away.*

"Hi," he said, leaping up to yank back her chair. "Thanks for agreeing to meet on such short notice. I really appreciate it." Then he flashed her one of his winning smiles and she sank down dizzily and allowed him to order her an aperitif. She felt as giddy and uncontrolled as the rawest ingenue, putty in his hands to do with as he pleased.

What he appeared to want, though, turned out to be far less exciting, a leisurely reminiscence, over an excellent meal in a nearby classy restaurant, about family concerns and her own direct lineage.

"Your mother is Patrice," he said idly. "Married, I believe, to Jonathan Sinclair. Is that right?"

"It certainly is. Jonathan's my dad, but she's been through it all before. First, Willard Hopkins, father of Will Junior and Charlie, with a quickie in the middle we try no longer to mention."

In spite of herself, she grinned. Henry had been an aberration they all now preferred to forget. Whatever Mom had been thinking at the time, she could not have got it more wrong. Lonely, possibly, or simply off her head. Now Élodie suddenly saw her own self starkly reflected in her impetuous parent. Patrice had always been considered the beauty of the family, condemned as a result never to be taken seriously except by the men she bedded and occasionally married. Grandfather Cornelius had always praised her looks in a caustic, rather slighting way that Patrice claimed had made her feel inferior, little more than a fun-loving airhead.

"Which is why, I suppose, she keeps on marrying."

"And she's the youngest?"

"No, that's Ethan. Named, I suppose, for your own maternal grandfather. This name business gets terribly confusing. He lives alone in Kentish Town and works for the BBC. Maybe you've met him." Dominic didn't respond, just jotted down something in a small black notebook and slipped it back into his pocket. Keen disappointment was clutching at Élodie's throat and she tried not to look too hard at him. What had brought all *this* on, this sudden family concern? For a man who'd neglected his mother, it was strange behaviour indeed. Surely he hadn't come all this way just to discuss her antecedents? After a lifetime wandering the world because he so much hated any sort of involvement? Or so he said.

Dominic, however, was giving nothing away and still appeared enthralled by the Annesley clan. She realized she knew very little about him. Except that he sang like a siren and fucked like a tiger, an occupation she'd far rather be involved in right now.

"I don't know how to ask this," he eventually said, apologetically, "but were they actually married, do you know? Your father and mother when you were conceived?"

Hang on. "I assume so," said Élodie stiffly, startled. "Why on earth do you think they might not have been?" It must be there on her birth certificate, surely. She was suddenly alarmingly unsure.

"Oh, family hearsay. I don't know." He looked uncomfortable and bent to scratch his ankle. "Things I've picked up. You know how people talk. Not that it matters, of course."

She did indeed know. Put her mother and two surviving aunts together and all mayhem always broke out, the way they liked to shred each other. She wondered if they'd turn up at the family reunion, Aunts Eunice and Aimée and her own beloved mother. It was a pity Claire had died so prematurely, because she'd always given good gossip too. She grinned.

"I hate to disappoint you, but I think you've got that wrong. Ma left Willard to run off with Henry, but I'm pretty sure she was well divorced before she got together with Dad. Still, I suppose you never can tell. Kids don't necessarily get told these things."

Thinking of Connecticut and their respectable little circle, the notion was beginning to amuse her hugely. Wait till they heard back home. Life was complicated enough without anyone casting aspersions on her mother's reputation. These days the reformed Patrice was a stalwart of the church who helped arrange the flowers and even wore a hat.

"So tell me about Madeleine," he said, switching the subject, and off they went again on another apparent irrelevancy. Madeleine's mother was the slightly loopy Aimée, who talked to her saucepans and knew each of her plants by name. By the time they were finally finished, she was tired and slightly headachy and they said very little as he walked her home through the still thronging late-night streets. She almost feared he wasn't going to come in, his mind seemed so set on other things. But he did and, once there, the old magic returned and they fell on each other like ravening wild things and he ended up staying till dawn.

"Who exactly are you?" asked Élodie dreamily, as she lay there beside him, studying his peaceful profile in the growing light. "And how come you're so interested in all this family stuff?"

"Don't really know. Guess it's just habit. Trying to identify my roots, if you like. I've always been an incurable snooper and our family seems to have more secrets than most."

"That's because there are so many of us."

"Maybe."

"What happened to the music?" she asked him after a while.

A slow smile spread and he lazily opened one eye. "I guess I just grew out of it," he said.

He caught up with Isabelle when he got back to Oxford, phoned her rooms and heard the familiar panic in her voice.

"Hi, how're you doing?" She was such a dear, silly, flustered thing, strangely awkward for one so awfully clever. Prettier too than she'd ever been encouraged to realize. He could picture her now, waving her arms about like a windmill, thrown by this unexpected telephone intrusion.

"Oh, Dominic, it's you. I wondered where you'd got to." Had lain awake nights worrying, if he only knew it, fretting that she'd done something to drive him away. It had been weeks since their last meeting and she'd feared he'd left forever. Just hearing his voice now brought her out in a relieved sweat.

"I had some business to attend to, but now I'm back for a while. Why don't we get together tonight and you can catch me up on your news?"

He smiled at her gasp of grateful acceptance and imagined her thrown into an even worse state at the prospect of having to meet him in a public place. Odd how cousins could be so different, yet still have so much in common as well. Those noses, of course, and their sharp, bright minds. Their susceptibility too, which he shamelessly manipulated for purposes of his own which he planned they should never discover.

They met at seven in the Mitre and he was touched to see she had made a bit of an effort and was wearing, slightly self-consciously, a light paisley shawl over her habitual uniform of sweater and denim skirt. Her legs were bare and her feet in mannish sandals, but he was sure he detected a hint of eyeliner and rouge. If only someone would tell her to shave her legs. He kissed her chastely on either cheek and ordered a couple of lagers.

"Go grab a table in a nice secluded corner," he ordered. "Where we can talk without fear of interruption." Not that he had anything he particularly wanted to say, but she might, if he was skillful, be maneuvered along the right roads. She was a sweet, endearing thing and it was certainly worth a try. And Harry was growing impatient; it was time to deliver the goods.

Charlie Annesley, sixth child and third son, had always been something of a drifter. Two years younger than the golden Roland, he had grown up in his shadow and when Roland died and his mother fell to pieces, it was Charlie more than

167

the others who had really suffered, ignored and rebuffed because he was still alive. Tom, a year younger, had an altogether different personality which had seen him through, but Charlie became reclusive and shy and in 1963, when he was still only nineteen, had sloped off to Canada and never returned. His only child, Isabelle, was born four years later after a halfhearted courtship of a girl he didn't love. What he had done in those intervening years was not a matter of record. He had always been a secretive sort of bloke and, even now, she felt she'd never really known him.

"So you don't think he'll be coming to your reunion?"

Isabelle was surprised he knew about that, since he wasn't in the direct bloodline.

"I wouldn't imagine so." For starters, he didn't have the money and her presence in England was not sufficient incentive. Sad but true; she'd never felt he cared. Her mother too was largely out of it, a bitter women who felt she'd wasted her life. Which she had, in a way, on the bottle. It had taken adulthood and this move to Oxford to instill in Isabelle a proper feeling of family. She was grateful to Clemency for taking her under her wing; to the others too for becoming substitute sisters. She confided in Dominic how awed she felt, being here in this seat of learning where her grandfather had been such a star. As a child, he'd made her feel lumpy and awkward. She wondered what he'd say if he could see her now.

Dominic walked her home and gave her a fraternal squeeze. He'd love to give her dinner, he said, but had other pressing things to do. Some other time, perhaps, when things were less fraught. As soon as he reached his own rooms, he picked up the phone and called Harry.

20

*T*his time it was Madeleine's turn to play host. They were well into August and needed to make firm plans for the birthday trip to France. Clemency had received enthusiastic responses from most of the people invited and now was thinking that a hard core of them, the female cousins, should drive down a few days earlier in order to sort out accommodation for the rest. She had dashed off another note to Mémé—didn't want to rattle the old lady unnecessarily by presenting her with a gang—but was careful not to state the purpose of the visit or quite how many were likely to show up. Provided the weather was mild, and in early autumn in France there was a fair chance it would be, they ought to be all right; otherwise, it might be wise to ask individual families to bring tents. There was loads of space directly around the house, with grazing fields beyond the vines she was sure they could coerce for the purpose. And, of course, that great empty barn she remembered so well which could accommodate all of them, as well as their belongings, and still have space to spare.

"Isn't it crammed with farm equipment?"

"Not these days, I wouldn't imagine. Unless Mémé leases it to a neighbour."

The actual birthday was on a Wednesday. If they aimed at leaving the previous Saturday, it would give them time to take the journey in leisurely stages, see a bit of the countryside and still arrive well in advance of the pack to sort out the catering and basic arrangements.

"I'll bring the cake," said Clemency, who loved to bake, ticking it off her list. "And Teddy will contribute a case or two of fizz." The Range Rover was getting more burdened by the minute. Soon there would be no room for passengers.

"That's the week after August Bank Holiday," said Madeleine.

"Labour Day weekend in the States."

They arrived in Chepstow Villas around twelve and trooped up to the large, airy flat. Élodie glanced around in appreciation while Cherie was openly gawking. On this occasion, she'd managed to leave the kid. A harassed neighbour with five of her own had agreed to take him for money, though only reluctantly, since his odd behaviour was widely discussed and you could never be absolutely certain quite how he'd behave. She had kept very quiet about the kittens and had unloaded the queens on another local breeder. An infection, she'd explained, though the grown-up ones were clear. It broke her heart to dispose of their little dishes, but she couldn't face the reminder and there was no way Ashley was ever going to have another pet, not while she was in charge.

"What on earth got into you?" she had asked him severely, cuffing his ear and shaking him hard, but he'd stared at her blankly and turned away, as if those sad, raglike bodies had been nothing more than cheap toys out of a cracker. Now she was trying to blank the whole episode. She was pretty certain that he was too. This day out with her cousins was exactly what she needed, provided nobody brought up the subject of cats.

Madeleine had a cat of her own, an elegant brown Burmese with a coat like a horse chestnut. In the spooky way cats have, he made an instant beeline for Cherie, causing Clemency to laugh and say he could probably smell the kittens. But nothing more, which was just as well. Cherie simply cuddled him and he fell asleep on her knee.

Madeleine showed them around, then took their bar orders, gin and tonic for Clemency and Isabelle, white wine for Élodie and a spritzer for herself. Cherie, uncertain, settled for medium sherry because it was what her mother always drank. She was impressed by the array of bottles in Madeleine's streamlined chrome and glass cabinet. If this was what single life in London was about, then she was all for it. If it weren't, of course, for that permanent millstone around her neck. The kitchen was gorgeous, cool and elegant like its owner, without a sign of anything cooking or preparations for a meal.

"I've made reservations," explained Madeleine, catching Clemency's glance. " 'Round the corner at an Italian place over a pub. Hope that's all right. My treat, of course."

Extravagant, thought Clemency, but it wasn't her business and she could see that this flat was scarcely used at all, a trophy showplace for an affluent businesswoman, with none of the comforts that surrounded her at home. Well, good for Madeleine, she added generously to herself. If this was the sort of life she preferred, then go for it. The cat was as leggy and immaculate as Madeleine herself, with fur that looked synthetic and smelled faintly of chocolate fudge. But the bedroom was sterile and rather too perfect, with its starched white linen and piles of elaborate pillows, and that Clemency found a little saddening. Madeleine was so beautiful and so nice. Shame she'd apparently not yet found her destiny.

"Well, chaps," she said, raising her glass in general welcome, always the natural leader even in someone else's home. "Here's to us all and our spot of French leave."

With six Cartwrights, Isabelle, Cherie and Ashley, there was clearly no more room in the Range Rover, so Madeleine said she'd definitely drive and offered Élodie a lift. It would be a chance to get to know a little better the cousin with whom she felt the most empathy.

"I can pick you up in Paris," she said, "if you'll give me a bed for the night."

Élodie brightened. She had intended going by train. The TGV was so fast and efficient, but she liked the idea of tootling along with her cousin. She took off so little time these days, a break would be just what she needed.

"There are some spectacular chateaux along the Loire," she said. "We could detour and spend a couple of nights on the road."

Clemency butted in as usual. "There's one near Chamonix that we've visited before. It would be fun to meet up and have a family dinner. Lovely scenery 'round those parts. And in September the leaves will just be starting to turn."

"What about Harry?"

"What about him?" As always, his name brought forth gales of crude laughter, though Clemency conceded that she really ought to include him. It could be awkward when they arrived if she didn't.

"Let's hope he leaves the family at home."

"And Dominic?" There, it was out. Madeleine's question seemed to fall into a void as they all turned to stare at her in silence.

"Not a direct descendant," said Clemency fairly stiffly. "Though maybe we could stretch the point and include him.

What do you think?"

"No," said Élodie, just a shade too sharply. She wasn't prepared to share him yet, to watch her cousins jostling in that all-too-obvious way, when she now was confident that she finally had his heart. At least for a while. Madeleine looked surprised. This was a bit of a *volte-face,* she thought. She had seen the longing in Élodie's eyes and wondered what had happened to cause her to change her mind. Well, she'd see what she could discover when they were off on the road together.

"Knowing Dominic, he's likely just to turn up," said Isabelle. He had a habit of vanishing and reappearing again like the Cheshire Cat, which these days kept her in a permanent state of flurried confusion. She'd have to think of something suitable to wear just in case, though her wardrobe was woefully limited. Not that Dominic was likely to notice; lately he'd been acting like a brother.

"Who's Dominic?" asked Cherie, surprising them all.

"You don't know Dominic?" said Clemency, amazed. "My, he really must be slipping." Though secretly she was rather glad; he had won a special place in her heart and she didn't want him spread too thin. Especially now with Teddy acting so strange.

At three-thirty, having put the world to rights, drawn up individual lists based on Clemency's master plan and all agreed to bring flashlights, candles and insect repellent, they spilled out into the street and strolled back to Madeleine's flat. Clemency felt like a spot of shopping, but none of the others was keen, which was a first. Madeleine needed to get back to the office; there was a hot deal hovering that she dared not neglect. Élodie was heading for Waterloo, privately thinking there were trendier shops in Paris, while Cherie, reluctantly, had to trek back home to Solihull for the kid. Isabelle wavered, then, as always, gave in. She really shouldn't, but Clemency was so persuasive and she knew she needed guidance in picking out the right things. And there was, after all, the holiday to consider with just the faintest chance that Dominic might come.

"We'll try Oxford Street first, then move over to Covent Garden," said Clemency, gripping her arm. She hadn't brought the car into town, had left it at Marlborough Station. If they were through in time, she might give Teddy a surprise and grab a lift back with him from the warehouse. So they all waved goodbye and went their separate ways and Clemency marched Isabelle down to the Bayswater Road and onto a bus to Selfridges.

"What you need," she said thoughtfully, studying her cousin, "is a lightweight trouser suit in something that doesn't crease." They were roughly the same size, with identical coloring, but Isabelle was awkward and managed always to look a fright. Colour coordination was what she needed, something plain and serviceable with alternative accessories. Clemency was in her element organizing someone else's life and simply itched to get her hands on Isabelle. She knew she had to tread carefully since she'd no idea of Isabelle's finances, but she could at least point her in the right direction and give her the encouragement she knew she'd always lacked.

Two hours later, their arms full of purchases, they turned the corner into St. Christopher's Place and dropped wearily onto outside seats for coffee in the piazza. A day well spent, thought Clemency with satisfaction. Two new summer out-fits for Isabelle, plus scarves and belts in contrasting colors, and some snazzy tailored pants for herself. Just time for a breather before Isabelle caught her train, then Clemency would go in search of her husband. If she caught him in a better mood, he might even spring to an early supper. She thought of including Isabelle, then dismissed it. She'd already had a basinful of her and would quite like to talk to Teddy on his own. Lately he hadn't seemed quite himself; she hoped there was nothing wrong.

The warehouse in Endell Street seemed strangely silent, but it was almost seven and they'd probably closed for the night. Clemency rang the outside bell and waited for ages to be buzzed in. She walked up two flights of stark concrete steps and into the huge lit loft that housed the wine. Rack upon rack of the best French vintages stretched endlessly in front of her like library shelves. Here her husband was at his hap-piest, browsing among his beloved bottles, checking and listing and ordering new stock.

"Hello, there!" she called, though the place looked deserted. But the lights were still on and someone had let her in. She wandered slowly between the racks, breathing the subtle perfume of the finest French grapes. In just a few weeks she'd be seeing them on the vine. Perhaps Teddy could do some business locally while they were down there. A special vintage in honour of Mémé. Now, *that* really would make a birthday to remember. At the end of the room was the office where Teddy worked and she could now see movement behind the glass. Bless his heart, he was still there, working away. What effort he put into this business he'd built up, in order to keep them all in such material comfort. She'd make an extra special fuss of him tonight; if he'd something on his mind, it was time she got it out of him. She hoped it wasn't a health thing; he had lately looked a bit peaky.

"Clemency!" said Teddy, breathless and amazed, swinging around to confront her, his face a mask of confusion. This was his inner sanctum, where few were ever invited. Clemency stood in the doorway and quietly surveyed the scene. He wasn't actually working but was in shirtsleeves with a glass in his hand, whiskey not wine, and a large one at that. And he wasn't alone. A slim young woman with hair cut like a choirboy's was perched on the corner of the desk and chortling away, though the laughter died on her lips as Clemency entered.

Teddy jumped to his feet. "You know Alison?" he said clumsily, and the young woman smiled and nodded slightly, sliding her glass away from her as though she were doing something she shouldn't.

"Indeed," said Clemency airily, not exactly sure if they had actually met. Teddy had so many employees and she wasn't always attending when he spoke of his work. Twenty-seven at the outside, she'd guess, neatly turned out but without a lot of flair. And she could do with a spot of makeup on that rather pasty complexion.

"I'd best be going," said Alison, slightly breathlessly. "I'll see you tomorrow, or are you going to the country?"

Teddy glanced at Clemency, but his expression was quite blank.

"No," he said firmly. "I'm staying up overnight. There's a lot on at the moment," he explained to Clemency, "and I'd

176

no idea you were coming."

She'd mentioned it, she surely had, but lately he'd been so preoccupied.

"I thought we'd have a spot of supper," she said, waiting for the girl to leave. "And then you could drive me home."

"Sorry, there's no chance of that. I've an early meeting in the morning." He glanced significantly at Alison as she began to pick up her things. "I'll take you to Neal Street for a fast plate of pasta, then put you on your train." And it seemed, for once, he was not about to budge.

Clemency said goodnight to Alison and they left her to lock up. They walked in silence till they got to the restaurant and Clemency found herself for once at a total loss for words. It was perfectly spontaneous, to drop in on her husband, yet he was making her feel guilty as if she had no right to be there. Something was wrong, though she couldn't quite think what. That whey-faced young woman had looked so knowing and the parting glance he'd shot her had spoken volumes. Maybe he was in financial trouble; she hoped it wasn't that. Over the years, she was forced to admit, Clemency hadn't paid much attention to the business. He made the money, she ran the home. That had always been the deal, and it worked. She would never bother him with minor things to do with the children; all of a sudden she was wondering if he had secrets too.

A smiling Italian greeted them in the stark but fashionable trattoria. Twice in one day; she would normally have mentioned it, but tonight something made her hold her tongue. Pasta was healthy and would do her no harm. A Mediterranean diet was said to extend your life. She ordered only mineral water and nibbled at a bread stick while Teddy studied the menu in detail and bought some expensive wine.

"Everything all right, sweetie?" she finally said brightly, and was shocked by the lack of reciprocal sparkle in his eyes.

"Why should it not be?" he countered rather too sharply, and, for the first time ever, quite knocked the wind from her sails.

"We've been talking about the trip to France," she told him, making an effort, but he brushed it aside as the waiter brought their plates, then told her he wasn't sure he could join them after all. Clemency was horrified; they always did everything together.

"I'm not sure I can get away," was all he would say. "There's stock-taking to be done and Ali can hardly manage on her own."

Ali. There she was again, and something icy gripped at Clemency's stomach.

"We really ought to talk about the future," she said carefully. "I'm assuming, of course, that we've got one." She didn't understand why she added those words; they just tumbled out of her subconscious.

Teddy stared at the tablecloth for what seemed an endless moment, then slowly raised his eyes to look at his wife.

"That depends," he said slowly.

21

T hings were looking grimmer by the day, and now Harry was itching to be off and on the road. The official inquiry was scheduled for mid-September, by which time, all going according to plan, he ought to be safely out of the country. On a one-way ticket. Without going into any real detail and fudging around the edges a little, he had managed to convince Lavender that the trip was mainly business, with a duty visit to his grandmother thrown in.

"No point in your tagging along," he told her. "Terribly dreary and you know how carsick you get."

Besides, it was the start of the new school year and the kids had enough on their plates as it was without being uprooted at an unsuitable time. Vivian had to have extra math coaching, while the girls were committed to ballet and elocution. Start them off young, was Lavender's motto, with her ramrod-straight back and impeccable vowels.

"We'll do something fancy at Christmas," he promised. "Belize, maybe, or even South Africa. Or a Kenyan safari. You can start collecting brochures."

All lies, of course; he had no intention of returning. His mind was already way into the future, one that did not include his nearest and dearest. He'd done the marriage bit, was up to here with domesticity. Like his grandmother before him, from this point on Harry Annesley intended to go solo.

The pressing problem was going to be money, though he'd start by emptying their number two account, the one reserved for long-term expenses: further education, daughters' weddings and the like. With luck, she wouldn't notice, not till he'd covered his tracks, then it was up to her what the selfish bitch did. From now on in, she'd be on her own. Let her try running sniveling back to the bank-manager father and see if they could cram the kids into the retirement villa in Hove. Harry had always felt cheated by Lavender. She deserved her comeuppance and now she was going to get it. He'd see to that.

Everything had conspired in the past two years to erode the fortune he had spent so much effort accruing. The building delays, the unforeseen setbacks, the wobbly state of the market and now this latest crisis. In his heart Harry knew that it was his carelessness alone that had caused the building's subsidence and the unfortunate workman's accident. But he was not in the habit of owning up; that was a fool's game. If he stayed around for the inquiry, he could well be facing a criminal trial and professional ruin, maybe even a custodial sentence. He was not prepared to risk any of that, the loss of his reputation, all he had ever worked for.

He was pinning all his hopes on the understanding of his grandmother, a free spirit like himself from whom he had inherited his talent. Mémé would understand, he knew that now instinctively; after all, she had also fled the coop more than thirty years ago. He loved that house, he always had, and knew he could work wonders with it, provided she'd allow him a free hand. He'd start by ripping out most of the windows and opening it up to the elements. A glassed-in conservatory over part of the courtyard he'd glimpsed, with a tasteful lap-pool in Italian marble mosaics. And electricity, of course, or even solar paneling. It would be a hard task, but one he'd really enjoy, to bring it up to scratch and into the late twentieth century. He was bound to make a killing when he sold it, enough to live in luxury for the rest of his career.

The house was not that far from the Spanish border. With luck and cunning, if things really turned against him, he could cross it stealthily and start a new life in Barcelona or Madrid. Gaudi had long been one of his major idols. The idea of following in the great architect's footsteps gave him a childish kick.

But first it was imperative that he be allowed to plead his cause. This harebrained plan of dividing everything between the lot of them had to be stopped before it went too far. As the oldest of the grandchildren and also the first of the males, primogeniture must be invoked; he was certain Cornelius would have agreed. He'd see she was all right in her dotage, that could be part of the settlement, but she couldn't have that many years to go, not if he struck lucky. So the vital thing now in this battle of wits was to stop the girls from getting there first.

"Harry's definitely coming," reported Clemency. He would, as it now turned out, though she hadn't yet told the others, be the sole adult male on the journey down. She could easily handle the Range Rover herself and it would mean that much more room for her load of passengers. And women alone always have more fun. They are far more adaptable and able to let their hair down. Provided they could keep Harry under control.

Élodie was doing sterling work on the route, investigating possible overnight stops, consulting her Parisian friends about the best way to bypass the major cities. Lyons was always a bugger, she knew, and everyone had alternative suggestions to promote.

"Is he bringing those frightful children?" she asked. Two days on the road with the opinionated Vivian was likely to be hell on wheels. Not to mention Lavender with her attitudes.

"I think not," said Clemency, unusually vague. She was still silently reeling from the blow Teddy had dealt her. How could he, after all these years of such unswerving devotion? Had he lost his mind entirely, or could it be attributed to a midlife crisis, something in which she had never before believed? She was still too stunned to be bitter but suspected that might come later.

"She laughs at my jokes," was all he would say, to which there was really no answer. It had been years since Clemency had stopped listening to him at all, but that surely was true of most marriages. A team, that's what they'd always been, and a staunch one at that. She had fed him, loved and supported him for sixteen years. So what if the children were now inclined to take precedence? In the scheme of things that was natural; he was a man in his forties who could hold his own. This break was probably exactly what they both needed. An eternal optimist, she was already beginning to bounce back. If he preferred that skinny schoolgirl to his witty, voluptuous wife, then let him try doing without her for a while. He would soon come to heel. She was confident of that.

She was still slightly worried at Mémé's continuing silence. There'd been no response at all to the letter she'd sent off weeks ago. She hoped it hadn't gone astray and that the old lady would not be too startled by their arrival. If there'd been a phone, she'd have chanced a call. As it was, there was no real way of checking—no friendly soul in the village who could just pop around, apart from the local gendarmerie. And that would be taking things a bit too far. Best let it be and assume that all was well. She thought wistfully of Dominic, then dismissed him briskly from her mind. Now was not the time for romantic dallying; she still had the reunion to arrange.

Madeleine too was feeling a touch bleak. No word from Dominic and she still smarted from the way he had turned down her invitation. But in Paris her cousin Élodie was in paradise. Exhausted by a long night's lovemaking, she now lay sprawled provocatively across *café au lait* satin sheets, wearing nothing but tiny diamond earrings and a strategic splash of Obsession. Her heart overflowed with a passion she had rarely known, with one single subject dominating her every waking thought. Him, her lover, her destiny finally found. Her dream come true, her beloved Dominic Carlisle.

Who was standing silently in the shadows smoking while penciling notes into a slim black book. All over her work-table, maps and guides were spread, the route to Uzès jotted on slips of paper, with telephone numbers and a list of possible overnight stops. Somewhere way off in the Champs-Élysées a church clock chimed six. He mustn't linger here too long; there were things he had to do, Harry to call, serious matters to discuss. He glanced back quickly into the darkened room at Élodie's recumbent form, decadently sprawled, displaying all she'd got. Dirty work, maybe, but someone had to do it. And he certainly wouldn't have trusted Harry.

Ashley was in a fever of excitement at the prospect of this holiday. Not that he really understood the concept of abroad, just that teachers and the other kids at school all seemed to envy him, which made him feel just great. Cherie, still not certain she was doing the right thing, watched him closely for signs of abnormal disturbance, but his manic humming was muted for a change and a benign smile of happiness lit up his face as he scanned his treasures for those he couldn't bear to be without. She stood in the now-cat-free bedroom, sorting through well-worn clothes and agonizing over what to take, though the choice, as always, was depressingly sparse.

Maybe her first instinct to bypass the trip had been correct. But Clemency's offer to fund them had been too generous to pass up. Sighing resolutely, she turned back to the closet.

T-shirts and track shoes would have to do, with her trusted satin jacket thrown in for good measure since Clemency had mentioned something about staying in a chateau, where she hoped the nobs wouldn't be dressing for dinner. Well, what they saw was what they would get. Cherie lit another smoke and grimly surveyed her puny pile.

"Here," she said, tossing Ashley his one-eyed bear. It only came out on rare occasions, to comfort and encourage in case he was scared of the dark. "Stick that in your rucksack if you can find the space." He wasn't a bad kid, really, all things considered. The truth was, these days she wouldn't be without him.

To Isabelle's amazement, she had a call from her father. He rarely ever kept in touch and certainly never phoned. Charlie had always been a bit of an outsider; after his retreat to Canada, he truly lost touch with the family. She'd always felt he had a bit of a chip on his shoulder. The next in age after Roland, his mother had lost all interest in him after the tragedy. And he hadn't made much success of his life since, though he was inordinately proud, in his understated way, of Isabelle's own academic success.

"Go to it, girl," he had told her proudly. "Sock it to them at Oxford and show them what you are made of." Annesley stock, was what he meant; fighting talk from a failure, but a sentiment honestly felt. And now here he was, on the telephone, having just received her letter about the trip. He wallowed in small talk for a good few minutes, then came to the point awkwardly and with embarrassment.

"I'll be interested to hear how your grandmother is faring." The woman who had deserted him just when he needed her most. "Send us a postcard if you have the time. Oh, and see you give her my love."

"I'll do that, Dad." She certainly would. All sorts of unforeseen good might come out of this trip. And repairing a few bridges on behalf of her father would be an excellent way to start.

22

*T*he house in Oxford, though huge and accommodating, was chilly and inclined to be drafty in winter. Chilblains and runny noses were a regular fact of life, so once the war years were finally over, Cornelius transferred the lot of them back to Maine for the summer vacations. As the family steadily grew, this became an increasingly complicated maneuver. With seven of them still infants and Patrice in diapers, it took organizational skills of almost military precision which Odile, still in the flush of youth, was fortunately well up to. Friends and colleagues thought them crazy, but Cornelius was determined that their American heritage should not be denied them. It was not their fault that they'd been transplanted to a foreign land; he wanted each one of them to have a free choice of nationality. By the time baby Ethan came along in 1950, it was a well-established custom and the Annesleys practiced gypsies.

It was therefore not too surprising that they'd ended up so far-flung: four in England, three in America, one in Canada. Roland, of course, was dead. Only Agnes had chosen France, and she wasn't even Odile's daughter.

"Why did she do it? Take the veil." Isabelle was still puzzled; it hardly fitted in with the Annesley absence of faith, and Agnes, more than any of them, had been a fabled sybarite. Clemency shrugged. They were taking their first break at a roadside café outside Bordeaux and the children were running wild among the tables.

"Who knows? Only Agnes herself, and she's taken a vow of silence. Though Mémé perhaps will be able to throw some light."

It was something she'd often wondered herself, the unseen half aunt who had deliberately turned her back on the world. And at only twenty-nine, when she'd still had so much to offer.

"She was wild and beautiful and living up a storm in New York." She had often heard her mother talk about her, the impetuous beauty with an entourage of lovers who, failing to find satisfaction with any of them, had ultimately married herself to Christ. Why people did things was very often a mystery. If only they could meet her, they might discover more.

"She's only sixty-seven now," said Clemency, musing. "Why would anyone want to throw their life away like that, I wonder?"

"She was called?" suggested Isabelle.

Clemency didn't agree. "Not from all the stories I've heard." The sisters—her mother, Aimée and Patrice—had been adamant about that. Some secret, they'd suggested, which she'd chosen to share with nobody. Eunice, the oldest, living austerely in New York, was the likeliest to know, though they were not sure she would tell. She was four years younger than Agnes, twenty-five when she went away.

"Is she coming to the reunion?" asked Madeleine.

"Eunice? I certainly hope not," said Clemency with a chuckle. Quite why Aunt Eunice was portrayed as such an ogre was not easy to tell after all the years they hadn't seen her. In its way, her own life had been far more tragic than Agnes's, forced by her mother's defection to abandon a promising teaching career to return to Oxford to cope with the brood.

"I don't think Eunice ever quite forgave her," said Clemency. "So I'm sure she'd begrudge her the cost of an international fare."

"Not even for curiosity's sake?" suggested Élodie. Rather to her surprise, she was really enjoying this trip. Madeleine turned out to be excellent company and it was good to get away, even if only for secret time in which to purr and gloat. Dominic was elusive, but that was all part of his allure. He'd be there waiting when she got back, she felt confident, even though he'd left her, like the first time, with scarcely a word or a backwards glance. She'd been tempted to talk to Madeleine about him, but natural caution held her back. And they'd be on the road for a couple more days; time enough for confessions later, should she ever feel the need.

Maine in the thirties was a very poor state, most people scraping a living on the land or down the mines. The Annesley family, on their annual visits, were viewed as local gentry, well-heeled and educated with an affluent lifestyle unusual in those parts at that time. With a steadily expanding family, they needed live-in servants, so that during the summer months at least the weathered wooden house on the edge of the rocks was usually humming with activity. The house had been in the family for generations and was now jointly owned by the surviving siblings. Clemency had been there often, they all had, and the cousins shared a mellowed nostalgia for childhood holidays when Cornelius was still alive and living with Mad Aunt Effie as his housekeeper. But Cornelius had died an angry and bitter man and his widow, Kay, rarely went there anymore or kept in touch with the family.

It was hard to imagine how Mémé could bear to have left it, however much she might have hated Oxford. Surely, without having to disrupt the family, she could have prevailed on her adoring husband to end his tenure in bleak, cold England and return to Boston or even Bowdoin College, his alma mater. And why did she have to flee at all in order to become a painter? The rugged Maine coastline, with its abundant foliage and luminous water, was far more evocative to Clemency's mind than the sere, burnt flatness they were driving through right now on the highway heading towards Lyons. If ever she could be bothered to move from Wiltshire, Maine was where Clemency thought she might well end up. She liked a bit of drama in her scenery; the Annesley blood was powerful in her veins.

And how could she possibly have borne to abandon her

children? To forsake eight because of one who had died made just no sense at all. The five in the back had finally lapsed into silence, all played out and quietly recharging their batteries. Even Ashley's interminable humming had mercifully ceased; Clemency glanced back and was amused to see Cherie crouched among them, small and sticklike, a lot like a child herself, apart from the familiar half-smoked cigarette in her mouth.

"I wonder what really happened," she pondered. "The reason for Mémé's defection."

Isabelle, seated beside her in the front, had nothing really to add. Because of the vicinity of Quebec to Maine, she had many times visited the house herself and shared her cousin's deep affection for it. Even if circumstances had made her father reluctant to return.

"I guess we'll never know," she said. "Unless she just couldn't bear to be there anymore."

"But you'd think a tragedy like that would have only drawn them closer." Their grandparents' marriage was famous for its passion, an enduring love that had made the children feel excluded. Clemency thought fleetingly of Teddy and inwardly winced. She was tempted to unburden to Isabelle, then quickly thought better of it. Matters like that were best left unspoken and she was keenly aware of Cherie sitting sulkingly behind her.

"All right back there?" called Clemency, eliciting a grunt. They were making good time and should reach the chateau by six. And that made her think of Harry, who was going to be meeting them there. Clemency sighed at the very thought but promised herself she'd be good. No point in displaying her inward aggression towards him; Cheltenham Ladies'

College had taught her that. At least so far their journey had been uneventful, just five spirited women traveling in convoy with a bunch of sleepy kids. She'd had sufficient drama in her life to appreciate this break. With luck the next few days would be peaceful; rapprochement with Mémé after all these years and a reunion to grace the family albums. And after that, she'd get back to real life and sort out this wretched business with Teddy.

The thing about Maine that she'd always particularly liked was its total absence of crime. You didn't lock doors, you left your ignition keys in the car. Your porch was always open, day and night, to neighbours and friends, and nobody ever took advantage of it. Why, Clemency wondered, would such a state of innocence exist? Just because everyone else was born straight, how could it have been that there were no bad pennies, not in that rural paradise in which they had all been raised? Particularly since most of them were on the breadline and must have encountered temptation at times. And even after the war, when the soldiers returned, the same state of affairs continued to prevail. Roosevelt was dead, Truman had taken his place. Poverty was still rife, the people continued to be dirt-poor. Yet the crime rate remained at rock-bottom and the newspaper headlines were filled with nothing more threatening than the blueberry harvest, the Bangor Lobster Festival or occasional human stories about long-lost siblings being safely reunited after the war. Amazing.

There had been a minor scandal, some years before she was born, when an Annesley housemaid had met with a violent death in the woods beside her home which bordered the family property. Seventeen and a virgin, so the newspapers had proclaimed, but Aunt Effie had always maintained with a wink that she was not quite as pure as she was cracked up to be and had received the wages of a sinful life not a moment before it was due. Though how she had access to things the newspapers didn't know, she was never able to explain.

Poor Aunt Effie. Her own life had been wasted taking care of those selfish brothers and waiting for a Prince Charming who failed ever to materialize. They laughed at her and said she wasn't quite right in the head, but Clemency remembered her as sparkling with merriment, bright and coquettish and always a good sport. Women had come a long way since those days, single women at least. Which made it all the more shocking that, having survived all those narrow, deprived years, the poor old thing had met such a violent death while doing her own thing and living inoffensively in Jersey. It could surely never have happened in Maine.

They had never apprehended whoever was responsible, and that in itself was reason for alarm, unless it had been a casual unmotivated slaying, which seemed probable. Usually these things went in groups; a random killer was likely to kill again unless, as on this occasion, he had left the island by boat and moved elsewhere. According to Harry, the Jersey police had no theory he was aware of and had doubtless closed the file by now, since both women were dead and out of the way, with no family on the spot to nag them and keep them on their toes. Aunt Martha was Dominic's mother. Why, she now wondered, did he not involve himself more, since it was her he had been returning to see when the murders had occurred? Could he really be that detached? He certainly didn't seem so. But then nothing about Dominic turned out to be straightforward; that was all part of his charm.

Pandora too had reached an untimely end, which was that much the more shocking since she had been that much younger and had managed to cram a lot into her life. Her murder on the golf course had sent ripples of horror through the family, even though, in her lifetime, she too had endured her measure of ridicule. Poor chatty Pandora, with her small brain and honeyed bouffant, who had been so vigorously attached to them all, she had earned the mean nickname of the "Annesley bicycle."

What a terrible tragedy that had been, even though they'd all liked to make fun of Pandora. Not the brightest person in the world, she could never manage to keep her mouth zipped but had liked to spill it all out, making enemies along the way through her brittle, yet harmless, prattle. To think, if Charlie hadn't got away, she might have ended up as Isabelle's mother. The thought amused Clemency greatly and she cast her cousin a cautious sideways glance. It might have been all to the better, who knows, had some of that lively airheadedness been injected into the sweet but suety Canadian grind.

Isabelle returned her gaze curiously and Clemency pulled herself together.

"I was thinking of Pandora," she told her inconsequentially, then swiftly changed the subject by offering to let her drive.

Harry was waiting for them at the Chateau Margaux, having taken a faster road and not stopped for any of the breaks

192

incumbent on the transportation of a carload of restless children. Isabelle turned through the fine old gates at exactly a quarter to seven and Harry, pacing the terrace in irritation, was out there in a flash, gin and tonic in hand, berating them for keeping him waiting for his meal. Clemency checked her watch in surprise; surely sophisticated Harry didn't eat this early, especially when unencumbered by small fry. They all pecked cheeks and compared notes about the road and Madame appeared, gracious in somber black, and led the way to the suite of rooms they had booked in advance. When they straggled down to the dining room, having dumped their bags and scrubbed off some of the grime, Harry was already seated at the table with a flagon of the local red wine, chewing bread and gloomily surveying the limited menu.

"Charming," muttered Clemency at this blatant lapse of manners, and Madeleine shot her a complicitous grin as they strolled over to join him. The table he'd chosen was not large enough to accommodate all eleven of them, so Clemency quickly called for Madame and, ignoring her boorish cousin's protests, calmly had them reseated. If he preferred to take his meals away from the children at home, that was up to him. There was nothing she could do about that, but here she remained in control. The whole point of this expedition was for a bit of clannish mixing—why bother to bring the children at all if they were to be ignored? Fortunately, the journey had tired them so, once they had consumed platefuls of the excellent local cassoulet and mopped up the juice with rough bread, Isabelle and Cherie led them back upstairs while the others joined Harry outside on the terrace, to savour the gathering darkness and the mysterious nocturnal stirrings of the countryside.

Harry appeared unusually jumpy and found it hard to sit still. Guilty conscience? wondered Madeleine, almost as if he thought something or somebody were on his tail. He hadn't explained Lavender's absence, not convincingly, and although it was doubtful that any of them would miss her, it did seem strange considering how boastful he'd always been about his tight little family and overachieving children. When pressed, he muttered something about the pressures of charity work and Lavender's crowded calendar, not to mention Vivian's private tuition, which made it sound as though the child were unusually gifted, not just lagging behind. Clemency didn't care; she was not particularly competitive and preferred her own unruly mob to those starchy, strangely inhibited Annesleys. Her boys would be up at the crack of dawn, kicking a ball around and exploring the terrain, while the insufferable Vivian, with his fancy airs, would be practicing the piano or playing with his Gameboy. Yet she sensed from Harry's manner that something was seriously amiss. He was sweating heavily and kept glancing around him whenever passing headlights illuminated the trees or he heard distant tires on the gravel of the drive.

"Expecting someone?" she asked him eventually, but he shook his head and inquired instead about Mémé. No, she told him, she had not received any answer and could only surmise that Mémé had got her note and was not too dismayed at the thought of this invasion. Harry recalled the lack of telephone at the *mas* which would be, in some ways, a blessing. He always carried his mobile but had turned it off; there were times when it was preferable not to be easily contactable and he did not want Lavender or the law pursuing him down here, not till he'd perfected his plans. There were answers he needed to questions he had not yet posed and he hoped this group pilgrimage would provide him with some of them. He had known his cousins, on and off, all their lives but never till now really focused on any of them. As the oldest of the grandchildren, his closest contemporary apart from her brothers was Clemency, whom he'd heartily disliked since their early quarrels in the playroom. Not the type of woman he could ever find attractive; too bossy, too opinionated, altogether a pain. Yet there were things he needed to find out, so he pulled himself together, smiled at the group benevolently and offered them all a nightcap.

"Garçon!" Madeleine winced as he snapped his fingers and the portly figure of Monsieur came lumbering from the bar. The man was a pig and she'd always known it. She remembered all too vividly why she persisted in keeping him at bay. Handsome in an angular, Annesley way with those probing, pale eyes so very like his grandfather's. Charming too, when he cared to put his mind to it, he was nonetheless not a person she could ever like or trust. If it weren't for their shared ancestry, she doubted she'd even know him; Madeleine was fastidious about the kind of company she kept. And she could see that Élodie clearly felt the same. Her lip practically curling, she was listening to him in silence as he bragged and postured and dominated the conversation in a way she found repulsive, particularly in a man.

This, after all, was Élodie's adopted country, yet Harry acted dismissively if she so much as opened her mouth. "Rubbish!" he'd say, as if he had the right, as though she were his wife or daughter or someone else he felt he could overrule. So Élodie kept her silence and sat there in the dark quietly smoking till Cherie and Isabelle joined them and pulled their chairs into the circle.

"They're all nicely settled, more or less," said Isabelle, flushed with the success of getting them all into bed. Clemency beamed at her, appreciative of her effort, and waved to Madame in a friendly way to indicate she should bring two more glasses. Harry, of course, was impervious. Let them fend for themselves.

"I think they're planning a pillow fight," said Cherie, relieved not to be in sole custody of Ashley, suddenly aware what it might be like to have sisters.

"That's okay. Provided they stay in their rooms and out of sight, let them do what they like. It might help to wear them out." They had another long day's driving ahead of them tomorrow. Five children packed together was quite an undertaking.

Cherie, devoid of her customary armour, looked young and appealingly vulnerable. Her hair, for once, was not pinned up in an untidy bunch but swung around her ears in a becoming mass which framed her narrow face and set off those huge, fringed eyes. In jeans and plain white T-shirt, she looked scarcely older than the children. Madeleine moved up to make room for her on the wicker seat, while Clemency leaned over and poured her some of the nectar-ridden golden wine. They were a good group, companionable and at ease. If only Harry would cease his incessant talking and relax and enjoy the felicities of this magical night.

They were rescued unexpectedly by a sudden visit from Monsieur, looming through the dusk to inform Harry he was wanted on the telephone. Harry looked startled but struggled to his feet and Clemency couldn't decide whether it was panic or relief she saw on his face. It looked a lot like the former, but what could prosperous Harry have on his conscience?

"And who in the world," she wondered aloud, "could possibly want to get hold of him here?"

23

They were all of them there that summer that Roland died. Henry, father of Harry Junior, fresh over from England with his wife and cute little five-year-old; Aimée, newly married, with her handsome half-Norwegian husband and, of course, Eunice, the fledgling teacher. Even Claire, heavily pregnant, with her two little boys. Tony Broadhurst had been delayed but hoped to join them later if he could get away. Clemency had the pictures to prove it, the lot of them grouped on the lawn around the flagpole, ages ranging from twenty-four-year-old Eunice to Ethan, the baby at ten. And a smiling Cornelius, for once relaxed and gracious, in tennis whites with his shock of silvering hair, seated in the center of them, his arm draped protectively around his wife, still as slender and youthful as her daughters.

Agnes too, she had joined them that summer, up from Manhattan where she'd been living up a storm, here to catch up on lost sleep she said, and allow her liver to recover. Not that there was a lot of chance of that, with the boys all there too, racing their old jalopies and motorcycles along the quiet country roads and raising hell in the local bars. There she was, grinning in the back row, tall and rangy with her distinctive long, dark hair and her father's heavy eyebrows which lent her so much character. And Roland beside her, fresh-faced and angelic, with those oddly luminous eyes that were so much like her own. There too was poor Pandora, tagging along for yet another free holiday, not yet quite an Annesley but clearly fervently hoping. In a skirt that was daringly short even for then, forerunner of the mini that was soon to sweep the nation.

How Odile loved those children, treating them indulgently though still with a measure of European strictness. Each one of them in the photo was simply and neatly dressed, the girls with clean hair and spotless, shining faces; the boys rugged and handsome, all built in the image of their father, apart from young Ethan, who was a shadow of his mother. He ought, by rights, to have also been her favorite, but that position was reserved for Roland, on whom she doted, eighteen years old at the time of this gathering, the fifth child out of nine.

Ellen, the former wife, had ceded her place with dignity and withdrawn to a small family-owned estate in New Hampshire, thus allowing the usurpers to occupy and overrun the house that had once been hers. Clemency had never understood that; how could a woman give up her rights quite so meekly, especially when her husband had publicly wronged her? It helped, of course, to have money of your own, and Ellen hadn't been short of a bob or two. But possession was still the main issue. Clemency felt certain that, in Ellen's position, she would not have gone down without a fight.

The old clapboard house literally creaked with activity and

the hired help enlisted from the village spent long hours in the cool, spacious kitchen, churning out meals for an endless line of ravenous mouths. The Annesley children were popular with the locals and Odile always maintained a state of open house. Boating trips, tennis parties, clambakes, picnics; all were welcome and the neighbours' kids joined them in droves. Far better to have them here underfoot, she reasoned, than out of her sight, getting up to God knew what. Roland was a handful, and so were his younger brothers. At least in this sprawling homestead they were blessed with plenty of space.

Clemency wasn't born yet, but Guy and Mark were both there. Harry too, the oldest of the grandchildren, at five already a mini adult who claimed he remembered it all. And lurking right at the edge of the group, a small dark-haired urchin, barefoot and with ragged trousers but, even then, a most disarming smile. Clemency's heart clenched: Cousin Dominic. Now, where in the world was he hiding at present? She'd not heard a word from him in ages.

"What's Dominic doing there?" she asked before she could stop herself. Had they shared a childhood? She'd no recollection of ever meeting him before.

"Let's see," said Harry, grabbing the album from her. It was breakfast the next morning and he appeared to have calmed down. "His folks lived up in Damariscotta just then. Must have come over with the other kids to play."

He remembered his cousin as a lively, likable child, always good for a laugh or dare, fearless and quick-witted as his uncle Roland. At that time Harry and Dominic had been virtually inseparable, though they had inevitably drifted apart in the intervening years. Now Dominic was back on the scene and, for personal reasons, Harry was attempting to build bridges, though he'd no intention of sharing that with Clemency. The less she knew the better.

Roland was always the ringleader, even though not the oldest, but when Agnes showed up it quickly became her gang. Ten years older and as spirited as he, she shed her city sophistication to run wild with the rest of them. Henry and the older girls were now responsible young adults, with mortgages and babies and careers they liked to discuss. But from Roland down they were still an unruly pack, ever dreaming up new hair-raising dares and crazy challenges to terrify their mother. Diving from the rocks at the foot of the lawn was a traditional Annesley sport.

"Careful, now," warned an anxious Odile, watching them constantly from the house. "Those currents can be treacherous, the water not always safe."

"*Calme-toi, Maman,*" Roland would say as he hugged her. "We're no longer children and know what we're about." Slim and tanned and naked like some glorious water sprite, he'd cavort across the grass and then arc into the water. Followed by Agnes in the briefest of bikinis, her long hair streaming behind her, to surface as sleek as a seal.

Odile relaxed when she saw what fun they were having, relieved that, after the traumas, no lasting harm had been done. She knew the fault of the marriage breakup rested entirely on her, but her love for Cornelius had been so great, there'd been nothing else she could do. Besides, he was older and far more mature and his passion had been as strong. A single look had been all it took and they had committed themselves for life. Perhaps if Eunice had not been conceived, the outcome might have been different, but she doubted it. By the time of the *coup de foudre,* his feelings for Ellen had worn thin and only his devotion to Agnes had kept him at home at all. Or so he said.

"It was written in the stars," Cornelius told her by way of comfort, and gave her another baby just to prove it. Still, she'd always, up till now, worried at the destruction of another woman's happiness but was finally convinced, as she watched that woman's child play, that no lasting damage had been done. Agnes was one of her family now and she loved her as fiercely as the rest.

Something was up that summer, something Harry hadn't properly understood. Lowered voices behind closed doors, grown-ups preoccupied and brushing him aside whenever he reached for a cuddle. And visits from the local police about some incident in the village. Eventually Cornelius did intervene and the boys, Roland, Charlie, and Tom, were summoned to his study and summarily chewed out. He had grounded them for the rest of the summer; forbidden them to leave the boundaries of the estate until he lifted his ban.

"So what was it about?" asked Clemency, but Harry didn't know. He had tried asking Ethan, who'd been out with them that night, but the older boy had brushed it aside and withdrawn to his flower painting without a word. These days he claimed to have forgotten it altogether, though Harry had his doubts. He was an odd one, Ethan, always had been, living in a strange, repressed world of his own. No one knew why he'd developed that way; he wasn't at all like the others.

"Something to do with one of the maids, I think, and the uncles were somehow involved. Something pretty nasty that they wanted hushed up. Grandpa was in a constant state of

rage and Mémé had her work cut out to calm him and protect her boys."

Agnes hadn't helped, of course, with her drinking and
generally over-the-top behaviour. She was picked up twice
for drunk driving and Cornelius had threatened to send her
back to New York. Or over to her mother in New Hampshire, where she pleaded she'd die of sheer boredom.

"She was a bit old, wasn't she, to be hanging around with
kids?" They had said that at the time, but Harry shook his
head. He remembered her vividly from those early days
with her long brown legs and sinuous body, usually draped
in too little clothing, provocative and challenging to men of
all ages. She was a riot in the village and the locals all
adored her. How she had survived unscathed was amazing
when you considered how she drank, and her later dramatic
decision, to take the veil, was just another bombshell in a
perpetually turbulent life. No one could understand why she
did it and they weren't likely to find out now. The Poor
Clares were reputed to be the most austere of orders who
devoted themselves to prayer and contemplation and never
emerged from their convents. Trust Agnes to go to
extremes.

Odile had always wished that some of the older girl's fearless spirit would rub off on her own firstborn. But the French
provincial narrowness showed loud and clear in Eunice. It
startled her mother, when the child was still small, to recog-
nize her own mother's disapproving spirit peeping from her
eyes. Odd how children could inherit such disparate traits.
Isabelle, with her scientific knowledge, tried to explain it to
her cousins.

"You're not going to tell us that we're all prepackaged,"

challenged Élodie. "Whatever happened to free will?"

"And no matter what we may inherit from our parents, always remember we are totally unique," added Madeleine. She was, at any rate, and was not about to change her mind because of some dusty theory of poor Isabelle's who hadn't yet remotely begun to live. She liked the sound of her outrageous aunt Agnes, longed to meet her and possibly elicit the truth. But the story appeared to peter out at that point; not even Ethan could throw light on the subject. Effie had been there, of course, but no one ever took her seriously. There were things that had occurred that only she could know. Yet no one had listened and now she was dead.

The rest of that summer continued uneventfully. The boys behaved, the police ceased troubling them, their father eventually was persuaded to lift his ban. There were reports in the local paper of stirrings in the village, but Eunice had the mean habit of snatching the juicy bits away from prying eyes and pretty soon even those rumblings ceased. A man was being held for questioning; that was all they were allowed to know.

"But *what* had happened?" Clemency was exasperated. Harry shrugged; he genuinely didn't know. Families were like that in those days; none of this freedom of speech and late-night cable TV.

"If Effie had lived, I'm sure she knew it all," he said.

"Or Ethan," said Clemency thoughtfully. He had been ten at the time.

Odile sat and painted on the lawn, alert and upright like a bright little robin, in jeans and a faded linen smock with her hair twisted high on her head like a girl's. She loved having the grandchildren with her and was always content to mind them while their parents and the other grown children took off in their cars to play golf or sail the sloop. Agnes was supposed to be back in New York; she had landed a job with a fashion magazine but kept on postponing her departure.

"That was Agnes all over," Madeleine's mother, Aimée, had said. "Willful and headstrong, always sailing too close to the edge."

In the end, of course, they'd withdrawn the offer, but Agnes had simply laughed. She was out of control that summer and no mistake, but her stepmother indulged her and her father was engrossed in his book. She was as beautiful and wanton as a sun-kissed wood nymph; there were pictures there to prove it, with Roland always at her side. Roland the glorious, with his open face and laughing eyes, standing on the brink of manhood, his whole future stretching before him. While poor, foolish Pandora mooned after him and Charlie trailed after her in turn without her ever noticing. An odd chain of circumstances that led in the end to disaster. Not one of them escaped entirely unscathed that summer. It was the beginning of the breakup of the family.

It was Labour Day weekend and the children were starting to pack. Claire, unwell, had left prematurely, anxious to get home before the labour pains began. Odile had fussed over her and implored her not to go. Flying in her condition was considered to be unsafe, but she wanted to be with her husband and have the baby at home.

"Take care, *chérie*," begged her mother, hugging her close. She hated it when they left her, fearing not to see them again. And she adored her two small grandsons who had brought her such joy all summer.

"Darling Maman," Claire had said with a laugh when they parted. "Giving birth is the easiest thing in the world, as you should know since you are the expert. Come and visit us at Christmas and help wet the baby's head. I'll be fine, I promise."

She wasn't, though, as Clemency well knew. It was all part of her own early history, though the details remained obscure, and for one significant reason. The loss of that baby had been eclipsed in Annesley memory by a death so much more shocking it had driven all else from their minds.

"It was Sunday evening," said Harry. "I do remember that. And Roland wasn't home yet, even though Grandpa had said he must be. The pastor was dining with us and he wanted us all on show. Clean hands and faces and don't say a word till His Reverence addresses you. All that New England stuff that Grandpa set so much store by. He might have been an intellectual, but at heart he was also a snob."

Odile had served a great roast in the dining room and they'd all been gathered around the table—Agnes, Eunice, Henry and his wife; Aimeé and her bridegroom. Charlie, Tom and Patrice. Even young Ethan with the two little boys, Dominic and Harry himself. Not forgetting Aunt Effie, who was always there and adored that pastor like the risen Christ.

"Sounds like our place," said Clemency with a grin. When her own family gathered, along with her brothers and their wives, they could equal the total of the previous generation. "But think of all that food they had to prepare, the cooking and basting and general hard work without the benefit of modern kitchen gadgetry. With no refrigerator or super-deluxe dishwasher."

"We had them then," protested Isabelle. "Surely we did." They weren't all savages, even in Maine.

"Not of today's standards. And not at the holiday home."

But they did have servants, women from the village. Effie did most of the organizing, of course; she loved nothing better than to be in the thick of things, while Odile sat perched like a bird on the edge of her chair, sipping a seltzer and dazzling the poor pastor with her still-radiant good looks. When she took the trouble, she could outshine the lot of them, and that included Agnes, which was no easy feat.

The meal was almost over before Roland put in an appearance, and then he only skulked on the porch till his father spotted him and ordered him inside. He was shaken and subdued and they could see that something was up. Odile took one look at him and told him to wait in his room. She would bring him some food when she had the time; until then he was banished.

"And that," said Harry, stretching his legs, "is really all we know." It was getting late and time they hit the road. The traffic beyond Lyons was likely to be heavy and he didn't want to risk arriving after dark. But Clemency wouldn't allow him to end it like that; she needed to know the full story.

Harry was vague. The truth was, the youngsters, himself and Dominic and probably Ethan as well, had all been dismissed after the main course, since Cornelius was such a stickler on bedtimes. But it was all in the past, he could embellish it as he liked. For once in his life he had Clemency hooked.

The next day was Sunday and they'd all got up late. It was

the official end of summer, with a feeling of fall already in the air. The sun was mellow, the grass scorched dry. There were blueberry pancakes with maple syrup for breakfast and they sat outside on the covered porch and ate in silence as they watched the turbulent sea. Odile behaved as if nothing had happened, as though Roland had not been in trouble last night. She sent for fresh coffee and pressed them all to pancakes until one of the boys who'd already left the table gave a great shout from the bottom of the garden and set them all running to see what he had found.

Roland's watch and goggles lay neatly on the rocks but no sign of the boy himself in the choppy, boisterous waves. They summoned the coast guard and searched for him for hours, but his body was never recovered. The tide which Mémé had warned them of so often had claimed its prey again and taken another Annesley. All hell broke loose and the village was in an uproar. Christmas Cove, a famed beauty spot, was noted for its water sports and the community wanted to hush things up. There was an inquiry, of course, and in time a memorial plaque on the wall of the church. But Roland had gone, like a shooting star, and the reverberations from his death, in one way or another, touched them all.

Clemency was silent. What, she wondered, could possibly have happened that far-off summer to have ripped the family apart so completely and tipped her grandmother over the edge? They'd be seeing her soon, so maybe now she'd tell them. It had been almost thirty years ago and could hardly still be a secret.

24

*H*aving babies came ridiculously easily to Clemency, who had reveled in it since her early marriage at the age of twenty-one. Camilla, Piers, Emma and Humphrey had followed each other with languorous ease; for a period of at least six years Clemency seemed always to be pregnant. But she carried it well. Her skin glowed, her hair shone, she walked as proudly as a wind-borne balloon, serenely displaying her burgeoning girth. Teddy doted on her and cared for her as delicately as a cat with its kitten. Nothing was too much effort for him; he did the shopping, the ironing, even occasionally cooked in order to allow her the peace in which to concentrate on the miraculous creation of yet another new life. And the thing that Madeleine envied her most was that he read to her at night, carrying home great meaty tomes to share with her by firelight or in the comfort of their bed. Dickens, Trollope, Henry James, even, ambitiously, when Humphrey was on the way, *War and Peace*. They had been through them all together in that special intimacy that reading aloud provides. And she'd carried this habit on to the children, they both had. One or the other of them would read to them each night, *Alice in Wonderland, The Wind in the Willows, Winnie the Pooh,* the immortal classics on which they had both been raised.

Clemency was tall for a woman, but her husband was even taller and bulkier. She leaned against him like a sapling against an oak and rested her head on his sturdy, unyielding shoulder. She'd seen him and wanted him and that had been that. Their marriage was strong and enduring and neither had ever stepped out of line. Not, at least, until now. The world saw them as the perfect couple and envied their single-mindedness. The brave, glamourous Cart-wrights, so very much in love and united against the world.

What they didn't see, however, what Clemency and Teddy carefully hid, was the occasional frightening attack of the blues which descended on Clemency like a summer rain cloud, usually when her hormones were acting up. Postnatal depression the doctor had originally blandly labeled it, though it seemed to have no predictable pattern but would throw her into a fit of black despair at times when she least expected it. It was partly for this secret reason that she'd had so many pregnancies so soon. When she'd failed to throw off the blues after Camilla was born, she had reached her own conclusion about the cause and briskly told Teddy that she needed another baby right away, if only to sort out her precarious chemical balance. And he'd gone along with it as he did with everything, concerned and benevolent to the ultimate degree.

The fits of ragged weeping that occasionally tore her apart were a well-kept secret from the rest of the world. And when she embarked upon one of these crying jags, Teddy had become past master at scooping up the children and safely removing them out of her way.

"There, there, my poor love," he would say, caressing her head. "There's nothing out there to hurt you. You know that, dearest." And Clemency would curl into the protection of his arms and cry herself out until all the wretchedness was spent. She had no idea why this happened and it only did so rarely; once the storm was past she was as right as rain again, the familiar ebullient mother of four with a sparkle in her eye and a smile as infectious as measles.

Later, when the children were no longer tots, she'd tried discussing it with her mother, but Claire had proved surprisingly vague and also, Clemency sensed, evasive. Why that should be, she really couldn't tell, but there was quite a distinct edginess if the subject ever came up. Yes, she had suffered herself from postnatal depression. The loss of a full-term baby had taken her months to recover from and only the blessed arrival of Clemency herself had brought the relief she had so much needed. But there the conversation always ceased and Claire would change the subject as if there were something remotely improper about discussing your menstrual cycle with your daughter. Strange, that, but obviously generational. There was no way Clemency would ever act that way with either Camilla or Emma.

Dreams were another thing Clemency suffered from, and suffer was certainly not too strong a word for the appalling nightmares that sporadically assailed her. Dark things would chase her through horrendous landscapes that bore no relation to anything in her conscious world and Clemency would jerk awake with terror and clutch at Teddy's arm like something crazed. He would soothe and calm her and hold her tight, smoothing her hair like one of his own children until her panicked breathing returned to normal and her heart regained its measured pace. Nobody knew why this would happen. None of her four brothers had ever experienced anything like it, nor could throw any light on why she should suffer so. They knew of no suppressed trauma from early childhood that might still hold possession of her psyche, and if they didn't know, then no one did, for they had always been there for her, as they still were.

These days a modern psychotherapist might have all sorts of theories, but Clemency resolutely resisted such a lure. She didn't believe in the sickness of the mind. Whatever bogies beset her subconscious, she was determined to defeat them by means of her own innate strength.

"I'm not having anyone poke around in my head," she declared. Psychobabble was all a lot of nonsense and by her age any baggage she might be carrying should surely have resolved itself. Returning to her childhood roots, as she was on this expedition, intrigued her, though. She had been scared, she remembered now, but surely only by the huge, dark house and not by anything tangibly sinister. It probably wouldn't even look that large in the rational light of adulthood, though she determined to ensure that her own intrepid four would enter it boldly and be charmed by its rustic simplicity.

"Loads of good places for Hide-and-Seek," she promised. "And trees to climb and a great big barn to explore." And lots of fresh air and healthy country food. The sort of rugged adventure park of which idyllic memories were made. They'd all had Maine as their childhood backdrop; these children, thanks to Mémé, would now have France.

It would be good for Ashley too, she observed. The poor, pale mite looked as if he never got sufficient fresh air or vegetables, cooped up on that grim council estate she had heard about but never seen. She liked the way he was visibly coming on with the encouragement of her children. His voice was now often raised in confident assertion and they seemed to have accepted him for what he was, with fewer sideways glances as though they thought him odd. They were good kids and she was proud of them. Whatever else they may or may not have done, Teddy and she scored well as parents.

"D'you think we should stop for more food?"

Élodie gave a snort of amusement, but Clemency was serious. Élodie had already checked out the supplies in the back of the Range Rover, hidden away beneath piles of anoraks and bedding, there presumably in case unexpected famine should strike. Boxes of cereal, homemade jam, soap and candles, packets of fire-lighters. But Clemency remained unperturbed.

"We'll stop in Uzès on the way through," she instructed Isabelle, back at the wheel. "And pick up bread and vegetables and fruit and something for dinner tonight."

Cherie was keeping right out of it. She had never known anyone to think so much about food or set such store upon quality of produce. They had already stopped for a picnic lunch and strolled through a local market buying goat's cheese, tomatoes and olive oil. More food than she and Ashley consumed in a fortnight, but tasty, she certainly had to concede that. At the rate they were going, they'd both be putting on weight. She plucked at the waistband of her junior boys' jeans and couldn't help grinning at such a ludicrous thought.

"You don't think Mémé may have plans of her own?" Madeleine was concerned they might offend their grandmother. After all, in the old days she had always been the center of things, the hostess extraordinaire, ever the provider. Things, though, were different now and they were Mémé's uninvited guests. She was old and possibly arthritic and might not have enough money for extras. It was so long since anyone had seen her, they could have no accurate notion of how she scraped by these days. But they had to be prepared. The very least they could do was supply their own food; and take her out for a hearty meal if there was time before they left.

It was after three and Harry was growing edgy. "Let's get a move on," he urged when they stopped for a powwow. He could not forget that locked and unwelcoming house; no matter how much Clemency might reassure him now, he would not be easy until they were actually there and inside. He wondered if that vile old caretaker was still hanging around the premises. He wanted no friction, just a warm reunion with his grandmother after all the years. To set things straight, to remind her of who he was, her senior grandchild and, surely, natural heir. There were things he needed to talk about urgently, preferably without this gaggle at his heels. He'd also quite like to get a sneak preview of what exactly these wretched women were likely to inherit if he failed to stop them.

"Okay, okay," said Clemency. He was beginning to get on her nerves again; the sooner they got there, the better for them all. "Let's go."

Almost the worst thing that Teddy had done was show no remorse for his terrible treachery. He had returned that weekend in much the same mood as usual, hugged the children and greeted her with a kiss, then bundled them all into his car for pizza and Cokes in the village. Save her cooking, he had told her breezily, though he knew from experience that her oven was rarely idle. If it was a truce he was seeking, he certainly never said so, but kept up his cheeriness until it was time for bed. Then he pecked her perfunc-

213

torily and rolled over on his side, effectively eclipsing from her the true state of his mind.

If this was what happened when a marriage started to splinter, Clemency thought miserably, she might just as well end it now. She could not believe his heartiness, then or for the rest of the weekend, appearing with her at morning service, mowing the lawn and then playing rounders with the kids. She half hoped he'd mention it but also was dead scared. Once the words were out, there'd be no way of unsaying them.

But they'd survived. He had left on Monday morning for a hectic round of meetings and mentioned casually, as he drove away, that he'd not be coming to France. Too much to do, at the height of the buying season. He casually tossed her the keys to the Range Rover and told her he knew she'd cope. Quite what she was to make of it, Clemency didn't know. Was he off to join that girl of his, in his cozy little Covent Garden love nest? Quite suddenly she realized, with a chill, that these days she hardly seemed to know him at all. Nor understood the inner workings of his mind; familiarity had sounded the knell of trust.

How long it had been going on she still had no way of knowing. And became aware, with a sickening lurch of guilt, just how many months it had been since they'd talked. Really talked, and not just discussed the children, or the humdrum daily matters that form the patois of most marriages. She depended on him and loved him, at least she thought she still did. But when, in the thick of Uzès in the late afternoon as the sun was preparing to set, she thought for one giddy moment that she'd caught a glimpse of Dominic, she knew from the uncontrolled thumping of her heart that she was no longer certain of anything at all. Had Teddy sensed her attraction to her cousin and could that be the reason for his lapse? She could not believe he could really be straying, that that anemic young woman had what it took to snatch him away quite so easily.

"For God's sake!" said Harry after a further period of indecision. "I'm sick of all this hanging around. Let's get out of here."

They had loaded up with food, then gone in search of fresh basil. Then Clemency had spied a dear little shop that sold baby clothes and was in there in an instant, despite the fact that she was far too old, surely, to be thinking of adding to her family again. One of his reasons for being glad he'd left Lavender behind was this infuriating female thing about shopping which could easily take over an entire trip if a chap didn't keep very vigilant. He was itching to be off because of the things he needed to do. Preferably before nightfall, since the house had no electricity. In the end he left without them, roaring away in a huff.

"I'll tell her you're on your way," he said sarcastically. "Or ought it to be kept as a surprise?" He'd grab the best room, hopefully with a bit of privacy, and unwind in a long, hot bath while scoring brownie points for being the attentive grandson. When he switched on his charm, Harry could captivate any woman. His grandmother should prove a piece of cake; by the time they caught up with him, he'd have her under his spell.

"Well, thank goodness for that!" said Clemency once he'd gone, struggling back with kitchen utensils and a bunch of fat red garlic. She was relieved to see the tail of Harry's sleek car, had found it unnerving to have it constantly behind her, like a predatory shark on the scent of fresh blood.

"Maybe he'll get lost," suggested Élodie with a giggle.

"No such luck," said Madeleine, who had watched him with the map.

Unseen by any of them, they were all being watched, as it happened, by Dominic, who sat in the square with a Kir and hid behind his newspaper. He prided himself on his superior tracking skills and had kept them in sight almost all of the journey down. He surveyed them now as they drifted along between the plane trees, casually dressed and very much in holiday mood, laughing and loitering and making impetuous forays into shops, acting as though they had all the time in the world with no particular destination in mind. He found each one of them intriguing and the more he studied them, the more ensnared he got. Which was something that didn't sit well with him, after going to such pains to remain uninvolved. For years he'd been an anonymous traveler, wandering the world doing his own thing in an attempt to sort himself out, and he'd only really come home when he did in order to make his peace with his mother. Too late. Without Harry's involvement, he would probably have been gone again by now, but curiosity had detained him and now he had serious business to contemplate. It was good, he'd discovered, to have a serious purpose once more. Harry's phone call could not have been more opportune.

They were a handsome bunch, these cousins of his, and he enjoyed his private surveillance, catching them unawares. There was Clemency, the forceful den mother, herding them merrily, making them all laugh. And the slender, chic Élodie, who had given him so much pleasure, with her raw

216

sexuality and lack of inhibition in bed. He wondered idly where she'd got that particular trait; it didn't seem awfully Annesley, though her mother had notched up three husbands. He liked her forthright attitude to carnal matters yet feared the growing light of passion he glimpsed occasionally in her eyes. He was not in the mind-set yet for settling down and had an uncomfortable instinct that perhaps she was. Better to cool it, despite the powerful attraction. He had a job uncompleted and needed to keep a clear head. Besides, there was the blood thing; the five of them were in trouble enough as it was with the ill-advised first-cousin marriage of their grandparents.

His eye strayed past her to Madeleine, elegantly licking an ice-cream cone, and lingered there tenderly, liking what he saw. Now, that one was unquestionably a cut above the rest, aloof and classy, fashioned from finer clay. With her delicately chiseled features and porcelain complexion, and that sleek blond bob with never a hair out of place; Miss Frigidaire incarnate, he looked forward to watching her thaw. But this was neither the time nor the place; action was what was called for right now.

The clock in the square tolled a solemn five and he realized how much time they had already wasted. Maybe they didn't want to get there at all, were deliberately dawdling because they were scared. Well, the longer they left it, the tougher it would be. There were shocks in store aplenty as it was, in that grimly repellent old house, without them waiting for the sun to set. If only he was able to urge them to get on their way, but he was loath to break his cover. At least for now.

25

*N*ight comes suddenly in rural France, and before she knew what was happening, Clemency found herself obliged to switch on her lights. Madeleine, tailing her, flashed hers on too in support and they bumped along a rough country lane that turned suddenly into not much more than a track. On both sides lay vineyards, the bushes groaning with grapes, and the earth all around them was dry and parched by the sun. There was a deafening humming of crickets in the air but no other sound at all apart from the occasional birdcall.

"Country living," murmured Madeleine with a mock shudder, pining already for traffic and fluorescent yellow lighting. Beside her Élodie giggled and lit another cigarette. She was hungry and it was starting to grow chilly; the sooner they got there, the better. Poor Clemency, traveling with all those kids, but the Range Rover was slowing now and indicating a left turn. The first thing they saw was an aluminum windmill, then, just beyond it, the looming bulk of a house.

"We're here!" said Madeleine excitedly, craning to see through the gathering gloom exactly what sort of homestead they were coming to.

"Can't see any lights," said Élodie, but Madeleine reminded her there was no electricity. In London that had sounded rather quaint; now that they were actually here, all her doubts began to surface. No hair dryer, no kettle, no television, no iron. How on earth were they, creatures of modern civilization, to be expected to survive at all in this primitive foreign backwater? But the Range Rover had halted outside massive gates and Clemency was out of it and wrestling with the iron bolts. No sign of Harry. Trust him not to be there when they could use a little help.

"Mummy!" shouted Piers triumphantly. "The door at the side is not locked." They all unwound themselves from their separate vehicles and followed him into the closed courtyard. Where Harry's car stood neatly parked but no living thing so much as stirred.

"Spooky!" said Humphrey with relish, but Clemency told him sharply to hush. Her own kids were robustly ebullient, but she was less certain of Ashley. Raised without any kind of a father figure, poor little scrap, she hoped he'd be able to stand up to this adventure and acquit himself well. His pale little face was screwed up with consternation and a sneaky thumb was inching towards his mouth. She longed to sweep him up and give him a reassuring hug but restrained herself in the presence of his mother. Cherie displayed no emotion at all, just stood there smoking and looking faintly cynical. *So this is France, so what?* her expression implied. *Let's get on with it and meet the legendary grandmother.* There was still no sign of life.

Clemency advanced to the glassed-in porch and tentatively tried the door. It was unlocked.

"Come on in," she hissed, edging her way into the gloomy interior and, one by one, the rest of the party followed.

"Wait!" said Clemency, "while I find my flashlight." From the back of the Range Rover she lifted a wicker basket crammed with candles and toilet-paper rolls and a ball of string. Whatever had she been expecting? Madeleine couldn't help laughing.

"It looks as though you've brought everything but the

kitchen sink."

"Well, you can't be too prepared." Clemency remembered her childhood terror as she swung the powerful beam of her flashlight across the silent kitchen.

"Matches!" she commanded, and Élodie handed her hers. From each of the walls extended an ancient gas bracket and these Clemency now lit, throwing a pale, rather ghostly light over the room. The stove was cold and the huge black pot upon it scoured and empty. The scrubbed wooden table in the center of the room was bare. But a basket held fresh bread and there were tomatoes, onions and potatoes in a brown paper bag; someone had been planning to eat, even if not expecting company.

"Hello!" called Clemency tentatively, crossing the flags in her sandals and opening the door that led into a passage. "Mémé, are you there, dear?" Perhaps the old lady was upstairs sleeping; she didn't want to startle her.

The main part of the rugged old house was a huge vaulted hall more than two stories high where, centuries earlier, the animals had been kept. Long narrow windows ran vertically down on either side of the main front door, which was heavily locked and barred and looked as though it had not been opened in years. A rising moon threw ghostly light in slanting patterns across the flagstoned floor and their voices, even modulated, echoed unnervingly in the great silent space.

"Not what you might called homey," whispered Élodie. It was like bunking down in a planetarium. She could imagine long-dead labourers slumped around, drinking from pewter tankards and throwing mutton bones to their dogs.

"Did you ever see the original movie of *Wuthering*

Heights?" asked Madeleine. All they needed now was for Laurence Olivier to come striding in, whereas what they'd actually got was Harry. Who was where?

Above them ran a gallery, off which, presumably, led the bedrooms. Life in those days was all conducted upstairs. Two matching staircases rose to meet it, one on each side of the main front door.

"Do you think perhaps we should go up in case she just can't hear us?"

Clemency fished in her basket and produced more matches and a clutch of candles. She found a group of china holders on a spider-ridden shelf that had not been swept in years and carefully inserted candles in them for each of the others to use.

"I'm not going up there by candlelight," said Cherie, appalled, shocked out of her sneering indifference. Nothing would induce her to; she'd sooner sleep in the car.

"Don't worry," said Clemency, sounding calmer than she felt. Suppose Mémé had not received her note, was not even here to receive them after their journey. Well, there was lots of food, thank goodness for her foresight, and they'd make up some beds for the children, who were visibly starting to droop. Boldly she swung her beam up towards the gallery, where something unseen took flight into the darkness with a sudden rush of tiny clawed feet. Cherie screamed.

This wouldn't do. A fire was ready laid in a small antechamber that was snug and heavily curtained, at the rear of the great cavernous hall. Clemency put a match to it and the children crowded around; now all they needed was a hot and comforting drink, with perhaps something slightly stronger for the adults. She returned to the kitchen and lit the gas on the stove.

"Won't take long now," she called as she filled a pot with water. Pasta would be cheering; she'd just throw together some sauce. "Where the hell has Harry disappeared to?" Just like a man.

Isabelle was lugging the rest of their stuff from the cars. Sleeping bags and blankets, and a basket of windblown apples. Surely only Clemency could have thought to bring those so far. They were welcome, though. With something to chew and the fire to soften the darkness, the children were starting to perk up again, game for more adventure.

"I'm going up," announced Madeleine determinedly, grabbing a candle and beginning to mount the stairs. As a sign of solidarity, though she couldn't have felt less like it, Élodie followed her, practically hanging on to her skirt.

"Mémé," they whispered as they opened each door in turn and peered inside, but every one of the many bedrooms seemed deserted, with no signs of recent occupation. Until they came to the studio and the smell of fresh paint hit them squarely in the face. Candles aflicker, they advanced into the room and gazed at the mass of stacked canvases as they marveled at Mémé's industry. They had wondered what she had been up to all these years; now they knew. Madeleine reached up and lit the gas.

"Come look at this," she said, whispering as though in a hallowed space. She'd removed the cloth from the painting on the easel and found herself confronted with the image of her grandfather, startling in the uneven light but with eyes as haunting and all-seeing as ever. Involuntarily, she took a sharp step back and collided with her cousin.

"So she does still care," said Élodie thoughtfully. Then

why in the world had she left him so abruptly?

With her customary calm efficiency, Clemency created a meal from nowhere and soon had them all seated around the kitchen table in the mellow light from the fluttering gas flares which was already beginning to seem familiar and less threatening. With the warmth from the fire and the enticing aroma of tomatoes and garlic, things weren't looking quite so bad after all. She had vivid recollections of meals here in the old days, with Mémé presiding, delighted to have her there. Perhaps she'd just slipped out for a moment, to visit a neighbour or something. If she'd left her life's work stacked so trustingly upstairs, she certainly hadn't gone far.

"Look what I've found," said Madeleine triumphantly, revealing a dusty wine rack that was more than half full. Clemency produced a corkscrew and dusted off some glasses. At least they'd all got here safely, and here, just now, was preferable to being at home. Her tension slowly began to ebb. Right on cue, as she ladled sauce onto steaming pasta, they heard rapid footsteps outside on the terrace and the glass door opened abruptly. Everyone jumped as the candlelight flickered dangerously.

"That smells good," said Harry, sweeping in. His shoes were caked with drying earth and his hands were quite filthy.

"What on earth have you been up to? We thought we'd lost you," said Clemency.

"Just looking around," said Harry nonchalantly. "Move aside, Cousin, so's I can clean up a little." He ran cold water over his hands at the sink, dabbing at his face with a kitchen cloth where a branch or something had made a slimy mark. He took for granted the meal they'd prepared, just grabbed a plate and helped himself.

"It's as dark as the grave out there," he remarked.

"But no sign of Mémé."

"None whatsoever."

While the others got sorted out bedwise, Madeleine and Élodie lingered on in the kitchen and helped Clemency clear up the remains of the meal. Not that there was a lot to clear, just plates and forks, the bare necessities. They also opened another bottle. While Clemency was rinsing plates and Madeleine waiting for the coffee to brew, Élodie sat toying with a neat pile of pebbles she had found on the corner of the table.

"What's that you've got?" asked Clemency idly. The thing about childless women, they simply weren't used to putting themselves out. She might have sorted out mugs and sugar and cream. Made herself useful, for heaven's sake. Found herself an ashtray and asked if anyone minded.

"Just pebbles," said Élodie, tired from the journey. And groped for a match as she started another cigarette.

"Where'd you get them?"

"On the table. They were here when we arrived."

"Funny thing," said Clemency thoughtfully. "That reminds me of something I recently heard." It all came back to her, the friend who had been to Greece and told the story of the pebbles on the table. The sign of a soul, newly dead, passing through. A sort of final signing-off.

"You're kidding!" said Élodie, horrified. "You're just making it up."

"No," said Clemency, getting a secret kick out of it. "That's apparently how it happens. The antidote, should you ever need to know, is to place a saucer of milk in the places where you feel the spirit still walks."

"And then?"

"Don't know. That's as far as the story goes. Something to do with setting the spirit free. Allowing it to move on to the next stopping place."

"Well, thanks a bunch for making me feel at home here!"

They made up makeshift beds in a couple of the bedrooms, leaving the connecting door ajar in case the children woke up in the night. Once they were safely tucked in, the women settled down to chat while Harry imperviously sat at the table and continued to drink. The kitchen was huge and spacious with a walk-in pantry and Clemency couldn't wait to get to grips with it in daylight. Strong, unwavering moonlight now flooded through the windows in the hall, giving it the feeling of a ghostly cathedral, and she was already beginning to adjust to the soft flicker of candlelight.

Since the house still had no telephone, they decided to leave finding Mémé till morning and turn in. The drivers were exhausted and the wine going fast to their heads. Harry had his mobile, of course, but could think of no one appropriate to call. They knew none of the names of Mémé's friends and what neighbours there might be were too remote. They sorted out temporary sleeping quarters and efficiently allocated washing facilities. The bathrooms were creepy, with no light from outside, heavily festooned with spiders' webs and rusty pipes which made a racket when used. In order to see anything at all, it was necessary to light the gas, and that, Élodie found, was arguably worse than having to wash in the dark. By gas or candlelight the periphery of one's vision obscured what might be lurking just beyond it, waiting to run over your foot. She'd almost rather pee outside and clean her teeth from the well, but the presence of so many children stiffened her spine. If *they* weren't scared, then she mustn't falter, but she couldn't help longing for the rationality of Dominic and the welcome shelter of his protective arms.

"Close the shutters when you go to bed," warned Harry. "Or you'll be bitten to death by mosquitoes in the night."

They were just closing up in the kitchen, rinsing out the sink and hanging the dishcloths to dry, when Madeleine stopped dead in her tracks, listening like a pointer, her eyes widening in alarm.

"What's that?"

"What?"

"Listen."

Harry snorted, but even he fell silent. *Now* what was it with this scatty band of dingbats? At first they could hear nothing apart from normal night sounds, then there was a slight bump against an outside wall and the window rattled impatiently.

"There's someone out there."

"It's just the wind."

Silence again; they could hear each other breathing. Élodie glanced nervously at the pebbles on the table.

Then another thump, a hard one this time. And the sound of something falling, something metallic.

"Christ!" said Harry. "You're right."

Madeleine wondered wildly if Clemency had thought to bring a gun and gasped as Harry opened the door to the porch.

"Be careful!"

He stepped outside and they bravely crowded after him. High clouds were scudding across the sky and the moon peeped through them, shedding an uneven light. The trees were stirring in a rising breeze, but the sounds they had heard had been more deliberate. Someone was out there, skulking in the shadows. Someone trying valiantly not to make a noise.

Harry displayed enormous courage as he gestured to them all to keep quiet, and then set off to patrol the grounds.

"Should we go with him?" hissed Élodie in the dark.

"Christ, no," said Madeleine, clutching her arm.

"Perhaps it's Mémé coming home." But Mémé wouldn't be slinking in the darkness, pushing her way through the bushes like an intruder. There was total silence for at least five minutes; then, just when Clemency was thinking they ought to join him, Harry shouted from somewhere among the trees and they all went running, shining their flashlights. He was grappling with someone on the ground, but they could see he already had the advantage.

"Over here," said Harry, breathing hard. "Don't let the blighter get away."

But the captive was now face down on the ground, arms pinioned behind him by Harry's foot, making no attempt to break free. The women encircled him cautiously and Clemency shone her beam on his face.

"Good heavens!"

"Evening, all," said Ethan Annesley shakily. "I decided to come after all."

He'd left his car parked at the side of the lane and decided to explore the property on foot. He hadn't let them know, it had been an impetuous decision, but he'd got some last-minute leave. And had realized just how much he wanted to see his mother; after all these years, he was still a boy at heart.

"Come on in," said Clemency, helping to brush him down. "I'll brew up some coffee and I'll bet you're famished." Ethan nodded; he was a bit. They all trooped back into the house, laughing as the tension broke. Funny old Ethan, what a card he was! Hadn't even thought about telling them he might come.

"Luckily there's plenty of room," said Clemency. "The attic's still empty, if you don't mind climbing a ladder."

Élodie ended up sharing a bed with Madeleine, cuddling up to her on the high, hard mattress, and despite Harry's warning they left the heavy shutters ajar for the moonlight to filter in.

"Night-night," said Madeleine from beneath the musty eiderdown. This curious echo of childhood was, she found, oddly comforting.

"Sleep tight," chanted Élodie on cue. "Mind the bugs don't bite."

The same childhood memories, the same meaningless nursery mantra. They might have had different upbringings but had a lot more in common than they realized. Two sleepyheads lying side by side on the pillows, one dark and curly, the other fair and sleek, but with identical straight noses and that provocative tilt to the chin. And, could they only have known it as they floated off into broken sleep, identical fantasies of future delights with the same infuriating man.

26

*M*ummy, come and see what we've found." The children had been up for ages and were running wild in the garden.

"Not now, darling," said Clemency abstractedly from the stove, dishing up eggs and bacon to the troops around the table. Mémé was weighing heavily on her mind; she hoped the surprise party was not going to turn into a fiasco. Suppose she'd gone away for the winter, but where on earth would she have gone? She was saddened by the realization that after pretty nearly forty years, they knew virtually nothing of their grandmother's way of life.

But the paintings were still there and the house had been left unlocked. Plus fresh food had been left in the kitchen which hadn't been brought by Harry. And when Clemency had tested each of the beds, not all of them were damp and in need of airing, as they surely would have been if the house had been empty long. There was also no mail or milk on the step, though in the country that didn't necessarily mean a thing. The house was more or less tidy. Inspiration suddenly struck; maybe somebody came in to clean it. Someone from the village who might at any moment show up and put them all out of their misery. There had to be some sort of rational explanation. They just hadn't thought of it yet.

"Mummy," begged Piers, tugging at her apron. "I really do think you should come."

"I'll go," said Isabelle, anxious to please, an echo of Mad Aunt Effie if she did but know it.

"Won't you have more breakfast?" The kids could wait.

"Ethan? Harry?"

If Isabelle wasn't very careful, she could find herself kow-towing to their every whim, and that was a recipe for certain disaster.

"No, really it's okay." The morning was bright and golden and she could do with some exercise. She pulled on ser-viceable boots with thick socks and followed the child into the garden.

Élodie laughed, but not unkindly. "She really is an angel, isn't she? Mad Aunt Effie updated."

"Only not mad. Just sometimes seems that way."

"It's all that book-larnin'," said Clemency in broad Wilt-shire. "Goes to their heads like something rotten. Don't ever do to edycate wimmen."

"But she's really such a pet."

"Oh, absolutely."

With Isabelle to back Clemency up, this trip could turn out to be a breeze. The shy Canadian had endless patience and genuinely seemed not to mind spending time with the kids. Perhaps she ought to have taken up teaching, if she weren't so overburdened with impressive Annesley brains. There were times when your heritage could be a positive obstacle. Take poor little Ashley, for example: where on earth did he spring from with his odd, compulsive ways? Unless, God forbid, he was some sort of throwback to Hugo, who had died so young.

Harry and Ethan were still lolling at the table, drinking endless cups of coffee and chatting about their lives. In the bright light of morning Ethan didn't look quite so strange, though he was pitifully thin and unhealthy looking, with a bit of tissue paper stuck to his chin where he'd cut himself shaving. Well, at least he had made some effort for them all; Harry hadn't bothered. He sat there in his undershirt and shorts with hair that needed combing. He was still a good-looking man, however, and reminded Madeleine of Grandpa's portrait on the easel upstairs.

With much of last night's tension removed, he was more at his ease and no longer quite so frenetic. A few days' break could be just what he needed to help lessen the strain he was obviously under. Despite her disapproval, Clemency couldn't help feeling motherly; that was the way she was made. She had tried asking brightly about Lavender and the children, two could play at this armistice game, but he had brushed aside her questioning and abruptly changed the subject. Now he was cross-examining Ethan about life at the BBC. Well, this was no time to gloat, thought Clemency. Look at the mess she had made of her own marriage.

Ethan was monosyllabic but clearly glad he'd come. The only one of his generation who had bothered to make the journey. He caught her looking and smiled at her shyly and she suddenly saw his strong resemblance to Mémé. He wasn't bad-looking if he weren't so shabby and could do something about that disastrous hair. Like her mother and aunts before her, she wondered about his sex life; she'd heard some rumour that he had a girlfriend back home.

But now was not the time to inquire. A grave-faced Isabelle was striding back, with Piers still hovering beside her.

"I think you'd better come," she said quietly to Harry, and the look she shot at Clemency almost stopped the blood in her veins.

. . .

231

They hadn't noticed it before because they'd arrived after dark and, in any case, it was virtually hidden in the foliage behind a stack of cut wood. The children had been playing one of their elaborate games and that's how they'd stumbled across it. It might be something perfectly ordinary but did look chillingly sinister, especially in their present slightly jumpy frame of mind, a narrow trench of freshly turned earth, dampish to the fingers and darker than the topsoil despite a summer of blazing sun. Harry stood slowly considering it, scratching his head. His thoughts were whirling and he really didn't know what to do. It was obvious what they'd all be thinking, he just didn't want to be the one to put it into words. It was . . . inconvenient, to say the least, and the longer they delayed it, the better. Besides, the kids were still hanging around; it just wouldn't do if they were to become alarmed or scared. Clemency and the others had now joined him and they all stood there staring, wondering what should be done. He looked at Ethan to help him out, but his uncle was simply standing there, blank-eyed.

"I hesitate to start digging," said Harry, "because it's probably something perfectly straightforward, done by the gardener for purposes of his own."

Did Mémé even have a gardener? It certainly didn't look like it. The place was a wilderness and so far they'd seen no hide or hair of that brutish Frenchman Harry had encountered so many years ago. Luckily even Clemency seemed to see Harry's point. They had really no right to meddle in Mémé's absence, especially if, for whatever reason, she didn't even know they were here. Any bumbling interference might well destroy an asparagus patch or something else perfectly innocent. This was deep country where folks made their basic living from the land.

Harry was all in favour of letting it be, but Isabelle still seemed worried and Clemency began to share her concern. They were, after all, supposed to be responsible adults and this land they stood on belonged indirectly to them. If they didn't take charge, who else was going to do so? She turned to Ethan, who was Mémé's son, but could see he would be no help.

"We could always call the police," said Isabelle thoughtfully. "Just to find out if they know where she might be." Which certainly made good sense. Mémé had lived in these parts half her life and generations of her family before her.

"I don't suppose it could do any harm," said Clemency. Small communities always hung together; that was part of the point of them. But it was fairly plain to see that Harry didn't agree. He stood there scowling, looking all of a sudden quite truculent.

"If you're feeling squeamish, you can always leave it to us," said Clemency, more sharply than was warranted. She wondered what was up with the guy, normally so assertive, the first to get in there and cope. Having known him from childhood, she could read him like a book, and Harry definitely had something on his mind; he'd been behaving oddly since they started out. And Ethan was clearly going to be no help. He just stood there blindly staring at the ground. What they really needed was someone to take charge, Teddy, for instance, or Dominic. She wished she'd invited him along. Then pulled herself sharply together. They didn't need a man, for heaven's sake. They were five able-bodied women with these two ineffective men. To prevent a threatened fit of trembling, she marched briskly back to the house to swap her sandals for proper shoes. She would drive into town.

"You surely can't be serious!" said Harry in alarm, but he could see there was nothing he could do to stop her now. The more she watched his dithering, the more certain she was she was right. Now she came to think of it, he'd arrived here well ahead of the rest of them and stayed out of sight an inexplicably long time. Whatever it was he'd been up to, lurking alone in the garden, he'd given no satisfactory explanation, and the more she focused, the more suspicious that grew.

She looked up at him now as she finished tying her laces and saw the dislike quite clearly in his eyes. I wouldn't trust him as far as I could throw him, she thought, and that was what finally tipped the balance. There were things afoot here that none of them understood. The sooner she got the gendarmes in, the better. Not just for Mémé but for everyone's sake.

27

*E*unice Annesley put on her glasses and dialed her sister's number in Connecticut. She liked to check up on her at least once or twice a week, but the Portland trip had caused a gap in that routine and she was anxious to know what she might have missed in her younger sister's far more glamourous life. Patrice picked up on the second ring. She was sitting outside on the sunporch with her coffee and the latest copy of *Architectural Digest*. Always trying to improve herself, was Patrice, a habit she had had since childhood.

"So you're there."

Hearing the clipped tones of her oldest sister made Patrice

start and spill her coffee. Of course she was there; where else would she be at ten to nine on a weekday morning? Tuesdays and Thursdays were her library days and she rarely played tennis before noon. Eunice had always had this knack of managing to make her feel guilty no matter what.

"I'm here. And you, presumably, are back." Conversations between the sisters quite often kicked off like this. Though close in blood, they had never been remotely on the same wavelength and Eunice still resented the life she felt she had missed.

"I thought you might have left for France."

"Now why would I want to do that?"

"On this harebrained expedition to visit Maman that Clemency seems to be organizing."

Oh, that. "No, we were in Europe already this year. And Jonathan's too busy right now to get away." Not that they could afford it, with the way things were with the markets at present. They had thought about visiting Odile in the spring but had received no response to their note. And, after all these years and the way that she'd behaved, Jonathan had felt inclined to leave it alone this time. He was very protective of his wife, didn't want her bruised any more. Fat chance of that, though, with Eunice weighing in. If he could have had his way, he'd have banned her from the house.

"You're practically the youngest." *The prettiest,* was what she meant. That innuendo was always there, needling her. "I was sure you'd be right there." *Holding Maman's hand, the way you always used to; sitting on Papa's knee.*

All the bottled-up resentment was still there in Eunice's voice. Sixty-two years old now, yet she'd never really forgiven her mother. Never forgotten the way she had fled, leaving her oldest daughter to cope. Eunice was twenty-five at the time, in her first year of teaching at PS 6. It was a dream of a job, all her ambitions resolved in one, and she was loving it in Manhattan, teaching those quite extraordinary kids. She'd even got a budding romance on the go, with the English teacher whose name was Evan Brookes. Eunice still kept his picture on her dresser, though all that had vanished in a flash the day of her father's call. But he'd published a couple of novels since then and she'd bought them in hardback and brooded on what might have been. It said on the jacket flap that he was married.

The sorrow in Cornelius's voice had been tangible; he could barely finish his stumbled explanation.

"Come home," he'd said. "Your mother has left me. There's chaos in the house and the kids are running wild."

She hadn't wanted to go, New York was home to her now, but family duty had always sat heavily upon Eunice and she couldn't see that she had any other real choice. Besides, though she didn't admit to it, his obvious need made her feel important, wanted even. Cornelius Annesley was not an easy man, brilliant and talented, with an acid wit and a viper's tongue. He brooked no insubordination and couldn't tolerate fools. His ten living children regarded him with awe; the boys in particular tried hard to keep out of his way. Yet he loved his wife like a wino loves the bottle, was absolutely addicted to her in every conceivable way. They often embarrassed their children by the way they canoodled in public and Eunice had caught them leaping apart when she'd entered a room without warning. It wasn't quite proper, she'd always felt, since he was over forty when he'd met Odile and twenty-two years her senior.

He also loved his other little girls, Aimée, always so zany and bright, and Patrice, the family beauty. He liked to show them off to his colleagues, the two cute schoolgirls he had sired so late in life. Handsome, sardonic Professor Annesley had a human side after all, he could see them thinking. Others, of course, might privately think he must be a bit of a dirty old man, though none would ever dare voice that opinion.

But the one he unquestionably loved the best was his first-born daughter, Agnes, who was so much like him in so many ways, with the same expressive eyebrows and rapier tongue, and the same daunting stare from those oddly silver eyes. Agnes was nine when she burst into their lives and even then, at five, Eunice had felt displaced. Used to being her father's pet, at least until Claire and Henry came along, she had felt pushed aside with the arrival of this noisy, mercurial child. Agnes was also American and therefore somewhat exotic. She had quickly taken charge of the older kids and only relinquished her leadership when the end of summer came and she was obliged to return to her mother. Eunice had instinctively hated this interloper and hoped never to see her again. Agnes was bright and fearless and altogether too knowing; she made the lumpy English child feel inadequate and slow.

"Are the girls going?"

"Yes, I believe so. Madeleine and Clemency, they're all getting on so well." Élodie sounded so happy these days and was constantly zipping over to England. Patrice, used to being cocooned in the heart of a huge family, was happy for her daughter that she'd found some connections of her own. She'd always felt slightly guilty that she hadn't been able to provide a stable home, though the boys, oddly enough, seemed throwbacks to the past, with their pleasant, biddable wives and cozy little families. And the girl cousins sounded really great, even Charlie's Isabelle, who had also turned up in England. Strange how the Annesleys moved around. Eunice still blamed it all on her mother. Because of her, she'd been born out of wedlock and British and had spent most of the rest of her life regretting it.

"And Aimée, what of her?" The familiar ice in Eunice's voice fairly crackled so that Patrice found herself squirming—get off my case.

"Oh, I don't think she'll go, she's far too busy with the garden." Eunice had just returned from Maine; how come she couldn't find out these things for herself? She had always terrorized her younger siblings and her mother's unexplained defection had put them totally at her mercy. For years, until they'd been old enough to flit, the younger Annesleys had feared and resented Eunice. A chip off the old block in spades, they'd all agreed, though their father could be compassionate at times when he was able to tear himself away from his constant grieving.

"Will Junior's thinking of going too," said Patrice brightly. "He's got to be in London in any case around that time, on bank business. He thought it might be a lark to tag along. Ethan too."

Eunice merely sniffed. Snoopy as she was, she really hated it when someone told her something she didn't already know. And now she was starting to regret her decision not to attend her mother's party. As head of the family she ought to be there, if only to keep an eye on things. She wondered fleetingly about Agnes, then dismissed the thought. There was no chance of her ever emerging from her convent; Eunice relaxed. Maybe she needn't bother.

Aimée laughed when Patrice reported this call. She was fresh in from the garden in Maine and washing the dirt from her hands. She looked out of the window and across the lawn to the small wooden bridge near the steep fall of rocks where the accident had happened almost forty years ago. She'd been twenty that year and just back from her honeymoon on the French Riviera. She would never forget the drama of that morning, with Charlie—or was it Tom?—racing up all white-faced and upset from the shoreline and Maman running back with him, like a creature demented, to the spot where he'd discovered Roland's things. She was far too self-contained to cry, just stood there wringing her hands while they fetched Papa. And Cornelius had come, grim-faced, from his study, where he was writing the thesis that was later to earn him a Pulitzer Prize.

They had searched for Roland for several days, but his body had never been washed up, at least not on this stretch of coastline, which was probably all for the best. The thought of poor, distraught Maman having to view the bloated corpse of her favorite child, like the drowned Shelley on the beach at Lerici, was too horrible to contemplate, even after all these years. As it was, she had refused to allow them any sort of memorial service until Papa had overruled her and arranged a private service for family only, with a discreet marble plaque on the wall of the local church.

Aimée walked into the winter parlour, where her dead brother's photo still hung on the wall. It was a formal portrait, taken at his high school graduation, but you could see the humour in his eyes and the hint of a mischievous smile at the curve of his mouth. He was a handsome boy, Roland, and filled with a devilish spirit that had kept him in trouble throughout most of his short life and more or less guaranteed, in hindsight, that he was destined to die before his prime.

Charlie, Tom and Patrice had probably been the ones to suffer most; Ethan was really too young to take it all in. But with Roland's death the light went out in their mother's life so that the younger children found themselves trapped in a void, abruptly deprived of the warmth and nurture she'd wrapped them in like a fleece since babyhood. Sometime that fall, after she'd finally given up hope, she permitted Cornelius to close up the summer house, which had not been winterized, and transport the lot of them back to cold, damp Oxford and the home she had, from that point on, begun to regard as a prison.

Aimée herself had just made it under the wire, safely married to Jack and living in Portland, but the others had never really recovered from the tragedy and it wasn't too many years before Charlie too slipped away as soon as he left school and moved to Canada to start a new life and try to forget the mother who had forsaken him.

The last time Eunice ever saw her mother was just before Christmas that year when she'd arrived unexpectedly in New York and begged a bed off her daughter for the night. It was not entirely convenient; Eunice and Evan were just beginning to notice each other, at that delicate stage in a budding courtship when everything hangs on timing and getting the signals right. The last thing she needed in her cramped little studio apartment was her mother sleeping on the foldaway bed, but she could hardly refuse her, particularly now when Odile was still acting strange and not yet back to herself. Papa would expect it of her, she reflected sanctimoniously, as she made the sacrifice with a fairly bad grace, begrudging every second she was likely to have to spend with this wayward parent who still seemed slightly off her head.

She was mortified, therefore, when, on Odile's arrival, she had discovered her real reason for this visit was mainly to see Agnes, not herself. Agnes needed her, was all she would say by way of explanation to her eldest daughter. So why didn't she stay with Agnes, then; but Agnes was sharing and there simply wasn't room. The two had spent a couple of days together shopping so that Eunice had barely got a look-in. All of a sudden, her priority ceased to be Evan; her early jealousy came flooding back and she hated her mother for not preferring her. Agnes came around to the apartment for supper, tall and flamboyant with her sweep of dark hair but paler than usual, with distinct circles under her eyes, and the two of them stood and muttered in the kitchen while Odile prepared one of her exquisite suppers.

"If your father calls, tell him I've gone to bed early," she mysteriously instructed Eunice while she chopped. It made no sense, but then, nothing seemed to these days, and Eunice just wished to see the back of them both and be left with her dreams, waiting for the phone to ring.

Agnes ate virtually nothing, said she was feeling under the

weather, and left for an early night, which was not like her at all. When Eunice asked her a few terse questions, Odile was evasive and peculiarly vague. When, in heaven's name, was she going to shake off her dolour and return to the real world for the sake of her living children, if not herself? She left early next morning, to stay a few days with Aimée, and that was the last time, as it later transpired, that Eunice ever saw her or Agnes again. Claire had lost her baby and was acting very strangely and all her mother would say was that she felt she should fly right back to be with her in her distress. Christmas was going to be a bad time all around. By sticking together and sharing their grief, they would try to help each other to cope.

Which, of course, only served to sour Eunice even more. Everyone came ahead of her with Odile, Roland, her sisters, even the interloping Agnes. When, she implored of her favorite saint, was it ever going to get to be her turn?

28

*T*wo gendarmes, reeking heavily of Gauloises, bumped along the track in an antiquated Renault, followed by a plain, unmarked van containing a couple of overalled workmen. Clemency led them silently through the undergrowth to the dug-over patch behind the woodshed, where Ethan and Harry were still loitering. Isabelle had swept up all the children and forcibly led them away and out of sight, while the rest of the women had returned to the house, scared and apprehensive. Suddenly what had started as a bit of a lark was beginning to look very dark indeed. The gendarmes poked at the disturbed soil with their boots and one of them stooped and trickled a little of it through his fingers. They spoke in low voices in rapid colloquial French which even bilingual Clemency had trouble following.

"Everything all right?" she asked brightly, but they blankly ignored her and went on conferring with rapid hand gestures that made it all the more dramatic.

"What's the score?" asked Harry, wandering over.

"Don't know. They are speaking too fast for me."

"Any suggestions of where she might have got to?"

"None," said Clemency, who had been through it all at length in the police station. "They say they rarely see her these days, that she only comes into town to shop and hardly seems to socialize at all. As far as they know." But why would the police bother watching one solitary old lady? Even though this was such a close community and her family had lived here for generations. Things couldn't be the same now as they were back in the old days; people had grown less caring, the gendarmes themselves more lax.

Finally they turned and beckoned to Clemency and the two men to join them.

"About time," muttered Harry, not well pleased, but Clemency frowned and touched his arm. The last thing they needed right now was one of his outbursts. She meekly did as she was bid and the others followed. Then came more routine questions as to who each one of them was and why they were there.

"Christ!" said Harry under his breath. "Get on with it."

But the gendarmes were not to be hurried. They asked for individual identification and were not satisfied until they had all returned to the house and everyone had fetched their

243

passports and driver's licenses.

"You'd think it was we who were under suspicion," said Élodie.

"We probably are," said Harry. "Prime suspects." And he wasn't joking.

Eventually, after a great deal of hawing and humming, the gendarmes walked back to the van and banged on its side, whereupon the workmen jumped out and started unloading shovels and a lethal-looking pickaxe from the back. Plus a rather sinister tarpaulin that sent a shiver down Clemency's spine. Lord, she thought, they're actually going to do it. Excitement ran like wildfire through the group. They followed like a flock of nervous sheep as the workmen strode over to the woodshed.

"*Allons!*" said the bossier of the gendarmes, indicating that the rest of them should stand well back. The pickaxe proved unnecessary since the earth was fairly soft, and the spades quickly got on with their deadly work. A low, sinister rumble sounded from beyond the vineyards, where the sky was rapidly turning a threatening dark purple.

"Just what we need now," said Harry, startled. "A thunderstorm to add to the fun." He was severely rattled by what was going on and the inspection of his passport hadn't helped. He had planned to remain as incognito as possible; the very last thing he wanted right now was the bloody police poking their noses in. Certainly not till he was ready to go, to slip across the border into the safety of the wilderness beyond the Pyrenees. But first there was the question of money to be sorted; he was damned if he'd forfeit his inheritance without a fight.

Clemency glanced at Ethan, who was tense and white as a

sheet. Poor devil, he must be terrified. It was his mother they were trying to find. She strolled across and took his hand and he gave her a tentative smile.

"Hairy stuff," he said. "Not quite what I expected. Buried treasure and all that." But the smile didn't reach his eyes.

Deeper and deeper went the spades and the first fat raindrops began to fall.

"Bugger!" said Harry, stepping back beneath the trees. He had shaved and changed and was wearing his better jacket. Élodie watched him with amusement, he really was such a prat. Fancy lugging Savile Row to the fastness of rural France. With only the family to impress; you'd think he was strutting his stuff on the Riviera.

"Shall I fetch you an umbrella?" she taunted, but Harry ignored her as beneath his contempt. But his attention was distracted; they were getting closer, he could see something starting to emerge.

Dominic watched them from behind the trees, safe in his car on the track which skirted the vines. He was wearing dark glasses and a battered old straw hat, posing as a farm labourer with the stump of a hand-rolled cigarette in his mouth. Even the vehicle suited his borrowed image. He had leased it in the village in exchange for a handful of francs. Soon the workers would be here to start stripping the bushes, but by then, with luck, he would be long gone. From a metal tube in his capacious pocket he drew a compact telescope, which he skillfully adjusted. Good stuff, this modern equipment; he could travel light and still get the job done effectively.

Dominic was as interested as the rest of them in what the

workmen were about to uncover. If he'd got here sooner things might have turned out differently, but Harry's imperfect memory had led him on several wild-goose chases he now regretted. He stepped out of the car to get a clearer view. The pile of displaced earth was growing higher; any second now they would see what lay beneath.

"Dominic?" Isabelle could scarcely believe her eyes. There she was, spread out on a rug, deep in an Anita Brookner novel, while somewhere offstage the children were playing; she couldn't see them but could hear their voices. And right in front of her stepped a man and it was Dominic, oddly dressed but him nonetheless. She'd have known him anywhere.

Caught unawares, Dominic wheeled around, then cursed himself for his lack of caution. He was losing his touch.

"Isabelle!" His heart sank. He hadn't noticed anyone was there, even though the rug she lay on was tartan and there was a wide wicker basket clearly visible beside her. His tracking skills, of which he was so proud, had let him down woefully at the crucial moment. He had to get rid of her, and as quickly as he could. The last thing he needed was that gang of children clustering around him and ruining his cover. Luckily the weather was on his side.

"It's raining," he said as the drops began to fall. "Better run for it before it sets in. Looks like a thunderstorm, and in the countryside that can be dangerous. Try the barn. It's the nearest shelter."

Apart from the car, of course, but she didn't seem to think of that. Just leapt to her feet obediently and started folding the blanket.

"Children," she shouted, "I'll race you to the barn. The last one there gets to do the dishes." And off she sped. He did find that funny and grinned as he resumed his watch. If she wasn't so sweet he would find her ludicrous, but her innocence was genuine and it touched his heart.

The barn door was heavy, but Piers managed to shift it and they all got inside as the heavens opened wide. Isabelle had thought to bring a towel in her basket, so they all grouped around her and she dried them off in turn. This was fun. Unaware of the grim proceedings over at the house, the children were having one whale of a time. Even little Ashley had a glow in his cheeks. Fresh air and laughter were doing him a power of good.

"It looks as though it might be setting in." Isabelle surveyed the sky, then pulled the door closed. She hated thunderstorms, was secretly scared of them, but felt obliged to put on a brave face for the children. And maybe this was a blessing in disguise if it kept them away from what was going on over there. The police were still there, their vehicles were lined up in the courtyard, and although they were only yards from the house, she felt it was healthier for them here. She peered around the gloomy interior, at the rusting farm equipment that looked as though it belonged in a museum. An old farm cart stood covered in sacking with an unwieldy contraption, all wicked-looking blades, which must have been some sort of antiquated reaping machine. And in the corner, draped in furry spiders' webs, a vicious scythe that might have belonged to Father Time.

"Come away from there," she warned as Ashley went to examine it; then, with sudden inspiration: "Let's all play Hide-and-Seek."

Black plastic was what they saw first, embedded in the dark, dank soil and firmly secured with sticky tape and rope. Clemency clutched at Ethan as the workmen meticulously loosened it, then attempted to raise whatever it was to the surface. *Oh my God.* Harry was slowly beginning to feel quite sick; this was not what he'd envisaged when they'd started out. And the rain didn't help. It came sluicing down from the angry sky so that the men were standing in a mire in minutes. The gendarmes, now wearing their waterproof capes, had given up trying to control the Annesleys. They all crowded around, as close as they could get, as the cigar-shaped package was lifted out of the hole. The workmen stood back, their task for the moment done, and one of the gendarmes drew an army knife from its holster and made a neat incision in the plastic. Clemency thought she might faint.

One look was confirmation and then the gendarmes took charge again. The tarpaulin was brought and draped across the bundle and the family were banished from the scene.

"They're not going to tell us," said Harry, stunned, through gritted teeth. He watched a gendarme talking on his radio and knew they were in for a long, officious ordeal. Might as well return to the house and at least get dry. There was a bottle of Glenmorangie in his luggage that he might be prevailed upon to share, at least with Ethan. The gendarmes nodded their assent, so the rest of them trailed, bedraggled, back through the sopping undergrowth and Clemency lit a fire with hands that shook with more than just cold. Don't let it be what I think it is, she pleaded in her heart. It would be too terrible if they'd come all this way for this. In some ways she felt responsible.

The children had all run off, whooping with delight, and Isabelle looked around frantically, seeking somewhere easy to hide. They'd allowed little Ashley to be the first seeker; she could hear him counting loudly as he stood in the corner and covered his eyes. A wooden ladder led up to a hayloft and Isabelle scurried to it and started to climb. A bit of a cliché, but he was only five; better not make it too difficult the first time or else the poor little chap might lose heart. The sloping skylight was filthy, letting in only murky light, but she could see that, beyond the mounds of hay, there was some ancient, discarded furniture, including a rusty truckle bed. How strange. Perhaps the labourers stayed here while they were picking the grapes. She hoped she wasn't intruding, then saw at a glance she was not. The place was quite deserted and looked untouched by time.

". . . ninety-nine, a hundred!" shouted Ashley from below, so she ducked behind a hay bale and waited to hear him ascend. There were metal pegs driven into the loamy wall with a couple of old jackets on them and a frayed, wide-brimmed straw hat. Ashley was moving around the barn; she could hear him quite clearly as he banged about. There was a yellow oilskin tobacco pouch on the table and when she unrolled it, she found the tobacco was fresh. Someone had been here recently; she looked guiltily around, afraid of being spotted, and not just by the little boy beneath. There were squeals of laughter, someone had been caught, and then a deeper, more serious voice, an adult, presumably sent to summon them home.

Isabelle rose and stretched from her crouched position and

crossed towards the stairs. Time to go back to the house and find out what had happened, to leave this childhood playground and return to the adult world. Too late. Someone, she hoped not Ashley, was starting slowly to climb. She thought perhaps she should hide again but found she had left it too late.

Dead a few weeks, was the pathologist's cursory opinion, and the body was repackaged and reverently placed in the van. The gendarmes shook their heads awkwardly and offered their formal condolences. There would have to be an autopsy and they preferred it if everyone stayed put. It was obviously murder, there could be no doubt of that, undoubtedly the grim work of the as-yet-uncaught "Provence Predator" who had been terrorizing the French countryside for a number of years. Madeleine was ashen and Élodie was shaking; it was Clemency, as always, who assumed command. There was no sign of Harry or Ethan, who both seemed to have wandered off.

She would have to contact the other guests and tell them the party was canceled. She would drive into Uzès right away and put in a call to Teddy. At least he still had his uses; she couldn't face telling each one in person that the grandmother whose birthday they'd come to celebrate had had her throat cold-bloodedly cut and been buried in the garden.

"The children," she said, as she piled on more wood. "It's time they came home for their tea." She didn't relish having to break the news, but it would have to be done sooner or later. Isabelle appeared to have vanished too; they must still be playing in the barn.

"I'll go," said Cherie; unusually willing. She was feeling

unhinged and quite sick with horror and suddenly badly needed her arms around her child.

29

*A*shley appeared to have done it again and picked up another stranger. She was glad to see him mixing so well yet was still badly shaken by the day's events. Who was it this time? She wanted no more surprises.

"G'day!" said the stranger as Cherie approached, and it was then she noticed his female companion. They were both fit and tanned, in shorts and hiking boots, with their laden backpacks lying at their feet. New Zealanders. She might have known it. Cherie had been born with an unnatural dislike of the unfamiliar.

"Is this Mas des Vignes?" he asked with a bright smile. "The little fellow doesn't seem to know."

Who the blazes could this be, now? Cherie, on her guard, was at her least attractive and scowled with all the hostility she could muster. Totally unfazed, however, the stranger held out his hand. He was quite well built, with sun-bleached hair, and appeared entirely at his ease.

"Rusty Annesley, at your service," he said with a bit of a flourish, and blinked in surprise when Cherie practically fainted.

Of course she knew about him, she always had, the legitimate son her father had sired before he left his second wife to run off with her mother. Aunts Rita and Irene had made quite sure of that, painting as bad a picture as they could of the decadent toff who had ruined their sister's life. She knew

251

but had scarcely given him a second thought, and now here he was before her in the flesh, firm-skinned and vitamin-packed, smiling at her benevolently, still extending his hand.

"And you are?"

The question was respectful enough, but Cherie wanted to snarl. He'd caught her completely off her guard, devoid of makeup or even clean clothes, and suddenly that mattered to her, far more than she might have imagined. The girl was smiling too, revealing the most perfect, whitest teeth and one tiny dimple at the corner of her mouth.

"Tonya," she said by way of explanation. "We're here from Auckland for the party."

At first Cherie wasn't certain what to do. Instinct warned her not to give too much away, but both still smiled at her trustingly and some answer was clearly required.

"Cherie Cole," she said reluctantly, hiding behind her mother's name. "And this is Ashley."

"Well, hello, there, Ashley," said the girl, stooping to meet him at eye level. Ashley beamed and touched her hand and Tonya looked up, her eyes full of laughter, only to encounter Cherie's blank scowl.

"Have we got the right place? The Annesley reunion?" Cherie still hadn't answered, but her son wasn't to be deflected.

"Annesley!" shouted Ashley, excited. "That's us! Our house is just down there."

Rusty hefted his backpack on to his shoulder and took the child's trusting hand. Tonya did likewise on the other side and, like a ready-made family, they proceeded jauntily down the lane, leaving Cherie to follow alone and thwarted, still foaming with inner rage at the intrusion.

When Thomas Annesley had left Pandora, her own children were still barely toddlers. He ran off with Sylvia, whom he met on a plane, and the result of that union was Rusty. Cherie had heard that story many times; what she hadn't expected was to like him.

"Have you been to New Zealand?" he asked politely over his shoulder, still innocent of the special relationship he had with this scowling antagonist. Cherie merely grunted. He had no right coming here, so confident and relaxed, without any warning so she'd know what to expect. It wasn't right; it wasn't fair. Just when she'd finally found some family of her own, here came her older half brother to usurp it. Throughout her short life people had spoiled things for her, most particularly men.

She changed the subject; where were the other kids? And where was Isabelle, who was supposed to be minding them? Ashley explained about the game of Hide-and-Seek and told them someone had come into the barn and frightened them.

"Who?" demanded his mother, instantly on the alert, but Ashley didn't know. It was dark, he said, and the person had shouted. In French, he thought, but he couldn't be quite sure.

"I ran and ran," he said in explanation.

"And that's how we met him." Tonya finished the sentence for him. "Something seems to have scared the little man."

By mutual unspoken agreement they both unshouldered their backpacks and the four of them headed wordlessly for the barn.

Inside it was really dark. The rain had eased off, but the night was drawing in so that all they could distinguish in the gathering gloom were looming shapes that Cherie found quite spooky.

"Stay outside!" she hissed at Ashley. Rusty lit a match.

"I ought to have brought a flashlight," he said with a laugh. "There's always something I leave behind."

The children had gone, presumably back to the house, and not a movement disturbed the dusty staleness. Here time had stood still and the centuries pressed upon them. Cherie moved instinctively closer to the others, fearful of a menace she couldn't quite define. Something touched her face and she gave a little squeal of terror, but it was only an old horse harness dangling from a beam.

Rusty lit another match, then gave her hand a squeeze. "It's okay," he whispered. "There isn't anything here."

Cherie found his proximity reassuring. Maybe he wasn't so bad after all. The girl seemed nice too. She wondered if she was his wife and felt inside her an odd little pang. Everyone seemed to have someone, apart from her. Except, of course, for Ashley, waiting obediently outside.

There was the faintest sound in the corner and Tonya nudged Rusty forward. Despite the cathedral-like atmosphere, she spoke in a normal voice.

"Up there," she said, pointing, and they could just make out the outline of a ladder. They moved cautiously across the shaky wooden floor and Rusty peered hopelessly up into the dense blackness, his match inadequate with so little light. Again something landed on Cherie's face and this time Tonya felt it too; it seemed to be dropping from above. Cherie brushed her hand across her face and it came away sticky and salt-tasting. With a gasp of intuitive horror, she backed towards the door and the light and held up her hand in the last rays of the sun. It was blood.

Rusty was quite amazing and took charge right away. They had to get help, he told them, and adequate light with which to explore. It might be nothing, but then it might; there was still no sign of Isabelle and that did seem odd. Cherie, despite her nausea, liked his calm air of control. This was what a man ought to be, not some futile layabout like the youths she knew back home.

"Go across to the house," he told them, "and send the men back here. I'll stick around in case something happens, but tell them to be as quick as they can."

He looked a little like the photographs in Clemency's albums, of Cherie's father at approximately the same age, keen-eyed and fearless, a bit of a hero really. Roland, Thomas and Charlie had much the same look, but secretly Cherie preferred her own dad and guessed he had been the best of the bunch. Regardless of what Aunts Rita and Irene might say. It wasn't his fault if women had fancied him. She had a secret passion herself for Leonardo DiCaprio and drifted off to sleep quite often, dreaming of what might be. Rusty had the looks of an action man, clean-cut and positive yet with a gentle smile.

"Run now," he said, giving Ashley a little pat on the head. "And don't forget to bring back a flashlight."

Isabelle's throat had been slashed from ear to ear so that the corpse in the hayloft greeted them with the parody of a grin. Élodie leaned against Clemency in the light of the hurricane lamps, pressing her handkerchief to her mouth.

"I can't believe this is happening," she said. The night-mare grew worse by the minute.

Blood was everywhere, soaking into the hay, and Isabelle's T-shirt had been ripped right off her, revealing one voluptuous breast dangling by only a ribbon of flesh.

"Oh God!" Élodie turned away in anguish. Luckily the children were safely out of the way. "How could anyone have done that to her?" And why conceivably would they want to?

Clemency took her arm and drew her close. She was shaking like a leaf herself and almost out of control. Rusty, Harry and Ethan held their lamps and Rusty poked around in the hay to see what he could find.

"Careful, now," said Harry sensibly. "Don't disturb the evidence. The police will want to see it."

Isabelle had been hiding, Piers explained, and they hadn't found her by the time they had run away. Someone had come, he said, confirming Ashley's story. They hadn't seen him properly, but he'd shouted and warned them off.

"He was wearing dirty overalls," said Camilla, "with dark glasses and a hat."

Harry turned to Rusty and shrugged. Could be any of the farmworkers; the vineyards were teeming with them. At this time of year there was a sudden annual invasion. They came from miles around to help with the grape harvesting, Spaniards, Algerians, Catalans, the lot.

"And they'd all carry knives," said Harry. "Which makes everyone equally suspect."

The gendarmes gave Isabelle's body a cursory inspection, then, after a rapid conference, carried it ceremoniously into the front parlour and placed it on the table.

"They can't do that," gasped Madeleine in horror, but that, apparently, was the local custom. They remained obdurate despite her objections; it was Mémé's house, not theirs, and the gendarmes were in charge. Obviously a police pathologist would have to do his grisly job, but not yet. It was late, it was dark and the gendarmes were going home. They had placed her in a makeshift coffin and this they draped with a blanket. No one was to go in there, they ordered, though they couldn't lock the room because the key appeared to be missing.

"I can't believe this is happening," groaned Élodie again, slumped in the kitchen by the warmth of the stove.

The parlour shutters were closed and barred, but Clemency lit candles and placed them around the coffin. She couldn't bear to think of poor Isabelle lying there all alone in the dark. How scared she must have been and how horrendously butchered. Clemency had only glimpsed her injuries but knew she would never be able to get them out of her mind. Somewhere out there in the creeping darkness a maniac was hovering, waiting to strike again. Mémé's murder was bad enough, but this one was unimaginable.

Food was out of the question. "Let's try to get some rest," she said. They banked up the fire in the small, curtained chamber, the one cozy spot in the house. There they all snuggled, their heads on each other's shoulders, for the long, dismal vigil until daylight returned.

30

*T*he addition to their numbers of the two New Zealanders actually turned out to be something of a plus. Rusty had quickly asserted his quiet authority while Tonya was proving a wizard about the house, scrubbing

257

floors, sweeping away spiders' webs, cheerfully setting about the chores none of the others could face. She wasn't his wife, they quickly established that, just a longtime girl-friend accompanying him on his travels. Cherie was relieved, though she wasn't quite certain why. Tonya was so friendly and unassuming it was impossible not to like her.

They were all so shell-shocked they stuck together in a pack. No one could face the grisly reminder of the horror that lay just behind the parlour door. Before they departed, the gendarmes had discovered that the lock to Mémé's writing desk was smashed. Someone had forced the drawer open, though for no apparent reason, especially since the rest of the room appeared untouched. The barn had been declared out of bounds and, at first light, a group of gen-darmes had returned and roped off the whole area while they searched for vital evidence.

"No point hanging around here," said Clemency, trying hard not to think about poor Isabelle's bloodied corpse. "We might as well go off on an expedition." Anything to get them out of the house and take their minds off it all. The children were grieving for Isabelle, whom they had lately grown to love. They hadn't been told any of the gory details, simply that she'd had a dreadful accident which was cer-tainly not the fault of any one of them. What Clemency would have preferred was to have taken them all back to England right away, but departure was out of the question until the local police gave permission. They had impounded their passports as it was, which was making Harry seethe with rage and impotent frustration.

Cherie, entirely unnerved, clung to the company of her newfound sibling and followed him around like a trusting little dog. Rusty smiled benignly and encouraged this desperate bonding. He found his waiflike half sister incredibly touching and saw through her streetwise toughness at a glance. He was excellent with Ashley too, kind and patient and endlessly accessible, ready with a bear hug or piggyback when it was needed.

"He'll make a wonderful father," commented Clemency, and saw the quick flash of endorsement in Tonya's eyes.

Collioure was their place of choice, a small, picturesque fishing village on the coast, just two hours' fast drive down the motorway and close to the Spanish frontier. Rusty drove the Range Rover and everyone but Madeleine climbed aboard. Harry and Ethan preferred to stay at the house, which was just as well as far as the women were concerned. Harry was growing so edgy, he was an irritant to have around, while Ethan wandered off on his own, sunk in a miasma of agonized despair. Clemency, watching him, could think of no way to help ease his obvious suffering. It was something he would just have to work through on his own.

"Who's going to ride with me?" asked Madeleine as she opened the door of the Porsche. But today, unusually, none of them was in the mood for a thrilling ride but preferred to cram in together for solid creature comfort.

"We'll see you there," said Rusty. He would have liked to race her but knew he didn't stand a chance against her more powerful engine. Clemency, who had been there as a child, suggested they meet up at noon in the chapel right on the water's edge. It was quite a famous tourist spot, impossible to miss. Madeleine, as it happened, was content to travel alone; the past few days had been so horrific she needed the space to think. A fast drive in her supercharged car with cool jazz blaring was what she craved most.

She reached Collioure by a quarter past eleven, well ahead of the Range Rover, as she had known she would. It was a bright autumn morning with the leaves just turning color and she locked the car in the center of town, where its scarlet sleekness stood out flamboyantly, and went for a leisurely stroll. Artists with easels were dotted along the seafront and she leaned on the wall to drink in the salt air. She found herself, inevitably, thinking about her grandmother, whose sad little slaughtered body they had watched being raised from the earth. This was definitely her sort of place; Picasso, Dufy and Matisse had all lived and painted here in their time. They had famously clustered at the Café Les Templiers, which still proudly held their signatures in its visitors' book. Mémé would surely have loved those inspiring connections. She had probably come here as a younger woman to soak in the atmosphere and paint the immortalized *caiques,* the brightly colored anchovy boats.

What possibly could have compelled a sparky, intelligent woman like that to make such a dramatic life change and abandon her husband and children so completely? Small wonder poor Ethan was so obviously upset. After years of solitary brooding, he had finally made his decision and traveled all this way to confront the mother he had lost. Only to find himself doubly bereft with his questions still unanswered. Mémé's mysterious motivation would now go with her to the grave.

She found the chapel easily, right there on the harbour wall, and since she had so much time on her hands, went inside to explore. It was a quite incredible interior, a former lighthouse with rounded walls and a steeply arched dome. It was dark and womblike with a powerful smell of incense and lit by a sea of sputtering candles. The wall facing the door was dominated by a vast and intricate gold altarpiece, which could only be viewed in its full splendour by the insertion of a two-franc piece into a modern slot machine. French pragmatism at its least attractive; Madeleine could think of nowhere in England she had encountered commercialism like this. She snorted at the tawdriness of the church but scrabbled in her purse nonetheless and made the obligatory contribution. The coin should allow her about two minutes' viewing time, but she had more in hand, should that turn out to be necessary.

The result was simply staggering. The entire altarpiece lit up like a stage set, allowing her to examine at leisure the artistry of a bygone age. She was stunned and thrilled to be here viewing it, especially alone, which greatly enhanced the aesthetic impact. She was glad she had driven on ahead; some moments were designated not to be shared.

So engrossed was she in her careful study that she only barely heard footsteps approaching from behind. Until he spoke close to her ear, when she practically jumped out of her skin.

"Madeleine? Can that really be you? How utterly wonderful to find you here."

Dominic; it could be no other. His voice had echoed in her dreams often enough. She turned to face him warily and found him standing right up close, fully at his ease in a blazer and open-necked shirt, tanned and relaxed and smiling all over his face.

"I thought I spotted your car in the square," he confessed. "So it was short work tracking you down to the obvious tourist spot."

He looked adorable, she couldn't help admitting, and the smile he beamed at her was warm in the extreme. Madeleine melted. Just when her heart was at its bleakest, along came Dominic to swamp her once more in his magic. She felt so suddenly vulnerable, she longed to fall into his arms. After all she'd been through in the past couple of days, she was as weak as a baby, all resilience gone. If he only knew how much she desired him, but she felt compelled to maintain her frosty image.

"All alone, are you?" he asked as he fed in another coin. Madeleine nodded. His presence so close did something vital to her hormones; she hesitated to speak in case he heard the tremor in her voice.

He looked at her shrewdly as though he detected some of this. He stood beside her at the altar rail and his hand, apparently accidentally, brushed hers.

"Once you're through here," he said in an intimate tone, "we'll go off somewhere together, just the two of us, and have that long talk I've been wanting for some time."

She felt on the verge of swooning; he could have taken her on the spot.

"I can't tell you how much I have longed for this moment," he said, stroking her hand quite openly and sending a thrill of anticipation down her spine. But right at that very moment the lights went out abruptly and they were plunged into shocking darkness.

Rusty elaborated on the journey down and Cherie leaned

forward in her seat to soak up all he was saying. He had been barely crawling when his father walked out, but that had been Tom's pattern throughout his life. The chase had always been what turned him on. Once a conquest was made, he would callously walk away. It wasn't his fault, was the family opinion, just something he seemed to have got genetically, not improved by his mother's abandonment. Like his sister Patrice, he had spent his adult life in the relentless search for love.

"First there was Pandora," Rusty explained. "From what I gather, she was the one who did most of the chasing, though he wasn't her first choice, not even close."

Cherie remembered the family albums and the miniskirted Pandora, with those great goopy cow eyes, gazing up at Roland as if she would like to devour him.

"Roland always had that effect. Mesmeric was how my dad described him." Despite the early desertion, Tom had always remained in touch. No matter what his morals might have been, he had been good and caring at heart. Just easygoing and feckless without his mother to rein him in.

"She would have had Charlie after Roland died, but he craftily evaded her by buggering off to Canada. So Dad was actually only her third choice and even then he was several years younger. There was no stopping Pandora once she set her heart on something. And for some strange reason that she never explained, she had her heart set on becoming an Annesley."

Pandora had had two sons of her own, Robert and Tommy Junior, whom Cherie had yet to meet. More half brothers she hadn't known existed. The family grew more complex by the minute, yet it gave her a strange, warm glow inside.

Ashley might not have a father, but all of a sudden he'd acquired a whole clutch of uncles. She drew him closer and kissed his glossy head; some good, after all, was to come out of this nightmare experience.

"Your mother, Betty, was the barmaid at his local." Rusty glanced back at her in the mirror in case he was divulging something she might not know. But it was old news to Cherie; her aunts had done their poisonous work well.

"From all accounts—well, from what my ma could discover—the union was a happy one. Might even have lasted if it hadn't been for the accident. They were kindred spirits and seemed to rub along well."

Clemency glanced at Cherie in alarm to see how she was taking all this. But Cherie sat enthralled as a child, her chin resting in her hands and her dark, fringed eyes fixed obsessively on her brother's head.

"By then, of course, Ma had lugged me off to Auckland. To start a new life away from the bastard, Tom. But Grandma kept in touch, with sporadic letters. She had a strong feeling of family even though she had ended up abandoning them. Strange, that, don't you think? What a creature of extremes she must have been. I only wish I'd had the chance to know her." No one in the car could argue with that.

They were drawing closer to Collioure and the traffic began to thicken. Clemency glanced at her watch; they needed to get a move on if they were to catch up with Madeleine on time.

Behind them, at the front of the chapel, the candles still fluttered in the draft from the curtained door, but the sudden withdrawal of bright illumination left Madeleine momentarily blinded. Dominic's hand closed firmly on hers and she felt his warm lips on her neck.

"I can't tell you how long I've been waiting for this moment," he murmured while his fingers caressed her throat, and the smell of his cologne, imbued with sheer animal maleness, left her weak with enchantment, entirely unable to resist him. She leaned instinctively against his chest and felt his arms close around her.

Sudden urgently running feet interrupted their electric reverie and a shrill voice shouted, "Madeleine, are you there?"

Bright light flooded the altarpiece once more as a two-franc coin was dropped into the slot, and there stood Piers and Camilla, triumphant, having raced the others, who were still parking the car. Madeleine got a grip on herself and turned back to her companion. But there was no longer any sign of Dominic, who appeared to have vanished completely.

"He was definitely there," protested Madeleine. "I was talking to him." *And he was about to kiss me,* though she didn't add that. They all stood around her in the sunshine outside and Madeleine looked in vain for any glimpse of Dominic. Élodie, she was aware, was eyeing her with an element of ice, but she couldn't help that. What had happened, had happened; that was all there was to it.

"What's he doing here?" Clemency wanted to know. "Did he tell you that?"

He hadn't said a word, not about factual matters. Madeleine was hard put to explain their dialogue at all.

"He spotted my car in the square and tracked me down.

That's all I know. Where he's staying or why he's even here, I really can't tell you. We didn't get as far as that. He was only there a few minutes."

So why had he disappeared so abruptly? It made no sense. But then, nothing Dominic did seemed to these days. He made a practice of being mysterious, part of his stock-in-trade. Maybe a pose, but who could tell? She still didn't know what he did for a living apart from being some sort of academic.

"Did you tell him about Isabelle?" demanded Clemency. God, no, how awful, nor about Mémé either. Whatever would he think when he came to find out? Madeleine was consumed with shame, but it had all been so sudden and she had been caught off guard. But try telling that to the cousins, particularly Élodie, who was still beady-eyed.

"Well, he can't just have vanished." They all looked around. "We should be able to spot his car in a place as small as this."

"What was he driving?"

"I'm afraid I didn't see." It was dark, it was sudden; they were alone in the chapel. And her head was still reeling from the fallout of his caresses.

"Maybe he's still in there," said practical Rusty. But they decided not to search for him, since he'd exited so abruptly. Who knew what he was up to and, when all was said and done, who cared?

"Whatever he's playing at, he must have his reasons."

"And will doubtless show up," said Clemency. "Perhaps when we get home."

Back in the Range Rover, on the long drive to Mas des Vignes, Tonya took over the driving while Rusty continued,

266

for Cherie's benefit, with his abridged family history. The children were sleepy and Clemency was content just to relax and listen. Two shocking deaths had drained them all of energy. It was a relief to close her eyes and hear the comforting twang of his soft New Zealand accent.

"We got the photo, of course," he was saying. "Guess Gran must have sent it from France."

"What photo?"

"Of the wedding."

"What wedding?"

"What do you mean, what wedding? Your parents' wedding, Dad's and Betty's."

Cherie sat up abruptly and Clemency shot awake.

"They were married?"

"Well, of course. Surely you knew that. They were killed when the car hit a lorry and turned over. On the way from the reception in the pub."

Cherie couldn't believe what she'd just heard. Then how come no one had told her before? Even the aunts appeared not to know; they couldn't be so mean-spirited they'd deprive her of information as dynamite as that.

"Probably they didn't know," said Rusty. "There were no wedding guests, just the witnesses, and the registry office took an official photograph, which eventually was sent to Gran."

He noticed Clemency's inquiring stare. "Apparently Dad had her listed as his next of kin. All those ex-wives and abandoned children; it must have been simpler."

"And Mémé sent a copy to your mother?"

Rusty nodded. "To me, as his son."

Cherie was silently reeling. All these years she had

thought herself a bastard, and now she found she was an Annesley through and through. To hell with Harry with his patronizing superiority. She was as entitled as he was to her share of Mémé's legacy. Her blood was every bit as good as his. She pulled the drowsy Ashley closer into her lap and covered him with kisses to prevent them from seeing her tears.

31

*H*arry was methodically ransacking Mémé's house. While Ethan hovered ineffectually in the doorway, he was wrenching out drawers and emptying their contents on the floor.

"Careful how you go." Ethan was offended. This, after all, was his mother's home, and these her personal things; although he was equally fascinated, he felt that Harry might show a little respect. Apart from which, the police would be keeping a check. They hadn't by any means finished with the murder inquiry, and until they had come up with at least one definite suspect, each of them must be equally under surveillance.

But Harry felt far too distracted for niceties like that. He had hung around quite long enough; now pure, blind panic was beginning to make him reckless. He couldn't leave as he'd planned to do because they had confiscated his papers, but the longer he remained here, the more trapped he felt. And the more all logical thinking was fast going out of the window. Any second now Lavender and the English authorities were likely to be breathing down his neck and summoning him back. It was vital he get safely away now and across the Spanish border before they caught up with him.

Mémé had written to let them know how she planned to dispose of her property, but the crucial question was whether or not she had actually drawn up a will. And signed it. And even though the girls had been promised her personal possessions, there was still no clue as to who was to get the house and its extensive land, by far the most valuable asset she could have. Harry still had hopes, perhaps deluded, that he—as the first of the grandchildren—might get the lot. It seemed only fair and who else could be more deserving? The older generation were all well set up and lived overseas, apart from Ethan, and he was such a wimp.

The real question was, if the will existed at all, where was it most likely to be stashed? Safely with her lawyers in Toulouse or somewhere here in the house, which he felt on the whole was more probable. He remembered his difficult exchange with the stuffy old gentleman who handled the family affairs and the chilly brush-off when he'd phoned to make inquiries. News of her death must surely have reached them by now; it had, after all, been widely reported in the papers. Any lawyer on his mettle would have appeared on the spot with the relevant papers in his hand. Or would he? Perhaps there was a plot to protect her from herself. Or maybe she had continued to defer the necessary legal work. Desperation was making Harry greedy; he moved through the grim, forbidding house with all the fervour of a professional thief.

"What are you actually looking for?" asked Ethan. It was reasonable to suppose that, if she had died intestate, her estate would go automatically to her living children. As a matter of course according to English law, though he was not even remotely mercenary himself. There was no way of telling, however, how these legal matters stood in France; he wished now he had allowed Emily to accompany him on this trip. Her calm self-assertion would have stood him in good stead just when he needed it most. Harry was insufferable, but then, he always had been. All Ethan really needed now, to add to his impotent misery, was Harry's youthful partner in crime to show up, the cocky and overconfident Dominic Carlisle. And from what he'd heard in the past few days, even that was not an impossibility.

But even Harry alone, intent on pursuing his inheritance, was unstoppable. Drawer after drawer was wrenched from its socket and stockings and old letters and pieces of antique lace went flying in all directions. Not to mention the dust and various startled creeping creatures, unused to such activity.

Now, just you pick that all up, Ethan longed to tell him, but instead went meekly along behind the maelstrom, restoring the scattered knicknacks as far as he could. Wait till Clemency returned, she'd soon put a flea in Harry's ear. But it was typical of Harry and his type to wait until the dominant female was safely off the scene before wreaking their selfish havoc. Dim memories of his own confused childhood emerged occasionally to remind Ethan of how things once were, when Eunice was in charge and Mémé already a thing of the past.

Harry had finished with Mémé's bedroom, with its heavy crocheted bedspread and camphor-scented drawers that contained only linens and basic country dweller's underwear, a far cry presumably from the chic little Frenchwoman who had, more than sixty years before, fatally captured his grandfather's heart. There were family photographs grouped on the dresser, and a Bible and magnifying glass laid touchingly by the bed. A carved sandalwood box contained hairpins and pieces of jewelry, and a bowl and pitcher completed the traditional interior. Mémé had evidently lived a monastic life.

Ethan was uncomfortable. He hated to watch Harry, with uncaring hands, roughly push through her few hanging dresses and check the contents of her hatbox and valise. Yet still he could not tear himself away, feasting his eyes on a life he had never seen firsthand, a detailed museum of his mother's unknown life. It made no sense, but then it never had. He fingered the glass of a framed iridescent butterfly and longed for the sound of returning wheels outside.

Harry's nose was twitching like a bloodhound's on the scent. He had worked his way through all the six bedrooms and lingered over the paintings in the studio. They had both stopped, startled by the authoritative face of Cornelius, then Harry had dropped the cloth back into place and continued his relentless search. It had taken most of the afternoon and now the light was beginning to fade.

Right at the end of the corridor, a heavy carved cabinet blocked their way.

"Is there another room behind that, do you suppose?" asked Harry, eyeing it speculatively.

"Shouldn't imagine so. Why would anyone want to block it up?"

Harry peered around the piece of furniture and exclaimed in triumph as he identified a door.

"There is a room. Well, a door, at least. Help me shift this and we'll see what's behind it."

But Ethan had had enough. He was tired of watching this scavenging son-of-a-bitch working his way through his grandmother's house before she was even in her grave.

"Leave it," he said curtly. "You've done enough damage already." And watched while Harry stomped away, angry at being thwarted.

Without a word, he thumped down the stairs, a nervous Ethan trailing in his wake. They had done the kitchen and also the dining room and now there was only the parlour left. Harry thoughtfully glanced at the firmly closed door and Ethan convulsively clutched at his arm. He wouldn't dare!

"No way."

"Why not?"

That was where Mémé kept her writing desk; that, now he came to think of it, was the obvious hiding place. But Ethan was clinging to him like a limpet and Harry had trouble shaking him off.

"You can't go in there."

"Try stopping me."

"Isabelle's in there."

"Well, she's hardly going to mind."

He wasn't as brave as he liked to pretend but was damned if he was going to let Ethan see that. She was in a box and covered with a blanket; what harm could it do if he poked around a little? Preferably now, while the coast was clear. Once the idea had occurred to him, he was pretty certain that that was where he'd find the will. It was only logical.

"You can stay out here, old chap, if that's the way you feel," said Harry. Then turned the knob and strode into the room.

Clemency's candles had long since burned down and the room was pitch-black, as the windows were shuttered and barred. There was a strange, sweet scent in the air that Harry preferred not to think about. He was about to go in search of a hurricane lamp, then remembered they'd left them all in the barn. He'd just have to make do with the ancient gas flares, though the flickering of their strange sepulchral white light always made him a little queasy. Secretly he was glad that Ethan was still with him, even if he had apparently lost his nerve.

"Come on, get on with it and help me case this room. As soon as we're through, we'll knock off and have a drink."

Isabelle's coffin sat squarely on the table which acted as a makeshift catafalque. Someone, probably Clemency, had placed beside it an earthenware jug of freshly picked wild-flowers and the wax from the burnt-out candles lay pooled at each of the corners.

"Leave her in peace." Ethan's tone was sharp, but Harry, having come this far, had no intention of backing off now. Isabelle, the unworldly, was the last person to mind. A new kind of insanity gripped him. He'd started the job and so had to finish.

There was no point examining the writing desk, though Harry did give it a cursory glance. Whoever had forced the lock must have been looking pretty desperately for some-thing; he now had a nasty suspicion it was for the will. If another person was also on the trail, then the whole damned thing became instantly more urgent. There was always the chance that he was already too late, but he thrust that thought from his mind. He wondered who else could be involved; in all probability her murderer. Even though the police still had this cockamamy theory that her death had just been a random killing by the so-called "Provence Predator."

"If you wanted to hide something away from prying eyes, where would you put it?" asked Harry. "To be really safe."

"The fridge?" suggested Ethan, who had found himself inevitably drawn in. But there wasn't one in this ancient house. "But why should she want to hide it?"

Harry shook his head. He couldn't figure out the answer either, but something had clearly gone badly wrong, leading eventually to his grandmother's brutal killing. Who was likely to be in it as deep as he was; who else could share his frenzied motivation? Only another relative, and most of them were now accounted for. The gaslight sent shadows flickering about the room. He tried to avoid looking at the coffin, but his eyes, inevitably, were drawn to it like a magnet. For one blood-chilling moment, he fancied he saw the blanket twitch, but it must have been only the flicker of gaslight combined with a fertile imagination.

"Let's get on with it."

There were rows of dusty books in a glass-fronted cabinet and these Harry now went through meticulously, taking out each one in turn and riffling through its pages. It was clear from the dust and the musty smell that no one had looked at them in ages. Fastidious Ethan wrinkled his nose. They were all in French and the paper was thin and yellowed. A throwback to his mother's parents before her; sometime when he felt up to it he might bring Emily here to look them over. Though, the way he felt now, he doubted he could ever face setting foot again in this hateful, doomed house.

The books seemed to be leading nowhere, so Harry shoved them back untidily and turned his attention to the rest of the room. There were large, gloomy paintings on each of the walls, undistinguished oils without Mémé's light touch; Harry dismissed them as being irrelevant, more things left over from an earlier age. What he was after he hoped would prove to be far more valuable. The deeds to the house and its surrounding acres. Best of all, a legal will leaving everything irrevocably to him.

Directly behind the coffin, on an armoire set against the wall, were rows of old photographs in tarnished silver frames. Harry began to edge his way towards them, but a horrified Ethan stuck out an arm to stop him.

"Leave them alone; they are far too close," he said.

Harry brushed his uncle aside, then gave him a withering stare. At moments like this he resembled Cornelius, the same sardonic expression and lacerating tongue.

"Pull yourself together, man," he said with contempt. "What possible difference can it make to her now? She's dead."

He leaned one hand on the corner of the coffin in order to reach the nearest of the faded family groups, then moved closer to the gas bracket to get a better look. Despite himself, Ethan went too and the two of them stood there, in the ghoulish flickering light, looking back in time to an earlier, happier age.

"They all seemed to wear white all the time," said Harry.

"Well, they had loads of servants. And it was always summer."

Packing himself gradually into the space behind the coffin, Harry worked slowly through the photographs, studying each one minutely. He wasn't sure what he was hoping to find but was caught, as always, by the handsomeness and poise of his immediate ancestors. There were several more recent portraits and these were the ones he lingered over. Clemency and her gang of kids, Élodie's graduation And then a professional black-and-white shot, mounted ornately on silver-embossed card, of a beaming couple signing a register.

"Who's that?"

"My older brother Tommy."

"With Sylvia? Surely not Pandora."

"No," said Ethan thoughtfully, scratching his chin. "I guess it must be Betty Cole, the third one. I did hear a rumour that they'd actually got spliced, though it's the first time I've ever seen that picture."

"You mean Cherie's mother?" Harry was shocked. He leaned back against the table without realizing what he was doing and only pulled himself together when he felt the coffin rock. How could it be that this vital piece of family gossip had evaded him so entirely? He found himself positively shaking as the implications sank in.

"Purely academic, of course. They were killed that same day on the way back from the boozer. Hand in hand as newlyweds to that great saloon bar in the sky."

It mattered, though, and Harry was oddly shaken. If Cherie's parents had married after all, then she was automatically legitimized. Which gave her equal rights with the rest of Mémé's grandchildren and made her another possible contender to the will. He moved on mindlessly down the rest of the row of photographs and found the one of the family grouped on the lawn. He was rapidly losing it but refused to quit. He wondered what other secrets his grand-mother had concealed and if there were more unsuspected heirs about to pop up out of the woodwork. This frame was larger and heavier than the rest and there were smaller snap-shots slotted in on top, of Agnes at the height of her regal beauty, of Tom and Charlie in tennis whites, and a small one of a seraphically smiling Roland.

Ethan had had enough. He was acutely aware of the corpse on the table, just inches away from Harry's elbow, and was scared she might suddenly sit up. He had heard such stories though wasn't sure he believed them.

"Let's get out of here," he hissed. Even the gloomy kitchen and cavernous hall were preferable to this claustro-phobic room from which all life had been long since sucked.

"Wait a minute." The larger photograph was slightly smaller than its frame and Harry could detect a scrap of paper just visible behind it. He turned the frame over and scrabbled at its fastenings. Ethan jolted his elbow, but he shoved him away impatiently. Then Ethan attacked him in sudden rage, catching Harry off balance and causing him to drop the photograph. Both lost their balance and stumbled against the table; there was the startling tinkle of shattering earthenware and the flowers flew everywhere, followed by the ominous drag of sliding wood as Isabelle's coffin crashed slowly to the floor.

With a great gasp of horror, Ethan shot out of the room, but Harry remained there on the spot, transfixed. Isabelle could wait, she was not going anywhere, but in the struggle, the ancient photo frame had sprung apart and a piece of folded paper had fluttered to the ground. He bent to retrieve it and squinted to read the faded handwriting. It wasn't the will but something a lot more intriguing.

Harry lit a candle and stood there, by the fallen coffin, studying the tattered document in his hand. The ink had faded and the handwriting was barely legible, but slowly, word by word, he managed to decipher what it said. And that drove all thoughts of the will right out of his head. For what he held was a birth certificate that appalled and delighted him both at the same time and made his eyes practically bolt from his head.

32

*T*omorrow would be September the ninth, Mémé's actual birthday, and Clemency was wondering how they should observe it. All family members had now been informed of her death and been asked not to come because of the police investigation. Though little appeared to be happening on that front. The gendarmes were still out there in the barn with a large section of the garden taped off and much coming and going on the part of the forensic team.

But perhaps it would be respectful and right if they were to celebrate, quietly on their own, the passing of their distinguished grandmother on what should have been her eightieth birthday. Clemency stood there at the stove, making bouillabaisse just for something to do, slowly stirring the thick, fragrant stock to which she would later add fresh chopped fish. Everyone else was huddled around the fire, sick with anguish, trying hard not to think of Isabelle. The children were busy with a jigsaw and Ethan was scrunched up in the corner, trying to read an old French book by the light of a single flickering candle.

Harry was acting more oddly than ever, pacing the great hall with a slow, measured tread, grinning and muttering to himself in turn and casting meaningful glances which his cousins had stopped trying to decipher.

"He's bonkers," said Madeleine, joining Clemency in the kitchen. "I always suspected it; now I know for sure."

Clemency laughed, her reverie disturbed. The terrifying incident of Isabelle's fallen coffin was still uppermost in her mind; she was thankful to have had the calm support of Madeleine and Élodie. What a nightmare this would have been without their solid good sense. Teddy had been rock-like when she'd called, had offered to drop everything and fly straight down, but there seemed little point with so many of them there already and she hoped they would all be given leave to get away soon. Cherie was enchanted with her newly found lost brother, and Ashley, unusually, appeared less shaken than the other children. Tonya was quietly doing sterling work; it turned out she was an infant teacher back home, good at organizing games and keeping their minds off reality. Which was just as well, considering all that had happened.

They had got back to the house the night before to find chaos reigning and Harry in a weird, wild mood. The parlour door was wide open, with all the gas brackets flaring brightly and, horror of horrors, Isabelle's coffin upended on the floor. The blanket had come adrift and the lid, which was not screwed down, was half off. Harry was no use at all, off on some flight of fancy of his own, and Ethan had taken to his room with a nervous headache. Rusty had dropped them off, then driven back to the village for fresh bread, so it was the women, as usual, who had had to cope once Tonya had herded the children away to help light the fire. They had raised the coffin bodily, the four of them, and clamped the lid back shut. Though not before Clemency had caught a sickening glimpse of what lay inside and been shaken to see the patches of rusty blood that had soaked through the makeshift winding sheet.

"What do you suppose is really going on?" Madeleine fetched them each a glass and opened a bottle of the local wine. "Do you think it's the work of a rabid mass murderer or someone far saner, methodically bumping us all off?" Put that baldly, it was even more alarming. Clemency pondered as she went on stirring the stew.

"I don't know." Although the famed "Provence Predator" had been active in France for years now, there was too high a percentage of slaughtered Annesleys for it possibly to be just a coincidence. After all, Martha and Effie had been murdered in Jersey and Pandora on a golf course in Spain.

"Of course, there are also the ones we don't yet know about," said Madeleine thoughtfully, picking up on her mood. "Cherie's parents, for instance. What of them?"

Clemency stared at her. This was getting truly ghoulish.

"You surely can't be serious," she protested. "That was just a random car crash with both of them reportedly drunk. You can't believe there could be any sort of a connection?"

"Maybe, maybe not. But it all needs looking into, don't you think? These murders appear to be getting more frequent. Almost as though someone is closing in."

Clemency shuddered. The thought made her blood run cold.

"Don't say that, that's awful!" she said, truly shocked. "Do you think we ought to tell the police? Or will that simply muddy the waters still further?" She was longing to get away from this place and go home; remove the children from the unhealthy atmosphere of violent death and return to face up to Teddy and their personal problems. She felt strong enough for that now. Nothing that had happened in the security of their marriage could begin to match up in dreadfulness with what was going on here. Against this background of carnage and horror, a small domestic hiccup should be easily sorted out. But Madeleine didn't know about that, whatever she might suspect, and Clemency was not in a mood to discuss it now.

"What I'd like to know," said Madeleine, both elbows on the table, "is, if it isn't random, and I cannot believe that it is, what sort of motive can this killer possibly have? To hunt down our relatives so relentlessly and kill them all off in cold blood?"

"And over a period of years," mused Clemency, rinsing the fish. She crossed to the knife rack suspended above the sink and selected a heavy chopper with a lethal edge.

"Careful with that," muttered Madeleine, inching away. "We don't want more bloodshed than is absolutely necessary. And keep it away from Harry," she added with a nervous laugh.

What about Harry? There he went, pacing back and forth, his footsteps clearly audible, occasionally pausing and letting out a manic chuckle. The two women glanced at each other in mock alarm, then Madeleine briskly refilled their glasses while Clemency attacked the fish. And what, now they were on to it, about the strangely elusive Dominic? His recent unscheduled appearance in Collioure had disturbed

Madeleine far more than she cared to admit. She longed for him to return and bring everything out into the open. Even if it was not to have a satisfactory ending, she would rather know now than later. Also, where he stood with Élodie, who still seemed to carry a proprietorial attitude towards him.

"It's this house," said Clemency eventually, carefully splitting a wicked-looking rascasse. "It is creepy and unsettled, unraveling at the edges. I am sure it's affecting us all in some subtle way."

"Please don't say that. Not while you've still got that weapon in your hand."

Élodie stuck her head around the door.

"Why all the hilarity? What are we missing?" She spotted the opened bottle and fetched herself a glass.

"Come on, spill the beans," she said, pulling up a chair.

Madeleine outlined the course of their discussion and Élodie nodded thoughtfully and gave it her gravest consideration.

"A family killer. Well, that's a novel idea. In which case we'd better barricade the doors tonight and make sure all the shutters are firmly bolted."

"Please!" said Clemency. "You're making me quite scared." And with one hefty swipe, she brought down her chopper and savagely beheaded a sea bass.

Drinks on the terrace followed by late lunch under the vines; that seemed most suitable for a quiet family celebration of the actual birthday. Low-key and tasteful; something to take their minds off it all. Time to get out the photograph albums again and look at them quietly with Rusty and Tonya, who had brought a selection of their own. Time for reminiscence and some of the age-old stories. This was what a family gathering should be and they'd all of them journeyed a long way to get together.

"You can make the speech," Clemency directed Ethan. As he was the only member present of the older generation, she felt that was appropriate and would give the poor man something constructive to do. Soon, presumably, they'd be allowed to bury Mémé; at present her sad little corpse lingered in the police morgue.

Isabelle's body was still there in the house, though, a looming presence in the parlour where Clemency industriously lit the candles and replaced the flowers each morning. Teddy had got through to Canada on the phone and broken the news to the parents, but neither seemed inclined or able to make the journey over to France. The mother sounded distant and distraught; not entirely sober, was Teddy's practiced guess. While Charlie was merely pathetic and had broken down on the line. His racking sobs were upsetting, but at least it was reassuring to know someone cared. He had lost both mother and daughter in a single shattering phone call, though how long Mémé had actually lain there in the earth, the gendarmes were not yet prepared to divulge.

"Did she suffer?" was mainly what Charlie wanted to know about Isabelle, and Teddy, lying, said he didn't think so. There was no point in adding to the poor man's obvious anguish; let him remember her as she had been and not as the brutally butchered corpse her cousins had had to view.

"She was always such an imaginative child, destined to go a long way." Charlie had been inordinately proud of her, with her prizes and degrees and the eventual move to elitist Oxford in the sanctified footsteps of her grandfather. Charlie had, of course, in reality lost his mother decades ago. Yet the actuality of her death had brought it all flooding back. On an impulse, after he'd finished with Teddy, he called both Aimée and Patrice in the States. Just talking to his sisters might prove to be some sort of solace. They had, after all, shared so much while they were growing up. He drew the line, though, at talking to Eunice.

September the ninth dawned a little shakily because of an ominously leaden sky. Lately the weather had been growing unsettled. Although it was still stiflingly hot, there was steady rumbling from threatening summer storms, inter-spersed with sporadic bursts of violent rain and hail. Clemency, waking early, pushed back the covers and climbed out of bed. On the unexpected arrival of Rusty and Tonya, she had taken the decision to move herself into Mémé's room. The forensic people had given the all-clear and she was careful not to disturb any of her grandmother's precious things. Somehow sleeping here seemed fitting; she had always been Mémé's favorite as a child.

She pushed open the unlatched French door on to the veranda and wandered outside barefoot. Across the miles of vines which were all she could see, the bruised sky was streaked with an ugly red, bad auspices for the celebration she was preparing. She planned that they should eat in the open air, under the trellis where the vines would provide some shelter. Nothing else in the house was stirring; everyone else slumbered on. Clemency pulled on a thin cotton robe and padded down quietly to the kitchen to set a pot of coffee brewing. There was a lot to get through; she would start at once.

Some way away, not far from the Pont du Gard, a heavy-duty army truck, bound for Marseilles, slowed down at a junction to allow a hitchhiker to dismount. There was very little traffic about; it was still pretty early. Even the grape pickers would not emerge for another hour. The solitary stranger, tall and forbiddingly gaunt and dressed from head to foot in sober black, reached inside for a single bag, raised one hand briefly in curt salute and strode away. It was a twenty-mile hike through fields to Mas des Vignes, but there was no hurry. The family reunion was not until today. Plenty of time for a leisurely stroll, with a great deal of remembering to do.

33

*T*he whole lot of them were out there in the courtyard, lounging around drinking pink champagne under the trellis to avoid the burning rays of the midday sun. The day, which had started out somberly, had revived itself in honour of Mémé's birthday and suddenly this was southern France at its mellow best, clear and golden and imbued with the scents of honeysuckle and lemon verbena; the late dog days of summer, a truly glorious time. The clamour of the crickets was positively deafening and the distant thrum of tractors in the vineyards came wafting to them over the breeze. Clemency, watching as she put finishing touches to the canapés, rejoiced to see them all out there together, laughing and getting along as smoothly as their parents' generation before them. This get-together, macabre though the circumstances might be, was turning out to be a good thing, a fitting tribute to the stubborn old lady who was the progenitor of them all.

"It's a shame we didn't think to bring the camcorder," she remarked. But Teddy always took care of things like that and they'd parted so explosively, it had not seemed much of a priority. She hadn't, in fact, given it a thought till now.

"I'm only surprised Harry hasn't produced one of his own," commented Élodie cynically, expertly spooning caviar onto gulls' eggs. "He must be constantly recording those terrible gifted brats of his. You'd think he'd never have one out of his hand. Wait till the next Christmas letter, it'll doubtless come in full color."

Clemency laughed. What had looked like a total disaster was turning out remarkably jolly, despite the continuing presence in the house of poor Isabelle's battered corpse. Blood relations were definitely best; they had all rallied around and managed to put the best face on things. Were connecting now as closely as if they'd been together all their lives. She thought of those old snapshots, with the Annesleys grouped on the lawn. In an odd, sad way and, against all expectations, this long-anticipated reunion was turning out to be an imprint of the past.

She carried a heavy tray out to the long table they had set up under the trellis while Élodie wandered off around the group, doing her stuff with a bottle. Ethan, looking unexpectedly revived, was standing in his shirtsleeves, skillfully slicing the turbot. The long white apron that Clemency had wrapped around him gave him the look of a genuine Frenchman and she saw him suddenly through different eyes, as a man of undiscovered dimension who cared only to reveal the surface. Just a few days of sunshine had taken the waxen pallor from his skin, and a jaunty beret, worn as a joke, covered the disastrous haircut and made him quite nice-looking. Ethan had potential after all. She patted him affectionately and he gave her a quick grin. She would like to get to know him better; had hopes of it in the future. The point of this sort of gathering was to cement what existed already and make up for lost time.

"*Ça va?*"

"*Très bien.*" He made a convincing chef. The eyes behind his battered spectacles were gleaming, his mastery with the kitchen utensils quite telling. The children, starving as seagulls, clamoured noisily around him and got in the way, but he smiled at them benevolently as he expertly sliced and served. For a useless bachelor, he was putting on quite a performance. Clemency was impressed.

"You can come and officiate at my house anytime," she said.

"I might just take you up on that."

Which brought her thoughts naturally to Dominic; she wondered where he had gone. If Madeleine had encountered him at Collioure, where had he been hiding himself since then? And if he had bothered to drive all this distance, how was it possible they'd seen neither hide nor hair of him since? It just wasn't natural. He always claimed to have business in France but was strangely evasive when it came to pinning him down. Exactly what his business was he never had explained. She had met him posing as a wine importer, yet he seemed to be a bona fide scientist at Oxford, while also showing an unusual interest in the family. These facts didn't add up unless something extra was staring them all in the face.

"Penny for them." Madeleine was watching her, seated unseen in an alcove of the boundary wall, shoes kicked off and skirt pulled up to display her shapely legs.

"I was wondering about Dominic," said Clemency baldly, and saw with satisfaction the start of emotion Madeleine tried so hard to hide.

"What of him?" Her ivory skin revealed just the faintest wash of color. Madeleine was blushing; well, whatever next?

"Where is he now? And why bother to come here at all? He wasn't invited, isn't a direct descendant. And how, come to think of it, did he get to know about the reunion in the first place?"

Madeleine shook her head. "Maybe he didn't." She was as confused and benighted as Clemency and the rest of the cousins. The more she knew of Dominic, the more she found he intrigued her, but she felt too vulnerable to be discussing that now. She always played her emotional cards close to her chest and was scared of revealing too much, even to Clemency.

"Have you thought of asking Élodie?" The sharpness returned to her tone. But Clemency, on this golden day, would not allow herself to be drawn.

"None of our business, really," Clemency said cheerfully. "Just wondered what was going on."

You and me both. Madeleine had thought about little else for days but wasn't about to divulge that now. Clemency was plenty nosy enough as it was. Let her wonder as she liked; Madeleine would remain mute. Though she couldn't forget the touch of his lips on her neck and shivered when she thought of what might have happened if only those bloody kids hadn't interrupted. She wondered when, if ever, he was likely to return. And what, in God's name, he was up to right now.

Tonya, as always, was playing with the children, and Rusty, patrolling the courtyard, was deep in discussion with Cherie. He had worked out how to get the fountain going and the refreshing tinkling of water into the stone basin made a restful counterpoint to the murmur of conversation. A fat, contented bee landed on Élodie's outstretched hand, but she was far too somnolent even to shake it off.

"Where's Harry?" No one had seen him for ages, but that, in truth, was something of a relief. Whatever had happened to him? Lately he seemed to have changed, he was less aggressive and more amenable, though his eyes occasionally still rolled wildly in his head and he had taken to muttering and laughing under his breath.

"Do you think he might be having some sort of breakdown?" Clemency, alert as ever, was strongly aware of his changing moods.

"Who can tell?" murmured Élodie, her eyes still firmly closed. "He has always struck me as slightly batty. I've told you that already."

They had carefully removed pages from the photo albums and mounted them on sheets of white card. Tonya had roped in the children to help her and the results were surprisingly professional. These were now neatly tacked to the cloister walls so that all could examine them at their leisure. It made an effective spontaneous exhibition; Clemency was proud.

They had no camcorder, but many had brought cameras.

"Come on, everyone," called Clemency when the sun was

at its highest. "Gather 'round and let's get some group shots." No point coming all this way and not recording it for posterity. She looked at her children with their healthy, glowing skin and wondered if they too might reconstruct this occasion sometime in the future. She hoped so. Families should certainly stick together.

Harry turned up eventually and they called him in for the photos. In a spotless shirt and well-pressed chinos, he was looking distinguished, an echo of Cornelius. His dark hair was greying in a most becoming way, almost as if he'd had it touched up. With vanity like his, Élodie had her suspicions, but she was feeling too relaxed to rile him about it now.

"Now, Harry, you take the center chair right there," bossed Clemency. "With Madeleine and Élodie each side of you." She secretly thought that that focal point belonged to her, but no one had suggested it and he was the oldest grandchild. Piers and Camilla were busy snapping with their Instamatics, but Clemency ordered them into line. Adults were grouped on chairs behind the table, with the little ones seated cross-legged on the grass. Cherie, aglow with happiness, stuck like a limpet to Rusty's side, though Tonya held back, since she wasn't officially a family member, and offered to do the honours with the camera. Rusty turned out to be a bit of an enthusiast and carried a rather impressive secondhand Pentax. They would get good pictures, something they all could share. Élodie went around again with the bottle to top up the festive feeling. Then Clemency noticed Ethan back at the makeshift bar, still wearing his ridiculous beret and skulking around the remains of the turbot. She hauled him over and seated him in the center, displacing

Harry by order of seniority, which gave her a small smug feeling of triumph.

"Smile now," said Tonya, kneeling by the fountain. "Say cheese and all keep your eyes on the birdie."

Ashley giggled and started to pull faces, but Cherie leaned over and tapped him sharply on the head. Hush now, these photographs would be important. Family feeling had finally overwhelmed her; she was both pleased and proud to be a part of such a group.

Dessert was served, a lavish confection of two sorts of chocolate and thick whipped cream, bought in the village and hidden away till today, and more of Teddy's excellent wine was uncorked so that few of the adults were feeling any pain.

"Speech!" shouted Harry, lighting a showy cigar. And Ethan, with a bit of prompting, shyly rose to his feet. For a man who preferred not to communicate, he turned out to be surprisingly good. But then, as Clemency pointed out, he was the one true professional among them. If Ethan, with all those years of BBC training, couldn't deliver a decent speech at a family gathering, which of them could? He had done his research effectively by questioning each of the cousins in turn and had pulled together a moving patchwork of reminiscence that brought spontaneous tears to Clemency's eyes.

Especially when he grew more sober and paid touching tributes to his mother and Isabelle. With lowered voice, he raised his glass and the others rose to join him in a silent toast. In an odd way, this was the end of an Annesley era. The clan would continue, but the major players were gone.

While Mémé's mystery remained unsolved, together with the secret of who was doing the murders. In an attempt to lighten the mood, Clemency persuaded the children to sing, pretty French folk songs they had learned at school, and Ashley aped them though he didn't know the words. Everyone laughed.

"It's as well Harry left his own awful brats at home," whispered Élodie. "Else we'd have had them showing off and playing their bloody instruments."

"And demonstrating their ballet steps," agreed Madeleine. "Grotesque."

Cherie turned her head to smile at them both and the look on her face was pure happiness. She was a sweet little thing now that the chip had gone; pretty and sparkling without the deadpan makeup and actually quite bright. I wonder if we can help her in some way, pondered Madeleine. It would be good to do something to lever her out of that ghetto.

By midafternoon they were pretty nearly spent, lightheaded and drowsy, unable to stay awake. By mutual consent, the dishes were quickly cleared and everyone headed in their own directions to sleep off the effects of the monumental meal. They left the terrace doors wide open to allow the air to circulate. This house was so well fortified with its medieval closed courtyard that no one without a specialist's knowledge could possibly breach its security. Besides, they were miles away from anywhere. Only the vineyard workers knew they were even there.

None of them heard, therefore, the quiet click of the concealed side door cautiously opening, nor the stealthy tread of feet on the flagstones as a latecomer joined them and stood outside, peering in. It appeared the feast was already over, the family gone to their siestas. But the afternoon sun remained high in the heavens; there was a great deal still to be done.

34

Silence reigned throughout Mas des Vignes, but Harry was fully awake and alert as he lay on his bed and planned his immediate future. Life was closing in on him faster than he had intended; he was still desperate to get out of here, to put the Spanish frontier between him and the pack before they sniffed out his trail. He had left his cell phone firmly switched off because he didn't want Lavender discovering where he was. By now, she would imagine, he'd be well on his way back to Paris for some fictitious meetings he'd dreamed up. If the British authorities were keen to interview him, he felt he had muddied his track quite a lot. But he knew it couldn't last forever. Find the will, ascertain its details, discover the legal provenance of the property and then get out. No matter who or how many might try to stand in his way. Harry was desperate and in it up to his neck. Nothing was going to stop him now; just let them try.

He swung his legs off the bed and slipped his feet back into his espadrilles. It was a good time now, while the others were all snoozing, to do a bit more nosing around to see what he could turn up. The birth certificate was safely in his briefcase, stuck between some architectural drawings, out of sight. At first he hadn't quite believed what he was reading, but slowly the pieces began to slot into place. He recalled Mad Aunt Effie sitting burbling on the lawn and that last long summer before Mémé's abrupt defection. He had often wished he'd listened more attentively then, but now he had the evidence and was only waiting to strike. With dynamite like that hidden innocently in his briefcase, the chances were he could dispute the will regardless of what it might say. Once he had located it.

He opened the door cautiously and cocked his ear for signs of movement below. Not a sound. The old house slumbered peacefully, with only the steady buzz of cicadas filtering in from outside. The sunshine and champagne, plus that mammoth meal, had done their work effectively; he couldn't have hoped for better results if he'd slipped each one of them a Mickey Finn. Harry stepped onto the landing, then slowly and carefully descended the stairs. The kitchen was piled with the wreckage of the meal, which for once the women hadn't waited to clear. He paused by the stove and selected a knife from the rack. He was not quite certain why he might need it; just felt it wise to continue to take precautions.

Outside, the courtyard was deserted, with only the leisurely plashing of the fountain disturbing the absolute peace. The sun was beginning to sink by now and the heat was far less intense. He could see distant grape pickers still going about their work, but they wouldn't be interested in anything he did, were unlikely even to see him. He knew where he was headed, was certain now where this quest was going to end. The house had turned out to be one giant red herring, with its rambling corridors and that mysterious locked room. What he was looking for, Mémé's best-kept secret, was likely to be stowed off the premises, he'd just realized. She was, after all, a sly old bird who had kept them all guessing for decades.

After that, he would deal with Clemency. Nothing would give him more pleasure. Still grinning ferociously and with new resolution in his step, Harry Annesley headed towards the barn.

Clemency lay under a single sheet and dreamed of Teddy and the shelter of his arms. She refused to allow that whey-faced trollop to have him; she would fight, to the death if necessary, to enchant him and win him back. She saw now that she might be guilty of neglect. Life, since their wedding, had been such a haven of blissful security, she had allowed her natural defenses to relax. Yes, she took him for granted, but only because he allowed it. She loved him every bit as much as ever and the fear of losing him filled her with sudden panic. All thoughts of Dominic had instantly sped; Teddy remained her single great love. She was damned if she was going to let go of him now.

She stared at the whitewashed ceiling of Mémé's room and wondered what she'd thought about, lying right here, in the long lonely years of her self-imposed exile. It was a cool, calm room with a soothing view, the place for an artist to rest and seek inspiration. Clemency wished she'd inherited Mémé's talent, but her child-raising skills were all she seemed to have been dealt. Élodie and Harry, and possibly even Ashley, were the ones with the artistic gifts. It was odd how characteristics could be handed down even from people you'd never actually known. Harry was frighteningly like his grandfather Cornelius, though wilder, more ruthless and far less controlled. She had heard his impatient footsteps as he hurried from the house and wondered what mischief he was up to now. But the champagne and rich French food lay heavily on her stomach; she closed her eyes again and drifted back into painless slumber.

Madeleine and Élodie lay side by side, barely talking, enjoying their private dreams. Both still thought of Dominic, though from slightly different perspectives; Élodie lasciviously of nights of torrid passion, Madeleine chastely of what might have been. And could still be, if only he would return and explain. Where was the fellow now, and what made him so damned elusive? She longed to discuss him but didn't quite dare.

Cherie was curled into a defensive fetal ball, still fully dressed but more relaxed than usual. She was semi in love with her dazzling new half brother and dreamed of returning with him to New Zealand when he went. Better opportunities, he had told her, fresher air and wide open spaces; altogether a cleaner environment in which to raise a child. She'd seen pictures of his mother's oceanside house, a pleasant wood-built bungalow surrounded by lots of lawn, and mentally compared it with the sordid concrete jungle she inhabited now. In such an environment she knew that Ashley would flourish and she liked the idea of him growing up with an authentic male role model to guide and help him along. She even liked Tonya, rather to her surprise, and appreciated the time she spent with Ashley and the way he had warmed to her immediately. Ashley had excellent instincts; knew without question when it was safe to trust. Though she remembered how instantly he'd been drawn to Dominic and his racking agony when the bastard had shrugged him aside.

How she'd ever afford the fares, she really didn't know,

but there was still her nan's will to be located and read. Maybe that would cover it; she had a comfortable feeling it might. She sucked her thumb in imitation of her son and dreamed cozily of a future she had never imagined before.

Long, sloping shadows extended across the grass from the cypress trees when Harry reached the barn and forced open the door. The police had finally withdrawn and even their plastic security tape had been removed. Isabelle's body still lay in the parlour, apparently forgotten, but he bet they'd be back again before too long, churning things up and asking uncomfortable questions. The sooner he got out of here, the better, but he was not going empty-handed. So far Dominic had failed to deliver the goods, a bitter disappointment after Harry had gone to such lengths to locate him.

He glanced around at the rusting antique implements and saw signs of where they had searched among the straw. Isabelle's death had been unfortunate, but then she'd always been a bit of a ninny; what was she doing up there snooping in the first place? Women like Isabelle and Clemency always irritated him, too breezy and socially committed for their own good. Madeleine was far more to his taste, the reason he had chosen an arctic maiden for himself. Élodie scared him, rather, though he'd die rather than admit it, while Cherie he found of no consequence at all, entirely to be overlooked. But this was getting him nowhere; the sun was sinking and the light fading fast. Without a torch he'd be hard-pressed to search properly. Better get a move on while he could.

He made a sporadic check of the barn's main area but could see the forensic team had been pretty thorough.

Nothing there, so far as he could see, designed to hide secrets or precious possessions. Simply cobwebbed hardware from an earlier era, museum pieces yet with no apparent value. He paused as his gaze moved on to the wooden ladder. Rather against his instincts, he knew that was where he had to go. Last time he'd been here, there'd been kids all over the place and their noisy excitement had driven away any terrors. Now the whole place stood silent and abandoned, the air quite still, draped in the musty past. It had to be done; there was no going back now. Harry took a firm grip on himself and slowly began to climb.

Ethan couldn't sleep, so got up again and prowled the upstairs corridor. Rather to his surprise, he had enjoyed today, had liked being there in a central, avuncular position, making a contribution, entertaining the kids. He would bring Emily here, he thought she'd really like it. Once the will had been sorted and they knew where exactly they stood. This doughty old building had lasted many centuries; he tapped the solid woodwork and admired its timeless strength. Some of his nephews and nieces found it spooky and unsettling, but he knew his Emily was made of far sterner stuff. All it really needed, she would say, was a bit of a dust and a lick of fresh paint. With perhaps some curtains and a rug or two on the flagstones. He had never been very domestic, but the idea, in theory, was tempting. His face softened as he thought of his goddess and imagined her presiding over meals in the great hall.

Of course, it would all depend on the will, though he knew in his heart that the house should come to him. To be nominally shared with his siblings, of course, though he doubted the others would ever be bothered to visit. They all had their own far posher places and this younger generation could wait their turn. They would get it in time, according to the laws of heritage; he was certain his mother would not want to be unfair.

The door to Harry's room was ajar, so Ethan peered inside. The covers were rumpled, but the room was unoccupied. Harry was off on another of his wild-goose chases, hunting, no doubt, for that elusive will. A huge wave of irritation instantly swept over Ethan. How dare that young whipper-snapper be so relentlessly pushy. Though only five years actually separated them in age, they were of different generations, and traditional Ethan greatly resented this constant intrusion on his past. What would Odile have had to say about it all? She had come here deliberately to shut herself off from the world.

The huge carved cupboard at the end of the corridor had been pushed aside so that the door was now quite obvious. Ethan approached it with beating heart but, when he tried the handle, found it locked. Now, who in the world had been up here, and when? He tried to peer through the keyhole and could see right through, so no key was in the lock. So someone had been in there, then locked it from this side. Stranger and stranger; he naturally suspected Harry.

Now what latest madness was the blighter up to, and where had he gone off to? In a sudden frenzy of wild frustration, Ethan loped down the stairs and out into the deserted courtyard. He would track Harry down, he couldn't have gone far, and finally have it out with him before he did any real damage.

"What's that out there in the courtyard?" asked Clemency

idly. It was almost seven and she was filling the kettle for late tea. The light was fading and all she could make out was a shape. Football-sized, but where on earth had it come from? It certainly hadn't been there when they started their mammoth siesta.

"Looks like a turnip or even a small pumpkin," said Madeleine, coming to join her at the window. Her head was still aching; the last thing she felt like was food.

Tonya and Élodie were valiantly attacking the dishes, while the kids could be heard squabbling offstage, probably wanting their supper. At that age they were indomitable. Ashley, thumb in mouth, wandered in.

"Go and investigate," instructed Élodie. "And if it's a pumpkin, stick a candle in its mouth."

"But it isn't Halloween yet."

"Just go."

Ashley, unusually biddable, strolled off into the twilight, while Élodie clutched at Clemency's sleeve and made a crude joke about Harry. It was good, this jaunt. All inhibitions were falling away and they were bonding like anything, the cousins. She was glad they'd come; it seemed they all were. Despite the horrendous tragedies, lasting good would come out of the reunion. From wherever she now was, Mémé would surely approve. Watching her family gradually regrouping, drawing back together as a clan.

"Pasta, do you suppose?" suggested Clemency doubtfully, checking out the leftovers and eyeing the diminishing stock of untouched food. "Or shall I make soup? Personally, I doubt I could eat another thing, but those kids are bound to want something."

"So go for it," said Élodie, wringing out her cloth. The

thing about kids was they ate what they were given; at least Clemency's seemed to, since they'd been properly raised.

From somewhere out in the shadows, Ashley screamed.

"Now what's up?" muttered Élodie tiredly. Bloody kids.

"Ignore him and maybe he'll go away," said Madeleine, who'd had a basinful. "But don't tell Cherie I said that or we'll never hear the end of it." To her mind, Ashley was grossly overindulged. He might have grown up normal if he'd only been left alone. That was the trouble with single-parent homes, an uneven balance of what was actually important. Cherie's guilt at not marrying the father combined with a chronic shortage of funds. Madeleine had never actually wanted one herself but was certain she would do better if circumstances should ever change. Which prompted within her an involuntary visceral twinge and conjured up images of Dominic at his best.

Ashley screamed again, this time with a rising hysterical note.

"Oh Lord," said Élodie, dropping her cloth. "What is it with these kids?"

She opened the terrace door and strode outside to where Ashley stood motionless, fixed to the spot, apparently turned to stone. It was slightly too dark to take it in instantly, though she saw at a glance that it most definitely wasn't a turnip. Nor football, nor pumpkin, nor any other innocent thing.

It was a human head with a stupefied expression, an apple crammed into its mouth. For a moment she thought it must be a plastic horror mask, something the children had brought with them for a lark, then took in the real blood seeping from the severed neck and promptly hit the flagstones as she passed out.

"Harry?" quavered Clemency from right behind her. His hair, she noted inconsequentially, was slightly mussed and the look in his strange, silver eyes entirely baffled. Whoever had done this had caught him unawares. And the apple rammed so savagely into his mouth denoted a touch of macabre humour.

35

*F*OUR HUNDRED MILLION POUND PROPERTY BOTCH-UP screamed the headline on the *Evening Standard*, and then, in smaller type: WORKMAN PERMANENTLY CRIPPLED. ARCHITECT CULPABLE, HEARING TOLD.

Teddy Cartwright, walking abstractedly back from a morning meeting, was startled to see his wife's first cousin staring out at him from the center of the front page. Now what new thunderbolt could have assaulted the Annesleys? He couldn't believe they could suddenly be in so much trouble. He sorted through his change for thirty pence and read as he cut across Covent Garden. What had that prize ass been up to now? He could scarcely wait to find out. Mortar, he read, incorrectly mixed, a cardinal sin in the building trade. After all his experience and years of constant bragging, it was shocking really that Harry could have made such a blunder. Must be getting careless in his old age; Teddy read on. The workman was asking for three million in damages and the financiers' insurers were out for Harry's blood. He was in it over his head, poor chap. Despite an age-old antipathy, Teddy felt a twinge of sympathy. Couldn't have happened to a more worthy candidate, but still. When all was said and done, Harry was part of the family and those innocent children didn't deserve to be so betrayed. Especially not at a time like this, when the whole bloody lot of Annesleys seemed to be self-destructing like flies.

He wondered exactly what was going on in France, how Clemency and the rest of them were coping. Due to their recent glacial dealings and the lack of a phone at Mas des Vignes, she had hardly been in touch at all, apart from imparting the ghastly details of the murders, leaving Teddy to worry alone. He knew he should be out there too, adding his weight to the police investigation, comforting his children through this terrible trauma, generally taking control. But Clemency had been adamant; she didn't want him there, and when she laid down the law, that was it. As it was, there were enough of them there already, hanging around being ineffectual, simply taking up space. His added presence could only cause confusion. And someone was needed back here at home, to field calls and generally pass on the awful tidings, to keep the rest of the relatives informed. Which wasn't at all pleasant, as Teddy had discovered. The imparting of gruesome news is never easy; more often than not the recipient is inclined to lash out in grief and blame the messenger. But there Teddy really came into his own. He was calm and warm and accustomed to listening and, in his own way, could provide some sort of comfort.

He hated to be relegated to second place like this, yet also knew he had forfeited his family rights. He had let her down, as it had later turned out, at the time when she most needed him, though no one could have foreseen these terrible happenings when she'd bowled off defiantly and left him on his own to sort out his mess.

He couldn't blame her; she had acted with great dignity. She had always had style, had his wife. Intrinsically fair, he had a kind heart and knew he had lately been behaving like a cad. But a woman like that would drive any man to drink with her constant mothering and spoiling and organization. Clemency, at her worst, was like an express train out of control: implacable, unstoppable, like a hockey captain on speed. Feeling his blood pressure beginning to lurch upwards, he deliberately slowed his pace and tried not to get too overwrought. It would work itself out; these things usually did. This total break, while the family was supposed to be on holiday, was probably the best decision they could have made. At least he knew she had the backup of her cousins; he thought a lot of Madeleine and Élodie and was certain they would help her cope, even at a time as grim as this. It gave him space to sort out his tangled emotions; to properly weigh the pros and cons and reach a mature decision.

Ali had certainly brought light into his life, but love wasn't everything, at least not the purely sexual kind. She made him feel ten years younger, true, amusing, sexy and free. But what had started off as an office flirtation had rapidly grown serious and out of control. Clemency's confrontation had proved the final straw. For sixteen years he had put up with her frightening efficiency; right now he felt he needed some autonomy of his own. Yet he missed his children and, goddammit, he missed her. Ali's earnest youthfulness just didn't fill the gap. Too many evenings of movies with a message, jazz concerts and wine bars were beginning to take their toll. He was no longer young, he had to face up to it, and wasn't at all sure how long he could stand the pace.

Later, back at the warehouse, he wondered if he ought to ring Lavender. He didn't like her, never had, found her arch and condescending and a bit of an obvious phony. But their consorts were related and furthermore traveling together, and the probability was that she was all alone. The press would be besieging her; she might not be able to cope.

She sounded quite dreadful when he finally chanced a call. No, she'd not heard a word from France and reporters were camping in her garden. The children were frightened, they'd been jeered at at school and she frankly wasn't certain if Harry was ever coming back. As far as she knew, he should be by now in Paris. Perhaps Teddy would check with Clemency next time they had a word. She'd just had a disturbing summons from the bank, requesting she go in there immediately. When she'd asked sharply what it was all about, she'd been told it had to do with their number two account. Which was reportedly overdrawn, an impossibility.

If only Harry would ring. It wasn't at all like him not to stay in touch. He had his cell phone, after all, and would know she must be out of her mind with worry. If, that was, he knew anything at all. It was possible that, in rural France, the newspapers had not yet got hold of the story. If they even cared.

Teddy was startled. "But surely he's told you what's going on out there?" The man must be a monster not to have filled her in on Mémé's death, no matter what else he might have been up to.

"No, what?" Surely not more trouble; Lavender couldn't face it. Confronted with ruin and public disgrace, what else could there be to go wrong?

Teddy told her, as gently as he could, about the terrible murders of both Mémé and Isabelle but wasn't at all sure she was able to take it in, she was already so distraught. He did his best to calm her and thought about popping over. But he'd only incite the press pack further and there wasn't anything useful he could do. Not, at least, till Harry got back in touch. So he told her to stay out of sight of the windows and to keep the children inside at all costs. He asked about food and she said she had a full freezer. He suggested she pour herself a strong gin and tonic, gave her the number of his private line and urged her to keep her chin up. But it did sound serious, more so than he had realized, so then he started worrying all over again about his own children and wondered how Clemency was coping out there without him.

The thing about families, they were very insidious, there to ensnare you just when you least expected it. Nearly everyone in the world had some sort of family; those that didn't lamented the lack. It was a universal bonding thing, parents worrying about children, children about parents. In recent years, since people had started living so much longer, most of his peer group were facing similar problems. Where once it had been routine to ask a person how they were, these days the ritual question was, "Are your parents still alive?" Followed almost invariably by shared commiseration on how difficult it all was.

Teddy was determined not to end up as a burden, but since Clemency, almost certainly, was likely to outlive him, he knew he had nothing much to fear and could leave his whole future confidently in her hands. He smiled. Constant loving, regular nutritious meals, a comfortable home, a warm bed.

Bossy instructions about what to wear, how much exercise to take, clothes that were mended and regularly laundered. Nights nodding off in front of the fire with his paper, his slippers and a dog's head on his knee. And later, when the children were grown and the grandchildren came along, a continuing haven of playing happy families, surrounded, like Cornelius Annesley, with a crop of healthy descendants. That's what "for better or worse" was really about; not just the bad times, the good ones too.

Provided, of course, that he managed to win her back. Chilly, ambitious Alison, whose parents had split when she was still a child, would undoubtedly just dump him unsentimentally in a home. The moment he grew short of breath and his sexual performance fell off.

Clemency had always been Teddy's girl, right from the moment she first bounced into his life, a great exuberant schoolgirl with her glossy, abundant hair held back by a velvet ribbon. The Broadhurst family had been good to him, welcoming him in when he first came home with Guy, inviting him for Christmas while his parents were abroad, instantly accepting him as part of their extended family. With four boys and Clemency, the house had been always crowded, but Claire, their mother, had easily coped and passed on her homemaking skills to her daughter. Teddy missed his mother-in-law still; her early death had come as a blow to them all. He felt that, of the sisters, she had probably been the best. Definitely nicer than Eunice and more stalwart than Aimée or Patrice, she had also been closest to her own mother, had shared some special bond that the others seemed not to have.

He wondered what she would think of things now, of this

frightening carnage that was cutting them all down. Again he felt guilty that he hadn't been there to shield them. Somehow he had let Claire down when she had trusted him with her beloved only daughter to cherish and look after for the rest of his life.

No one could have cared for Clemency more than her mother; that was part of what was wrong with her now. She had been a so much wanted child, the single girl among four brothers, that her overwhelming personality had developed from the smug certainty of always knowing herself loved. Thin-blooded Alison, from her broken home, needed him rather pathetically. That, if he was honest, had been the initial attraction. She clung to him, had made him feel that much more masculine. But confident Clemency flowed through life, taking everything as her due. Even though that often irritated him intensely, he acknowledged what a true life force she was. He needed her strength and optimism, longed to reach out to her now.

He would go to her, as soon as he could. If it wasn't already too late.

36

*N*ow Harry's coffin lay next to Isabelle's in the parlour while what was left of the Annesley family, distraught with uncontrollable grief and terror, clustered together in the kitchen drinking endless mugs of tea. No one had much to say. Even the children, though shielded from the wilder excesses, were silent and staring, shell-shocked by what had occurred. Ashley had been put to bed, heavily sedated after what he had seen, with his mother sitting beside him in case he suddenly woke. But the other children were too scared to go upstairs. Clemency didn't blame them. She admired Cherie's amazing courage at being up there alone with just a candle, though actually Cherie was so dazed with horror, she was quite impervious to her surroundings.

At first the gendarmerie had wanted them to vacate the house, but sheer logistics had prevented a late-night exodus. By this hour there was nowhere practical they could go and the gendarmes insisted that they all stay together, since they would need to question them intensively once they'd had some sleep. They decided, therefore, to wait for first light and then devise some sort of a plan. Besides, it was the barn that was once more the center of activity. The forensic team had been summoned back and had sealed it effectively off. Harry's body had been found on the edge of the hayloft, his neck neatly severed, the wicked-looking scythe beside him. Someone had lately deinfested it of cobwebs and sharpened the blade to a razor's deadly edge. Whoever it was must have been lying there in wait, confident that sooner or later he'd come snooping. And then shown the macabre humour of a sick and twisted mind, to risk being seen in the court-yard as he made his ghoulish delivery.

"Who could have hated him quite that much?" asked Clemency, surprised yet also relieved that her initial suspicions had proved unfounded. Her cousin, with his posturing and pontificating, might have been a bit of a pain at times, but she was glad he hadn't turned out to be a killer. Though somebody was.

"And why the apple in his mouth?"

"Because he was a bit of a pig?" suggested Élodie irreverently. She had recovered miraculously from her sudden fall, though had a lump the size of an egg on the back of her head.

"Or simply to shut him up." Madeleine gazed somberly out into the darkness and tried to make sense from her whirling thoughts. All their idle chat about family killers had become alarmingly real. No one could seriously believe that this latest atrocity was the work of some faceless "Provence Predator," though whoever had done it must have abnormal strength. Or specialist's knowledge of how to sever a neck.

"A surgeon, maybe," posited Rusty.

"Or a butcher."

"Actually," said Clemency sensibly, "most ordinary farmers are used to disjointing carcasses. I'm afraid it hardly narrows the field at all, must makes it fairly probable it couldn't be one of us."

"You hope." It was all getting so horribly out of hand, anything suddenly seemed possible. Madeleine wanted to rush to her room and barricade it securely to keep the rest of them out. Though she couldn't face the darkness, not alone. And there was no way Élodie was likely to budge. She'd seen the ghastliness face-to-face. She felt she would never be able to sleep again.

The policemen all had mobile phones, so Clemency had called Teddy and he was coming in on the earliest flight. She was glad of that. Strong she might be, and capable and brave, but she'd reached the edge, she really had, especially with her children to protect. They hadn't yet notified Lavender. No one relished the idea of breaking the news, and the leading gendarme rubbed his nose and hemmed and hawed and decided eventually a personal visit might be best. They had no idea of the workings of Harry's mind, but when the gendarmerie contacted Interpol, they were instantly alert and suggested a meeting at Scotland Yard before they informed the widow of Harry's death.

"Just to be on the safe side," explained the cop. No point opening up too soon what looked like becoming a right can of worms. And since he was traveling and not yet expected back, not a lot of harm could be done by the temporary silence. After all, dead is dead. Harry Annesley, for the moment, would keep, was the opinion of both lots of police. And once the London newspapers got on to it, it would blow sky-high their stealthy investigation.

Ethan paced the flagstones of the great hall, too shaken with horror even to have logical thoughts. The vast dark cathedral ceiling loomed high above him, and the two wooden staircases, outlined by flickering candlelight, climbed into nothingness, their connecting landing obscured by shadow. This was not a welcoming house; he could not have lived here very long himself. Not without considerable modernization, and certainly never on his own. It was archaic these days to exist without electricity, a stubbornness in his mother he would not have expected. Just what exactly had been her secret it was probable now that they would never find out. To leave the brightness and normality of the houses in Oxford and Maine in order to hide herself away in this grim fortress simply made no sense. Odile had always been a sociable being, at her happiest when surrounded by her beloved children, with the husband she doted on at her side.

Ethan had suffered enormously from his mother's abrupt

departure. She'd been snatched away when he was at his most vulnerable, leaving him to face puberty alone with only a resentful older sister and grief-stricken father to bring him up. Eunice, embittered by what she saw as her lost youth, had taken out her frustration on the younger children, with the result that none of them could stand her now. One after another they had all jumped ship, Charlie to Canada, Tom to wander the world, Patrice into a string of unsatisfactory relationships while she desperately looked for enduring love. Ethan alone had been stuck there at home, missing his mother but emotionally inadequate, entirely unable to express his loss.

He peered up into the gloom above him. It was silent up there and he thought of Cherie's lonely vigil. The kids were going to bunk down by the fire, behind the heavy curtain in the small, claustrophobic den, the one safe place in this great rambling building. To set an example, the adults would go to their rooms. But not yet. He could hear the clanking of saucepans in the kitchen and knew that Clemency would be back at the stove. Bustling and energetic, she could never remain still for long, but he sympathized with her motives and applauded her solid good sense. He liked and admired women who could cope, liked all of his nieces, in fact.

Oddly, he was glad he had come on this journey despite all the traumas and the horrors all around him. There were things that had had to be done, of course, but they were inevitable and could have occurred at any time. It had given him the chance to get back to his roots, to restore the feeling of kinship he had lived without for so long. He peered up into the gloom above but could detect neither movement nor sound. Yet someone must be lurking somewhere; even through his loneliness, Ethan felt he was not alone. Those women huddled together in the kitchen deserved what protection he could provide. The only man among them now was Rusty, who was little more than a kid. Ethan felt the compulsion to do something, to let them know his own inner strength. He thought of that locked room upstairs and his mind was made up. Carrying his candle in its porcelain holder, he returned to the kitchen to borrow a flashlight.

"Where are you going?" asked Clemency sharply. Too much had been happening; she wanted none of them to stray.

"Upstairs," said Ethan firmly. "I won't be more than a minute." The oxtail stew smelled quite heavenly, though he doubted any of them could eat.

"Well, look in on Cherie and see if she wants some supper. That child should be asleep by now. Tell her to come down and join us."

The bedrooms all had interconnecting doors and Ethan walked silently through them till he reached Cherie's. She had lit the gas lamps and was sitting there motionless, not reading or anything, just gazing blankly into space. Ashley was sleeping, a slight, defenseless bundle, and Ethan's heart went out to him as he recognized one like himself.

"All right?" He spoke softly, but she still jumped out of her skin.

"Jesus, you scared me." She lit a cigarette. "I thought you were the bogeyman that Ashley's been rambling about."

Ethan perched beside her on the bed and watched as she tenderly stroked the boy's damp hair. She was an odd little creature, a real street fighter, but beneath the veneer he could see she had heart. And what Ashley had been through was

313

enough to drive him batty. He remembered so clearly his own youthful trauma, staggering home crying through the woods the night his brothers tried to lead him astray. His own mother had been there for him then too. He saw quite suddenly how like Odile Cherie was: small and severe and filled with fierce determination, with her thick dark curls and that sharp little nose. A Rochefort, if not an Annesley, through and through. There was no doubting Cherie's pedigree when he saw her like this.

He told her about supper, but she said she wasn't hungry. Would stay on up here for another half hour and join them later when she was sure the boy wouldn't wake. Ethan nodded and squeezed her shoulder, then picked up his flashlight and proceeded into the next room. He had a sudden conviction that the clue to everything lay in that mysterious locked room, if only he could get in there.

The heavy carved cabinet had been shifted to one side and he saw now it had castors and could easily glide. Castors that had been freshly oiled since Harry had first investigated it. There was room now just to open the door, so he tried the handle with a beating heart. It was locked.

Shining the powerful beam of Clemency's flashlight right on the lock, Ethan bent and tried to peer through. Although the room beyond might be in darkness, he could detect no light or anything at all. The key was clearly in the lock this time; the door was locked from the other side.

He was on the point of walking away when something halted him dead in his tracks. The faintest sound, like the murmur of the breeze, and it came not from the kitchen below but from the other side of the door. Voices quietly talking, he was almost sure of it. Within the locked room. At first he thought it must be the police, still working away as they searched for further evidence. Then he realized how late it was and remembered he'd heard their vans drive off a good two hours before. He stood there in a frenzy, wondering what to do, then gathered together all his resources and reminded himself he was no longer a scared child but a fully grown man with a formidable brain. If Clemency could handle things so calmly, it was high time he showed them all what he was made of. Ethan squared his shoulders and boldly knocked on the door.

"What's up?" Rusty looked up startled as Ethan hurried into the kitchen, with a strange light in his eye and showing more energy than any of them had seen from him during this trip. Whereas normally he skulked like a shadow, all of a sudden he had become a flesh-and-blood man of action. Ethan crossed the kitchen and searched on a cluttered shelf for another flashlight.

"Quick," he said. "There are people up there. Talking in the room behind the locked door."

"You're kidding!" Bad taste, thought Élodie, to joke like this when they were all already so badly shaken.

"They're there," insisted Ethan, thrusting the torch into Rusty's hand and indicating the door. But when Clemency rinsed her hands and looked like joining them, Ethan shook his head.

"Not this time," he said importantly. "Best wait downstairs while we see what's up."

"Men's work," said Madeleine with a shaky smile. She was rather impressed by her uncle's sudden bravery. There was clearly more to Ethan than was initially apparent. She found it attractive; was suddenly proud of him.

But Ethan and Rusty were back in a few minutes; neither could hear anything now and Ethan was beginning to doubt himself.

"Wait," said Clemency, struck with inspiration. "Whatever actually lies behind that door must abut onto the barn."

Ethan stared. She was right.

"The barn is really just an extension of the house. So if there's a room there, with people in it talking, there's probably also an entrance from the other side." Else how could anyone, who was flesh and blood, come and go without being seen? Simple once it was pointed out. Ethan struck his forehead in exasperation.

"Clemency, you're a genius," he said. And they all started pulling on their outdoor shoes for a trip to the barn door across the courtyard.

"Stay with the children," whispered Clemency to Tonya, who shrugged with good humour and sank back onto her chair. She had got them playing Racing Demon and their spirits were returning. Soon, she estimated, they'd be calm enough to be coaxed upstairs to bed.

"Should we all go?" asked Madeleine, suddenly anxious, but Clemency already had the door wide open and was leading the procession, flashlight in hand.

They'd forgotten about the police precautions and were halted by a red-and-white barrier with a stern warning notice saying, *INTERDIT*. The whole of the barn and the area all around it had been sectioned off with blue-and-white tape and they could see without approaching further that an industrial-sized extra padlock had been slotted through the latch on the main door. Nothing doing; entrance totally blocked. They scoured the area, looking for light or something, but the barn stood silent and gloomy as it must have done for years. Rusty turned to Ethan and turned up his hands helplessly, but Ethan was already having his own doubts and beginning to think it had been nothing but the wind after all. Certainly it was blustery.

"There's a storm coming," reported Clemency.

Back in the kitchen, they opened another bottle and sat around the table for a proper powwow. The light of battle had still not faded from Ethan's eye, and though he now had his own doubts, his dander was properly up. Something was going on up there; he could swear he hadn't imagined it. And someone, they had to face up to it, had been killing off the Annesley family at a fast-increasing rate, which was not a joke. Since the local police seemed to have no leads so far, the family really ought to be doing something themselves. Soon, or who knew where it all might lead?

"We need to be clearheaded," said Rusty. "And think through who it could possibly be, even the least likely."

"We'll make a list," said Clemency, opening her handbag and searching for a pen.

"Are we assuming it's somebody family?" asked Élodie, and after a moment of exchanged glances, they all nodded.

"There's no point including strangers," said Rusty. "Or where on earth would we start?"

The same person, by the law of averages, could be assumed to have killed Mémé and Isabelle and Harry. That went without saying. Three savage murders all in close proximity on private land.

"And Mad Aunt Effie and Martha," prompted Madeleine.

"And Pandora on the golf course in Spain. And possibly

Cherie's parents."

Rusty started listing the surviving Annesleys and, with some help from the rest of his cousins, came up with a formidable list.

"Which can easily be thinned down," said Ethan, taking out his fountain pen and beginning to strike off names.

"Who's still alive of the original nine?" asked Rusty. Ethan reeled them off. The three surviving aunts were safely in the States, while Charlie, they knew, was still in Canada, since Teddy had talked to him on the phone.

"And he'd never kill his own daughter," said Clemency, shocked.

"You never know," said Ethan darkly. "We're dealing with a crazy person here."

"Or woman," remarked Élodie, exhaling smoke. In some odd way, she was actually rather enjoying this, until a sudden thought struck her and she visibly froze in shock. Oh God.

"Élodie?" asked Ethan curiously, aware of her pallor and the sudden violent trembling of her hand. She shook her head. What had just occurred to her was too terrible to say aloud; she only hoped the others wouldn't get there first. Ethan sat there, staring at Rusty's list, and it was only a matter of minutes until the lightbulb went on in his head too.

"Dominic Carlisle," he said firmly, adding the name to the list, impervious to the concerted gasps from the women around the table. It seemed impossible, but it had to be someone, and Dominic certainly behaved in a very strange way. And Ethan still resented the blighter's airy intrusion into his life, the day he'd turned up and asked so many questions.

"But Martha was his mother," said Madeleine, ashen too.

"So what?" No one could be logically excluded, not at this stage in the game. And, apart from those present, no one else was very likely. Most of their relatives were accounted for or dead.

37

*C*lemency was awakened in the small hours by the cumbersome thunking of heavy shutters and the continuous growl of thunder as a breeze sprang up and summer lightning flickered among the vines. She sat bolt upright in the unfamiliar bed, for a moment scared almost out of her wits until, recalling where she was, she felt her clamouring heart slowly subside to its regular beat. Mémé's house in the middle of nowhere, on a fool's errand they were crazy ever to have embarked upon. Apart from the sporadic spluttering from outside and the eerie creeping light across the fields, the room was hot and intensely dark, with only the unlit candle at the bedside any sort of defense against unimaginable terrors.

This was a bad house, severe and unrelenting. Clemency paused, the temptation to lean across and light the candle balanced by fear of what its feeble beam might reveal. Only a couple of antique gas brackets lit this room and to reach them meant having to leave the spurious safety of the bed and tread across hazardous floorboards in impenetrable blackness while she fumbled with matches.

She remembered vividly from her childhood being this scared and recognized why it had been so long since she'd last returned. Out there in the darkness, along with the spiders and other nighttime unmentionables, nasty things lurked, waiting to grab at an unsuspecting ankle. She wished now she had taken Harry's advice and left the shutters firmly secured, only that would surely have been far worse, rampant claustrophobia in an airless room.

The thought of Harry only added to her terror and she longed to burrow back beneath the pillows, but the storm had driven away all thoughts of sleep and now she could just detect, from somewhere down below, the faintest sounds of stealthy movement before the air was rent by a blood-freezing scream of almost otherworldly awfulness.

What the . . . ?

Braver than she could possibly have imagined, Clemency risked the darkness to wrestle with the heavy latch of the door that opened onto the gallery and overlooked the great hall below. There beneath her, a smudge of paleness in the sporadic light, someone was standing in the arched doorway, close to where the dying embers of their fire still glowed. A figure apparently frozen into stillness, gazing up at the bend in the stairs where something dark and ominous had just swung into view.

"My God!" breathed Clemency, aghast and unbelieving. For what she glimpsed now, in the hard bright flickering light, she knew for certain did not exist. And even after all they'd already been through, that really scared her.

"Jesus!" said Élodie, instantly wide awake, not that she'd been sleeping after the horrors she'd been through. She knew she'd never again be able to close her eyes and not see Harry's ghastly head, with its popping eyes and slightly baffled expression. She gripped the sheet, which smelled heavily of dried lavender, and shrank rather than leapt as the scream was repeated. Next to her Madeleine was also fully awake. Instinctively they held hands.

"Mating vixen?" suggested Madeleine hopefully. Even her highly civilized Burmese could make strange sounds when aroused. In the city too; not just in the heart of the country.

"Nice try," said Élodie, rallying. "But it's not the season and that was definitely human."

They listened for all they were worth but heard nothing more. They looked at each other. Too scared to face the dark when they went to bed, Élodie had recklessly left the gaslights turned down low and the room was dancing with fitful shadows which failed to improve their present state of mind. She had also bolted the shutters. Somehow they'd strayed into a nightmare scenario which didn't seem to be getting any better.

They listened again; total silence. But this ancient pile was so fortified, the Campbells and Macdonalds could have ridden right through and they'd not be any the wiser.

"Do you think, perhaps, it was Ashley having a dream?" ventured Élodie. Madeleine shook her head. "That sounded to me like the real McCoy. Someone in deadly peril. Someone being murdered."

"You're not serious!"

They stared at each other in horror. Élodie's instinct was to dive back under the covers, but she couldn't let Madeleine think she was scared.

"So what do we do?"

"Go down, perhaps?" Even Madeleine sounded doubtful. "Take our candles and see what's going on." She was only acting brave; inside she was a mess. But she was older than Élodie by several years, and someone had to take the lead. Then a thought struck her.

"There's always the boys." She hated even to think it, but it was true. Men did occasionally have their uses, and this, most definitely, was one of them. "Rusty and Ethan? What's happened to them?" Dominic too, though she dared not say it. Just the thought of him, and the implications, filled her with a dread she could not face.

"Shall we wait a little and see what happens?" Élodie's kohl-smudged eyes pleaded eloquently from the pillow; Madeleine, relieved, squeezed her hand. It was cozy here in this barricaded room, like lying in a sickroom with your best friend at your side. They had bolted the door and shifted the chest of drawers. For no reason other than cowardice, just to be certain they were safe. Somewhere out there was a rampant killer, but the men were in the house to guard them and the police not far off. It would be all right provided they didn't move.

Both together heard the slightest sound outside, soft footfalls, barely discernible, then the grinding of iron in the lock.

"Jesus!" repeated Élodie. This time there was no mistaking it. Someone had just locked the door from outside and was stealthily moving away. They were neatly caught, like rats in a trap, and there wasn't a thing they could do.

"What the hell was that?" Along the corridor, Rusty shot awake when he heard the scream and moved to switch on the bedside lamp before remembering that there wasn't one. Beside him, Tonya groaned and snuggled deeper. Having expected not to be able to sleep at all, sheer exhaustion had rapidly overwhelmed her and suddenly she couldn't bear to be disturbed.

"Kids," she murmured. "Having themselves a fight." And lapsed back into unconsciousness, unaware that Rusty was leaping out of bed. Something was most certainly wrong. He reached in the darkness for his jeans and sweatshirt, then groped on the table for a flashlight. Again that chilling screaming, more frantic this time and coming apparently from somewhere below. Mindful, and who wouldn't be, of the murderer in their midst, he realized he ought to be rousing reinforcements before charging in there in his usual impetuous way.

Ethan was occupying the adjoining room, so Rusty cautiously listened at the door before nudging it open a few inches. Pitch-blackness, with even the shutters tightly closed; he could make out nothing, not even where the bed was.

"Ethan?" he ventured softly, entering a little farther while frantically trying to get his bearings. He listened for Ethan's breathing but could still not hear a thing. He edged his way carefully into the room till his knee encountered a chair.

"Ethan!" he hissed. "For God's sake, wake up! Things are going on downstairs. Something is horribly wrong."

Still no sound. He found the bed and felt around, but the covers were flat and he could detect no signs of stirring. So he switched on his flashlight and saw he was too late. The bed was empty, Ethan was gone. Out there somewhere in the treacherous darkness, perhaps at the source of the commotion. He tiptoed across the room by the light of his flashlight, eased open the outer door and peered into the corridor. Here the darkness was slightly less dense and he could make out vague shapes of furniture and things. It took a second for his eyes to adjust, then his attention was drawn to the far end of the passage. The great carved cabinet had been thrust to one side. The door to the locked room was ajar.

Stealthily and with thumping heart, Rusty approached. He could just discern a pale glow from within and devoutly hoped he wasn't walking into a trap. He paused a second, then pushed the door open wider.

"Come and look at this," said a quiet voice from inside, and there stood Ethan, opening cupboards and poking around. "I thought I heard someone passing," he explained. "Knew I'd never nod off, so decided to explore instead. And look what I've found."

His flashlight picked out a well-furnished room with solid fittings and sumptuous wall hangings. And large, dark portraits on the walls. With an easy chair and a tapestry footstool, close to a desk with an old-fashioned oil lamp. Rusty fingered the heavy brass base and found it warm. He felt in his pocket for a match and lit the wick.

"Good God!"

Good furniture, well cared for, and shelf upon shelf of books. American history and politics; philosophy, medicine, forensic stuff, as well as rows and rows of paperback novels in French. Poetry too. Piles of newspapers and periodicals, with a pair of gold reading glasses negligently tossed down, as if someone had just finished reading and gone for a stroll. And a bottle of four-star brandy next to an empty glass.

"What on earth is this and how come we never saw it?" Ethan remembered Harry's quest and could not believe they had managed to miss this room. The bed was grand and canopied, the wardrobe ornate and antique. One glance inside revealed rows of suits, immaculately styled and in perfect condition. There was also a strong smell of camphor which suggested they weren't often worn, but they were in mint condition and carefully pressed, with a row of matching neckties too.

Ethan was poking away at the wall behind the hangings.

"Clemency was right," he said triumphantly. "There's a door back here that must lead through to the barn."

"Locked," he reported after he'd fiddled with the catch. But the room was a definite hidey-hole, discreetly joining the two buildings, windowless and secure. They hadn't found it before simply because they hadn't looked hard enough. But it meant that whoever inhabited this space could come and go at ease without ever being seen.

"Do you suppose my mother had a lover?" pondered Ethan, hating the thought but feeling obliged to voice it.

"Maybe." Why not? Rusty was far more relaxed about it. She'd lived here alone, after all, for forty years. What she did with her life was up to her. He went on exploring. The piled-up newspapers were arranged in orderly piles and seemed to go back a few years. Some were so faded, they were barely still legible. He studied them more closely.

"Wow!" he said. "Come take a look at this." Story after story, all on a single subject, the legendary uncaught killer they had dubbed the "Provence Predator."

Rusty's eyes met Ethan's and they practically shook with excitement. What had they unearthed?

"Where's that list?" said Rusty, positively panting, and Ethan, after a few tense seconds, found it crumpled in his pocket. He spread it on the table, next to the newspapers, and they both pored over it to see who they had missed.

Which was when they heard the faint movement behind them as the door was suddenly kicked shut.

"Hold it right there!" commanded a chilly, imperious voice, and there was no mistaking the sickening click of a safety catch being flicked off.

"You stupid damned fools," remarked Dominic with contempt, once he'd finished frisking them for weapons. "Did you honestly believe you were sufficiently smart to outwit a killer of that sort of caliber?"

His smile was thin and no longer extended to his eyes; he was dressed in what looked like army combat fatigues. Gone was the velvet-jacketed dilettante who had played such havoc with the feelings of his cousins. Ethan ground his teeth. This was a man of action, cruel and ruthless, who had systematically hunted them down and had only now chosen to show his hand. A hand that was holding an ugly automatic which was leveled uncompromisingly at their chests.

And then they heard the scream again and all three of them froze. Dominic's finger tightened on the trigger and he stared at them as if they were strangers.

"Not one move," he threatened, "or you're both dead meat." And he locked the door behind him as he left.

"Clemency?" Cherie's voice was high and strained, for it was, it now appeared, she who was standing down there all alone, her small frightened face spotlighted like an icon by the single quavering candle she was holding. She, indeed, who had uttered that awful scream at the sight of the presence on the staircase, now indomitably approaching her in a relentlessly threatening manner. Hearing her name, the figure paused and slowly turned to stare across the yawning gap at Clemency, standing by her bedroom door, transfixed. Like the signal from a lighthouse, the summer lightning continued to flicker on and off, revealing the creature's face in snatches and striking primeval terror into her heart.

"*Clemence?*" rumbled a throaty French voice, and the man, for man it was—slowly scratched his belly then held out both arms towards her in the parody of an embrace.

"*Ma chère, viens et embrasse moi.*" He belched and lurched and stumbled down a few more stairs; he was clearly more than a little drunk. Clemency just stood there, rooted with horror, as distant echoes of childhood nightmares returned at the sound of that voice. That rusty, distinctive voice, with its strange mongrel accent that was neither one thing nor the other, came arrowing back at her from the long-forgotten past. Echoes from early childhood that she'd tried all these years to suppress, things her grandmother had never fully explained before banishing her peremptorily from the house forever.

"*Clemence!*"

That fetid breath, those fumbling hands. As she started to remember, she wished she didn't have to and felt an urgent attack of the shakes coming on. For here he stood, made flesh after all these years, the threatening dark presence who had haunted her subconscious and caused her to wake up, screaming, in the night. Teddy always put it down to bad dreams and cuddled her till the palpitations ceased, but Teddy wasn't here yet and the thing was horribly close with only the sparrowlike Cherie to protect her. Breathing heavily, he was clinging to the banister rail and slowly attempting to regain his tottering balance. Clemency saw, in the snatches of ghostly light, that he was huge and ungainly, more so than she remembered, dressed roughly in a workman's dirty denims with several days' growth of beard. A creature from the grave, in more senses than one. His massive paunch bulged above a wide leather belt into which was stuck, quite casually, a gleaming knife used for gutting rabbits.

"This way, Clemency! Take the back stairs!" Cherie's shrill voice had assumed command, jerking her back sharply to reality. If she used the rear staircase and headed through the kitchen, she could get to Cherie by a different route and bypass the ghastly presence in the hall. Provided she was surefooted enough; no time for faltering in the dark. In her long linen nightshirt, Clemency darted away while the nightmare figure continued to groan and bellow out her name.

"Clemence, Clemence. Où est-que tu vas?"

She groped her way through the kitchen without wasting precious seconds to light the gas and located her cousin easily in the bursts of lightning through the long Gothic windows of the great hall. She grabbed at Cherie's thin arm for support and felt how badly she was trembling. Cherie gave a little convulsive sob and tottered against Clemency with heaving shoulders, clearly close to the brink of hysteria.

"I only came down for a glass of water," she whispered. "Ashley was restless and I thought he might wake. And then, when I turned to go up again, this thing came looming out of the darkness and started to come after me." She gulped and brushed away childish tears. "Ashley's bogeyman."

"Hush, now." Petrified though she was herself, Clemency held Cherie till her breathing was steadier and took the candlestick out of her hand. If she extinguished the flame, they'd be less of a target, but she cringed at the thought of being near him in the dark. Particularly armed with that lethal-looking knife.

She thought of Mémé and poor butchered Isabelle; remembered Harry's decapitated head. Memories she would prefer to stay hidden came rushing to the surface with a volcanic force that she knew she couldn't stem. He might be slightly clumsy now but was always fast on his feet, a native of this territory, surefooted as a deer. She remembered those terrifying games of Hide-and-Seek, forced to run frantically through dense, unfriendly woods with him in relentless pursuit behind her, lazily laughing and inevitably the winner. But this, alas, was no longer a game. She recalled poor Isabelle and shuddered.

Where were the men now, just when she needed them most? Ethan and Rusty; her own valiant Piers? Above all, Teddy, on whom she had always relied? Not to mention the women, sleeping snugly above. How was it possible they could ignore Cherie's screams? Throughout the ancient farmhouse not a single thing stirred. She had a sickening realization that the walls were just that much too thick.

"Quick!" she mouthed at Cherie as she saw him moving again. "I'll distract him and you make a dive for it. Get to the cars and summon the police." Which was when she remembered two things. The keys were upstairs and Cherie couldn't drive.

At which point Cherie screamed again.

38

*T*he summer storm was gradually abating and the light growing paler by the second. This interminable night was heading towards dawn and the darkness on the stairs was visibly less dense.

"Clemence, Clemence," breathed the creature from the past, but Cherie, still taut with terror, had now been startlingly distracted. Clutching convulsively at Clemency's arm, she pointed up to where a second figure, dark and terrible, had silently appeared and was standing on the landing, looking down. Except, except . . .

"It's got no face!" screamed Cherie, burrowing her head into Clemency's bosom like a child.

With hammering heart, Clemency clung to her cousin and tried to soothe her by stroking her hair. She stared at the tall gaunt figure, which was barely discernible in the shadows. Like the angel of death or something still more terrible, it stood there absolutely motionless, while below the drunk swayed and moaned. This had to be a dream, she thought; nothing rational could be this bad. Soon she would wake and find it glorious morning, with lovely Teddy to hug and protect her and Mémé alive and restored to them again.

"What is it?" said Cherie urgently, risking another peek. She knew she should never have come on this loony expedition, or trusted this vile house with its secrets and bad vibes. Ashley's instincts had been accurate as always. There were dark things here that ought never to have been disturbed. She felt that she had let him down by putting his life in peril. The minute they got away from here, assuming they ever did, there'd be no more foreign travel, not for either of them. Except, perhaps, to New Zealand someday, where she sensed they'd be finally safe.

Silence prevailed and nothing stirred. All they could hear, as they stood there frozen with terror, was the rasping breathing of the thing on the stairs, who appeared finally to be running out of steam. At least for a while. He was doubled over and clutching at his stomach. Emotion, or maybe just drink, had struck him dumb.

Cherie still clung to Clemency like a drowning child, while Clemency, with renewed conviction, stood firm and faced him out. Reason told her he was only flesh and blood. Apart from the laboured breathing and repellent fumes of brandy and garlic, her memory was finally clearing and things she hadn't realized she knew were gradually starting to surface. If he was merely mortal, which it stood to reason he was, then he was also vulnerable and unable to see in the dark. And with the skinful he'd recently taken, it was likely he couldn't see anything at all. Certainly not the threatening figure hovering somewhere in the shadows behind him, which might, or might not, be flesh and blood too. There simply wasn't time to find out.

Cherie made a grab for the candle, but Clemency acted faster. In a split second's decision, she snuffed out the flame, causing her cousin to gasp and clutch her even tighter. Now there was nothing but fading moonlight to reveal the cavernous stairwell. The guttering lightning was pretty nearly spent, the embers in the fireplace finally dead. The gaunt, black figure melted effortlessly away. Clemency was now not certain it had ever been there at all.

"What did you do that for?" Cherie was close to hysteria.

"Hush now and listen," whispered Clemency, firmly resolute. "While I distract him, try and make a dash for it." It didn't matter where she went, provided she got away.

Suddenly Clemency was completely calm. It was true what was said, if you faced something squarely it was never quite as bad as you might think. She was strong and fearless and these days far fitter than him. Once he had been able to terrorize her, but only as a child. Now she was grown, she could give as good as she got. She recognized his weakness and despised him for what he'd become. All that brilliance, all that beauty, dissipated in the same way he had squandered his life.

This needed to be done, it was part of their reason for coming. A rite of passage that inevitably had to be gone through. Mémé had sent out signals which, fatally, they'd ignored. It was all up to Clemency now and she wouldn't let her down.

"Go now!" breathed Clemency, giving Cherie a slight push and willing her to make her escape before the forces of evil closed in. Then, gathering her courage and taking a deep breath, she walked slowly forward to her destiny, holding out both hands.

Teddy sat on the TGV as it hurtled south towards Avignon, and worried about his wife. All of a sudden he was gripped by a terrible anxiety and felt he couldn't get there fast enough. He had chosen the train because it seemed that much simpler, preferable to airports and having to change planes. But it still took eight hours and he was scared what he might find. Three violent murders had already taken place; they'd been out of touch for a whole twenty-four hours and a lot could happen in that time. Even with the sluggish gendarmes supposedly hot on the murderer's trail, he hated the thought of his wife and innocent children trapped there in peril at a madman's whim. With only the wimpish Ethan to protect them, and some unknown kiwi who had blown in out of the blue.

Alison had taken his departure pretty badly, but she was the last thing on his mind right now. She had cried rather drippily, not bawled as Clemency would have done, and accused him of destroying her life, that she no longer had anything to live for. There hadn't been time to comfort her properly; he had to get to Waterloo for Eurostar. But he had stopped feeling sorry as the taxi pulled away. He wasn't by any means heartless, just knew where his priorities lay. With Clemency and the children, to try and make amends. Provided it wasn't already too late; he shuddered even to think it.

He thought about his mother-in-law and how she had cherished her daughter. Bold and confident though Clemency always was, she was the child her mother cosseted most, even though there were four boys as well, two of them that much younger.

"Take care of her," she had begged him on their wedding day, and then, when she was dying, she had made the request again. Almost as though there was something he didn't know, some hidden agenda lurking beneath the surface. Yet Clemency had always been the embodiment of health, had sailed through all four pregnancies and was practically never ill. No chills, no fever, not even the common cold. She radiated spunk and vigour, an inspiration to them all. Clemency was a genuine life force; nothing ever seemed to get her down.

Apart, of course, from those occasional broken nights when she woke him with her irrational sobbing. And those strange dark periods after each delivery when she had withdrawn for a while from his embrace, suffering some mental torture of her own. But that, said the doctors, was all quite natural. Women's stuff caused by a hormone imbalance. Nothing at all to be fretting about.

Well, one thing was for certain, thought Teddy resolutely. Never again was he going to neglect her, not if he lived to be a hundred. He would finally heed Claire's request and smother her with love, demonstrate his appreciation in every possible way. Even though she would brush him off and tell him he was a dope. Despite his anxiety, he found himself smiling. What a dear, infuriating, impossible woman he'd married. He could scarcely wait to see her again and let her know how he felt.

"*Clemence?*" said the thing on the stairs again. She took both his hands in hers and raised herself slightly to kiss him lightly on both cheeks. Try to act normal, said a voice within her; he smelled disgusting but at least it had calmed him down. His blurry eyes focused and he gazed at her in wonder. She flinched as he disentangled one hand in order to stroke her neck.

"*Clemence, tu es revenue?*" he said, then burped surprisingly delicately as though in deference to her.

"*C'est ça.*"

He smothered her face with kisses then and pawed her like a dog while she patiently stood and endured it. Provided he stayed in this amiable mood, she might make it work, but already he was growing restless and trying to pull away.

"Viens," she said gently, coaxing him down the stairs. If she could only get him to somewhere safe, a room with a stout door and a lock with a key, she would effectively disable him and make him less of a threat. The handle of his lethal-looking knife brushed against her arm and she wondered fleetingly if she dared make a grab for it and throw it out of his reach, as far as she could. A ghastly vision of Isabelle's butchered corpse floated into her mind and sickened her with revulsion. This was no longer her boisterous childhood playmate, this was a conscienceless killer who wouldn't hesitate to destroy her too the second he grew tired of the game. The only way she could possibly survive was not to lose sight of that thought and try hard not to arouse him. Even drunk, he was dangerous and far stronger than her, and the booze might wear off before the gendarmes arrived. It was growing rapidly lighter now; surely they must be here before too long.

"I can't believe he did that," said Rusty, hammering ineffectively against the unyielding door. The exit to the barn was similarly barricaded and the room they were locked in was windowless.

"Steady on," said Ethan nervously, worried about the noise. He remembered Dominic's parting shot and was wary of provoking his anger. He was stunned by the coldness in Dominic's eyes, saw him suddenly in a quite different light, as a seasoned and ruthless killer. Whoever would have believed it, that bright, cheeky kid? Naughty, he'd certainly been, but a maniac—never. Yet the evidence of their eyes had been there and he'd locked them up as securely as if they were suspects themselves.

"Sod that!" said Rusty, kicking the door instead. Somewhere out there Dominic was prowling, weapon in hand, while Tonya was innocently sleeping. He remembered he'd left their door gaping wide and trembled at what could be happening now. "We've got to get out!"

"But how?" There seemed to be no answer to that.

"Why would he be doing this?" Ethan wanted to know. What reason could a person have for decimating a whole family, especially since he was not even in the direct line? He wasn't Odile's descendant, so could scarcely have expected to inherit. Which had definitely been Harry's motivation, and look what had happened to him. Ethan looked again at the pile of old newspapers and decided the answer might lie somewhere there. There was no point in panicking and lathering up a storm; till someone released them, there was nothing they could do.

"Here," said Ethan, suddenly taking charge. "Grab a pile of these, shut up and start reading." At least they could study his modus operandi, even if they didn't survive to pass it on.

Madeleine and Élodie were dressed and ready to go, in jeans and dark T-shirts with socks pulled low on their heads. Tired of being helpless damsels in distress, they had opted instead for action and set about devising an escape plan. The noise from downstairs had ceased abruptly and they could no longer stand the suspense of waiting for something to happen. Anything was preferable to being caught like rats in a trap. So they opened the shutters and extinguished all light. Outside, the dawn was breaking and the sky was mottled with pink.

Madeleine peered down. Their room faced outwards on to

the lane, with a sturdy vine creeping right below the sill.

"If we crawled along it like Tarzan," she said, "we could ease ourselves downwards and drop the rest of the way."

"You go first," said Élodie beside her. "Show me how it is done." With her crazy headgear and brilliant smile, she looked quite dashing and cheered Madeleine up. A twisted ankle was preferable to a knife in the back; she tried not to dwell on what might happen if they got caught.

"Each man for himself," she said brightly. "If one of us breaks their neck, then run like the clappers and get the police."

They shook hands like the troopers they were, then hugged each other fiercely with unfeigned emotion. Madeleine, poised on the windowsill, gave a jaunty thumbs-up sign, then launched herself into space.

All was proceeding smoothly until Clemency stumbled in the dark and lost her footing. In an instant he was on to her, like a lion upon its prey. He grabbed her roughly by the shoulders and she couldn't throw him off.

"*Non,*" she said sharply, hoping to calm him, but he still held on with a viselike grip. His breathing grew ragged as he sensed her weakness, and his hands slithered upwards and closed around her throat. Blindly she groped for the savage knife, dragged it from his belt and tossed it as far as she could throw. She would have used it herself if only she could, but knew she had neither the strength nor courage. Even *in extremis* she remained essentially civilized; despite what he'd done to her relatives, she could never go the whole hog. At least, while it remained beyond his reach, she had gained herself a little time.

She was truly shaken by what was happening and her

courage began to wane. She had always held a special place in this man's heart, right from the days when she came here as a child. She had seen it in his eyes; it was there still. It was for his sake, surely, that she'd been the one to be singled out; not Harry, nor one of her brothers, her alone. The privileged grandchild to whom Mémé had left her crucifix, invited here in the summers as a treat. But those visits had ceased abruptly one year and Clemency had not been invited back since, nor ever seen her grandmother again.

And now he was attempting to throttle her to death. The blood was throbbing in her head and her vision was starting to fade. Relentless fingers pressed into her windpipe and his eyes, close up, were bloodshot and flecked with fury. No point appealing to his better nature; the man had gone, the animal prevailed. She struggled with him valiantly but knew she just couldn't win.

Then two things happened, in such fast succession, she was never after able to recall which came first. As her knees began to buckle and consciousness ebbed away, a powerful arm snaked suddenly out of the darkness and hauled him off bodily by his hair. He let out a bellow of agony and let go of Clemency on the spot.

"Duck!" shouted a voice with an authoritative tone, and she dropped like a stone and lay still. There was a terrifying crack that resounded from the walls and a small dark stain appeared on her assailant's chest.

"Don't move!" So she didn't, just lay curled there in a ball, vainly struggling to recollect where she'd heard that voice before.

Then someone switched on a powerful flashlight and raked her adversary with its beam.

"Good God," said Dominic, with awe in his voice, for the dead man's throat had been skillfully sliced from ear to ear. "It wasn't my bullet that killed him after all."

39

*C*lemency?" said Dominic with true concern in his voice, tucking his automatic into his belt and crossing swiftly to where she lay. "Are you all right? What did that bastard do to you?" He dropped on one knee and touched her shoulder with infinite gentleness.

Clemency was lying as still as the dead, but her eyes were open wide and riveted on the staircase, where the tall gaunt figure had silently rematerialized and was now simply standing, motionless as before, draped like something from a Victorian cemetery, from head to food in absolute black. The bruising on her throat made it difficult to swallow, much less utter a sound. All she could do was tug urgently at Dominic's sleeve and nod frantically in the direction her eyes were fixed. With a reflex action swifter than a cobra's, Dominic's hand was back on his gun as he turned and saw what Clemency could see.

"Holy Moses!" he muttered under his breath, springing instantly into crouched combat position, both hands steadying the automatic. "Don't move," he hissed with just a hint of panic in his voice, for this new menace was something he couldn't fully comprehend.

Tall and unyielding and silent as the grave, it stood there like a terrible figure of doom, come here to warn them. But of what?

"Who are you?" challenged Dominic at last, his voice

echoing harshly in the cavernous hall. "And what is it you want?" What unnerved him most, as the darkness gradually paled, was that he could make out no details of the dark, hooded shape. As Cherie had screamed at Clemency hysterically, it appeared to have no face or other human attributes.

Nothing happened, it neither moved nor spoke, and each ensuing second made its presence there more menacing. Now Clemency would have screamed herself if only her throat weren't so damaged, but as it was, nothing disturbed the tomblike silence of the dark. Except for the distant crowing of a farmyard cockerel, signaling the arrival of dawn. Soon the gendarmes would be here.

"The flashlight!" hissed Dominic, still quite clearly unnerved. "It's lying there somewhere. Find it and switch it on."

Clemency was really reluctant to do that, scared of what further horrors might be revealed, but Dominic's steely tone brooked no argument, so she meekly did as she was bid. The first thing she saw, as the strong light beamed downwards, was the knife still there at her feet, viciously cruel and smeared with the dead man's blood. And then, as she swung the flashlight across the floor, it picked out the face of the dead man himself, now ghastly pale, with horribly staring eyes and a thick crust of congealing blood around his neck like a ligature. Clemency gasped, once again stunned by the sight. Apparition or not, the figure on the stairs possessed enough human strength to kill. Eventually she summoned the courage to swing the powerful beam in an arc up the staircase to illuminate what was standing there.

The robes, which merged with the shadows, were somber

and dusty black, while the face, if it had one, was almost entirely concealed by what Clemency now saw was a plain linen wimple, from beneath which glowed a pair of intensely burning eyes. She took an involuntary step backwards, clutching convulsively at her throat. There was no doubt now that this creature was flesh and blood, alive and apparently about to speak. But instead it simply floated forward and dropped to its knees at the side of the bloody corpse.

With hands so thin they were virtually opaque, it caressed the dead face and wiped the blood from its cheeks. Then shifted the head into the lap of its gown and, with exquisite tenderness, closed the staring eyes. The image of Mary with the dying Christ leapt unbidden into Clemency's mind and the *Pietà* parallel was doubly strengthened as the figure raised its eyes to heaven, intoning something under its breath and making the sign of the cross. Which was when Clemency took in the beaded cord and dangling ivory crucifix. This ghostly visitation was, in fact, an earthly nun, who was looking at her now and gently beckoning.

"Come here, my dear," she said, speaking at last. The voice was low and not easy to hear, but the message unmistakable. "Come, child, and let me look at you properly and see how life has treated you all these years. It has been so long."

Right at that moment, from the courtyard outside, came the glare of powerful lights and the intrusive squealing of brakes. The cavalry had arrived in the shape of a police van packed with uniformed gendarmes, with Madeleine and Élodie grinning perkily from the front seat.

· · ·

The heat of midmorning was reaching its zenith when a tired and crumpled Teddy Cartwright spilled from a creaky taxi in the courtyard of Mas des Vignes and stared uncomprehendingly at the silent tableau before him. The door to the terrace stood open wide in an attempt to allow air to circulate and a whole gang of people was grouped together in the stark, cool flagstoned kitchen. Clemency—thank God she was safe—sat serenely at the scrubbed pine table holding hands with a nun, while the Annesley cousins, a whole raft of them, were crowded around attentively, with a couple of earnestly jotting gendarmes thrown in for luck. What the blazes was going on?

With as much authority as he could muster after his hectic race against time, Teddy stepped into the room to join them, hoping to find himself welcome.

"Teddy, dearest!" croaked Clemency with unfeigned affection, rising and radiating happiness. There was something terribly wrong with her neck, which was swollen and turning purple with bruising, but otherwise she seemed to be in her usual exuberant spirits. "What a wonderful surprise. Come here and sit by me." So far, so good. Teddy, having kissed her, slipped gratefully into the proffered chair and accepted a glass of chilled wine.

"What's going on?"

"You might well ask. Allow me to present Sister Agnes, my long-lost aunt."

The nun acknowledged Teddy with a slight inflection of the head. She was an imposing presence whose ultra-thinness made her appear unnaturally tall. With her hood pushed back, it was possible to see that the bones of the face beneath the wimple were fine and strong, with eyes as bright and challenging as her father's, a warrior spirit undaunted by all that had occurred. In her day Agnes Annesley had been famed for her beauty, a whisper of which was still evident in her face. The gendarmes were keeping a wary eye upon her but so far had made no arrest. Agnes sat upright yet entirely at her ease; her voice, when she spoke, was low-pitched and almost rusty, a voice that had not been used for many years, with an odd hybrid accent that was a mixture of archaic French and dated American slang. With maybe a smidgen of ecclesiastical Latin thrown in.

"What are you doing here?" Ethan wanted to know. His temper had cooled the moment Dominic had released him and he was stunned to be seeing his half sister face-to-face after an absence of almost four decades. Was there no end to today's surprises?

"Odile sent for me," explained Agnes simply. Something about her stepmother's letter after so many years of silence, an understated note of urgency, had caused her to renege on a lifetime's sacred vows and hurry her on her way. Too late, alas; she would never cease regretting it. If she'd got here sooner Odile might still be alive.

"*Mais, madame . . .*" the leading gendarme interrupted as he flicked back through his notebook in search of relevant details. The lock on the drawer of the writing desk had been smashed, its contents taken, he pointed out. Clemency had never received her grandmother's note. How, then, had Agnes been permitted to receive hers? All eyes swiveled towards her, awaiting an answer. Agnes pondered, then gave a melancholic smile.

"He wanted to see me," she said with a shrug. "One final time while Clemency was here." He had tried to stop them, she realized that now, by destroying Odile's letters before they could be sent. And then by destroying Odile and the others. But Agnes had proved to be too much of a draw; he had risked a final gamble that had ended in his death.

"I don't understand," piped up Cherie, out of her depth. Ashley was off with the other kids again, safe with Tonya and beyond earshot. This reunion had turned into a right fiasco. And the pieces were only slowly beginning to slot into place.

"Why would he want to kill off all his relatives?" Assuming, that was, that he was an Annesley himself.

"That bit's obvious," said Clemency briskly. "He dared not risk the authorities finding out. This house had been his home for more than thirty years." Funny she never thought of it herself, not even when Odile failed to answer any of her notes. He couldn't allow them to find him there; it was his home too and he'd intended it always should be. In any case, where else could he possibly go, a man who had for years been officially dead? But Mémé, for her own reasons, had sent off urgent smoke signals and the fear of the pending invasion had caused him to kill her too.

"I still don't get it," said Cherie a shade petulantly. It was all right for them, they'd been family all their lives. "Who is that old geezer, and why the song and dance?"

"Why, Roland, of course," said Agnes, infinitely calm. "I thought you had realized that by now, my dear."

Eunice might have known, had she taken the trouble to join them, for as it happened she was the sole living witness of the chain of unfortunate events that had led to this day. But so suffused with self-pity had she been that the bizarre set of

344

circumstances had managed to evade her entirely.

"Forever looking for trouble, is Eunice," was her sister Aimée's uncharitable comment, "yet can't see the nose on her own face."

"Up her own backside," Patrice had agreed. "Thinks, for some reason, that the world owes her a living."

Which, in a manner of speaking, it did, at least in Eunice's eyes. Had her mother not left quite so precipitously, abandoning Cornelius to cope alone, Eunice would have remained in New York City and possibly married the man of her dreams. Might even have made it work. But Cornelius had needed her and that lure had proved too strong for her frail ego. She had turned her back on her one chance of love to seek a father's approval which had never been forthcoming. Cornelius had fretted and grieved for a while, then married a third wife and lost interest in his daughter. Eunice had returned to her adopted city to find life had effectively passed her by. The job was still there, but Evan was gone. She'd been taking it out on her sisters ever since. Yet that night Odile had stayed over at her apartment had been a crucial link in the chain of subsequent events. If only self-pitying Eunice had had the eyes to see, she might have found a new crusade in life, one that would have made her a softer and better person.

"I was desperate," said Agnes frankly, looking back. "And the only place I could think of to go was to Odile."

Her own mother, Ellen, was virtuous and kind, but this latest piece of outrageousness would have been more than she could cope with. Agnes drank too much, experimented with drugs, drove like a maniac and slept around. A product of her times, maybe, but consistently over the top. The little

345

Ellen knew, she blamed on her successor, the ruthless French ingenue who had sabotaged her marriage.

"Not fair, of course," said Agnes now. "Theirs was a rare and wondrous love. A once-in-a-lifetime bonding."

There was magic in the air in those early Camelot years, in the long idyllic summers she had spent with them in Maine. All those laughing children with scarcely a care between them; small wonder only-child Agnes preferred to be there instead of at home with her own deserted mother.

"She never really approved, of course. Nor, I may say, did Odile."

Unhealthy, Odile had thought it as she watched them constantly fooling. A blood relationship too close to be allowed to grow. Cornelius had already ignored one taboo by marrying his own first cousin; the sooner these siblings were separated, the better it would be for all. But things rarely work out for the best and this case was no exception. Everyone was listening hard, even the gendarmes. Agnes, as she warmed to her story, grew visibly more relaxed and a faint dab of color appeared on her waxen cheek as she gazed back into the past. What a looker she must have been, to be sure, thought Teddy. And what a tragic waste of a life.

And then, quite suddenly out of a clear blue sky, everything changed at once. A local girl went missing and the police came to the house asking questions. Things were hushed up but were never again the same. Then tragedy struck in full force.

"What happened?" asked Cherie.

"Roland drowned."

"But—"

Agnes held up one imperious hand. She was almost fin-

346

ished; soon they would know. And hopefully understand.

Now it was Ethan's turn to grab the spotlight. In their long confinement in the hidden room, he and Rusty had done their homework. As he'd suspected, the stack of faded newsprint had taken them right back to the postwar years when Roland was still just a schoolboy.

"He was always a bad 'un," he told them now. "I don't know how he got away with it, but he seems to have done so."

"Charm," said Agnes. "Which he always had in abundance. The archetypal sociopath, if only I had realized at the time."

Unsolved murders, missing children; all carefully clipped and accounted for in those chilling news stories he had so proudly preserved. Ethan's blood had grown colder and colder as he read on; this monster was his brother, they had shared a childhood together. Yet he'd kept this record of all his crimes like the doted upon favorite he had always been. Until that last Maine summer, when things had grown too close for comfort and his mother had found herself involved.

"Maman fixed things for him, as she always had, but this time nobody shared her secret. She was on her own. What her darling had done could never be absolved. She knew that clearly when she planned his disappearance."

Aware of the drowning of her husband's younger brother, she had arranged things swiftly before the police got too close. Roland was dispatched in the early hours of the morning on a lobster boat belonging to a friend. The rest was comparatively simple; she had always had Mas des Vignes. And, courtesy of his parentage, Roland had dual

347

nationality. There'd be no problem with immigration. He had formally committed no crime.

"So she knew she was going a year before she went." Ethan's eyes were now bright with tears. He remembered his wretched, wrecked adolescence, the sense of failure he had never been able to throw off.

"Someone had to keep an eye on him. And it was vital that our father never got to know." Agnes, stern and upright in the brilliant morning sunshine, was the image of Cornelius, a perfectionist who never relented.

"But what about the owner of the boat?" Cherie, enthralled, gazed at Agnes, enraptured.

"Lost at sea," said Agnes after a pause. "The boat went down without a trace." She looked at them pleadingly. "It had to be."

"And you?" asked Clemency, picking up the thread. "What was your problem and where exactly did you fit in?"

Agnes clasped her translucent hands and lowered her head in spontaneous prayer. They all sat silently, awaiting her answer, while a chill of anticipated dread coursed through Clemency's veins.

"I was pregnant," she told them eventually. "With Roland's child."

And it was then, as she turned to her in supplication, that Clemency finally knew.

40

So," said Dominic comfortably, lolling back with his head in Madeleine's lap. "Good old Cousin Clemency turns out to be less than whiter than white after all. The bastard child of a sociopath and a rebellious nun." He chuckled with delight as he licked duck pâté off his fingers. Madeleine swiped at him but couldn't help laughing too. She adored Clemency, she genuinely did, but, all things considered—it was rather delicious. All that holier-than-thou stuff, the perfect marriage. Though she had to admit that she did admire the way saintly Teddy had leapt to the rescue once more and the look in his eyes when they'd first heard the truth, besotted as ever, unswervingly devoted.

"She deserves whatever happiness she can find." With a pedigree that dreadful, she was lucky to have survived so well. Only the devotion of a caring grandmother had snatched her from certain disgrace and defamation and placed her in the arms of someone ideally suited to raise her. Claire's own baby girl had been stillborn; the timing could not have been more perfect.

"All those years," pondered Madeleine, "and she never knew. Growing up as the pampered only daughter, smothered with love by those wonderful brothers."

"Do I detect a hint of envy?" Dominic asked, but Madeleine shook her head. She was thinking of that garrulous trinity, her mother and her aunts, and wondering why none of them had ever spilled the beans if, of course, they knew. No, that undoubtedly was the key to it all. The one true way to keep a secret is not to tell anyone at all. Though old Aunt Effie had certainly known something and, according to Harry, had almost let it slip.

They had stayed on at the house just long enough to see everything tidied up. Roland was dead, by the hand of his half sister, and the police were assuming he had been responsible for the other murders. There would have to be a full-scale investigation, of course, but no civic action would be taken against Agnes. Two somber-faced clerics had arrived late at night from Normandy and she had peacefully accompanied them on the long journey back.

"Don't worry about me," she told Clemency as she kissed her. "I am not going anywhere anymore, the Church will see to that." She had done her bit, had helped right a wrong, and was now content to spend the rest of her days incarcerated. God would forgive her, of that she had no doubt. She felt at ease in the life she had chosen, had achieved the only purpose she'd had left.

The police had finally returned their papers and told them they were now free to leave. Those three sad bodies had finally been taken away, to join Odile's in the morgue until they were cleared for burial. So they'd cleaned the house and closed it up for winter and would await the decision of the lawyers in Toulouse about who it would belong to in the future. Ethan, they all felt, was fair, and his three surviving sisters. Which meant, he told them, that they could all feel free to use it, including Rusty and Cherie, whenever they wished.

"Help make it a happy house," he told them. "Bring back the spirit of those golden, long-gone summers."

First, however, he had plans for bringing Emily here, before it grew too cold and the dark nights really drew in. He would like her to see the paintings and help him remove them to safety. And he intended in the future to come here often, to tend his mother's grave and let her know that her long lonely vigil was finally at an end.

Rusty and Tonya preferred to hitchhike, but Teddy dropped off Élodie in Avignon.

"No," she told Madeleine gently, touching her cheek. "Two's company and you don't need me along as goose-berry." Besides, the train was faster and she had pressing things to do. A career to get on with and a cracked heart to mend. She was reasonably proficient at both these things and hoped that it wouldn't take too long.

"Take care of her," she told Dominic gaily, punching him in the biceps. Since the time she had first seen the two of them together, she had known she was just living a dream. She might appeal to his raunchier side, but Madeleine was the one who'd got his heart. Besides, if she was honest with herself, she knew deep down that they could never have lasted. What they had had together in the last fleeting months was just too hot not to cool down. Even if he hadn't, she would have moved on in time. Look at her mother; it was in her genes. And some good had come out of this dis-astrous reunion; she had all these new cousins now with whom to share her life.

"Besides," as she told Madeleine in the privacy of their room, "it's only fair that you should have him; I'm so much younger than you."

So here they were now, the two of them alone, parked in a country lane just minutes from the motorway. They had brought a picnic which Clemency had prepared and were drifting home to London and real life. Dominic's days of wandering the world were finally at an end, or so he told her. He liked this job of criminal profiling, knew he had an apti-tude for it and a job with the FBI if he cared to take it up. He hadn't told her that bit yet, felt that it would keep. First he had to get to know her properly and help melt the icy facade she had built up so carefully over the years. Trust was the thing, and he knew he would get there in time. But he owed a huge debt to Harry for dragging him in, in the first place; if it hadn't been for his cousin's greed and urgent need to discover the truth, he might never have remembered his erstwhile buddy who had always been so good at cracking puzzles as a child and vowed to be a detective when he grew up.

He raised his head and pulled her down to kiss him. She laughed and struggled but eventually gave in.

"Tell me," he said as they both came up for air. "I hate to mention this so soon but how do you feel about kids?"

Center Point Publishing
600 Brooks Road ● PO Box 1
Thorndike ME 04986-0001 USA

(207) 568-3717

US & Canada:
1 800 929-9108